N. C. HAYES

THE QUEEN OF RECKONING

THE REDFERN LEGACY:
BOOK TWO

Brett,
For fourteen years of friendship. For memes, margaritas, and endless shit-talking. For your enduring love and support— this one is yours.

Queen of Everything

Part One

Chapter
One

I sat before a pot of dirt, focusing my energy into my hands which hovered above its surface, waiting for something to happen.

"Remember," Lyra said as she stood watching nearby. "Focus your breathing, then say the words clearly and carefully." I nodded and took a deep breath, closing my eyes as I set my mind to the task before me. As slowly and clearly as I could without sounding ridiculous, I spoke the word that Lyra gave me that would apparently make this pot of dirt and seeds turn into basil. "Good," Lyra said. I was scared to open my eyes and break concentration but was unsure if anything was happening. "Keep breathing like that—"

"This is ridiculous." I heard Kenna's exasperated voice from her seat on the other end of Lyra's quarters. "How do we even know you're giving her the right spells? You could be telling her to say anything."

"I should give you a spell to improve your memory, Lady Kenna," Lyra snapped. "You have been shown many times now that these spells are well documented in your people's libraries. The Children use commonly known spells. I suspect you simply do not like hearing the words spoken aloud."

"Well— can she not simply *think* the words?"

"No, but I'd be happy to share which words I'm *thinking*—"

"Will you both hush?" I asked, keeping my eyes shut, "I'm trying to grow some damned basil here."

"If she—"

"Kenna, if you say one more word while I'm trying to concentrate, I'm going to ban you from my lessons and let Alastair take your place." The seer quieted down, and I resumed my attempt.

In the five months since I brought Lyra back to Sylvanna with Hannele and me, the witch had been able to blend into our household, now getting along cordially with everyone in my new family— except for Kenna. The fiery seer deeply disliked the witch who now lived in the bedroom next to hers, despite Kenna helping me in my quest to find The Children of the Onyx Temple— the coven where Lyra had learned her craft— in the first place. Kenna's inability to see anything touched by witchcraft had been an irritation when she first discovered that her sight on me was diminishing, but it was clear that not being able to read Lyra was a blow to her ego.

"That's it," Lyra murmured, "Keep going."

Lyra requested I start some early training a few weeks ago, once my magic and physical strength had mostly returned. Before we could start my formal lessons in her craft, she needed to have an idea of what sort of grasp I had on the witchcraft that ran in my veins alongside my sorcery. We had tried and failed so far to make her spoken spells work for me. Gone now was the hold I had on any element— even fire. I could no longer light fireplaces and lanterns as I once had without losing control of the flame. Lyra suspected my extended captivity in silver had something to do with it, but when it came to my unprecedented abilities, no one could be certain.

I let my eyes flutter open, and I saw that the surface of the soil was starting to shift and move. My task was to make the plant grow at an accelerated rate without losing control. My grasp on the earth element was weakest; On more than one occasion I had brushed my hand on some shrub or another, doubling or tripling its size in seconds. I had overgrown the healers' herb garden by mistake, as well as wilted a meditation garden beside Lehrun's temple that had been there since Prince Niklaus still ruled Sylvanna.

I stared at the pot, expecting any second that a plant would start to emerge. Sweat beaded on my brow and I pushed every ounce of effort I could into my palms as I repeated the word again.

The pot shattered.

"It was worth trying." Lyra sighed, brushing dirt and shards of broken clay from her apron front. She turned and brushed more dirt off a large black snake that sat coiled on the windowsill, soaking up the sun. Her familiar. Upon being moved, he lifted his head and stared in Lyra's direction. "Don't look at me like that, Petyr, you've got dirt on you."

"Are you finished with her?" Kenna asked abruptly. "There's still a lot to do today." When I turned to scold her, she simply pointed at the clock against the wall, which indicated that we had indeed gone well past the end of our lesson.

"That will do for today, my lady," Lyra told me. She handed me a packet filled with the remaining basil seeds. "I'd like you to practice again before you retire tonight. I believe you owe the kitchens some new herbs— see if you can grow it on your own and have it delivered to them." Indeed, Zale and Tory's kitchen herbs had been picked over in attempts to provide Lyra with a functional supply of ingredients. I was sure they would appreciate the gesture if I could ever produce something useful with my powers.

"Thank you, Lyra," I told her. "I'll see you in the morning."

"And you're sure you want to take such a long break after that? It will further delay your training."

"It's only four days," I replied, "And I told you, you are more than welcome to accompany us on our travels."

"I prefer not to be glamoured for such a long amount of time," she said, waving me off as we exited her bedroom-turned-study. "Enjoy your... dress fitting, or whatever it is." I waved over my shoulder just before the door shut. Kenna and I made our way to the dining room, where Gerridan sat across the table from Hannele, who looked rather peaky today, helping her with some exercise to improve the function of her arm. Her injuries being as severe as they were, Hannele's healing time had been quite the chore, even with her magic now returned to her. I faced Kenna.

"I'm serious Kenna, if you don't stop antagonizing her, I'm going to let Alastair take your place."

"Alastair has better things to do than sit in on your lessons—"

"And I have better things to do during those lessons than manage your mood swings," I told her. "I don't need a chaperone anyway."

"Two more days," Hannele said from the table. "And you'll have enough anointed power running through you that no one will worry about you being alone with a witch." It was true. The day after tomorrow was both my wedding day and my coronation, where I would be crowned the anointed Queen of Medeisia, at my soon to be husband's insistence. Not consort, not simply a king's wife—

which would have been plenty for me— but his equal, ruling side by side until the end of our days.

"Lyra isn't a threat," I reminded my friends. I met Hannele's eyes. "She saved us."

"We know, Shaye," Gerridan said, leaning back in his chair. "Lyra is fine, but old habits die hard. Let us be a little over-cautious until you get your extra claws at the coronation and then you can order us all away to your heart's desire." I rolled my eyes while he chuckled to himself.

"Are you ready?" Kenna chimed in. "You really do need another fitting."

"I think I had plans to spar first..." I glanced pleadingly at Gerridan. With Hannele still taking things easy, designing my gowns for the wedding and the coronation ball had been left mostly to me— which meant consulting Kenna, and needing to reign in her adventurous tastes. Luckily, Hannele's favorite Ayzellen dressmaker, Cecil, who had designed the gown I wore to Aydan's coronation, understood my tastes, and created a pair of dresses that I was truly excited to wear. However, with Kenna already being in a sour mood, I didn't feel much like fielding her comments today.

"Yes, you're right, we have a lesson," Gerridan replied, understanding my cry for help. He fidgeted with the gold ring on his left hand, and my eyes drifted to the matching band on Hannele's. "Give me a few minutes to help Hannele wrap her arm."

We had only been home for two weeks when Hannele and Gerridan took an evening walk and did not return for several hours. None of us thought much of it. Upon realizing what he could have lost, Gerridan finally set aside his feelings of inadequacy, and allowed his and Hannele's courtship to begin after nearly two centuries. They were doing their best to make up for lost time. It was nearly midnight when the pair came sneaking through the front door of our home, only to find myself, Aydan, and Alastair all still awake and having a nightcap in the sitting room. They were practically giggling, with guilty looks on their faces when Kenna entered the room. She took one look at the pair of them and her eyes widened, "You did *not.*"

The rest of us stared in confusion until Gerridan, with his arm around Hannele's waist, announced, "I'd like to introduce you all to my wife."

After a brief celebration in the sitting room, Aydan produced a set of keys from nowhere and pressed them into Gerridan's hand, insisting that he and his new bride spend their honeymoon at one of the Crown's private seaside cottages in Xarynn. After a minute or so of Gerridan trying to refuse, Hannele took the keys and thanked Aydan before we sent them off with a promise that their bags would be close behind them.

I met Gerridan by the sparring ring once we both changed into our gear and he had finished wrapping Hannele's arm. Alastair had been traveling a lot in the months since my return, and so Gerridan stepped in to practice swordplay with me, as well as continuing our training in hand-to-hand combat. I was nearly back to full strength, thanks to our training six days each week. It was the only break either of us got from our increasingly busy lives these days. Between the wedding and my coronation, as well as my lessons with Lyra, our ongoing negotiations with Nautia— and the ins and outs of life at court— we were all stretching ourselves thinner by the day.

"Where is our darling Aydan today?" Gerridan asked once we finished our third round. He handed me a canteen before removing his shirt, now drenched in sweat. I drank and gave it back to him, shrugging.

"He had an early breakfast with Priamos and Solandis this morning," I said. "He said something about popping over to Ayzelle for a few hours, and then he had a fitting this afternoon for his wedding clothes. His note said he should be home for dinner."

"I'll bet you're excited for the tour," he commented. "I haven't seen you two in the same room in days." As the wedding drew nearer, it seemed Aydan and I saw each other less and less, usually only for a few minutes before falling into bed exhausted each night.

"It will be a nice break," I agreed. The tour of Xarynn would begin the day after our wedding— four days in the seaside territory, which I had yet to visit since crossing the border into Medeisia a little more than two years ago. The Duke of Xarynn was apparently eager to meet me, and, Aydan told me, it was about time for the Crown to visit the import capital. Our family would accompany us and spend the first part of the trip in the Duke of Xarynn's home for a two-day official visit. From there, our family would return home while Aydan and I spent the final two days alone at one of the private residences belonging to House Aevitarus.

"Should we go another round?" Gerridan asked.

"As much as I'd like to," I sighed. "Kenna might kill me if I don't see the dressmaker today." Gerridan chuckled.

"Fine, we'll go again first thing in the morning— one final, grueling session before we take a vacation and get soft." I agreed to the early morning session before Gerridan took my arm and effuged us back home.

Kenna stood in the foyer, tapping her foot while I greeted Hannele and said goodbye in one breath. Gerridan looked apologetic as I let Kenna take my arm, and she effuged us to the dressmaker's shop.

Chapter
Two

Aydan did not make it home for dinner.

Instead, I ate with Gerridan, Hannele, and Kenna. Alastair arrived home unexpectedly toward the end of the meal, stating that he wasn't hungry, but joined us at the table for a drink. The Lord General had continued his correspondence with Nautia, now having frequent meetings with Gram, the Prince Regent of the mortal kingdom, to negotiate the possibility of a face-to-face meeting between Gram's nephew King Callum, and Aydan. Alastair had taken on the correspondence while Aydan and Gerridan were dealing with the loss of Hannele and myself. He and Prince Gram appeared to have some level of understanding with one another, so leaving the negotiations in his hands made the most sense.

"How'd it go?" Gerridan asked.

"Fine enough— treated me as a guest, as usual," Alastair replied, pausing to drink his wine. "The prince is ready to move forward, but convincing the King is proving troublesome."

"He's seventeen," Gerridan said around a large bite of roast duck. Hannele elbowed him in the ribs, and he swallowed before continuing, "The Prince Regent could simply force him to sit in on the meeting."

"No, he couldn't," Alastair said. "Prince Gram takes his role seriously— he's there to guide the King until he comes of age, not manipulate him into doing what he thinks is best. Anyway, the problem lies in the Callum's distractions, not his unwillingness to meet."

"Distractions?" I asked. "What— some hobby is keeping Callum from peace negotiations?"

"A woman, apparently," Alastair explained. "One of the palace witches. Gwendolyn, I think. The King is quite smitten with her." I set down my fork and waved my hand over my plate, banishing it to the scullery.

"He's young," I said, folding my arms on the table. "He'll get over it. There's plenty of time for him to come around. For now, we'll simply keep the doors of communication open between our courts and be sure to make it clear that we remain eager for peace."

"Well said, my lady."

My heart fluttered when I heard Aydan's voice from behind me. He had effuged into the room while I spoke. His hands warmed my shoulders and I felt him press a kiss to the top of my head. I looked up at him while he smiled down at me.

"You're late." I smirked.

"I'm sorry," he replied. "My task in Ayzelle took longer than I thought it would— and I couldn't put off that damned fitting again."

"I know the feeling," I replied, glancing at Kenna from the corner of my eye. I heard Alastair stifle a laugh. Kenna did not look amused.

"Will you come with me?" Aydan asked, offering his hand to help me from my seat. Before I could ask where we were going, we had appeared just outside the Great Hall in castle Ayzelle.

"What are we doing?" I asked, looking around to see workers bustling back and forth through the castle as they prepared for the wedding and my coronation. Both would take place at the capital.

"I want to show you something," he said, offering his arm. I took it and let him walk me all the way to the King's Chambers. Each worker we passed bowed or curtsied to us, and it took all my effort to be sure I acknowledged all of them in some way.

When we arrived at the west wing of castle Ayzelle, we came upon a corridor lined with paintings in frames.

"What is this?" I asked, noting that I recognized many of the paintings now on the floor.

"They're finally going to a public gallery," Aydan said. "These are all the paintings my father had hidden away in the King's Chambers. They're to be transported in the morning."

"They look so strange, off the wall," I told him, glancing around at the portraits and landscapes surrounding us.

"Come on, I have something for you," Aydan said, guiding me forward through the doors. On the far wall of the parlor room were two canvases, both covered in cloth. "Unveil them," he said, gesturing to the frames. I tugged on the first covering, revealing a familiar painting of a field of wildflowers. I saw it for the first time the night Aydan returned to Ayzelle and became king.

"Aydan, what—"

"It's yours," he said. "Put it wherever you want in our home. I told you I'd find a place for you to see it often." I kissed his cheek before reaching to unveil the second painting.

The canvas depicted a female soldier on horseback, the horse's front legs in the air while the woman raised her sword, clearly bellowing, to lead her army into battle. "Oh my," I said, "This is—"

"Look at the title," Aydan said, pointing. I leaned the canvas forward to peek at the back of it and, scrawled in ink, were the words: *Commander Eastly's Battle for Ayzelle.* I blinked away tears before turning back to face him. I buried my face in his chest and mumbled my thanks.

"A wedding present," he said, lifting my chin to kiss me.

"Your Majesty," a man's voice said from the foyer. Aydan turned to answer him. His eyes were pointed toward the floor and he held another painting, this one facing him so we only saw the back of it. "I found this one in a storage closet— thought you might want to see." Aydan gestured for the man to bring it over, thanking him as he stepped back. I turned to face the painting and gasped:

It was a portrait of my mother, Brina Eastly, and my father, Lord Ronan Redfern— their wedding portrait, by the look of it. Gone was the fierce warrior in the previous painting. Here, Brina was dwarfed by both my father's stature and his intensity. His long auburn hair was tied back from his chiseled, pale face, his striking gray eyes piercing through the canvas. My eyes. While Brina did look beautiful, it was as Alastair had said in his memory when I mindwalked for the first time all those months ago: she was diminished. A lady of the court, perhaps, but not the warrior she was born to be.

"Get this out of our sight," I heard Aydan say sharply to the worker who had presented the wedding portrait to us. I blinked and realized that tears were streaming down my face. I wiped them away quickly. "How dare you—"

"It's fine," I said, placing a hand on Aydan's arm. The man approached again with his head bowed.

"My lady, I did not know that it would upset you so," he said to the floor, wringing his hands.

"It's all right," I told him, "Just, please— yes— remove the painting. Put it back where it came from. Please." The man did not lift his head, but instead bent at the waist into a deep bow, before taking my hand and pressing his brow to it.

"My lady," he murmured. "Your mercy is unyielding." I took my hand away.

"It's... quite all right," I said with some confusion. I gave a sidelong glance to Aydan, who stared at the pair of us.

"Medeisia is truly blessed by the holy mother, Ehnara herself, to produce such a union." He reached for my hand again. "House Redfern has returned to glory, and our gracious Lady Redfern shall soon sit upon the throne, *anointed*— I can hardly—" I moved to take my hand away from the man, but he gripped it tight within his own, pulling me closer to him. Without warning my hand burst into flame, producing an inhuman scream from him.

Aydan was there in an instant. He stepped between us, the blue glow of the royal line encasing his hand and crackling like lightning as he gripped the man by his throat and threw him all the way back against a wall in the foyer. The man gasped for air and held his hand against his chest, weeping.

I blinked. Twice. Three times. Waited to feel my arms in Aydan's grip, or the sound of my own sobs to wake me from a nightmare— but it did not come. I watched as the King's Guard flooded the room, blades drawn, and Aydan crouched before the strange man, sternly asking his name.

"Knox Redfern," he choked out. My mouth went dry as I straightened my neck, folded my hands in front of me, and approached them.

"You are of House Redfern?" I asked flatly.

"Yes, my lady," he replied eagerly, "Your father was my first cousin—"

"I don't particularly care," I replied drily. "There is no glory to be held by House Redfern. My name is Lady Eastly. I do not claim my father's house— and frankly, neither should you. You have entered your King's home without permission and spout out such traitorous language—" I paused, taking a single deep breath as I looked directly into Knox Redfern's eyes. They were gray, like mine, like Ronan's. His held fear and awe as he stared directly back at me, and I wondered if he realized what the flames from my hands must mean. I turned to the Captain of the Guard. "Captain Adler, take this man to the dungeons. Keep him there for the night— then you can send him back to wherever he came from."

"My lady," the Captain said, inclining his head slightly. He looked to Aydan— who nodded once— for confirmation before indicating to his men to carry out my orders. "You heard her." Knox Redfern was wide-eyed as cuffs were slapped onto his wrists and he was hoisted to his feet before being led by the guard out of the room.

The chamber door shut, and I felt myself choke out a shuddering sob, clutching at my throat. Aydan gripped my hand. I felt my stomach drop again and we were in our bedroom, back home in Sylvanna. I was on my knees, trying to catch my breath. Aydan sat beside me, taking my face in his hands and breathing deeply, indicating that I should match his rhythm. For several moments, I attempted to do so, but try as I might, Solandis' words rang in my ears:

You are the head of House Redfern…you will be followed by your father's legacy.

I gagged. Ice formed over the palms of my hands and crept up my arms. Aydan snapped his fingers.

"Your Majesty?" It was Elise's voice, but I did not look at her.

"Please go collect Lyra from her room and bring her here," Aydan said softly.

"You want Miss Lyra in your private—"

"Yes, Elise. Quickly, please." Elise hurried away before Aydan said in a normal volume, "Gerridan."

Gerridan strode into the room, and saw us on the floor together, my sobs still not under control, my breath ragged, and ice encasing my arms up to my elbows. Aydan moved aside and allowed Gerridan to take his place before me. He placed his hands gently on either side of my face and I felt my breathing almost immediately return to a normal pace. The sobs diminished until I was left just with tear-stained cheeks and what I was sure was a red, blotchy complexion.

"What the hell happened?" Gerridan asked us. Before we could answer, Lyra appeared in the doorway. She swept in, squatted down beside Gerridan and turned my face to meet hers. She reached for one of my icy hands, taking it in her own and examining it.

"You panicked," she said.

"We were met with an unexpected situation at castle Ayzelle just now," Aydan said.

He explained the events of a few moments before. Gerridan blanched as he listened to the story, while Lyra's expression did not change. Instead, she turned to the King and his advisor and asked:

"Is it common for sorcerers to have emotional outbursts, when their powers first emerge?" The men considered.

"In some of the more powerful bloodlines, perhaps," Gerridan replied. "Royalty, to be certain— I remember hearing of Princess Irsa's tantrums when she and Aydan were children."

Aydan nodded. "Well into the teen years. She would have outbursts, usually of anger. I didn't see too many of them myself— except the time she ran off and got lost in Xarynn for a week—but I heard after the fact."

"And what happens when a sorcerer cannot or will not use their power for an extended period of time? Does it diminish?"

"It fills you up until it bursts from you without warning," I replied, remembering Aydan's words the morning after we met. "But I use magic— I use it all the time."

"You use sorcery all the time," Lyra corrected. "But we have yet to get control over your witchcraft— to quell it or put it to use. I believe your witchcraft needs a task to achieve or an emotion behind it in order for you to control it, and that you'll need to find a purpose for it or risk more outbursts like this. Getting a better hold on your emotions will help." She paused, considering me for a moment. "Sleep it off. The panic was you— the magic was simply a reaction to it. I'm sure you're tired…We'll work on the rest in the morning." She turned her attention back to Aydan and Gerridan: "Your Majesty. My lord."

"Thank you," Aydan replied. Gerridan gave a nod. Lyra turned on her heel and exited the room as swiftly as she'd entered.

"I'll let you both get some rest," Gerridan said as soon as the witch was gone.

"Thank you, Gerridan," I said. "I'll see you in the morning." The advisor winked at me before following suit behind Lyra.

When the door closed, Aydan said, "I am so sorry."

"You couldn't have known," I told him, wiping the last stray tears from my face. "There was no reason to think someone would sneak in with the workers." There had been multiple crews of builders and designers in and out of castle Ayzelle for the past few months, preparing for what would be the two biggest events in Medeisia for the next century. Most of the workers were from the villages in the surrounding area. The villagers had been eager to participate. Many were happy to have the extra work, but others, mostly the mortals, knew that it was unlikely another event of this size and importance would take place in their lifetimes. Extra security had been hired from Sylvanna and Xarynn for the events themselves, but the usual King's Guard had been monitoring the preparations on their own, stationed in their normal positions with a few individuals looking in on certain projects.

"I should have just brought the damned things here," Aydan said. I leaned into his chest and he wrapped his arms around me.

"But then we wouldn't have found him," I replied. "He might have interrupted the wedding or done something at the coronation. If it had to happen, I'm glad it was tonight." Aydan said nothing, but let loose a sigh and ran his hand up and down my back while we stood there, just being near one another. Despite what had occurred to get us here, it was nice to be alone.

"I'll draw you a bath," he said after a few minutes. He kissed the top of my head and let go of me, walking to the bathroom, where I heard the water start and smelled the perfumed oils and salts he was pouring in. I undressed where I stood, and unwrapped my hair from its braid, shaking it loose. Not bothering with a robe, I followed Aydan into the bathroom.

He offered his hand as I stepped into the tub and sank into the steam. I rested my head against the porcelain and closed my eyes. I felt Aydan reach his hand into the water, then felt a soapy cloth scrubbing my neck and shoulders lightly as he washed me.

"Much better," I heard him murmur.

"What is?" I asked.

"You went away for a little while there. Gerridan helped you calm down, but just now I felt like you were back in the room with me."

"I'm here," I assured him.

"Do you want to talk about it?" Aydan asked.

"What?"

"Where you went."

"I didn't go anywhere," I insisted. "I was here, I could hear you and feel you, I just… Froze. Like Lyra said, I panicked."

Aydan pushed his hand lightly on my back so I could lean forward while he ran the cloth over me. I brought my knees to my chest and hugged them. "That must have been quite a shock, to meet another Redfern."

"No, it— it wasn't that," I admitted. "It was… I couldn't stop thinking of what Solandis told me that night at the Grand Palace." I repeated her words back to Aydan. They were burned in my memory. Aydan sighed and set the cloth down. I heard him stand, then a rustling of fabric, but before I could bring my head up from my knees to see what he was doing I felt him step into the tub and sit down behind me. He wrapped his arms around me and pulled my body to his, letting me rest on his bare chest while he held me.

"I am here," he said in my ear. "I am yours, and I will be here until you tell me to go. You will not lose me." I didn't reply, just squeezed his arm, which lay over my chest, his hand gently gripping my shoulder. "You *are* the head of House Redfern," he continued. "Which means you get to decide the narrative from here on out. Lord Ronan alone will not define a house as ancient as yours forever." Again I said nothing, just nodded while I let myself relax fully against Aydan. We sat in silence for a long while, until the water was nearly cold.

Rather than let me go, Aydan effuged us into bed, and dried us both with magic so we were comfortable and warm, now holding one another beneath our sheets.

"What are you thinking?" I asked softly after another moment had passed.

"That I can't wait for the next two days to be over, so I can have you all to myself in Xarynn," he mumbled, sounding rather sleepy.

"Our friends will be with us for the first two days in Xarynn," I reminded him. "So you won't have me quite *all* to yourself."

"Right," he corrected. "Perhaps I'll have to arrange for a second property to send the rest of them to." I chuckled, and he continued, "Though they might make their own arrangements after the first night— I don't plan on keeping quiet once we've gone to bed." The tone of his voice and the suggestion in the way his fingertips drifted across the lower plane of my belly sent a white-hot current pulsing through me. Aydan pressed a lazy kiss to the back of my neck but before I could turn over to return some of the attention, his breath had steadied, and I realized that he had fallen asleep.

I kissed the back of his hand before letting his arm fall over my chest, and settled into his embrace for the night.

Chapter

Three

I was in the ring just before sunrise, waiting for Gerridan. Unable to keep my nerves at bay, I woke two hours before, tossing and turning for a while before I gave up and decided to head out. The previous evening's events had certainly rattled me, but it was what I would spend today preparing for that had me restless. This time tomorrow I would begin preparing for my wedding, and before the day was over I would be the anointed Queen of Medeisia. I needed to hit something. Gerridan would do.

By the time I laced and buckled my boots, Gerridan arrived in the ring, greeting me quickly before getting into position. We ran through the usual defensive drills. Gerridan put me in various holds that I would then escape from before we began sparring. We kept things predictable, so the other could block our strike without much calculation. We went on this way for a while, until I heard footsteps, and the gate to the ring squeaked open. I turned my head to see who was entering, but before I could register their face, I felt Gerridan's fist collide with my cheek, knocking me off my feet. I hit the ground hard, landing soundly on my ass.

"*Fuck.*" Gerridan was crouching beside me before I could even finish blinking away the stars in my eyes. "Shaye, are you alright?" I blinked again and saw that it was Alastair who had come to join us.

"You fucking idiot," I heard the general say sharply. "Look at her."

"Aydan's going to kill me," Gerridan muttered, touching my face gingerly. I winced, then started laughing.

"She's delirious," Alastair scolded.

"No I'm not," I said, still laughing. I held out my hand. "Help me up." Gerridan obliged, helping me to my feet as I continued to chuckle through the pain. "Gods, Ger, you really got me." I touched my cheek which I imagined must be bruised. It was definitely swollen.

"Shit," he said, as he walked me to the low wall that lined the ring and helped me sit down again. "I'm going to get Jemma."

"There's no need—" I started, but he was already walking away. By the time I watched Gerridan effuge from the edge of the ring, Alastair was sitting down beside me.

"I was going to see if I could step in for some swordplay this morning," he said. "But that seems to be out the window." He examined my face again, shaking his head. "I can't believe he did that."

"In all fairness to Gerridan, I turned my head to see who was coming in the gate."

"He punched his future queen in the face." Alastair joined me this time when I burst out in laughter.

"Luckily it will heal before the morning," I said. "Immortality has its perks." Alastair half smiled but said nothing. "Is something wrong?"

"Wrong? No," he replied. "I intended to speak with you after some swordplay, but it can wait."

"What is it?" I asked, "It's still early, I have plenty of time before my lesson with Lyra."

"I—er, well, I wanted to discuss potentially taking on another position within court," he said.

"You want to step down as Lord General?"

"No, not at all," he clarified. "Just— something additional. I'd like to, with your permission, begin the formation of the Queen's Guard." I furrowed my brow.

"The King's Guard is sufficient, I think—"

"It's not for lack of sufficiency," he said. "As an anointed monarch, you'll be entitled to a private guard. They would work alongside the King's Guard and protect the home and members of the royal family, just as the King's Guard does— but ultimately would follow direct orders from you above all else."

"And you think this is necessary?"

"Maybe not now, but someday you might need that security. Queen Euna's Guard was the only reason she was able to keep her throne at all." The last anointed Queen— Aydan's great grandmother— and the footsteps I would be following from here on out. She had been imprisoned upon trying to take her place on the throne after her husband's death. I considered it for another moment.

"If Aydan has no problem with you setting time aside to recruit for the formation of a Queen's Guard, then I don't see a problem with it either."

"I already discussed it with him," Alastair said with a nod. "He encourages it."

"Then go ahead," I told him with a half-shrug.

"It will be my greatest honor." He bowed his head with exaggerated sincerity before settling into a quiet calm.

"I think Brina would be happy with us," I said, a little abruptly, after a moment. "I've been thinking about her a lot, with the wedding and everything...I know I didn't know her, but I think she would be happy that you're my friend. That you make sure I'm taken care of."

"I'd hope so." He paused again, then nudged me with his elbow. "And I hope you know that I would care for you just as much if Brina was not your mother."

"I know," I said, letting myself lean into Alastair's side. He wrapped his arm around my shoulders.

Though I loved all my friends deeply, Alastair and I had a particularly close bond. It had started of course with the general's love for my mother, whom Alastair had considered a sister. But since coming home from the Onyx Temple, I found myself spending as much time with Alastair as I could, missing him when he went to Nautia every few days. His quiet, thoughtful demeanor was a welcome presence in our stitched-together family of joyful, boisterous gamblers, always full of mischief, ready to argue or crack a joke. I could see why Aydan had made Alastair his Lord General. His careful consideration of all positions made for an effective military leader.

We enjoyed the morning in silence for just a few more moments before Gerridan effuged back into the ring, Jemma in tow. Alastair offered me his hand to help me stand.

"My lady," Jemma said with a curtsy. She stepped forward and began to examine my face. She turned and scowled at Gerridan. "You said it was in a life-or-death situation."

"It is for *me*," Gerridan mumbled. I scowled at him as well while she continued.

"You dragged me away from delivering a baby to address a bruise?" My face flushed, as did Gerridan's.

"Jemma, I'm fine," I told her. "Return to your patient, I'm so sorry. I'll put some leopard's bane on it tonight and I'll be fine in the morning." Throwing a look of disapproval in Gerridan's direction, Jemma effuged away in a huff. "She was delivering a *baby* and you thought you needed to bring her out here?"

"Do you remember when I said Aydan is going to kill me?"

"Shut up, he's not going to kill you." I rolled my eyes. "Kenna might." Alastair laughed before reaching for my hand. I took it, and we effuged back home, leaving Gerridan where he stood.

When we arrived in the sitting room, the house was awake. Gerridan followed closely behind us, ducking sheepishly into the dining room to join everyone else, who would be eating breakfast by now. I followed, while Alastair headed up the stairs to his bedroom. When I entered, Kenna took one look at me and dropped her fork, letting it clatter against her plate. Gerridan drank deeply from a steaming cup of tea now in his hand while Hannele winced but said nothing.

"I'm fine," I insisted before Kenna could start in on us. "I'm going to get some leopard's bane now. It will heal by morning." I noticed then that Aydan's chair was empty. "Is Aydan still asleep?"

"He's meeting with Captain Adler at castle Ayzelle," Hannele explained. "Tightening up security again, after last night." I nodded, not wanting to bring up last night's events again, though there was no doubt everyone in our household knew what happened by now. It was one of the many things I was still growing accustomed to— my life, my whereabouts, who I speak to, were all topics of concern for my friends, soon to be my shared Cabinet with Aydan. Had I been raised among the noble class I'd been born into, this might be an easier adjustment for me to make.

I took a raspberry and chocolate filled pastry from the tray in the center of the table— my favorites, made by Tory, one of our cooks— and ate it where I stood. Kenna scowled back and forth between Gerridan and me, deciding if it was worth the energy to scold us anyway. She apparently decided against it, picking up her fork and diving back into the eggs and sausages on her plate. I winked at Gerridan from across the room before pouring myself a cup of tea. As I added milk and honey, I said to no one in particular, "I'm going to take a bath." Each of them nodded or gestured that they had heard me before I took my cup and left, heading toward mine and Aydan's bedroom.

When I entered, it was clear that Elise had already come in to clean. Our bed was made, and the curtains were open, letting the morning sun pour in. I set my teacup down on the table near the fireplace where my familiar, Catchfly, was curled up in an armchair. She slept, warming herself in the beam of sunlight that hit the chair cushion this time of day, purring as she dreamt, likely of whatever her next meal would be. I patted her gently before walking to the bathroom to draw myself a bath. While water filled the tub, I stepped back into the bedroom to take off my sparring clothes. When I looked in the mirror to unwrap my braid, I saw my face where Gerridan's punch had landed— angry red and purple blotches covered my cheek and up over my eye. Lovely.

I glanced over to the bed and spotted a folded sheet of stationary. As I brushed out my hair, I walked over and grabbed it. A purple flower fell from it as I unfolded the page and read:

> *Shaye—*
> *I'll be in Ayzelle until this evening. I've arranged for us to dine privately when I return if you'd be so kind as to join me. Enjoy your lessons.*
> *All my love,*
> *—A*

I sighed, then folded the page and placed it in a box on my vanity where I saved Aydan's letters. I left the flower there as well, before returning to the bathroom and stepping into the steaming tub. The tour could not come fast enough.

Chapter Four

My lesson with Lyra was largely uneventful. We would not begin my true, formal training until my return, but she gave me a few everyday tasks that could be replaced by witchcraft, like lighting candles and filling pitchers, to try using spells on. Small things that could prevent an outburst like the night before. When none of them worked Lyra quipped, "Don't worry, someday you'll master it and your servants will have to find something else to do." I scowled at her. "Only joking."

"Watch it," Kenna replied before I could.

"It's fine, Kenna," I said.

"She should remember who she's speaking to," she said. "Tomorrow you'll be Queen, and—"

"And it was just a joke," I finished. "No harm done. Drop it." Kenna crossed her arms and stared out the window, ignoring us until the end of the lesson when I asked to use some leopard's bane, and Lyra offered bloodwort too.

"Blend them together. You'll likely heal by morning regardless but together this will guarantee it. Should help with any soreness as well—"

"You're sure this is bloodwort?" Kenna interrupted, snatching the bottle from Lyra's hand.

"Of course I'm sure. It's a simple herb. Any healer will have it."

"Well you're not just *any* healer, now are you?" Kenna asked.

"What exactly are you implying?"

"I think you know—"

"Kenna, get out," I said. She gaped at me. "We discussed this. You will not disrespect Lyra in her own quarters."

"Provided to her by my King—"

"Take it up with him then." We stared at one another until she finally turned and left, slamming the door behind her. I looked back at Lyra, who had busied herself with pouring the herbs into a jar, murmuring her words over them until a purple glow engulfed her hands. When she took them away, the dry flowers had become a paste. "I'm sorry," I told her as she placed the jar in my hand.

"Don't be," she replied as she wiped her hands on the tea towel she'd tucked into the waist of her skirt. "I can't say that I wouldn't be just as suspicious as she is, given the circumstances."

"She could stand to be more polite," I said with a sigh. Lyra chuckled.

"Perhaps, but I like a challenge." She picked up Petyr the snake from his perch on the windowsill and began stroking him as he wrapped himself around her hands. "When you return from your tour, we will begin your true lessons," she said, getting back to business. I would start my year and a day— the traditional length of training for witches. For mortals who sought this path, at the end of their year and a day they would embrace the title of witch and the magic they earned would halt their aging. What that title will do for me, we did not know.

"Things like this?" I asked, holding up the jar.

"Some," she replied. "But herbal medicine is common knowledge even amongst mortals. When you return from Xarynn, you'll need to be prepared for dream work— and then I'm going to see what we can do to harness your mindwalking abilities." I gulped, and she added: "I know you're still taking that tincture. You must stop before then." I nodded, lowering my eyes. The tincture that kept me from experiencing horrific nightmares had been a topic of discussion several times. I knew the day was coming when I wouldn't be able to put it off any longer.

"I'll start weaning off of it after the wedding."

"Good. Go put on your salve and get some rest. Big day tomorrow." She winked.

"Don't I know it," I sighed. Lyra gave me a sympathetic look, as if she could sense the nervous energy bubbling under my skin.

"Tomorrow you will wed the man you love," she reminded me. "The rest... well, I wouldn't say it doesn't matter. But it is not nearly as important as that."

"Thank you. You're right," I said with a smile. I looked at the clock. "I should get going."

"My lady." She bowed her head. I smiled at her again and stepped out of the room to find Kenna pacing the hallway.

"I can't believe you threw me out," she said when I shut the door behind me. I moved past her, making my way to the stairs.

"I can't believe you would put me in the position to do so," I replied. Kenna followed me down into the sitting room, where Hannele was napping on a sofa with an open book on her chest. I waved my hand, spreading a blanket over the top of her and continued walking to the dining room. "You are going to have to get over this hang up you have with Lyra," I told her.

"She disrespected you."

"It was a joke— you say jokes ten times more disrespectful than that before I've had breakfast."

"She's not one of us," Kenna continued. "She's not family, she shouldn't speak to you that way."

"Ken...look," I said. "I can't order you to be friends with her, or to like her. But I trust Lyra. She saved my life, and Hannele's. She's brought great risk to herself to come teach me how to use this power— all for the sake of a better future between our people and the covens. So I'm asking you, as a friend, please try to be nicer to her. Help make her comfortable here." Kenna remained silent, glancing down at the floor with her arms crossed. After a few seconds she nodded. "Thank you." I squeezed her shoulder. "I need to go get ready."

"For what?" Kenna asked quickly.

"Aydan has something planned for me. A private dinner." Kenna chewed the inside of her cheek. "What?"

"Oh, nothing— don't worry about it. Go— have a nice night. I'm going to go find Gerridan..." She trailed off as she turned to leave the dining room. I looked after her, scowling for just a moment, wondering what she could be plotting.

When I entered our bedroom, I stopped in my tracks, wondering if I had somehow walked into the wrong place. The bed was gone, replaced with a small table and chairs, already set for two. The floor was filled with candles, surrounding the perimeter of the room, leaving a wide circle for the table with a path to the doorway I now stood in, and another leading to an open set of double doors that had not existed a couple of hours before, revealing a previously nonexistent veranda, also lit with candles. And in the midst of all of it stood Aydan, adjusting a table setting. He looked up when I gasped.

"You're early," he said.

"We finished up quickly… Aydan what is all of this?"

"A few hours of solitude," he said as he approached and kissed me. "The past few weeks have been relentless. Tomorrow will be even more so. I thought—" Aydan paused, taking note of the angry purple bruise still on my cheek. "What the hell—" I winced as he brushed his thumb over it.

"Gerridan thinks you're going to kill him," I said. Aydan's eyebrows shot up as though he might be considering it while he continued examining the injury. "It was an accident," I clarified. "I let my guard down and got distracted in the middle of him throwing a punch this morning in the ring."

"Well, I won't kill him tonight. I'm otherwise occupied." I laughed. "We really should get something on that though." He snapped his fingers and a black leather case like a small traveling trunk appeared on the tabletop. Aydan led me there to sit.

"That's a healer's case," I said.

"Mhm." Aydan opened it and began sifting through some jars. "I was a medic in the army," he reminded me. He held up his left arm, his sleeve rolled up to reveal the tattoos on his brown skin, reminding me of their purpose— a symbol of his rank and his service to the territory and to his grandmother, Lady Solandis, its patroness. "These were awarded for lives saved, not lives taken."

"What are you looking for?" I asked as he continued to rifle through the case.

"I could have sworn I had leopard's bane—" I held up the jar given to me by Lyra. He cocked an eyebrow. "The trick is to mix it with—"

"Bloodwort?" I finished. He smirked. "Already done." He snatched the jar from me and opened it up, sniffing the contents.

"Well," Aydan said, dipping a finger into the jar and beginning to spread the salve over my cheek. "Looks like my techniques have spread even to the covens." I rolled my eyes and smacked his arm lightly.

"Or you're not as innovative as you think you are."

"Of course I'm not," he replied, still smirking. "Isn't that the fun of being King? Pretending you're good at everything?"

"Not if I have anything to say about it." He finished applying the salve and I looked up at the mirror which still stood in the corner of the room. The paste-like substance was a brownish yellow color, now spread across my cheek. "Well that's attractive," I commented, turning my head to see from a different angle.

"You certainly are."

"I was being sarcastic, my love."

"I wasn't." He tucked a loose strand of hair behind my ear. "You look beautiful. Yellow sludge and all." Aydan leaned forward in his chair to kiss me deeply. Again. Then a third time, and Aydan's hand was cradling my face, refusing to break from me. It only took seconds before the eager kisses became wandering hands; One remained on my face while the other explored the bodice of my dress, grazing my breasts over the top of it, his thumb dragging along my collarbone. I threw my arms around his neck, and soon found Aydan lifting me from my chair and laying me down on the floor. I began fumbling with the laces at the front of my dress which held the bodice together, and Aydan broke our kiss to lift the edge of my skirt, running his hand up my leg, caressing my thigh, his hand gripping roughly as he began to kiss my neck, down my chest and toward my breasts—

Three sharp knocks sounded on the door. I jumped.

"*No.*" Aydan called out. His voice dripped with irritation.

"Open up." It was Kenna.

"Aydan darling, it's an emergency." Gerridan was at the door as well. Aydan sighed and stood from the floor, helping me up as well before crossing the room and unlocking the door. He attempted to simply stick his head out, but our friends pushed past him.

"Hey—" I cried out, turning away from them as I finished re-lacing my bodice.

"*Very* nice," Gerridan said, looking around the room at the candles, the new veranda, and our dinner set up. "Too bad it has to go to waste."

"What are you talking about?" Aydan asked, looking between his advisor and seer. "What is the emergency?"

"Stag night." Gerridan winked.

"Hen party for you." Kenna jerked her chin in my direction.

"No." Aydan shook his head. "Not happening, we have plans, we have to be up at dawn—"

"It's tradition."

"You know we aren't leaving without you. You might as well comply." Kenna leaned against the table and examined her fingernails while she spoke. Aydan groaned and ran a hand down his face.

"I suppose there's no arguing with these two," I told him. Ignoring our audience, Aydan wrapped his arms around my waist and pulled me in tightly.

"I could just remove Gerridan from his position... Banish Kenna from the house..."

"Yes, but then there would be all the trouble of finding a new Chief Advisor before we leave for the tour," I replied. I heard Gerridan make a noise of protest but did not break Aydan's gaze. He kissed me again, eagerly, and when my arms found their way around his neck again our friends' protests became even louder. We parted, and Aydan pressed his forehead to mine.

"I suppose I won't see you until the ceremony," I said.

"I suppose not."

"I'll be the nervous one in the fancy dress," I joked. "In case you lose track of me."

"I'll be with you the whole time," he replied seriously. He squeezed my hands once more before kissing my cheek and murmuring, "Goodnight, my lady." Gerridan clapped him on the shoulder and they disappeared from the room.

A second later, Kenna gripped my arm and I felt the familiar dropping sensation of being effuged, before my feet landed on stone floors. I looked around and saw what appeared to be an apartment suite. The light gray stone of the walls and floors told me that we were in the Grand Palace of Sylvanna.

"Make yourself at home," Kenna said, summoning a drink to my hand. I realized this must be her suite.

It was similar to the one I had occupied following Aydan's return to Ayzelle, in that it was a single, large room, with what I assumed was a bathroom behind a door opposite from me. However, there was no bed. Instead, there was a large circle carved out of the floor filled with silk cushions and embroidered pillows. There were short tables placed every few feet carrying food and wine that one could lazily reach for while they lounged in a sea of comfort. As I could have expected, Hannele was sitting on a teal cushion, helping herself to the nearby food. What I didn't expect was Lady Reyna Hazelwren to be beside her, or Lyra to be sitting opposite them.

"Ladies," I said, looking between the witch and Lady Reyna, "I didn't expect the two of you to be here."

"Reyna and I ran into one another last week and I thought you'd both enjoy the visit," Kenna explained. "I extended the invitation to Miss Lyra this afternoon following my outburst." I glanced at Lyra, who shrugged before drinking deeply from her glass. She was not glamoured. Reyna saw Lyra's true face the day the witch brought Hannele and me to her doorstep. If she had questions about Lyra's identity, she had not expressed them to any of us.

"Well— er, thank you all for coming," I said as politely as I could, hoping that my face wasn't expressing how much I'd rather be back home with Aydan right now.

"You must be so excited," Reyna said, beaming. "After all the planning, it must be a relief for the big day to finally be here."

"It is," I said. "There's hardly been time for anything else."

"Sometimes I wish I would have been able to plan a wedding with Charles," Reyna said. "But then I see how exhausted one gets during all of it and I must say that I'm grateful for our elopement." She took a drink. It was the first time I had heard her say Charles' name out loud. Her late husband, a mortal man, died in a sparring accident while she was still pregnant with their daughter. Aydan was once reluctantly betrothed to Reyna in an arrangement made by her father and Aydan's grandmother, but when he found out that Reyna was in love with Charles, Aydan helped the two of them sneak away to elope. Despite knowing it was all arranged, I found it difficult to quell my jealousy when I learned of Aydan's previous engagement. However, it was Reyna's doorstep that Lyra, Hannele, and I wound up on when we returned from the Onyx Temple, and it was Reyna who called in healers and the rest of the Cabinet to make sure we were cared for. I doubted I would ever be able to repay her.

"Yes, exhausting is the word," I finally said. "Although Kenna has been kind enough to take on much of the stress on my behalf." The seer shrugged.

"Can't have my future Queen's hair falling out over flower arrangements," she mumbled.

"I always knew I would elope if I ever married," Hannele commented.

"That's because you and golden boy have been pining over each other for two hundred years," Kenna replied, rolling her eyes. "Honestly I'm surprised you two didn't stop at the temple on your way home from Hazelwren." I stifled a laugh, while Hannele shot Kenna a look. I heard Lyra chuckling to herself from her cushion, which drew Kenna's attention.

"And what about you?" Kenna drawled. "Was your wedding just absolutely *magical?*"

"Oh, are you married, Miss Lyra?" Reyna asked politely. Hannele met my eyes briefly— we were all too familiar with Lyra's husband.

"Unfortunately," the witch replied flatly to Reyna before turning her attention to Kenna. "And no, it wasn't." She swirled her wine.

"Were you forced to elope too?" Kenna smirked. "Didn't get the big reception you always wanted?" Lyra stared at her.

"Kenna, stop it—" Hannele said. Lyra cut her off.

"I only found out the day before that it was happening at all, and I spent every minute until it was over begging for it *not* to happen." She took a drink before continuing. "My husband was trained in his craft across the sea, by worshippers of Thiirmot." I glanced at Reyna, who blinked, but did not otherwise react to hearing Lyra speak of witchcraft. Bless her. "He came to us with news from his clan, whisperings of plots coming from their sister coven— or so I gathered. I was not privy to their discussions. The Mothers were impressed with Deimos and asked him to stay on in their court. After some negotiations on what titles and prizes would be awarded to him, an agreement was made. I, apparently, was the greatest prize of them all." The rest of us were silent. "My unwillingness didn't matter to the Mothers, or to my husband. Truth be told it seemed to make things more appealing for him. I told him I didn't want him, that I didn't want any man at all. But, after the wedding, I was his to do with what he liked." The memory of Deimos groping me in his dungeon flashed in my mind. "I escaped from my mortal family's stifled ways only to find myself trapped by the same place that gave me my freedom. As the Mothers' Keeper I held more power than most in the Temple, but for the last forty years I've been Deimos' prisoner. I'm sorry that you both have some experience in that department," Lyra said, looking between Hannele and me.

"You really need to work on your party conversation," Kenna chuckled. I felt the flames beneath my palms rising and it took some concentration to keep them from engulfing my arms.

"*Kenna,*" Hannele scolded.

"She's right," Lyra mumbled. "My apologies, ladies, that's certainly not a story to be told the night before a wedding." She raised her glass in my direction. "You are a lucky woman, Lady Shaye. Few in this world get the chance to encounter true love, let alone keep it for a lifetime." I raised my glass in her direction as well, and we both drank. Lyra added to Kenna, "My apologies again, Lady Kenna. It can be difficult, I'm sure, to hear stories of other peoples' troubles when you've lived such a charmed life—" Kenna's glass shattered in her hand.

"Shit," I whispered, willing the glass back together and summoning the wine from the rug it had soaked.

"My life has been far from *charmed*, Miss Lyra," Kenna said through gritted teeth.

"That's not what she meant, Kenna, leave it," Hannele said. Reyna had gone pale.

"Of course it's not, how could anyone like her know the things I've— She couldn't even fathom—"

"I know. But this isn't this place."

"Fine," Kenna huffed. She turned to me. "Sorry Shaye, this isn't what I wanted for your party."

"Don't worry about it," I replied, wondering now what it was that she had endured. I knew very little of Kenna's past. "What are the gentlemen of the Cabinet up to tonight?"

"Gerridan glamoured all of them and took them to a pub in the village," Hannele answered. "Lucky bastards." I tried to hide my agreement to spare Kenna's feelings.

"I don't see why we couldn't join them—" Reyna was interrupted by a knock at the door. Kenna, looking irritated, stood from her cushion and moved to answer it, only to be faced with Lady Solandis, holding a large white box in her hands.

"My lady?"

"Lady Kenna, I am sorry to intrude, but I hoped I might have a moment with the bride to be." I quickly glamoured Lyra to look mortal and moved to stand as Kenna stepped aside, allowing the Lady of Sylvanna to enter the suite. Solandis looked around. "I haven't been here since the renovation. I like what you've done with it."

"Thank you, my lady," Kenna replied. "It made more sense to have it as an entertaining space, since I spend so much time at the King's private residence."

"Indeed," Solandis said before turning her attention to me. "Lady Shaye, I am sorry to interrupt your party. May I have a word in the next room?"

"I— yes, of course," I said before moving to follow her through the door to what I had assumed to be a bathroom, shooting Hannele a look that I hoped said *Don't let Lyra and Kenna kill each other while I'm gone.* When I entered the next room, Solandis waved her hand, shutting the door behind us, and I saw that it was a dressing room. Kenna's many gowns hung on racks lining the walls, and dozens of pairs of shoes were placed neatly on a large unit of shelves toward the back. There was also a large vanity, filled with creams and cosmetics I didn't recognize, and a purple velvet chaise, where Solandis now stood with the box sitting on top of it.

"You are looking well, Lady Shaye," Solandis told me as her eyes drifted up and down my figure. Her gaze paused for a few seconds on the salve spread on my cheek, but she did not mention it. "You've recovered nicely from your ordeal." The lady had only seen me once since my return to Sylvanna, when I was still mostly bedridden, coming for a brief visit to Aydan's private residence to pay her respects and offer congratulations to her future Queen.

"Thank you, my lady," I replied, tilting my head and dipping down into a brief curtsy. Aydan suggested I stop curtsying to the various lords and ladies in Ayzelle and Sylvanna alike following our engagement, but Solandis was different from a council member. Until tomorrow at least, she still outranked me. "I'm glad to be feeling so much better before such an important day."

"Tomorrow will make history," Solandis agreed with a nod. Her stiff words, her tight posture, were both a result of the thousand years she'd lived and ruled as Lady of Sylvanna, alongside her husband, Lord Priamos. She did not look a day older than me or Hannele or Kenna, but the sorceress who had led the overthrow of the tyrant prince who once ruled this territory held her age in her aura. "Which is, as I'm sure you suspect, why I'm here."

"Oh?"

"It is, er, traditional for the groom's mother to deliver a gift— an heirloom, to welcome the bride into the family. Astra is not here to do it herself, so..." Solandis gestured to the box.

"Oh." I tucked my hair behind my ears. "That's very kind of you, my lady." Awkward silence hung in the air. Aydan's grandmother had told me plainly that she did not want our relationship to carry on, as my family's ruined reputation threatened to taint the Crown. Now, here she was, bearing a family heirloom. A welcome-to-the-family gift.

"My daughter did not live long enough to see her son have any serious candidates for marriage," Solandis said. "Such a gift is chosen once the bride has met her future mother-in-law, as it is meant to reflect the recipient's taste, or fill a need. That is to say, I have chosen this item myself. For you." She motioned toward the box once again, indicating that I should open it. I placed my fingers along the edges of the lid, and was surprised, having expected to feel a dress box, to find now that I was touching it that the box was made of leather. I lifted it, gasping softly as I revealed a golden corset. Like many of the decorative pieces the Lady of Sylvanna wore, it appeared to be part jewelry, part armor, and I supposed depending on who saw it, could be interpreted either way.

"My lady, I—" I set the lid aside and ran my fingers along the white velvet lining of the box. "I don't know what to say. Thank you."

"Tomorrow, you will start the day as a bride," Solandis said. "And you will end it as a Queen. I thought you might like to look the part." She wiped her hands on her skirts before folding them in front of her again, her tattooed face expressionless as she added, "The piece should accompany any gown with ease."

"It's amazing. Thank you," I turned to face her fully. "Truly. I know… I know that we started off on the wrong foot, but I hope you know, my lady, that this means so much to me. I hope that in time I can prove your reservations about me wrong."

"My reservations have never been about you, Lady Shaye. I believe I've made myself clear on that topic." She sighed. "You make the King happy. You were effective as Chief Advisor, and you've suffered enough to know what hardship is. The people see you as one of them. I believe you'll be an effective leader, if you can keep your House from becoming the topic of conversation." My palms heated at the memory of Knox Redfern's groveling from the previous evening.

"I plan to do my best," I replied vaguely. Another awkward pause lingered around us until I finally blurted, "Well— I should get back…"

"Yes, yes, of course, my apologies for keeping you from your evening." I gave a swift curtsy before she effuged from the dressing room without any further bidding farewell, leaving me standing alone. I glanced once more at the contents of the box before lifting the large lid and placing it back on top. I summoned a slip of paper into my hand and wrote a brief note which read: *For the coronation gown.* I banished the box and its contents to Cecil the dressmaker's shop. He would know exactly what to do. My friends would have to endure the suspense.

When I returned to said friends, Hannele and Reyna were talking quietly while Lyra and Kenna tried their hardest to look at anything else in the room but one another.

"Sorry, ladies," I said as I rejoined them in the cushioned circle.

"What did she want?" Hannele asked.

"To give me a gift," I replied before sipping from the goblet in front of me, though I wasn't quite sure it was mine.

"Scary," Kenna commented.

"Terrifying," I agreed with a chuckle. I looked around the room and sighed before telling Kenna, "Ken, I'm sorry but I am dying of boredom here. Can we just glamor ourselves and join the boys at the pub?"

"Absolutely not," she replied. "You and Aydan will just sneak off together and leave the rest of us drinking on your behalf while you get a head start on your wedding night."

"Caught me," I laughed. "Well, then someone needs to get me drunk, and quickly, or I'm going to make a run for it." Kenna did not look amused.

"May I suggest a game?" Reyna said from her cushion.

"Please do."

"Well... first we'll need an ale glass and a few coins..."

The next morning, I slowly blinked my eyes open and immediately snapped them shut again when the sunlight pouring in through the window met my line of vision. Cursing the sun itself, I pressed a hand to my pounding head and after a moment realized that the pounding was actually a soft, continuous knock on the door of mine and Aydan's bedroom.

"My lady, it is time to wake up," Isolde's thick accent whisper-shouted through the door. "We must get you in the bathtub if we're going to have enough time—" I couldn't hear the rest of her sentence over the pressure that built in my ears while I leaned over the edge of the bed and vomited as quietly as I could manage onto the floor. I groaned softly as I cleaned it up, banishing the now visible contents of my stomach to the toilet and flushing it away. Fucking Kenna. The seer had bested me for the eighth round in a row of Reyna's cup game, leaving me giddy and drunk, before she pulled out a hand painted box filled with smoking herbs, packed them into a pipe made from a deer's antler and offered it to the rest of us. I, in my drunken stupor, had eagerly accepted, leaving my head cloudier with each inhalation. At that moment, it was the best decision I'd ever made. Now, I was ready to kill Kenna for offering me the pipe when I was already so drunk— that is, if I ever managed to pull myself out of bed. The knocking continued.

"My lady, I really must insist—"

"I'm awake, Isolde, thank you," I called out. Catchfly nudged my side for daring to wake her. "Would you please ask the kitchen for something to help my head? I'm afraid I had a few too many drinks last night." The door opened, and Isolde entered, followed by Elise, carrying a tray holding a tea pot.

"Lord Alastair already made the request on your behalf, my lady," Elise said as she placed the tray on the bedside table and poured me a cup, rather than forcing me to sit up and risk vomiting again. "He mentioned that your party ran a bit *late* and that you might not be feeling your best this morning." I scoffed. The late hour hadn't caused the problem and Alastair knew it. It was he who arrived at Kenna's door in the middle of the night to escort me home. All of us— save for Hannele, who had yawned dramatically and announced her departure about ten minutes after the drinking games started— had drunkenly protested, but Alastair insisted I sleep in my own bed tonight as Elise and Isolde would need to find me in the morning. He'd eventually convinced me to effuge home with him but had needed to nearly carry me to my room after my knees buckled upon our landing. Alastair tucked me into bed in the clothes I was wearing, and I fell asleep mere seconds after he left the room.

"Thanks, Elise," I said before taking a sip of the tea and making a face. It was one of Tory's concoctions, a nearly instant cure for hangovers that all of us needed at some time or another. I wondered what sort of mischief the Xarynnian cook had gotten up to in his life to have discovered such a useful mixture. Whatever it was, he had never told any of us the ingredients— or rather, as Tory only spoke Xarynnea, he had never told his husband Zale, who assured me that even he didn't know the recipe. I didn't really care— the cup could be filled with pureed fish heads for all I knew, and I downed the contents anyway. I squinted at the clock on the other side of the room. "What time is it?"

"Early," Elise replied, motioning for me to stand. "But we only have four hours until the ceremony and there is much to do. Off to the bathtub with you."

Half an hour later I was being pulled from the tub by Isolde, who insisted on washing my hair despite my protest, telling her that I was happy to do it myself. "A bride deserves pampering on her wedding day," she said. I fought the urge to remind her that my whole life was dripping with privilege and pampering, which would only increase after today. Instead, I bit my tongue and allowed her to massage soaps and scented oils into my scalp without further protest.

It was hard not to find myself ridiculous, even now. Me— about to become the anointed Queen of Medeisia. The gods-chosen Queen of all sorcerers, and yet, it was only a little more than two years ago that I still thought myself mortal like Uncle Gideon. There was a hollow ache in my chest that mourned the fact that he would not be here today. It was tradition in Medeisia for the parents of the bride to escort her to the edge of the aisle, and he was the only parent I had ever known. It would be a struggle to walk alone today, in just a few hours. But the smiling face waiting at the alter would be worth the nerves now shivering through me.

I toweled off and stepped into the silk robe Elise held before she directed me to sit at the vanity. Waiting there on a plate before me was a chocolate and raspberry pastry, courtesy of Tory, along with some bacon and fruit. "Eat," Elise instructed while she picked up a comb to begin running it through my hair. "You won't have time again until *after* the coronation feast, and I won't have you walking around with an empty stomach all day." I picked up the pastry and took an eager bite, chewing silently as Elise combed out my hair to begin her handiwork. When a knock rapped on the door, it was Isolde who crossed the room to answer, to be met with a delivery girl carrying a large gown box. Isolde thanked the girl and waited to shut the door before squealing with excitement that my wedding dress had arrived. But before Isolde could lift the lid, there was another knock. She scowled and opened the door again.

"I'm sorry to interrupt," said a timid voice. Another delivery girl. "But I have a few things here—" I almost choked on my bacon when the girl stepped aside and a stream of delivery girls and boys began to enter the room carrying enormous arrangements of flowers, setting them down on various surfaces, as if they had been instructed on exactly where to go. The last boy carried a stack of blue velvet boxes— three of them, the largest on the bottom with two smaller versions sitting on top of it. The boy approached gingerly and set the boxes beside me on the vanity before backing away quickly and joining his companions in a line. They all bowed and curtsied to me before turning on their heels to leave as quickly as they had come. I nodded in silent thanks before gaping at the flowers.

"Oh, Aydan," I whispered to myself as I stood to inspect the six enormous arrangements now taking up every flat surface in the room save for the vanity. They were mostly roses, though I also spotted peonies, gardenias, and ranunculus— all from the gardens surrounding the Grand Palace of Sylvanna— in shades of white, cream, dusty mauve, and blush pink— almost the same shade as the pink dress I wore to the eclipse festival nearly a year ago. My throat bobbed as my fingers brushed the delicate petals of the flowers nearest to me, sitting atop the small table between the high-backed armchairs by the fireplace. A card was sticking out of the top of this one, barely visible amongst all the blooms. I opened it, reading the short note in Aydan's familiar loopy scrawl:

A stem for each day you've held my heart. It remains yours, forever.
-A

I blinked away the burning in my eyes and folded the note again before returning to the vanity. I placed the note with all Aydan's other letters before turning my attention to the trio of blue velvet boxes beside me. I opened the smallest, revealing a delicate pair of earrings, made with clusters of no less than twenty tiny diamonds that surrounded a single, delicate, tear-shaped pearl which hung from the very bottom. The next box contained a bracelet that matched the design of the earrings—diamond and pearl, in a delicate swirling pattern. I had a suspicion as to what would be revealed in the largest of the boxes. When I opened it, despite being proven right, I still gasped as I beheld the swirling, exquisite diamond and pearl tiara in the box before me. Elise, who had been busy using her magic to dry my hair and had not noticed what I was looking at, peered over my shoulder and let out a light gasp.

"Those are the Queen's," she said.

"I guessed as much," I said. "I told him he should stop giving all of his mother's jewelry to me—"

"Not Queen Astra, my lady," Elise clarified. "That jewelry belonged to Queen Euna." I swallowed and let my fingers dance along the edge of the box. "Would you like me to put it away?" She asked, noting the uneasy look on my face. I swallowed.

"No," I said. "I will wear the earrings and bracelet during the ceremony. Save the tiara for the ball." Elise nodded and set the jewelry boxes beside the dress box and returned to her work on my hair.

While Elise worked my hair into curls and pinned them by hand— magic, she told me, would not allow her to be as detailed, and she wanted perfection— Isolde began applying makeup to my face. I was always fascinated to see the result of what the women transformed me into. They finished at the same time, Isolde completing her work with a final dusting of a barely-there shimmering powder on my cheekbones and began lacing me into my dress. Cecil had supplied clear instructions on how to do this. Elise was applying glamours to my back, erasing the old scars that peeked over the top of my shoulders, when yet another knock sounded on the door.

"Enter," I called out while Isolde helped me to step into the shoes Cecil sent along. The door opened and I heard female voices over the sounds of movement from the hallway. Hannele and Kenna entered, followed closely by an already-glamoured Lyra, all dressed in beautiful gowns also made by Cecil.

Hannele, who looked particularly weepy, said softly, "Oh Shaye, just look at you." I glanced at the floor length mirror on the opposite wall and saw it all put together for the first time: my reddish-brown hair was in soft curls gathered and pinned just at the nape of my neck, with a few strands pulled loose to frame my face, while my makeup was light, just enough to highlight my best features. Then there was the dress, which only me, Cecil, and Kenna had seen: layers of sheer fabric gave the gown the appearance of being made from nothing but gossamer and air. The sleeves sat off my shoulders, leaving them bare while the rest of my arms were covered by just a layer or two of the material. Cecil had gathered layer after layer, placing them on top of one another and creating sheer panels along my torso. Thicker sections covered my breasts while keeping the low-cut necklines Sylvannian fashion had popularized. The gown was a soft dove gray that matched my eyes, and in certain light appeared nearly lavender. I watched in the mirror while Elise fastened the earrings into my lobes and Isolde placed the bracelet on my right wrist. I was ethereal. All at once, for the first time, I felt like a bride.

"You all look lovely," I said, turning my attention back to my friends. Kenna wore a slightly less revealing dress than normal. Her gown was a light sage green, with her favorite design choice of no bodice, instead covering her torso with nothing more than a crisscross of fabric and using magic to keep things in place. Hannele, who also tended to enjoy a plunging neckline, had opted for a flowing coral pink gown that sat off her shoulders. Lyra, whose glamoured body had alabaster skin and raven black hair, with sharp, angular features and icy blue eyes, wore a similar design to Hannele's but in light blue. I glanced back at Hannele, whose eyes had filled with tears. "Han, what—"

"Oh it's nothing," she said, dabbing her eyes with a handkerchief that she'd summoned from somewhere. "I'm just so happy for you—"

"She's been blubbering all morning," Kenna clarified before wrapping her arms around me in a soft hug, careful to avoid crushing my dress. "You're stunning." Lyra nodded from behind her.

"The King is a lucky man."

"Thank you," I told them all before looking at the clock. "Is it time to go?" My palms heated slightly, and I wiped them on my skirts.

"Looks like it." Kenna looked at the clock as well. "We have about an hour, so we'd better get into position before Declan works himself up." I turned to Elise and Isolde, who were both misty eyed, standing near the vanity, and hugged each of them.

"Thank you," I told them softly. They curtsied in unison. "I'll see you at the feast."

"My lady," Elise said in farewell. I realized that it was the last time she would call me that. She seemed to realize it too. Like Hannele, Isolde now cried into a handkerchief. Without another word, I joined hands with Lyra while Kenna held Hannele's, and the four of us effuged to castle Ayzelle.

I paced the lounge where Hannele and Kenna dropped me off while Lyra sat watching and keeping me company. I was too nervous to sit; I could hear the rumble of people walking and talking as they passed through the castle and made their way to the ceremony site, which was outside on the castle grounds. Hannele had wanted to go let Gerridan know we'd arrived, while Kenna announced that she was going to make sure Lord Declan had not deviated from her instructions for the décor. He was the most senior member of the Ayzellen council, which granted him the privilege of managing large events such as royal weddings and coronations, but Kenna assured me that she would be damned if she was going to let Declan oversee my wedding. If he had deviated from her instructions, I surely would not envy him today.

Someone knocked. Not waiting for my response before entering, Gerridan and Alastair filed into the room. The former grinned widely while the latter wore a solemn look on his face. It was as emotional as Alastair would appear in public. Both men hugged me and kissed my cheek. When I pulled away from Gerridan I asked, "How is he?"

"Calm as can be," Gerridan replied.

"Really?"

"Gods, no," he scoffed. "He's as much a nervous wreck as you are." I punched his arm, and he laughed, batting me away. I noticed him sneaking a glance at the side of my face that had been bruised yesterday and exhale with quiet relief when he saw that it was healed. He looked me up and down and let out a low whistle. "Aydan's going to lose it when he sees you," he said.

"I'm going to lose it if I don't get out of this room soon."

"Almost there," Gerridan assured me. "A few more minutes and someone will come to collect you. We just wanted to wish you luck before we go and take our places." I thanked him, hugging them both again before they bid me and Lyra farewell. When the door clicked shut, I turned to Lyra, who now stood.

"If I burst into flame, promise you'll glamour me so the guests can't see—"

"You won't," she said.

Another knock, and Lord Declan entered the room.

"Lady Eastly, we'll be starting in five minutes," he said. "I suggest Miss Lyra find her way to the ceremony site." Lyra looked at me and I nodded once, dismissing her. An act that we put on for the council and other nobles outside of our house. When Lyra left, Declan continued, "I'll be happy to effuge you to—"

"That won't be necessary, my lord," said Alastair, reappearing behind Declan. "May we have a moment?"

"Of course." Declan stepped out into the corridor. "Please arrive in three minutes, my lady." He bowed his head and effuged.

"Shouldn't you be with Aydan?" I asked.

"I thought you might need— I'd like to be your escort today. If you want." I swallowed. "I don't mean to be presumptuous—"

"No. You aren't, I mean. I'm just kicking myself for not thinking of it first." Medeisian families did not give brides away the way Nautian ones did, but if Gideon were alive to see this day I would have asked him to escort me to the aisle. The Eastly line had ended with Gideon, and the Redferns were certainly out of the question. Alastair was the last living link to my mother. "I'd be honored, Alastair. Really." The corners of his mouth curved upward into a smile, and he offered me his arm before effuging us outside to the castle grounds.

We arrived at my end of the aisle, and an unseen orchestra was already playing. Despite my clutching Alastair's arm, I shook with nerves. The eyes of five hundred prominent Medeisians, sorcerer and mortal alike, were turned toward us. I could feel them staring at me, my dress, my hair. I wondered what they thought of me. Did they agree with Solandis? Or was Aydan's faith in me enough for them? It had been so long since anyone had heard his old moniker, the Wayward Prince, whispered around court that it seemed the courtiers had accepted the transition into Aydan's reign— but would they accept mine?

"You have to start walking now," Alastair whispered in my ear. I nodded to show that I had heard him but couldn't bring my mouth to speak.

In Medeisia, the bride and groom both make their way down opposite ends of a long aisle, meeting in the center, where the High Priest and Priestess waited in the middle of a large circle. Those witnessing the marriage fill the spaces outside the circle once the bride and groom meet, leaving no trace of the aisles. This seemed sweet when it was first explained to me— the thought of a couple's family and friends encircling them while they were joined for life. But now that I walked slowly to the circle surrounded by the courtiers and nobles who just a year ago had hated me, I wondered how any royal bride who came before me had managed to make it this far without fainting.

And then I saw him.

Coming over the slight curve of the hilltop on the other end of our aisle, Aydan was dashing as ever. His brown skin glistened under the late morning sunlight. His wavy black hair was combed neatly beneath the gold circlet that sat atop his head. He wore a dark emerald suit stitched with black. As we came closer to the center, I could see his crest sewn into the breast of his jacket, the rampant winged lion wreathed in roses. The sweat on my palms disappeared as soon as I saw his face, now the only one in view amid this crowd. Thank the gods he kept his composure despite the emotion I could see swimming behind his eyes. If Aydan started crying, I doubted that I would make it through the ceremony. I let out a breath as we came closer, and despite myself all I could bring myself to think was: *Don't fall, don't* fucking *fall—*

When we came to the edge of what would be the circle, the High Priest and Priestess both knelt in unison toward Aydan just before he stepped inside. I had almost forgotten about the kneeling. It had been an argument throughout the course of the wedding planning. I had not kneeled to Aydan since his coronation. A public curtsy here and there, yes, but never full-fledged, eyes-averted kneeling.

"It *is* tradition," Aydan had explained, looking somewhat embarrassed after seeing the look on my face when Kenna had told me what to expect of my wedding ceremony. "But not one that I would expect you to keep. You are to be anointed, there is no expectation—"

"When you enter the circle, Shaye will still just be a lady, and you will be her King. She is your subject. It is more than an expectation, it is simply how this is done." Kenna straightened the papers before her. I'd been shocked by her insistence. "There will be a good number of people in attendance who are wary of the Head of House Redfern becoming an anointed monarch of Medeisia. Shaye's adherence to tradition will be a comfort to them." I told her I would think about it.

Now here we were. Alastair appeared at the edge of the circle, and Aydan stood before me, his eyes scanning the dove gray dress that floated around my body. Here, now, tradition didn't seem like such a bad thing. Like the clergy, I sunk low onto my knee before Aydan. I didn't hear or see anyone bid me to rise, but after a few seconds of silence, I began making my way upward. It was time to begin.

The High Priestess bid us to join hands and then greeted the witnesses. "It is a fine day to celebrate such a historic union. Today, His Majesty King Aydan Aevitarus will wed Lady Shaye Eastly." I kept my eyes on the High Priestess and did my best to ignore the murmur in the crowd. I knew it would happen whether she said Eastly or Redfern, though it would no longer matter in a few minutes.

The High Priestess, and then the High Priest each took their time making speeches about duty and unity, prosperity and fidelity. I felt my hands start to shake with anticipation and the weight of a thousand eyes on me. Aydan squeezed them tighter with his own and I glanced up at him. His eyes were shining, and I had to look down at the ground or risk bursting into tears.

The clergy continued for another moment until it was time to say vows.

"The oaths you are about to make will be heard not only by these witnesses but by the gods themselves: Lehrun and Ehnara, the father and mother of us all. Your Majesty," the High Priestess said. "Will you take Lady Eastly to be your wife and your Queen? Will you honor, protect, love, and cherish her as your partner in all things?"

"I will." I looked to him again and he winked, trying to make me laugh. He got a smile out of me before the high priest began his turn to speak:

"Lady Eastly, will you take this man to be your husband and King? Will you honor, protect, love, and cherish him as your partner in all things?"

I locked eyes with Aydan and said, "I will."

"Then it is my honor and my pleasure to declare you husband and wife today, until the end of your days," the priestess said. To the crowd she added, "I present to you all: the King and Queen of Medeisia." This time when everyone sank down to their knee, I remained standing. I couldn't help but stare at them all. When they rose, the High Priest added:

"Your Majesties, you may seal your oath with a kiss." Aydan wasted no time, placing his hands on either side of my face and kissing me on the mouth as he effuged us back to castle Ayzelle.

When the ground reappeared beneath my feet, Aydan kissed me again, and again. My arms looped around his neck, and his around my waist, pulling me against his body. When we finally parted, he took both of my hands in his own.

"You look incredible."

"So do you. When I saw you come over that hill it was like I could finally breathe." He kissed me again.

"It is tradition for this to be given in private, after the ceremony." Aydan reached inside his jacket and pulled out a small box. He opened it to reveal a delicate gold ring topped with a large oval-shaped black gem, encircled with tiny white diamonds. He slipped it onto my left ring finger. "I had it designed with you in mind, but if there are any changes you'd like made we can send it to the jeweler—"

"It's perfect," I said, my attention darting back and forth between Aydan and the ring. "I'll never take it off."

"You'll have to in a few minutes for the ceremony," he reminded me. "But after that you may keep it on your hand until your final day." In all my excitement, I'd nearly forgotten the coronation. I buried my face in his neck.

"Do you remember when I dropped that tree on us that first night in Sylvanna?"

"Vaguely." I could hear a wicked grin in his tone.

"You told me you felt the presence of the gods during your coronation." I swallowed. "Do you think— What happens if they don't approve of me the way they did you?"

"They will."

"But what if—"

"If by chance the gods don't approve of you, if they shatter the crown from your head and turn the dyadic oil to acid, then I shall renounce my titles and we will live as peasants for the rest of our days."

"I'm being serious," I said.

"So am I."

There was a knock at the door and Gerridan poked his head through it.

"It's nearly time," he said. "Elise and Isolde are here to prepare you, Your Majesty." It took half a moment to realize that he was addressing me, and not Aydan. "Hannele and Kenna will wait outside to escort you to the temple."

"All right," I said.

"Give me another minute with my wife, please, Lord Advisor," Aydan said. Wife. *Wife*. I could listen to him call me that until the sun burned out. Gerridan grinned.

"As you wish."

The door shut again. Aydan placed his hand on my cheek. "You'll be fine. We'll get through the next hour, and then you will be the anointed Queen of Sorcerers." He kissed my forehead, and I couldn't help but melt despite my nerves.

"Promise me something," I murmured after a few seconds of silence.

"Anything."

"No matter what happens, no matter what titles we hold— promise me that before we are anything to anyone else, before I am a Queen and you are a King: that you are my husband and I am your wife. I want those to be the most important titles we hold."

Aydan placed his fist over his heart in salute. "On my honor, wife."

And with that, I had all the courage I needed to meet the gods.

Chapter Seven

It only took minutes for Elise and Isolde to undo their hours of work from this morning, removing all the intricately placed pins from my head and brushing my hair out so it lay down my back in a waterfall of curls. The makeup was removed from my skin with a wave of Isolde's hand before the pair helped me into a plain cotton shift that hung down a few inches past my knees. I removed my ring and placed it in Elise's hand.

"Hold this for me?" I asked. She nodded, her eyes looking a bit glossy as she placed it in her pocket and buttoned it closed.

When I stepped out of the room, Hannele and Kenna were both waiting for me, still in their gowns but now armed. I knew from having done weapons checks with them before that if I could see the blades at their hips, then they each likely had at least five more blades on them. No additional guard would be needed for this escort.

They curtsied. When the ladies rose, they paused, both folding their hands in front of them, waiting for me to speak or move.

"Well," I started, hoping I'd find something worthwhile to say. "I suppose we'd better get on with it." That would have to do.

I had not been to the temple since Aydan's coronation, but I remembered the way quite well. It didn't take us long to arrive, meeting the High Priest at the door. He held the same bowl of holy water as he had for Aydan.

"The tears of Ehnara," he announced, dipping his fingers into the water, and drawing a crescent moon shape on my forehead. My coronation had begun.

Having been a witness to this same ceremony so recently, there was an air of familiarity in the room as I stepped forward and stood before the altar to meet the High Priest and Priestess again. Then I was bid to kneel before the gods. The room was heavy with magic weighing down on my shoulders. I did my best to listen as the clergy took turns speaking, reminding the present witnesses just how monumental this occasion was.

The Dyadic Oil was brought forth, and the clerics continued to speak. My ears buzzed at the sight of the oil, and I became wrapped in warmth.

A strange voice, like two people speaking at once, not in my ears or in my mind, but somewhere deep within my heart asked, *"Are you worthy of this challenge?"*
I paused, swallowing before replying silently: "I believe so."

"Are you worthy of this challenge?" They asked again, more persistent this time.

"I am."

"Are you worthy of this duty?"

"I am."

"Are you worthy of this suffering?"

"I... I am."

"To defend the Crown comes at a great cost to all who bear it. You will one day learn its price, Daughter of Redfern."

"I will do so gladly," I answered. "No matter the cost."

"Then go forth and claim it."

Suddenly I realized that I had been covered in the mysterious shapes and drawings that the High Priest had painted on Aydan's skin during his ceremony. I didn't know how much time had passed, but I was about to be crowned.

It never occurred to the makers of the King's coronation crown that one for a Queen would ever be necessary. Queen Euna herself had designed her crown, and to carry on the tradition of reusing the coronation jewels, it would be presented to me tonight.

I felt warm again. The presence that questioned me during the anointing still lingered, no longer speaking, but surrounding me with comfort— a barrier between me and the heavy, overbearing magic that nearly threatened to crush me should the presence disperse. The High Priestess brought forth a large wooden box which I knew contained my crown. I held my breath as she opened it, and for a second, I wondered how many people in this room were old enough to have seen it the first time the Queen's crown was revealed.

It was enormous. Twin in design to the King's, the Queen's crown was tall and pointed, as if to mimic the rays of the sun. Rather than gold, however, this crown was made of triangular shards of diamond and moonstone, formed together in a circle and encrusted with raw sapphires along the brow so dark they were nearly black. The High Priestess placed it upon my head, and I felt my neck bend slightly with the weight of it.

I remained on my knees, letting the weight of the crown sink in, and waiting for the priestess to tell me to stand. It was then that I realized that Aydan left his seat and was standing before me on the dais between the High Priest and Priestess. I watched while the High Priest presented his king with a box and opened the lid. Aydan reached inside and pulled out a short dagger. Before I could process what I was seeing, he took the blade and dragged it across his left palm, sending blood dripping from the wound. My eyes widened, but the presence holding me in place did not allow me to react otherwise. Instead, I watched as Aydan dipped his finger into the blood now pouring freely from his palm, then closed my eyes when he reached forward and began to draw on my face and chest. He warned me that my coronation might differ from what I remembered of his but being painted in my husband's blood was not what I had pictured.

The warm crackling began in my chest, but quickly spread to my arms, hands, and fingertips before continuing down to my legs, then my feet. The High Priestess extended her hand to me, and when I took it, I saw that the familiar blue glow of Aydan's magic was coming from my own fingertips. The fiery blue light of the royal line, the unyielding magic which had held their throne for five thousand years now ran in my veins. Aydan's blood. It was his gift to me, the new matriarch of House Aevitarus.

I stood, and for the first time, faced the crowd of witnesses while power continued to surge through me. Each spot of blessed oil on my skin grew suddenly ice-cold, though I remained wrapped in warmth surrounding me. The glow that I'd witnessed in Aydan's hands so many times continued to grow, engulfing my arms up to the elbow while I felt this new magic intertwine with all the gifts that already lay within me.

I was the lioness.

The anointed Queen of Medeisia. Queen in my own right. My King's equal. Queen of everything if I wanted it.

It wasn't over. One by one, the lords of the Ayzellen council approached the dais, taking my hand as they knelt and swore fealty to me. The Sylvannian representatives followed. I didn't hear their words over the roar of new magic in my mind, like wind rushing passed my ears. The warmth of the presence strengthened for just another moment; the divine embrace of mother and father, before Lehrun and Ehnara departed.

My friends approached. Our family, our Cabinet. Hannele, Kenna, and Gerridan knelt one by one, their faces solemn as they looked upon me and swore oaths that I could not hear. They each pressed my hand to their brow as they finished, and I felt every ounce of their love in the touch.

It was Alastair's turn, and suddenly I could hear his footsteps as he approached the dais and knelt. My Lord General. The last thread of my mother's love. He pressed a kiss to my hand before looking up at me.

"Blessed lady and anointed Queen, I swear before you now, in the presence of gods and men, to act in faith of the Crown, to protect your throne with my flesh, and to do your bidding: through steel, through blood, with honor, all the days of my life." I met Alastair's gaze and dipped my chin in the slightest of nods, thanking him in my mind. I hoped he understood, and he seemed to, as he kissed my hand once again before pressing it to his brow like the others had done, then rose and moved to join them where they sat.

Aydan stepped forward to join me at my side. He would swear no oaths to me here, having done so already at the marriage altar. Instead, he extended his arm, and I lay mine flat atop it before we stepped down from the dais in unison. I allowed the blue glow to remain wrapped around my hands as we walked in step back down the aisle toward the temple doors. We were halfway there when the High Priestess' voice rang out:

"Long live the lioness! Long live the anointed Queen! Long live Queen Shaye!"

The crowd repeated: "Long live Queen Shaye!"

Chapter
Eight

Aydan delivered me to the doors of the prayer room, a small wing off the temple where I would now spend a period of silent contemplation. I wondered if the scholars or priests who'd come up with such a rule knew the direct contact that took place between gods and monarchs upon their coronation, or if this was all for appearances. If Ehnara and Lehrun had just taken the time to speak to me mere minutes ago, I doubted they would extend the same courtesy twice in a single night.

My husband dropped me off at the door without a word or so much as a kiss goodbye. He would greet me again when I emerged from the prayer room a fully formed Queen. For now, I sat here on my knees again, straining to hold up this crown and trying to process what had just become of me. An anointed Queen. Queen of all sorcerers, sovereign ruler of Medeisia until the end of my days. Aydan and I were bound for life. As solemn as the room felt, my heart soared anyway. My prince. My King— my *husband*. Mine, until the day I die. Should we be as lucky as his ancestors, that may not be for another thousand years. Centuries upon centuries to prove myself worthy of every oath I'd made today. Worthy of the challenge, worthy of the duty, worthy of the suffering. It seemed to only be a few minutes before I heard a soft knock.

"Enter," I choked out, shaking off any nerves that lingered.

"Your Majesty," a soft, familiar voice said upon entering the room. Elise's head was bowed. "I've come to help you dress. It's nearly time for you to join the ball."

"Of course," I replied softly, remaining in my place as Elise approached. Isolde trailed behind her, carrying a dress box stacked on top of the white leather gift box Solandis had delivered to me last night.

The pair got to work, first removing the crown and placing it on an empty stand that disappeared as soon as they let go. Back to the temple, where it would return to the care of the High Priest and Priestess until the next anointing of a Queen. My servants did not speak. The excited chatter that had taken place while dressing me for the ceremony was long forgotten and now replaced with a solemn silence that lay heavy on the air. I could feel my eyes glaze over while I stared ahead, attempting to at least pretend I was experiencing something holy.

Elise moved to lift my shift, and I raised my arms so she could remove it, stripping me naked in the temple. I fought the urge to shiver. While she helped me step into some undergarments, Isolde had already worked my hair back into pins. This time, rather than keep the soft curls at my nape, her magic brought it all high upon my head, with small braids woven throughout and Euna's tiara fastened firmly at the front of the mass of hair. I glanced down at my chest and saw that both the oil and the blood were gone, having been absorbed into my body.

When my hair was finished, Isolde waved a hand toward my face, then produced a mirror from nowhere. She had applied makeup to my face through magic, rather than taking her time with brushes as she normally did. I examined her work in the mirror: my eyes were lined in black, the lids were covered in a smoky powder that made the gray color of my eyes look fierce, and she'd stained my lips in a berry red just darker than the natural pink of my mouth. I nodded my approval to Isolde, and turned my attention back toward Elise, who was waiting to help me into my dress.

The gown for my coronation ball would need to send a message, Cecil had informed me. My wedding dress was soft, ethereal— the end of a fairytale. But *this* would be my first appearance as Queen. The gown should be beautiful, no doubt, but it should also remind all those who saw it exactly who it was they were looking at. Cecil's words had turned my arms to gooseflesh, and I grew excited as he showed me various sketches to approve of, adding and taking away elements as our minds changed. Elise took the top off the dress box, and with Isolde's help, lifted a mass of shimmering black from within it.

Like my wedding gown, the black dress was mostly layered gossamer. Tiny diamonds had been applied throughout the skirt to make it shimmer in the candlelight, and the bodice was mostly sheer black material with strategically placed lace appliques sewn in throughout. Elise and Isolde each took a side of the dress, creating space in the skirt for me to step into, before helping my arms into the delicate sleeves which sat off my shoulders. The effect of the gown would have been enough on its own, but there was still Solandis' gift to think of.

From its box, Elise removed the golden corset. She blinked at it a few times before placing it around my body and fastening the clasps.

The corset and dress both rested low in the back, exposing much of my scarred flesh, and I knew Elise's next step would be to begin glamouring me. Something stirred in my belly, and when she raised her hand to begin working, I stopped her.

"Let them see me," I said softly.

"Of course, Your Majesty," she replied with a nod. She produced a pair of black silk shoes and helped me step into them before returning to Isolde's side.

"Thank you both," I said, smoothing my hands down the front of my skirt. "I don't know if I'll see you before we depart for Xarynn, but I do hope you enjoy yourselves while the house is empty. It will be a well-deserved break."

"Thank you, Your Majesty," the pair said in unison as they curtsied.

"Enjoy the festivities," I added. "You're dismissed." The women effuged from the temple, leaving me alone once again. I did my best to shake the nerves from my chest as I walked with purpose to the door and pulled it open.

Aydan was in the corridor, alone, pacing slowly with his hands behind his back. He looked up when he heard the door, and my face heated when I saw his flood with emotion.

"Wow," he breathed before stepping forward to take my hand. He pressed a kiss to the back of it, then ran his fingers up my arms. A staticky tingle crackled under my skin, startling me. Aydan raised his hand and let his finger graze a tendril of pink scar that peeked over my shoulder, the static following where he traced. His eyes met mine and he raised his brows in silent question. I shrugged. A smile tugged at the corner of his mouth and he kissed my cheek.

"Shall we?" He asked, offering me his arm. I took it, and let my husband lead me to the Great Hall.

The rumble of voices from the Hall was nothing new to me, but I was not used to being the person the crowd was waiting for. Any anticipation in the air at previous events was brought on by nobles eager to whisper in Aydan's ear and bring themselves closer to the throne and the council. But tonight, they waited for me. I flexed my hand at my side a few times, trying to shake my nerves. Aydan placed his hand at the small of my back as a brief comfort before the herald announced us.

The doors flew open and we strode into the Hall to the sound of applause. The lords and ladies closest to me spoke in loud whispers as I walked by and they noticed my scarred back. I kept my focus on Aydan, and on looking for our friends scattered throughout the crowd. I spotted Gerridan with Hannele on his arm, both beaming. Hannele's eyes were glossy again. The rest of them were nowhere to be seen.

The crowd quieted as we reached the center of the room, and I swallowed, knowing they were waiting for me to speak.

"It is an honor—" I paused and cleared my throat. "It is an honor to be with you all tonight, to take up this calling at my husband's side. I thank you for your trust in me and vow to never take it for granted."

"Long live the Queen!" A voice cried out from the crowd. Suddenly all the lords and ladies who held goblets raised them in the air, repeating the words: *"Long live the Queen!"* before drinking in my honor.

Music started playing, and Aydan held out his hand. *Shit*, I realized. *It's time to dance.* I had been told about the expectation of opening the dance floor at the same time as the kneeling during the ceremony. To Kenna's surprise, the former was much more of a concern to me.

"I'm terrible at Ayzellen dances," I'd complained.

"She really is," Gerridan confirmed. I shot him a dirty look and he shrugged. "My feet have never recovered from Aydan's coronation."

"It doesn't matter if you're good or not, you'll be the Queen," Kenna replied. "It will only be a few minutes and then you can carry on with your night."

I held on to that thought now—*just a few minutes*. I took Aydan's hand, and we started the formal choreography that had me mirroring his movements. I was sure sweat was beading on my forehead as the weight of all the eyes in the Great Hall bore down on me.

"You're doing great," Aydan whispered when our steps brought him close enough for me to hear him. I shot him a disdainful look and he pressed his lips together, trying not to laugh. "Want to see a trick?"

"Sure," I grumbled at the next turn. Aydan pulled me in close, then took my hand as if to lead me in a turn, but rather than feeling myself spin I felt my stomach drop as my husband effuged us from my coronation ball.

My feet landed on familiar stone floors and applause erupted around us. We were in Sylvanna surrounded by the familiar faces of courtiers and friends alike. Aydan had me finish the turn before pulling me in closely and kissing me. Whistling and more applause rang out at the sight.

The crowd parted to allow Solandis and Priamos to approach. They both greeted us warmly. Solandis even kissed me on the cheek and mumbled her congratulations. She gave what appeared to be a look of approval to the golden corset she'd gifted me, and to everyone's surprise, after a moment of quiet, she and Priamos dipped into a deep bow in my direction. The rest followed suit, and it took all my willpower to not burst into tears.

"It is my honor to serve as your Queen," I told them all as they rose. "I hope to always remain worthy of the title." Priamos raised a glass he hadn't been holding a moment before.

"To the Queen!"

"*The Queen!*"

Chapter

Nine

The party was larger and rowdier than any I'd ever seen in Sylvanna. The usual music and dancing were fueled by non-stop wine and ale, enormous trays of food— including platters of fruit soaked in faerie wine that left one giggling after just a few bites— and desserts piled high on every surface. I barely had time to enjoy the refreshments beyond a bite here and there, as it seemed every few minutes I was being pulled back out onto the dance floor. Alastair and Gerridan each took a turn spinning me around the room, followed by Priamos, then a few of the lords of the Sylvannian council. Occasionally, I'd catch a glimpse of Aydan being pulled away to dance with our guests as well and lament the fact that we weren't spending the early hours of the celebration together.

I'd become hyper-aware of Aydan's movements since greeting him outside of the temple. The hairs on the back of my neck stood up when he came close to me, like a wild animal sensing a lightning storm. I kept a pleasant smile plastered on my face when speaking with the Sylvannian nobility, but beneath the surface I was overwhelmed by new magic vibrating under my skin.

Luckily, it didn't take long for the obligatory dancing and greetings to die down, and eventually I got my wish of a few moments with my new husband. I spotted him sitting at a freshly conjured table with Gerridan and Hannele, the latter watching unimpressed as the men clinked their glasses together and downed some sort of liquor.

"I thought the toasts were over," I said as I approached the table. "What are you two drinking to?" Aydan grabbed my wrist and pulled me into his lap before pressing a kiss to my shoulder and rubbing his hand up and down my back. My magic hummed happily in my veins at the touch.

"They're gambling," Hannele replied with a sigh.

I raised my eyebrows at my husband. "What's the bet?"

"Gerridan thinks that the Duke will attempt to seduce Kenna within a day of our arrival in Xarynn," Aydan said. "I think it will happen within an hour."

"That's not much of a bet," I replied. It was no secret that the Duke of Xarynn thought any unmarried woman to be fair game. I looked across the room to Kenna, who was begrudgingly handing a drink to Lyra. An attempt, I guessed, at fulfilling her promise to be kinder to the witch. I didn't expect it to last. "A better wager would be how soon Kenna will make an attempt on Lyra's life," I joked. "I give it another month." Gerridan and Aydan conspicuously followed my gaze to look at Kenna, who now appeared to be trying small talk with Lyra. A grin spread across Gerridan's face.

"I don't think it's Lyra's life you need to be worried about," he chuckled.

"What are you talking about?" I reached for a few of the wine-soaked berries from a dish on the table and popped them in my mouth. "I had to throw Kenna out of my lesson yesterday. She hates Lyra."

"Fifty gold pieces says those two will be fucking by the equinox." I nearly choked on the fruit in my mouth and Hannele shot her husband an exasperated look. Aydan stifled a drunken laugh.

"Must you be so vulgar?" Hannele asked. Gerridan replied by kissing her temple.

"That's insane," I said, glancing once again at Kenna and Lyra. Lyra's hands remained wrapped around her glass though she did not drink, while Kenna's arms were folded across her chest and she stared in the opposite direction.

"Then you won't mind taking the bet?" He smirked. "It's easy money."

"Ger, I'm literally the richest woman in the country. I don't need your fifty gold pieces."

"Make it more interesting then." Gerridan winked and took a drink from his glass that was suddenly full again. "A thousand?" Aydan let out a low whistle.

"You're drunk," I said.

"Indeed I am."

"I'm not going to take advantage of your poor judgment."

"If you're scared of losing, just say that," Gerridan taunted.

"Excuse me?" I replied. Aydan's hand tightened at my waist.

"He's trying to get a rise out of you," he warned in my ear.

"I'm not scared of losing," I said. "In fact, let's make it *actually* interesting. I'll see your thousand gold and raise you one of the Redfern estates." Gerridan's eyes widened.

"Alright Shaye, I get it, we won't gamble on Kenna—"

"Scared?" I asked, holding my hand out. Gerridan paused and glanced down at my hand before allowing his grin to return. We shook on it.

"You've got yourself a deal," he said.

"Thank the gods," Hannele said before moving to stand. "I'm going to get something to eat."

"Have some fruit," I said, offering the bowl. She waved me off.

"No thanks, I'm not in the mood for faerie-wine," she said before walking away toward the food tables.

"Since when is Hannele not in the mood for faerie-wine?" Aydan asked when she had gone. "She's been drinking both of us under the table for years." Gerridan flushed.

"She's just not feeling well lately. Nothing to worry about."

"She didn't drink anything last night at Kenna's either," I commented. It wasn't something I noticed at the time, but now that Aydan mentioned it, I hadn't seen Hannele drink much more than water in a couple of weeks. She'd been sleeping more, complained of feeling ill, and her healing was taking much longer than it should…

"Is there something we should—" Aydan started, but I cut him off.

"Let's dance." I stood from his lap and pulled him up from his seat, leaving Gerridan alone at the table looking rather pale.

Aydan and I were greeted by applause when we stepped onto the dance floor. He spun me a few times before pulling me in closely and improvising the steps. The song was slow enough that it didn't matter much what we did as long as we were moving.

"I was hoping to see more of you today," Aydan said. His lips grazed my ear and sent a shiver down my spine.

"I was hoping for the same thing. You'd think the couple getting married would be allowed a few moments alone."

"There's always Xarynn," he reminded me.

"True. Although the way the past few weeks have been going, I'm afraid we'll wind up too busy to enjoy ourselves once we're there."

He looked down at me and tucked a stray curl behind my ear before saying softly, "Let's go home. We'll get a head start on the trip."

"I don't think abandoning two parties thrown in our honor on the same night is the politest course of action," I said.

"May I let you in on a secret, my love?"

"What's that?"

"No one cares if the King is polite or not," he whispered drunkenly.

I stifled a laugh. "And what if *I* care?"

"Then, we have a problem. Because I planned on being *very* impolite for the rest of the night." He gripped me tighter, and before my laughter could escape my throat again, he effuged us home.

We arrived in our bedroom, where the walls were cloaked in candlelight.

"The same trick three times in one night?" I teased with a raised eyebrow. Aydan laughed and kissed my neck. I shivered, and blue light emerged from my hands. "This will take some getting used to," I noted, examining them.

"It will, but you'll be wonderful," Aydan said, brushing loose hairs from my forehead. "The head of two ancient houses should have all the powers of those houses, shouldn't she?"

"Yes, and luckily I share headship of House Aevitarus with such a capable partner, beloved by our people." I kissed him again. "Although, if he keeps effuging us from the parties they throw in our honor, I'm not sure we will remain so beloved."

"You can go back, if you want," Aydan quipped.

"You'd let me walk all that way by myself?"

"You can effuge now— I made sure of it when I gave you access to the powers of House Aevitarus."

"What?" Effuging was the one bit of sorcery that had remained out of my reach. Aydan tried to teach me a few times to no avail. He always seemed to brush it off despite my frustrations, saying that I would figure it out one way or another. He must have been planning this all along. Could it be that easy— Aydan simply gave me the power?

"Try it."

I centered myself, despite feeling a bit tipsy from the faerie-fruit. I remembered Aydan's instructions from a long-ago attempt to teach me the skill: *Focus. Know the exact spot you're headed to and go there— don't dwell on the how, just declare to yourself that you want to be there.* I placed all my attention on the vanity and willed myself forward—

My hips crashed into the front of the vanity as I slammed forward, effuging just a few inches too far. Effuging— I had *effuged.* My eyes went wide with excitement as I turned to Aydan, whose grin spread across his face.

"I did it," I gasped.

"You did," he confirmed. I focused again and appeared right in front of Aydan, knocking him off his feet and onto the foot of the bed. His head tilted back as he laughed at my apologetic wince. He held my chin and kissed me, pulling me down to straddle his lap.

"Thank you," I said when we parted. "That is such a relief."

"What's mine is yours, my love." The blue glow emerged from my palms again in response to his voice. My power reacting to his— or to *him,* I was not sure. It hummed beneath my skin as it had when we sat with Gerridan only minutes ago— a happy feeling. We sat on the bed, breath mingling as the currents of our power ran through us.

"I will never tire of this," I said quietly.

"Of what, my love?" His gentle hand stroked my cheek.

"This feeling—" I held up my light-engulfed hand. "This power you've given me, makes me feel so close to you. So utterly, wholly, yours— as you are utterly, wholly mine. I don't— I don't know if I'm explaining that very well…"

"I understand," he murmured. "My magic feels especially strong next to yours. The powers complement each other." He pressed a kiss to my neck and we stopped talking about our magic. We stopped talking altogether as our breath quickened and Aydan's hands began gathering the edge of my skirts, reaching for my bare thighs beneath.

My legs were spread as I straddled him, and Aydan wasted no time, brazenly dragging a finger up my slick center. He circled a few times, letting his calloused fingertips graze the edges of my most sensitive spot. I moaned and buried my face in his neck while he continued, and after a few more strokes he slipped his first finger into me. I was practically dripping, so it was no effort to add a second before Aydan began pumping his hand inside of me. Aydan hummed as he took his fingers back. He held them up, examining them in the candlelight. He let his fingers part, allowing the evidence of my arousal to shine. "Is that all for me?"

"It's always for you— all of it, all of me," I said, bucking my hips forward, desperate for friction. Aydan *tsk*ed at me and spread his own legs just slightly, not allowing me to even press my thighs together.

"Not so fast, my love." He licked one of his fingers clean before sticking the other in my mouth to do the same. "I'd like to savor you, if you'll let me." I flushed but nodded anyway and Aydan's hands continued their exploration under my skirts.

Another minute of toying with me passed before Aydan banished my clothes, shoes, and all my jewelry save for my crown. I didn't bother waiting and waved my hand to do the same to him. His cock stood at attention—practically twitching while I pushed closer to him, allowing us to touch, though he did not enter me yet. I ground my hips forward, gliding up the length of him.

"Gods, Shaye—" he groaned in my ear before continuing to kiss and suck on my neck. He slipped his fingers inside once again, earning a gasp from me. I rocked my hips, riding his hand until familiar pressure built between my legs and clouded my brain. "Good... good—" Aydan pressed the heel of his palm against me, and I yelped at my immediate release. I bucked forward again and again as I rode it out, and as the final wave subsided, Aydan withdrew. He stood and turned, laying me gently on the bed before sinking to his knees and going to work with his mouth. My hands gripped his hair and he moaned against me as I dropped over the edge again. Aydan rose to kiss me, his mouth and chin wet with my pleasure.

He crawled over the top of me and claimed my mouth with his own. Without breaking the kiss, Aydan reached down and held himself steady before sliding in all the way to the hilt. Sparks flew untamed from my fingertips at the sudden sensation of being completely full. My hands sparked again and again with each of Aydan's thrusts until a stray ember landed on the sheets and began to smoke. Without hesitation, I slammed my hand down on top of the smoldering fabric, smothering it. I gripped the sheets with tight fists while Aydan continued and soon my arms were glowing with blue light. Aydan noticed, and seconds later— to his apparent surprise— the light began to shine from him as well. Aydan reached a hand down between us and pressed his thumb hard against me while he continued to thrust.

"*Fuck*, Aydan—" I started to say, but was cut off by my own climax, and his name caught in my throat when I cried out. I pulled his face down to mine and kissed him, not breaking away even as his breath quickened and I felt him finally ride out his own release. Aydan rolled off me and nearly collapsed onto the bed, breathing heavily as he pulled me to his chest. Blue light danced up our tangled limbs while we caught our breath. After a few moments, Aydan kissed my temple and sat up.

"Do you want some water?" he asked.

"First," I said, sitting up and wincing. "I want this damned thing my head." The crown, which had remained on my head for the duration of our lovemaking, was now fully tangled in my hair and threatened to rip away at my scalp if I let go of it while sitting up. Aydan grimaced and gestured toward my hair. The crown untangled itself and was banished along with all the pins, while my hair fell into waves down my back. "Much better," I sighed, then said, "Water sounds fantastic."

"Coming right up." He stood and poured me a cup from the water pitcher near our bed before he made his way to the bathroom. I returned the cup to its place once I'd drained it and fell back on to the pillows, struggling to keep my eyes open while I listened to Aydan fumble in the darkened room. He approached the bed and began wiping my skin down with a warm, dampened towel, removing as much of the sweat and other fluids as he could. When I was clean, he offered me a nightdress which I took and pulled over my head while he cleaned himself up. Aydan climbed into bed. He pulled the blankets up over us before wrapping me in his arms and pressing kisses into my hair until we both fell asleep.

Chapter
Ten

It was midday before Alastair woke and spent the next hour waking everyone else besides me and Aydan. Finally, when it could wait no longer, we were greeted by a soft knock on our door, inviting us to join the rush of dressing and trying to organize the last few trunks of our belongings that would be sent to Xarynn ahead of us. This was made even more difficult by the fact that I had woken up and ran straight to the bathroom before vomiting up the contents of my stomach.

Aydan followed me and ran his hand up and down my back while holding my hair with the other as I retched a few more times.

"Do *not* let me drink while we're in Xarynn," I groaned. Two days in a row of nasty hangovers was enough to put me off alcohol for a good while. Aydan patted my back sympathetically.

"The faerie-wine will get to you if you're not used to it," he explained.

"I only had the soaked fruit," I whined. "And I only drank a few glasses of the Medeisian wine besides that."

"Must have mixed poorly for you. Here—" he produced a glass of water which I sipped carefully, not wanting to make myself sick again. Once I drained the glass Aydan banished it to the scullery and helped me to my feet. To my surprise, I felt much better, if not a bit groggy. Catchfly pranced into the bathroom now that all the unpleasantness was over and wove herself in and out of my legs, meowing her sympathies.

"Thanks, Catchfly," I said, scooping her into my arms. "Are you going to miss me?" She meowed once again in response, and I scratched behind her ears.

"We'd better get moving, if you're feeling all right," Aydan said. "The others will be waiting, and we still need to bathe and dress." I made my way toward the sink to clean my teeth and wash the taste of bile out of my mouth.

We arrived in Xarynn as the clock struck three. At Aydan's suggestion, I wore a cream-colored dress in a light, flowing fabric that the noblewomen of Xarynn wore regularly. The balmy conditions of the seaside territory meant that folks here did not bother with heavy fabrics or bulky jewelry, opting for comfort instead.

We had effuged, much like my first trip to Sylvanna, all at once, after our luggage had been sent and we all bid Lyra farewell, offering once again for her to tag along. She declined, insisting she had lesson planning to do, but reminded me again to start weaning from the sleep tonic. I promised her that I would. Our party landed outside the gates of the Duke of Xarynn's manor, standing in rank, waiting to be let inside.

The gates swung open, and we all stepped through, beginning our walk across the grounds to meet the Duke on the other side. He stood, flanked by two ladies that I'd never seen before— one petite with white-blonde hair and tanned skin, the other quite pale, ginger-haired, with a smattering of freckles across her nose— at the entrance to his home. As we approached, he stepped toward us, spreading his arms wide in greeting.

"Your Majesties," he boomed in his thick accent before dipping into a deep bow. "We are honored to have you with us. It has been so *long* since we have hosted the royal family— we are so grateful for your company." Gerridan warned me that the Duke was rather underhanded. Now I saw what he meant. Aydan's sister Irsa was just here two years ago on Zathryan's behalf, returning to Ayzelle only a few days before she died. For immortals, that was no time at all— but Aydan had not visited the seaside territory since his coronation. That, and the fact that new trade routes were being built which Xarynn did not approve of, meant that the port city was feeling neglected.

"Edwin," Aydan grinned, stepping forward to shake hands with the Duke. "It's a pleasure to be here, as always." I stepped ahead to join the men.

"My Queen," the Duke— Edwin— murmured as he reached for my hand and pressed a kiss to it. His thick mustache scratched against my skin and I fought the urge to snatch my hand away from his. He gestured for the blonde to join us. She curtsied. "My wife, Duchess Ylena."

"Your Grace," I greeted her.

"Your Majesty."

"And Lady Rowena," Edwin said. The ginger woman curtsied as well but did not speak. "I thought we might give Her Majesty a brief tour of the manor before showing you all to your rooms."

"I'd love a tour," I replied, taking Aydan's arm. The Duchess and Rowena each took one of the Duke's and we followed them inside.

Edwin's tour felt like an eternity. He led me to each wing, showing off his library, multiple parlors, and a games room, where he displayed his many hunting trophies.

We were taken to an apartment in the east wing, "So you may wake with the sun, Your Majesty," the Duke told me. Inside were several suites surrounding a common sitting room. Enough space for our Cabinet to all be near each other. The Duke lingered for just a moment too long to be polite, before inviting the married couples to dinner. We had of course agreed, despite the already late hour. With no chance to rest or enjoy our suite, we quickly got ready for dinner.

Now, I sat beside Aydan at Edwin's table in his private dining room. Gerridan sat on the other side of me and Hannele beside him. Edwin had offered Aydan a seat at the head of the table, but he declined, insisting that Edwin take it instead. Seated across the table from us were Duchess Ylena, Lady Rowena, and another tanned, blonde woman who had been introduced as Lady Elwen. The women all conversed happily with Hannele, while speaking to me only when I spoke first, keeping their replies short and polite.

When the first course of our meal arrived, Edwin informed us that he'd heard we enjoyed a more casual setting for meals, and thus had only ordered three courses from his team of chefs, rather than the usual five course banquet that the Xarynnians prepared for royal visitors. To start, we each were presented with two small dishes: the first contained three rounds of toasted drakebread, spread with a soft cheese made from sheep's milk imported from Keotis, and topped with figs brought in from Sewyth. The second dish was filled with ice, and atop the ice were four shells filled with a slimy, gelatinous substance that I had never seen before. I glanced around at my friends and my hosts and saw that they all were slurping the substance directly off the shell as if it were nothing. I attempted to do the same, but the second it hit my tongue I wanted to spit it out. Reluctantly, I swallowed, and attempted to cough politely before taking a large drink of water. No one seemed to notice, so I ignored the rest of the shells and soon enough, the second course arrived.

Servants delivered several covered platters to the table, arranging them so they could be easily reached before turning back and filing out of the room. A routine of theirs, it seemed. The Duke snapped his fingers and the covers disappeared from the platters, revealing overflowing dishes of seafood, likely caught just hours before. I had only ever seen the small blue-gray fish the fishmongers caught in the ponds of Nautia and didn't much care for them. The table in front of us held an enormous baked pink fish, head and all. I also noted two different plates of some sort of shelled animals. One contained the entire carcass of the strange, clawed beings, while the other seemed to be filled only with appendages. Large tureens, enchanted to stay warm like the ones used for feasts at the capital, contained some other now-cooked creatures swimming in melted butter and spices. Other dishes were piled high with vegetables that Edwin informed us were grown locally as well. Being in the Duke's private dining room, we were bid to help ourselves to whatever we may like. I continued staring at the strange fare, trying to decide which dish would be the tamest.

"Is something wrong?" Aydan asked, leaning in close to my ear so no one would hear.

"No, I just—" I whispered. Gods, I felt stupid. "I needed a minute to decide." I flicked my wrist and sent a piece of the pink-fleshed fish to my plate, along with a small pile of the vegetables. The fish seemed safe enough— and certainly appeared to be the easiest thing to eat. Everyone else had piled their plates with the shelled creatures and were now loudly cracking them open with small tools, tearing chunks of the flesh out of the shell and eating it. I took a polite bite of my food. It wasn't unbearable, but certainly not something I would choose for myself. Aydan, seeming to sense my nerves, warmed my thigh with a comforting hand.

"Tell me, Queen Shaye," Edwin said over the sound of his wife cracking open another shell. "Are you enjoying Xarynn thus far?" I pressed a napkin to the corner of my mouth before speaking.

"I am, though I haven't seen much of it, Your Grace," I replied. "I am excited to see the ports tomorrow morning."

"Oh yes, speaking of the ports." He turned his attention to Aydan. "I'm afraid, Your Majesty, that the team available to escort you to the site of the attack on the King's Guard will only be available tomorrow morning before they board a ship back to Keotis. If you still desire to make that trip, the port inspection would have to wait until the following day." I blanched at the mention of the attack that killed Stefan Whittaker and six young members of the King's Guard all those months ago. Their party was technically still in Ayzelle when the attack took place, but the Ayzellen side of the border had been tracked and examined dozens of times since. Aydan had expressed a desire to visit the site before examining the paths leading from Xarynn into Ayzelle, to see if there were any clear signs of the creature who left no survivors in its wake. He squeezed my knee, knowing the subject was touchy.

"The Queen does not desire to accompany us for the examination of the attack site," Aydan replied. "Perhaps she and Lord Hollick could go alone to the port for their tour while you and I head to the site with the escort team."

"Fine by me," Edwin replied. "I'll send Mr. Denby to accompany them." A chuckle escaped from Hannele.

"How is Denby? Haven't seen him in ages."

"As finicky as ever," Edwin replied with a smirk. "But an excellent advisor, nonetheless." My dinner companions all smiled knowingly, sharing in the joke while I pushed the food around on my plate.

Dessert came soon enough—more platters, this time filled with iced lemon tarts, lime and ginger ice cream, and tiny, jam-filled cakes topped with candied violets— and once we'd all had our fill, it was time to say goodnight.

The four of us arrived back at our suite close to midnight. Alastair was nowhere to be seen, while Kenna lay sleeping on one of the sofas in the sitting room with an open book lying face down on her chest. Hannele announced that she was exhausted and would be heading straight to bed. Gerridan followed, after reminding me that he and I would be heading to the port first thing in the morning, and to be ready shortly after sunrise. I agreed and bid him goodnight before Aydan and I made our way to our bedroom, leaving Kenna where she slept.

"You're quiet," Aydan noted as we started getting ready for bed. I cast a few orbs of light to the ceiling, sat at the vanity, and began removing pins from my hair.

"I'm tired," I replied, looking at him in the mirror as he stood behind me, "And truthfully, feeling a little overwhelmed."

"It's been a busy few days," Aydan agreed.

"I'm fine with busy. I just… Gods, I felt like an idiot through that whole dinner."

"What do you mean?" Aydan looked puzzled.

"Duchess Ylena and the other ladies wouldn't speak to me unless I spoke first, and even then, it was like they couldn't wait for me to stop talking. Edwin asked me one question and turned my reply into something to discuss with you. I didn't recognize any of the food, I didn't understand the jokes—" I cut myself off, hearing the ranting tone building up in my voice. "It just felt like I was sitting in on a party I wasn't invited to, that's all." Aydan stepped closer and put his hands on my bare shoulders, warming them while he looked at me in the mirror.

"It's not entirely unreasonable for you to feel out of place," he said before pressing a kiss to the top of my head. "You've changed roles so often in just a little more than a year. You've only been Queen for a day. You're doing wonderfully. Now, as far as the Xarynnians behavior tonight—" he smirked a little bit. "The

Duchess was simply following the tradition here. Ladies in Xarynn don't speak to someone of higher rank than them unless spoken to first. Ylena was simply attempting to be polite. Lady Elwen and Lady Rowena, however, were probably under the assumption that you did not approve of their presence."

"Why would I—?"

"Elwen and Rowena are two of the Duke's mistresses. His favorites, apparently." My eyes widened.

"He made his *wife* sit next to his *mistresses* during dinner?"

"They're friends," Aydan clarified. "Ylena, Elwen, and Rowena have known each other since childhood. They all seem fine with their arrangement, and if no one is being coerced or kept against their will, the Crown doesn't care much what they do. Edwin keeps those three at home with him and has a rotation of others that he visits from time to time." I blinked a few times, processing the explanation for a moment.

"And why would the Duke not deign to speak more than a few words to me all night?"

"That, I'm afraid, is my fault." Aydan ran his hands along my shoulders and up my neck. He let his fingers graze my collarbones. I raised an eyebrow at him in the mirror, noting the amused, glazed over look on his face. He sighed. "At my coronation feast, Edwin was very put out that he did not have a chance to speak to you." Gerridan had rushed me away from greeting him that night to join Stefan, warning me of the Duke's flirtatious nature and trying to save me from the uncomfortable experience of an attempted seduction. "When he came to congratulate me on my ascension to the throne, he expressed his disappointment in not being introduced to you by er, *complimenting* your appearance that night, and detailing to me everything he would like to do to you if you gave him the chance."

"I see." My face burned. "How exactly did you respond to that?"

"I told him that sort of talk would lead to the great displeasure of his King—"

"And what did you *actually* say?"

"That if he spoke like that about my Chief Advisor again, I'd take him out to the sparring ring to shut him up and that I couldn't guarantee his favorite accessory would still be attached to him when I was through." I erupted with laughter, and Aydan soon joined me, planting another kiss to the top of my head.

"Well, thank you for defending my honor, even back then," I told him.

"I always will. Until my dying breath, wife," he said with exaggerated solemnity. I rolled my eyes and started to reach around my back to untie the laces of my dress. Aydan helped me loosen them and then let me hold his arm to steady myself as I stepped out of the skirts. He banished it to the wardrobe while I pulled a nightdress over my head. "Do you want me to draw you a bath?"

"I'd better skip it," I said. "I have to be up with Gerridan in a few hours and a bath will just take up more time that could be spent sleeping."

"Are you opposed to all activities that would prevent you from sleep?" He asked, looking me up and down in my nightdress with my hair undone and hanging around my shoulders.

"I'm sorry," I half-groaned. "I'd love to, but I'll be kicking myself in the morning if I stay up much longer."

"Don't ever apologize for denying me." He kissed me on the mouth. "Go to bed. I'm going to take a bath myself and then I'll join you." Aydan kissed me again and I bid him goodnight. I immediately regretted agreeing to meet Gerridan so early as I watched my husband undress and then walk naked across the bedroom before entering the bathroom and shutting the door behind him. But once I climbed into bed and sank into a pile of down pillows, it was mere minutes before I drifted to sleep.

Chapter Eleven

Gerridan was waiting for me in the sitting room shortly after sunrise.

I wore another Xarynnian dress, today in lilac with a tiara of small golden sea stars and tiny pearls. My hair I let lay in loose waves, pinning the front pieces away from my face. I woke only hours after Aydan and I went to bed and found myself quite exhausted now.

I'd gasped for air and felt sweat beading on my forehead. Aydan quickly woke as well, sitting up next to me and rubbing my back as I caught my breath and settled myself into the present. I hadn't woken in the night like that since the immediate days following my return from the Onyx Temple. When Aydan asked me to describe my dream— a trick Lyra had suggested to make what I saw in my sleep more bearable— all I could come up with was an overwhelming feeling of dread. There were no images, just the sense that something was coming for me. Something was watching.

Aydan bid me to lie back down before curling up behind me. He gripped my hip with one hand and stroked my hair with the other. He assured me that we were safe, that it was all just a dream. When I settled completely, I reached for the hand that stroked my hair and pressed my lips to his palm.

"I hate that you're not taking your tonic," Aydan admitted while we lay in the darkness. "But I am glad I can comfort you more closely now than when we were being held in the Prince's Chambers." He pressed his face into my hair and tightened the hand on my hip.

"You could have comforted me as closely as you wanted, even back then." I smiled, knowing he was doing his best to distract me. Playing along, I feigned a stretch, pressing my backside into him. I felt him begin to harden. "All you had to do was ask."

"Now you tell me," he whispered roughly in my ear. "You have no idea how guilty I felt, with all those filthy thoughts about my guest running through my head each night." My breath shallowed as his fingers began to gather the fabric of my nightdress, finding the hem and slipping his hand beneath it to stroke my bare thigh. "One word from you and I would have…"

"Show me," I breathed. "Show me everything the Wayward Prince wanted to do to me."

And he spent the next few hours doing exactly that.

Now, Gerridan greeted me with a cup of tea in hand. He downed the contents in a single gulp before speaking. "Want a cup?"

"Please." A fresh steaming cup of strong tea appeared in his other hand and he passed it to me. By the look of it, milk and honey had already been stirred in. The first sip confirmed it. "Tell me again why we're doing this at sunrise?"

"None of the ships will have left yet," Gerridan said, his cup steaming once again. "Whenever royalty tours Xarynn, it is tradition for you to inspect one or two of the merchant ships leaving Medeisia."

"Inspecting for what, exactly? I don't know what a departing merchant ship is supposed to look like."

"No need," he said. "Denby will have made sure the ships we see today are up to royal standards. This is mostly an opportunity for Xarynn to show off, and for the people to see you." I blanched at that but drained my teacup anyway and banished it to the scullery. "Let's get going."

Mr. Denby was a strange man.

He'd been waiting in the courtyard when Gerridan and I arrived. He was tall and gangly, with a nervous sort of energy surrounding him. He was quite tan, like many residents of Xarynn, with sandy brown hair that curled at his ears, which were pointed. Mr. Denby was an elf. He was already bowing by the time we could step toward him, and the bow deepened when I bid him good morning.

"Your Majesty, it is a great honor to meet you. My name is Mr. Denby" He kissed my hand before rising and greeting Gerridan. "Lord Hollick, a pleasure as always."

"Hello Denby." He dipped his chin.

"Shall we begin?" And without waiting for an answer, Denby broke out in a brisk walk through the courtyard, toward the front gates of the estate. Gerridan snorted before offering me his arm and we took off after him.

The thirty minute walk from the estate to the port was narrated by Denby, telling us about the history of the estate and how the Duke's family came to be the patrons of Xarynn. This was all information I already knew, having read Gerridan's copy of *Houses of Medeisia: All Territories* when I first took the role of Chief Advisor, but hearing the history from someone who had such a passion for it was at least entertaining. After a while, Gerridan let us fall a few steps back so we could talk without Denby hearing.

"How are you adjusting?" He inquired. "We haven't talked much since we arrived. How are you doing with all that power?" I knew he wasn't talking about my royal status.

"It's strange," I admitted. "It's there and not— all the time. Like a whisper in my blood."

"That's a terrifying way to put it."

I chuckled under my breath and squeezed Gerridan's arm, letting the conversation fall quiet for a moment while we continued walking. Finally, the suspicion that had crossed my mind at the feast in Sylvanna became too much to bear, now that I had Gerridan alone, and I blurted, "When were you going to tell me that Hannele is pregnant?"

Gerridan stopped in his tracks and went pale. "When— How did you—"

"I grew suspicious at the feast the other night, but it seemed that you two were keeping something a secret for a reason, so I didn't want to pry in front of others. Tell me, am I right?" We started walking again.

"Gods, Hannele is going to kill me— yes, you're right," he nearly whispered. I bit back an excited squeal. "We were going to wait until everyone was home from Xarynn to announce, since that will be about the halfway point—"

"*Halfway?*" I dug my fingernails into his arm. "You waited until the pregnancy was halfway over to tell us?"

"It's tradition," he replied. "Especially among those with royal titles." Denby called over his shoulder that the port was just over the next hill. "Look, do me a favor and don't let Hannele know that you know. She's been quite ill most days and telling all of you has been something to look forward to."

"I won't say a word to anyone," I promised. "Except for Aydan."

Gerridan sighed. "I suppose that's the best I'm going to get."

"Your Majesty," Denby called out as we reached the top of the hill, "We've arrived. Welcome to the port of Xarynn."

I had expected docked ships and sailors loading goods. I had expected to see the water lapping up on the shoreline— my first views of the sea. What I didn't expect was the marketplace that had popped up around the port.

The dirt path that led to the docks was lined with merchant stalls, many of them selling fresh-caught fish or various types of the shelled creatures the Duke served at dinner the previous night. Others had huge displays of spices and herbs, or linens in vibrant colors. I walked slowly, still holding on to Gerridan's arm, eager to see everything. It had been ages since I'd walked through a marketplace, and there was certainly nothing in Nautia quite like this.

Denby did not rush me. He and Gerridan watched as I touched fabrics and smelled spices, the merchants selling them greeting me merrily in Xarynnea. I did my best to reply with the few phrases Zale and Isolde taught me, but anything beyond a greeting or giving thanks was handled by Gerridan.

I stopped at a small stall run by an elderly mortal woman making jewelry out of crystals. Her goods lay displayed on a simple table, sparkling and colorful against the raw wood slab that looked like it would give me a splinter if I were to rest my hand upon it. She was chipping away at a large geode, collecting chunks of white quartz on a cloth beneath her workstation. The woman dipped her head in my direction while I examined her creations.

"Where are the stones from?" I asked my companions. It was the woman herself who answered.

"The white quartz is from Keotis," she said in a thick accent, gesturing to the stone before her. "Amethyst came from the cave systems here. Most everything else is from Sewyth."

I picked up a particularly attractive piece—a bracelet made from large chunks of amethyst—and asked, "How much?"

The woman paused, glancing at my tiara and necklace. "You flatter me, Majesty, but my goods are not fit for the Queen."

"I think that's for me to decide." I conjured two gold pieces. "Will this cover it?" She blinked, and then nodded just once. I left the coins on the table for her and slid the bracelet on my wrist, examining the way it glittered in the sunlight. "What is your name?"

"Ana, ma'am."

"Ana, your work is lovely. Would you perhaps be interested in making a few custom pieces for me? I'd like to purchase gifts for my ladies."

"Aye," said Ana. "I'm not as fast as the sorcerers or elves, ma'am, but I can make whatever you like."

"Excellent. I'll send a note with the details before the day is out. Thank you, Ana."

"Your Majesty."

I faced Denby, who looked flabbergasted by the exchange. "Shall we continue?"

"I— yes, Your Majesty, right this way."

I took Gerridan's arm again as we continued, and I noticed the corner of his mouth twitch. "What?" I said without looking at him as I waved to a group of children watching us.

"Nothing, Your Majesty."

I made a point to purchase a few more items from the vendors— some herbs for Lyra, several yards of fabric from Auperene in a strange shade of emerald green, and a toy ship, which I held up for Gerridan, waggling my eyebrows at him before I purchased it. I banished each item to Sylvanna, except for the amethyst bracelet, which I continued to wear.

"Most of these ships will be carrying our exports to the Elf Kingdoms," Denby said loudly over the sound of waves slapping against the sides of the ships and men calling out to one another as they stacked boxes and barrels. "Today there is a large shipment of Sylvannian wheat headed to Sewyth—"

"I notice we don't export much to Auperene," I said.

"The fae do not care much for foreign goods, Your Majesty. We import many luxury items from them but our merchants and farmers cannot sell to the fae what they are not willing to buy. There are certain medicinal herbs, however, that they cannot do without in their hospitals and cannot grow on their lands, so they import from us. One may also find the occasional fae lord making private orders for his estate."

"I see." I leaned in to Gerridan's ear. "I want to discuss this with the extended council. We need to make trade more appealing to the fae." He nodded, making the mental note.

"*This* is Xarynn's largest ship," Denby announced proudly as we reached the end of the dock. "The *Pauline*. She'll be delivering fifty thousand gold pieces worth of salt to Keotis tonight." Salt was Xarynn's biggest export, and their current monopoly on the salt trade was quite lucrative.

I moved to step onto the ramp and make my way aboard the ship, but Denby put out an arm to stop me. Gerridan stepped forward.

"What the hell are you doing, Denby?"

The advisor had a strained, embarrassed look on his face. "My deepest apologies, Your Majesty, but I cannot allow you to board the *Pauline*."

"I'm to inspect the ships, am I not?"

"I— yes ma'am, but—"

"And how would you suggest I do so if I am not permitted to board?"

"I'm happy to take you to another ship, Your Majesty, but I'm afraid the captain of the *Pauline* does not allow ladies on board." Denby looked as if he'd rather throw himself off the side of the *Pauline* than tell me this. I could feel Gerridan's eyes burning into me, but I did not look at him. I did not know the best way to respond, but I knew I couldn't let Gerridan do so on my behalf. So instead, I said:

"It is a good thing then, Mr. Denby, that I am not a lady. Lord Hollick?" I held out my hand for Gerridan to assist me up the ramp, and left Denby scurrying along behind us.

Gerridan let me practice effuging us, and shortly after midday I managed to return us to the parlor in our suite at the Duke's manor.

"Shaye, I could just kiss you for that," Gerridan gushed upon our return, now out of Denby's earshot. I ignored him and approached a drink cart, my hands still shaking from nerves.

"Why are you threatening to kiss my wife?" Aydan poked his head out of our bedroom door. By the look of it he'd returned just shortly before us. "My love, I don't blame you if you're tempted, but I can tell you from experience his kisses are not as good as he advertises." Gerridan held up his middle finger to Aydan in response.

"It was nothing," I said, plopping myself down on one of the sofas, drink in hand.

"It was not nothing," Gerridan insisted. He turned to Aydan. "You should have seen it. We arrived at the port and Shaye started *shopping* at the stalls..." He proceeded to describe my every move at the port as if it were some sort of triumph. "You wouldn't believe the captain's *face*— and all he could do was watch while Shaye acted like it was nothing to walk aboard." I flushed, a little embarrassed. Aydan crossed his arms and leaned against the doorframe, looking amused.

"Impressive," he commented. I shrugged.

"Hopefully everyone else sees it that way." I held my ground in the moment when the captain of the *Pauline*— a mortal man named Matthias— stood seething as I made it a point to visit every storage room on the ship, but now I worried that I'd been too rash in an attempt to preserve my pride. The sailors all stood back and let me see their work, hats in hand and heads bowed. Captain Matthias never did speak directly to me.

"You showed an interest in the locals and put a challenger to your authority in his place," Gerridan said, waving off my concerns. "You did well."

"I agree," Aydan said from his spot in the doorway. "Had you allowed yourself to be banished from the ship you would have sent the message that men in this kingdom can tell their Queen what she can and cannot do." I nodded, but their assurance didn't fully calm my nerves. Desperate to change the subject, I looked around the room.

"Where is Kenna?"

"She had meetings with a few friends planned over the next couple of days." Alastair rounded the corner from his bedroom into the parlor as he answered my question. He planted himself next to me on the sofa. "She said not to plan on seeing much of her."

"Sounds like she won't be paying Lyra much attention," I teased, nudging Gerridan's leg with my foot to remind him of our bet. He clicked his tongue.

"The equinox is months away," he said. "I have time."

"Time to count out my gold pieces?"

"More like time to plan the décor for my new estate."

"Enough, you two," Alastair sighed. Gerridan and I both shook with laughter. "Home for ten minutes and you're already bickering like children."

"Just a friendly sense of competition, Alastair," I said, poking him with my elbow.

"Yes, a competition that I'm going to—" Gerridan started but was cut off by the sound of loud retching coming from his and Hannele's bathroom. He made a face. "I'd better go check on her… dinner didn't sit right…" he trailed off before quickly leaving us in the parlor.

"I hope Hannele is okay," Alastair frowned. "That's the third time I've heard her today. I checked on her earlier and she claimed to be fine."

"I'm sure she is," I said. Then, trying to change the subject again, I asked Aydan, "Should we dress for dinner?" Alastair scowled.

"Dinner isn't for… oh. I see. I'll be going now." A look, like a mix of understanding and embarrassment washed over his face. He stood and went back to his bedroom. He reemerged with a book in hand. "I'm going to go read by the water. You two… have fun, I suppose."

"Alastair," I laughed. "I wasn't—"

"You're on your honeymoon," he put his hand up. "It's none of my business. But between the vomiting on one end of the house and whatever you two are planning to do for the next few hours… I'll just leave." Alastair moved for the front door. When he reached for the handle, it opened. Kenna swept through the door, not stopping to greet anyone as she made her way to her bedroom.

"Careful," Alastair said to her. "It's a madhouse in there."

"Just bathing and then I'll be leaving again," she called over her shoulder. "But I'll see you all at dinner." Her door shut soundly, and a second later, so did the front door.

"You've chased everyone away," Aydan said, thoroughly amused. I stood and pushed him into the bedroom, shutting the door quickly behind me so Kenna would not hear us. Aydan laughed. "You really did want to take me to bed then—"

"No," I whispered. "I promised Gerridan I wouldn't tell anyone but you so I can't let Kenna hear me."

"Tell me what, exactly?"

Hours later, we were saying goodnight to the Duke and Duchess and preparing to head back to the guest chambers. Edwin's attention kept sliding over to Kenna, who paid him no mind while she and the rest of our Cabinet mingled with the Duke's advisors. Denby appeared rather flustered by the seer's scant dress. Aydan and Gerridan exchanged a knowing look and bit back laughter, remembering the wager that I'd foiled. Hannele clung to her husband's arm, glamoured to appear in better spirits than she did, and doing her best to pay attention to the conversation.

Aydan's mouth spread into a wide grin when I told him of Hannele's pregnancy, and it took all his willpower to not go knocking on their door immediately after finding out. I explained Hannele's plans for an announcement and swore my husband to secrecy. He promised he wouldn't reveal what he knew to Hannele, but when Gerridan finally emerged from their bedroom, Aydan nearly tackled our friend. I gave them a moment alone together, and when I returned, I found them wrapped in a hug, Gerridan looking rather misty-eyed from over Aydan's shoulder.

Now, our Chief Advisor was the picture of composure, laughing politely at a joke told by an advisor in Xarynnea. I smiled in their direction, trying to look like I understood more than I did. The advisor smiled back, but mostly kept their attention to Gerridan and Hannele, with whom they could communicate more effectively.

Tonight's dinner had been much different than the night before. The food itself had been a little less intimidating— still plenty of local fare I did not recognize, but I'd spotted a roasted pheasant and let out a small sigh of relief. We dined with the council of Xarynn, the small group of advisors led by Mr. Denby who answered to the Duke in mine and Aydan's absence from the territory. Tonight, rather than listening to my companions talk, we were met with discussions of policy. The meal quickly descended into a council meeting with a meal on the table instead of stacks of paper. Complaints were made about the newest trade route built by the Crown, connecting Sylvanna and Ayzelle directly for the first time in a century. I froze for half a beat when questioned directly by one of the lords— Harnington— about my design for the route and whether I was punishing Xarynn for some reason by taking opportunities for growth away from them. I'd managed to clumsily explain that that had not been my plan, and that we could discuss the impact of that route on Xarynn in the morning, when I could see the documented numbers and understand better what Harnington was referring to. He gave me a somewhat disapproving look and left it at that.

When we returned to the guest wing, everyone started toward their respective rooms to change clothes, agreeing to come out to the sitting room for drinks after we were all more comfortable. But as soon as the door shut behind us, Aydan asked, "Would you like to run away with me?"

"Only every second of the day." He grabbed my hand and I felt the familiar swoop in my stomach of being effuged. When we landed, I found us in a darkened room I didn't recognize.

The only light was the moonlight pouring in through the open balcony doors, through which I heard crashing ocean waves. We were on the beach or very close to it, to be sure, but— "Where are we?" I asked, looking around the simple room containing only a bed, a wardrobe, and a small table and chairs by the fireplace on the opposite wall.

"Xarynn," Aydan answered, tucking a stray curl behind my ear.

"Obviously," I replied suspiciously. Aydan chuckled.

"I thought we could use a little extra privacy," he said. "It's been a long day." His eyes drifted downward, examining my dress and its adornments.

"It has," I agreed with a sigh. Aydan's hand grazed my cheek. "What's wrong?"

"Nothing," I said honestly. "My mind is just racing. It's silly, I've only been royalty for a couple of days, but…"

"It takes some getting used to," he said sympathetically. "People hanging on your every word, policies and laws being written to match your desires… it's a big responsibility."

"I'd love to not make a decision for a bit," I joked. "Or just have someone tell me what to do." A smirk appeared on Aydan's mouth. "What?"

"I'd be happy to oblige you," he said quietly, dragging his fingertips along my collarbone, down between my breasts, and back again.

"What do you mean?"

"I could show you how it feels to take some orders," he said, continuing his pattern along my chest. "But you must be exhausted." I swallowed.

"I planned on being awake for a while longer," I told him, taking his hand and kissing his palm. "Show me."

"Well then, Your Majesty—" He cut himself off by pressing a hard kiss to my mouth.

I pressed my body as close to his as I could manage as he held my face in his hands. Pulling away roughly, he waved a hand in my direction, and with a flick of his wrist my crown had vanished from my head. I stood before him in the shimmering black fabric of my dress, nearly sheer as the moonlight struck me. His eyes, glazed with lust, ran over me again. Aydan sat down, a high-backed armchair appearing behind him where it had not been a moment ago. His posture was casual, his performance measured as he leaned fully against the back of the chair. "Take it off," he ordered. The rough command in his tone nearly set me alight. My breath shuddered and try as I might, I could not keep my fingers from trembling as I began to drag my arms from the long sleeves, pulling the bodice down to reveal my breasts, then my stomach, letting the layered, gauzy skirts drop to the floor before stepping out of the mass of fabric, still wearing the heeled shoes. He had not ordered me to remove those yet.

With another flick of his wrist, Aydan banished the dress from the room, leaving me standing naked before him. Aydan continued to play his game, his expression unchanged—but I noticed his grip on the chair's arms grow tighter.

"Come to me," he said, lifting a hand and curling his fingers toward himself. I obeyed, walking slowly to my husband, knowing that if I walked any faster, I would lose control and devour him where he sat.

I stopped when I reached the chair, standing between Aydan's legs and waiting. My breath already ragged from watching him stare, only able to imagine what he might have in store for me. I waited.

And waited.

A lustful smirk appeared on Aydan's face as the anticipation began to make me tremble. I was nearly panting and he hadn't even touched me.

After what felt like hours, my husband reached for my hip, dragging his fingers down in a straight line, grazing my thigh and returning upward. He continued in silence, dragging his fingers lightly over my body, never quite touching the places that would bring true satisfaction, until I was fully shaking and nearly whimpering. His hand came up between my legs and began to brush his fingers across the wiry hairs there— too lightly to touch the skin, but enough to create a sensation that sent my head spinning.

"Shall we begin?" Aydan murmured. I tried to reply, but the words tangled themselves on my tongue as I stammered out an incoherent string of syllables. He pressed his fingers just slightly harder, barely touching my skin now. "What was that?"

"Y-yes—" I couldn't form the words, instead I nodded pathetically.

"Oh, you can do better than that," he said softly. "Where are your manners?"

"P*lease*—"

"Much better."

Immediately, he slipped his first finger inside of me, as deep as it would go, curling forward as he pumped in and out. I cried out in relief while I stood there, letting the pressure build until I could feel my pulse pounding between my legs and in my ears. Aydan added another finger, only gliding in and out a few more times before I lost my balance and gripped his forearm. "*Aydan*—" My fingernails dug into his skin. I was about to erupt when—

He took his hand away.

My eyes widened and a whine escaped my throat. Aydan placed his hand back on the arm of the chair, staring at me. I was still bent forward, gripping him. I thought I might cry.

"Not just yet." His still-wet hand reached forward and gripped my chin. "On your knees, Your Majesty." He held his grip on me while I lowered myself to the ground and waited for him to unbuckle his pants. My body, so sensitive after the start of our game, was very aware of the cold stone floors beneath my knees. His pants now adjusted, Aydan sat erect and waiting. I reached my hand forward and he pushed it away.

"No," he said. "Hands on your knees." I obeyed and my knuckles turned white as I gripped them tightly. Aydan's fingers tangled in my hair as he pushed my head down and I took him in my mouth. I let out a muffled moan when I heard him swear under his breath. He kept his grip on me, guiding my head up and down several times before he took over, thrusting himself into me, jamming into the back of my throat. I thought the sounds escaping me might be the thing that sent him over the edge, but it wasn't long until he suddenly pulled my head away. His eyes were half closed and cloudy with pleasure. I leaned forward and took him back in my mouth, keeping my hands on my knees and moving slowly, gently now.

"You like that, don't you?" He asked. I nodded and took my mouth off him.

"I love it."

A groan escaped his throat and he grabbed my arm, pulling me to my feet. I stood waiting while he moved his pants back in place, leaving them unbuckled when he sat back down, beckoning for me to come closer.

"Sit," he said. I did as I was told, perching sideways on his knee so my legs sat in between his. He reached under me, scooping my legs up and draping them over the arm of the chair. He removed one of my shoes, tossing it across the room carelessly before rubbing my now aching foot. My eyes closed and my head hung back while he did the same to the other.

It didn't take long for him to move on to my breasts. One arm held me tightly behind my shoulders, keeping me secure while I lay across Aydan's lap. The other played with my breasts, squeezing them firmly and letting go, fondling my nipples until they peaked, and I was panting once again. He bent his head forward and took one in his mouth while his hand squeezed the other and he moaned into my skin.

Aydan sat back up, moving his hand from my breast to my legs, scooping his arm underneath them once again, and lifting them up, up, until my knees were nearly at my chest. "Hold your legs," he commanded. I hooked my arms behind my knees, placing one on top of the other so they wouldn't slip. "Don't move," he added sternly, then kissed my forehead. I almost came unraveled at the sound of his voice.

His fingers returned to grazing the hairs between my legs. He dragged them just hard enough that his fingertips became wet again but didn't fully enter. Aydan made long, lazy strokes down my center, drifting upward and pressing light circles into me, and moving back down just as I began to whimper. After a few minutes I could feel my arms and legs faltering as I struggled to hold myself up, and just as I was about to let go, Aydan thrust his fingers inside of me. Just like before, he curled them slightly, heightening the sensation as he moved, using his thumb to press outside, keeping a steady pressure the whole time. I could feel the ache rising again and my breath became ragged.

"Not yet," he said sternly as he continued at the same speed. I whined pathetically and did everything I could to hold off. "Don't you dare."

I tried to speak, but once again was reduced to blabbering and incoherent pieces of words. He continued, pressing harder, while he stared into my eyes and shook his head. I gathered my thoughts and with every ounce of effort I could muster I begged, "Aydan— please—"

"No."

I responded with a string of expletives erupting from my mouth. Aydan grinned. Another moment of torture and then, "Are you ready?" I whimpered and nodded eagerly. "Are you sure?" An inhuman sound escaped my throat. "Go ahead. Come for me." I didn't think I was capable of the shriek I let out. Aydan continued moving his hand. He didn't stop as I rode out wave after wave. He continued, letting me build up again. I hesitated when I reached the top, but Aydan did not stop me, instead pulling me closer to him, holding me tightly and kissing my hair while I finished again and again. My limbs were shaking, and I finally let go of myself, feeling as though I would dissolve into a puddle. My legs and Aydan's lap were soaked.

"Can you stand?" Aydan's voice was gentle in my ear. My legs shook, but I nodded anyway. He gathered me in his arms and lifted me when he stood from his chair. A flicker of his power piqued my interest, and I opened my eyes to see that his clothes were gone now too. He set me on my feet, and held my face in his hands, kissing me soundly on the mouth. "I'm not finished with you yet." The words heated me, exhausted as I was. He guided me the few feet to the balcony. Now outside in the warm summer air, I could hear the waves crashing against the shore. Aydan explored me while we stood outside beneath the moonlight and he kissed me deeply, his warm hands spread wide across my skin, kneading into my backside.

Suddenly, he broke the kiss from my mouth and turned me around to face the railing, dotting kisses along my neck and shoulders. He pressed himself against me and pushed his hand into my back, bidding me to bend forward. I complied, gripping the railing with my hands and pressing my hips into it as well, while Aydan slid, desperate and throbbing, into me from behind. He went slowly the first couple of thrusts, but soon lost all restraint, gripping my hips and slamming into me, once again bringing me to the edge. I didn't know if I was capable of falling over it again. He reached around me, pressing between my legs with one hand while he continued fucking me, and gripped my hair with the other.

"Come," he ordered in my ear through gritted teeth. "Do it. Come." The rough order was my undoing, and I cried out once again, my body shuddering against his. I soon felt him do the same. He held me from behind, running his hands along the front of my body while he rode out the end, effuging us back inside before pulling out.

I swayed on my feet and Aydan caught me, lifting me into his arms and carrying me to the bed. A flick of his wrist moved the covers, and he gently sat me down in the sheets before covering me with blankets. He sat down beside me and conjured a goblet of water.

"You should drink," he said. I nodded and took the goblet from him. I drank eagerly, realizing once the water hit my lips exactly how thirsty I was. When it was empty I set it on a bedside table and then rested my head on Aydan's shoulder. "How are you feeling?"

"Amazing." I grinned with my eyes closed. Aydan made a contented noise.

"I'm glad," he said. "I worried for a moment that it might have been too much."

"If it had been, I would have told you before now," I assured him. He stroked my arm as if to warm me, and only then did I realize I was shivering. "What is this place? Is it one of the Duke's properties?"

"No, it's mine," Aydan replied. "I bought it after I retired from my army service. I always stayed with my grandparents at the Grand Palace when I was on leave, so I never spent any money on anything. By the time I retired I'd saved nearly all my wages and had a decent sum of money, so I decided I wanted some place that belonged just to me— not the Crown, or House Aevitarus, or even my grandparents."

"So you wanted a place to bring your lovers where Solandis wouldn't see?" I teased. Aydan's head tilted back as he laughed.

"That may have been a contributing factor," he admitted. "But not the sole reason. I'm sorry you aren't the first that I've brought here."

"Doesn't matter," I said truthfully. "I'm the last. Besides, I'm grateful for the century of experience you put on display tonight." Aydan chuckled again and tucked me in closer to his body. Finally regaining some warmth, I yawned. "I feel like I could sleep for a year."

"Well, we only have until mid-morning," he reminded me. "Then it's breakfast and the Xarynnian council all day." I groaned. "I know. But after tomorrow the official part of the tour is over, and then you get me all to yourself."

"How shall I repay you for tonight?" I mused sleepily, struggling to keep my eyes open.

"I'm sure you'll think of something. Sleep now, my love."

Chapter Twelve

I stood in darkness, with no up or down— an almost familiar sensation despite the months between my last visit and now. The light of Lord Ronan's study glowed in front of me, and I approached.

"Ah," Ronan's voice rang out. "You again. I didn't expect to see you so soon after your sudden disappearance this morning."

"This morning?"

"Yes— has it been longer for you?"

"Months." I swallowed. "I'm afraid I don't have much control over my mindwalking."

"Mindwalking, you say?" Ronan asked. I nodded. "Interesting… However, as I told you earlier, I need your help— I'm terribly sorry, young lady, I don't believe you've told me your name."

"It's Shaye, my lord," I told him. He looked at me expectantly, and I realized he was waiting for my surname. I couldn't very well tell him my name was Eastly, or Redfern. Claiming House Aevitarus would raise a whole new set of questions. "Shaye Vesper." Confusion flashed over his face for half a second.

"Vesper?" Ronan looked me up and down. "Hm. Lady Shaye, I am Lord Ronan Redfern, Chief Advisor to King Zathryan."

"My lord, you've told me twice now that you need my help, but I don't see how I can be much help to you when I cannot even be in the same room as you."

"You wouldn't need to be," he said. "It would be quite an easy task— I simply need you to write a message and hide it in the

Grand Palace of Nautia." I gaped at Ronan while he stared back at me, waiting for my response.

"How— how do you expect me to do such a thing? In what way would that be helpful to you?"

Ronan placed his arms behind his back, the picture of a diplomat. "I've had many enemies in my life, Lady Shaye, and if the enemy I face now is not defeated, it could mean ruin for the entire kingdom." Zathryan. He was talking about Zathryan— his great enemy, the King he was sworn to, yet would attempt to usurp. My stomach churned. "It is proving difficult to achieve my goals on my own— if I simply had more *time* to understand the threat, perhaps my struggle now would not be so great."

"I'm afraid I don't understand how my hiding a message in the Grand Palace would help anything. Sneaking into the mortal lands is quite impossible, as I'm sure you know."

"The mortal lands?" Ronan was suddenly crestfallen. "In your time, Nautia has already succumbed to the rebellion?"

"I think there has been some confusion," I said.

"Yes, I believe there has been. When you said you were a mindwalker, I took that as confirmation of my suspicion that you are living centuries before myself."

"No, I'm afraid I am living in a time after your death."

"I see." I half expected him to ask when or how he died, but Ronan did not question me further on that topic.

"Besides, if I was visiting you from the past wouldn't you have received that message already?"

"Hell if I know," Ronan sighed, dropping the decorum and leaning back against one of the many tables in the study. This one had rows and rows of herbs drying on colorful linens. "Everything seems to be falling apart now— I thought maybe you could be my chance at turning this around."

"I'm sorry," I said to fill the silence. For what, I wasn't sure.

"Don't be." He waved me off. "Tell me— how did you come to be a mindwalker? Did the Children teach you?"

"I seem to have been born with this ability. It lay dormant within me for quite some time, as did my other powers, until about a year ago. I am a sorceress, but I also appear to be a born witch— the powers passed down through my family line."

"Fascinating," Ronan replied. "And who in the Vesper line first learned the craft?"

Shit. "I— uh… No one is sure. They never revealed themselves."

"I see. And you're certain you've mindwalked here?"

"What else would this be?" I asked. "If this is real, if I'm truly talking to you right now, I have to have mindwalked in my sleep."

"Do you worry that this is not real?" Ronan inquired.

"Worry? No. But if it's not, I am thinking of becoming a novelist, to harness my overactive imagination." Ronan chuckled, then considered.

"When you wake, go to the library in Ayzelle. Behind a brick— let's say the fourth to the left of the fireplace, along the bottom near the floor— I will leave you a box. If this is real, the contents will convince you."

"Why do you care if I think you're real?" I asked.

He shrugged. "I think you're interesting, Lady Shaye." There was a knock on the door. Ronan's eyes widened. He whispered, "I don't believe anyone else can see you, but— don't test it." I pressed my back to the wall, keeping myself covered in shadow while I stood next to a large bookcase.

Ronan cracked the door, peering through and then opening it wider. "Brina—" My mother came rushing in, and once the door was shut behind her, she threw her arms around Ronan's neck and kissed him. The action startled him for a second before he placed his hands on either side of her face and deepened the kiss.

"I'm sorry," she said tearfully when they parted. "Gods, Ronan, I'm so sorry for this morning. I don't care— I don't care about the witchcraft—" Ronan shushed her gently, wiping at the tears streaming down her face.

"I do not blame you for being scared, Brina. Frankly, my darling, I would worry if you weren't." She laughed softly through her tears. "You must know— I meant every word I said last night. I've never felt for anyone the things I feel for you." Brina flushed.

"And I meant all I said to you as well. I love you, Ronan." She toyed with a button on his jacket, looking away from his face. "I know that I'm not *titled*, and I'm just some mortal soldier…"

"You are so much more than that," Ronan said thickly, putting his hand under her chin and lifting her face to meet his gaze. "You are brave, and a fierce leader. You saved Ayzelle from invasion. You're beautiful—"

"The beauty will fade," she reminded him.

"Not to me," he said. "Never to me."

"My mortality will catch up to me someday, and I will have to leave you."

"Then I will take the Final Draught and follow close behind you," he declared. She shook her head in an almost exasperated manner, as if they had been together for years and he always told the same bad jokes at festivals.

Brina said, gesturing to the room: "I want to know everything. Promise me you won't keep me in the dark."

"Never," he said earnestly. "I will finish what must be done here, and then I will take you away to the countryside, where we'll live out the rest of our days as Lord and Lady Redfern." My mother blanched. "Sorry, I'm getting ahead of myself—"

"No, it's— marry me, Ronan." Surprise painted his face.

"You're serious?"

"I know I'm being forward, but—"

"You're not," a smile spread on his face. "Of course I'll marry you, Commander Eastly." Brina threw her arms around Ronan's neck and kissed him again. It deepened after a few seconds, and he soon appeared to forget that I was still in the room because he lifted Brina onto one of the tables, kissing her neck and reaching to unfasten her sparring pants—

I'd never been more grateful for good timing than when I woke up blinking at the black ceiling. The beach house was quiet, save for the sound of waves crashing. A gentle wind blew through the open balcony door, raising gooseflesh on my arms, while Aydan lay sprawled next to me, and his deep, steady breathing brought me back to the present.

Morning came all too quickly. Aydan effuged us back to our room at the manor and we got dressed for the day before emerging to join our friends, who had all gathered in the parlor.

"Nice of you to join us," Kenna said. "You abandoned our plans for drinks last night."

"We had to deal with a very urgent matter," I joked.

"You took her to the beach house, didn't you?" Gerridan grinned at Aydan. Alastair shook his head. Aydan didn't reply, and instead prepared a cup of tea, handing it to me as if he didn't hear our friend. "Excellent."

I didn't tell Aydan about my dream of Ronan and Brina. The topic would likely upset him or lead him to believe that I should be more upset than I was. Truthfully, I was more confused than anything. The dreams of Ronan were so different from the other dreams I'd had. Between these and the nightmares where I'd stumbled upon Aydan's brutalized corpse, or watched him be murdered, I certainly preferred the visions of my traitorous father, but what did they mean? What did any of it mean? I hoped Lyra and I would be able to come up with some answers.

"Aydan, how did your visit to the attack site go?" I heard Kenna say, pulling me from my thoughts. "Did you find anything useful?"

Aydan gave me a sidelong glance. He knew I did not want to hear the details of anything to do with the attack that killed Stefan and the young guardsmen travelling with him that day. He looked like he might try to change the subject, but I gave a brief nod, letting him know to go ahead. He plucked a pastry from a tray that sat near our tea service and said, "We didn't find anything new." He took a bite. When he swallowed, he added. "Although one of the escorts had quite the theory for me— she was there when the scene was first discovered. Said it reminded her of a dreary attack."

Gerridan snorted. Kenna coughed on the swig of tea she had just taken. "Should I know what a dreary is?" I asked.

"It's a... creature, I guess," Aydan explained. "From the Unknown Territories. They used to be quite the problem, I'm told, coming over the border into Medeisia to hunt. They're intelligent, but carnivorous, and have no problem going after humans. From what I gather they leave very little behind when they kill."

I blanched. "And your escort thinks they've returned? Shouldn't we take a concern like that seriously?"

"King Alune altered the wards himself to keep them out of the continent," Gerridan said. "The only way something like that could be altered is by someone born of royal blood— and Aydan hasn't touched the wards. They wouldn't even be able to get into Nautia. Trust me, drearies are not any of our concern. It was probably some sort of mountain lion, or a pack of wolves. Jackals. Something rabid."

"That's not exactly comforting," I mumbled.

"I know. I'm sorry. There's not really a comforting version of events," Aydan said. "But I promise, if there is an explanation for Stefan's death— for all their deaths— I will find it."

"I know you will," I said. "Thank you." Aydan bent down to kiss the top of my head before the room descended into idle chatter about our plans for the day. I tried to shake the discomfort I felt from discussing Stefan and turned to Hannele. "Are you feeling any better this morning?" I asked.

"I am," she said, with a small smile emerging on her lips. Her attention flitted between Gerridan and me. "And er, well— I have something to tell you all." She sheepishly explained that her and Gerridan's plan was to clue us all in when we'd returned from Xarynn, but didn't consider the close quarters we would all be in. "So, since everyone has been so worried about me being sick, I thought I'd reassure you all that I'm fine— better than fine, actually." When she said the words, shock washed over Alastair and Kenna's faces. Aydan and I tried our best to keep from looking at one another, or we'd give away the secret that we'd known before everyone else. Aydan joined Alastair in clapping Gerridan on the back while Kenna and I hugged Hannele.

"I can't believe I didn't see this earlier," Kenna whined. "That damned witch has completely ruined my sight."

"Well, I'm quite thankful for Lyra," Gerridan said before kissing Hannele's cheek. "Her block on your sight allowed my wife to have her surprise. We all know how great you are at keeping secrets, Ken." Kenna narrowed her eyes at him.

Hannele spent the next few minutes giving us what details she could. We were to expect the next Lord or Lady Hollick sometime near the equinox. Jemma had declared the pregnancy healthy and all appeared to be going well, aside from Hannele feeling quite ill most days.

While she spoke, a stack of letters addressed to the Chief Advisor appeared on a table next to Gerridan. He picked them up and started shuffling through the pages of the thickest one.

"Oh shit," he said out loud, turning a page over to check for more writing. "Fuck." He looked to me and Aydan. "The Elf King has died."

"Shit—" Aydan reached for the letter.

"Keotis and Sewyth are in turmoil— the King's final act was to completely uproot the line of succession. He stripped the Crown Prince of his title and put his sixteen-year-old daughter on the throne," Gerridan explained to the rest of us. "That letter is from the private council of Queen Frances of the Elves."

"Sixteen?" I repeated. "And they haven't named a regent?"

"Sixteen is the elves' age of majority," Gerridan informed me. "She doesn't require one."

"The King will have installed a capable council for her, no doubt," Aydan added. "I'm willing to bet that King Laurent had this planned for some time and waited until the last second to put his plan in motion."

"Old bastard," Kenna said. "He was likable enough, but gods, what a bullshit final act, to spring such a thing on your daughter like that." Aydan passed the pages to me now, and as I finished each one I gave it to Hannele.

"This says there is talk of civil war," I said. "Should we be concerned?"

It was Alastair who answered. "War across the sea isn't likely to involve us from a military standpoint, but it could affect trade badly."

"Frances and her advisors wrote because they want your support," Hannele said. "It's not written directly on the page, but it's a smart choice. Her brother— Lucas, I think—won't engage if she has the support of the other Known Nations."

"Then it seems we must show our support for the new Elf Queen," I said. "Gerridan, write up a response, please. Aydan and I will sign it right away. Tell them King Laurent knew what was best for his kingdoms, and Medeisia trusts in his choice for successor. Give Queen Frances our congratulations and tell her we look forward to continuing our good relationship with Sewyth and Keotis."

"I'll have it ready for your signatures in an hour," Gerridan said to Aydan and me. "Sorry to put a damper on the announcement, darling," he added to Hannele, who waved him off.

"Our work doesn't stop for our personal lives," she said before turning her attention to me and Aydan. "That being said, there is something I wanted to discuss with the two of you." She glanced at Gerridan, who gave her an encouraging nod.

"What's going on?" Aydan asked, looking between them.

"When the baby comes, I'll need time to recover, and I was thinking I might want to take more of a break than most would…"

"You'll be able to take all the time you need," I said. "We're not currently involved in any sort of conflict— we can do without a strategist for a while."

"Well that's just it," Hannele continued. "I'm not a vital position right now and I just— I've discussed it with Gerridan, and once the baby arrives I'll be handing in my resignation."

Aydan let out a long breath. "You're sure?" She nodded.

"I don't want to miss anything. And who knows? It might be nice to just be an advisor's wife for a while." I wrapped my arms around my friend.

"We just want you to be happy," I told her. "If that means stepping down, then do it."

"The position will be there for you if you ever want it back," Aydan added. "But no matter what, we'll still expect you at dinner." Hannele grinned, her eyes shining a bit having gotten all of that out into the open.

"So," Kenna said. "Have you thought of names?"

With the news of King Laurent's death, the meeting with the Xarynnian council was less confrontational than expected. Instead of complaining about the route between Sylvanna and Ayzelle, discussion of trade was focused on keeping good relations with elves. I mentioned my desire for the council to investigate why Auperene wasn't importing goods from us. There was a spattering of agreement to continue with that as a topic of discussion at a later date, and then the meeting was adjourned.

Aydan and I saw our friends off as they effuged back to Sylvanna. I made Kenna promise not to kill Lyra while I was gone. She agreed and added, "Who knows, maybe she'll start to grow on me someday." From behind her, Gerridan raised his eyebrows and smirked. I scratched the corner of my eye with my middle finger.

After we bid them farewell, Aydan and I paid our respects to Edwin and Ylena. The Duke appeared quite disappointed when he realized that Kenna had already departed and kept our goodbyes brief.

Now, we were getting settled at a seaside cottage owned by House Aevitarus. With all of Aydan's promises of ravishing me once we were completely alone, I hadn't expected to make it through the door upon our arrival. Instead, he gave me a tour of the cottage then started unpacking our trunks, and hung my dresses in the wardrobe for me. When he finished, he told me he was going to take a bath but did not invite me to join as he usually did.

While he bathed, I went outside to look at the view, but the vast sea unsettled my mind. Instead, I sat on the ground and plunged my hands into the sand, burying them in warmth. I tried saying the words that would control earth but nothing happened. Then, looking to the waves for inspiration, I said the words for water. Nothing. After a while I gave up and dusted off my hands before making my way back inside.

Aydan was reading. He lounged on the bed in a thin pair of black linen pants with no shirt on. I pretended not to notice his muscled chest and shoulders when I went to the bathroom and washed the last of the sand from my hands before summoning a gift Kenna had given me the week before. "Something honeymoon worthy," she had said with a wink when she gave me the box. I'd laughed when I first saw it: a nightdress made from a single layer of white fabric so sheer I might as well be naked. Tonight, the thought of wearing it sent my heart pounding.

When I walked out of the bathroom, Aydan didn't look up from his book. It wasn't until I was almost directly next to him, standing at the edge of the bed that he saw what I was wearing and set the book aside while looking me up and down. I reached out and stroked his hair, dragging my fingertips down his jawline. I did this a few times before asking, "Are you tired?"

"Not really," he said.

"Good." I continued stroking his hair. "I had an activity in mind, if you'd like to join me."

Aydan started to run his hand along my thigh. "Of course, I—" I smacked his hand away. He raised his eyebrows and the corner of his mouth twitched. "What were you thinking?"

Once more, I stroked his hair, but instead of drifting to his jaw, I grabbed a handful of the dark waves and held them tightly.

Aydan groaned and happily obliged when I said, "On your knees, Your Majesty."

Chapter
Thirteen

We spent two blissful days in the cottage. There was little sleep to be had, between sex and nightmares, but the break from home was well spent nonetheless. Upon our return, we were bombarded with messages and meeting requests from various members of the council. Before we could decipher what they were all so concerned about, Gerridan knocked on the door to Aydan's study to inform us that we would be meeting with the Prince Regent of Nautia in ten days. King Callum had agreed to allow a face-to-face meeting between us and Prince Gram first, and then would consider meeting with us himself based on Gram's report. For the first time since the Rebellion, a King of Medeisia would be setting foot inside the Grand Palace of Nautia.

We'd been home for a week when my exhaustion finally got the better of me. I was sparring with Alastair and found that after only twenty minutes or so of our usual drills I was so tired I could barely lift my sword.

"Go home and rest," Alastair finally said as I swayed on my feet.

"I'm fine, just let me use a waster," I said, eyeing the wooden training swords on the rack at the edge of the ring.

"When was the last time you slept, Shaye?"

"The whole night? Before the wedding," I admitted. "Lyra is trying to help me understand my dreams, so I went off my tonic." In our lessons each day, after trying to conjure my elemental magic, Lyra had me recount my dreams from the night before to her. After a few times forgetting details and confusing the order of events, I had been tasked with keeping a diary on my bedside table, so I could write everything down upon waking and it could be reviewed later.

"The dreams are that bad then?"

"Most of the time they end with me finding someone's mangled body, so yes," I said. Alastair made a face.

"I can't say I'm too fond of this lesson plan, but I can see why it would be important."

"It will be worth it," I said. "Better to know what causes them and how to handle it than to hide behind potions for the rest of my life."

"Either way, you should go get some rest. Take a nap, we'll try again in a few days."

Begrudgingly, I agreed. I had enough time before the council would meet tonight. A nap might do me some good. We packed up the ring and I effuged myself home, leaving Alastair in behind at his request.

"You're back early," Aydan said from his armchair when I entered our bedroom. Catchfly was sprawled in mine, snoring just slightly. It seemed Aydan had decided to complete his work in the light of the bedroom rather than his study, which he often complained was too dark. Stacks of papers littered the small table beside him. I leaned over the back of his chair, looped my arms around his neck, and pressed a kiss to his cheek.

"Alastair kicked me out of the ring and told me to go take a nap," I explained.

"That's not a bad idea," Aydan replied. "You've been exhausted."

"I know," I sighed. "I'm going to change and then try to get some rest until we have to prepare for the council."

"I can handle the council on my own tonight, if you'd rather rest," he offered.

"No, I should be there," I yawned. We had been going over safety precautions presented by Lord Declan at our last visit, and despite his over cautious nature, it felt good to be prepared for anything that might happen during the Nautia trip. Alastair, however, had assured us that none of it was necessary and that Gram was a gracious host.

Aydan kissed my hand. "Go lie down. I'll try not to keep you up."

I nodded and made my way to the bathroom, grabbing a nightdress from the wardrobe on the way. I debated bathing first, but after all the discussion of napping I just wanted to quickly wash my face and then climb into bed. Once I'd washed, I reached for a towel hanging from a small hook on the wall and managed to knock over a basket Elise left out for me, filled with clean and folded sanitary cloths ready for my upcoming cycle. *My cycle.* I groaned internally, dreading what the monthly discomfort would feel like combined with my exhaustion. I bent to pick up the sanitary cloths, and then paused. I counted the days since we'd been home from Xarynn. Then I began to count backwards.

Still in my sparring clothes, I left the bathroom and rummaged in the wardrobe for a satchel. When I found one, I threw it over my shoulder and tried to say casually, "I'm going to see Jemma for a moment."

"Why, what's wrong?" Aydan perked up in his seat.

"Nothing," I replied. "My cycle is… being strange."

"Do you want me to accompany you?"

"No, I'm sure it's nothing a few herbs can't fix." Many people visited Jemma when ginger tea and a hot bath were not enough to ease their monthly symptoms.

"All right, I'll just finish up here then," Aydan replied with a shrug. I bent down to kiss his temple before swiftly leaving our bedroom, my nerves bubbling under my skin.

An hour later, I returned to the house, choosing to walk rather than effuge. I had to resist the urge to take out the covered dish from my satchel and stare at its contents yet again, stunned by Jemma's words despite my suspicions: "Congratulations, Your Majesty."

The house was busy when I walked in the front door. Hannele, Gerridan, Alastair, and Kenna were lounging in the sitting room, passing papers around in their usual manner, going over Aydan's notes for the council. My eyes fell to Hannele's swollen belly.

"You were supposed to be resting," Alastair scolded when he saw me.

"Had to go see Jemma," I explained distantly. "Cycle trouble," I added when his face filled with concern. Before anyone could question me further, I mumbled something about running to get ready.

When I returned to our bedroom I clicked the door shut behind me and found Aydan standing before a mirror, adjusting his clothing.

"My offer still stands to handle the council tonight," he said by way of greeting. He turned to face me with a sympathetic look. "You're pale. You should really lie down…But if you're set on going you have plenty of time to get ready. No need to rush."

"Maybe," I said. I struggled to form words. "You should— um, I mean…"

Aydan knit his brow. "What's the matter?"

"You should sit down," I said. Slowly, Aydan made his way to the bed and sat on its edge.

"You're not exactly putting my mind at ease, my love."

"It's nothing to worry about— I don't think, anyway." I sat down beside him. "Um, I went to see Jemma. I told her what had been happening with me lately…she examined me, and well—" I reached into the satchel and pulled out the small dish. I removed the cover and handed it to Aydan to let him examine the contents. He stared at it, blinking in surprise.

"Is this a moonflower?"

"Yes." The healer had handed me the dish and a few moonflower blossoms, instructing me to chew them up and spit them out into the dish. I did as I was told, then watched as she placed a cover over the bowl. She chatted with me for a few minutes, and then removed the cover, revealing to me a new sprout growing from the macerated flowers before extending her congratulations. Aydan remained silent, staring at the dish for a few more seconds. "Will you say something please?"

"You're pregnant." It wasn't a question.

"It certainly looks like it," I said. Without saying anything else Aydan took my face in his hands and kissed me. "Are you happy?" I asked when he pulled away and I saw that his eyes were glossy.

"Of course I'm happy— are you?"

"I am, really— this just wasn't news I planned to receive today." I laughed. "It's so unexpected."

"Did she say how far along?"

"Our best guess puts me right around ten weeks." Between planning the wedding and preparing for Xarynn, I hadn't noticed my missing cycle, and I'd been blaming my exhaustion on nightmares.

"So, late winter then?" He'd done the math in his head.

"I believe so, yes."

"And everything is... fine? Normal?" That was the first question I had asked Jemma. The mortal women in my village growing up were all given strict instruction not to drink wine or liquor, to refrain from strenuous activity and avoid stress. I had been doing the exact opposite of that list these past weeks. Jemma assured me everything looked healthy, and that those restrictions don't affect sorcerers the way they do mortals. Alcohol wouldn't harm my baby, but it would make me quite ill, which explained the nasty hangovers I woke up with when I had more than the cup or so I normally drank with dinner.

"Jemma says everything is as it should be. We're both healthy."

"Wow," he murmured. "*Wow.*" Aydan grinned, and hugged me tightly, kissing the top of my head.

"What do we do now?" I asked. "Do we— do we tell anyone, or...?"

"Traditionally announcements from royalty would wait until the pregnancy reaches the midway mark. But we should tell the others here. Alastair might start interrogating us both if he sees Jemma coming and going too often," Aydan said. He looked at the clock. "And now, I really must insist that you try and get some rest. Let me handle the council."

"Fine," I yawned, unable to pretend any longer that I desperately wanted to attend this meeting. "Tuck me in then, Your Majesty," I joked. Aydan took this as a challenge and lifted me from the bed. His magic pulled the covers back and he lay me onto the plush mattress before tucking the blankets in tightly around me while I shook with laughter.

"Go to sleep," he said, kissing me once before loosening the blankets for me.

"All right," I yawned again. "You win. Goodnight."

Chapter Fourteen

Aydan and I elected to tell our friends after keeping the news of my pregnancy to ourselves for only one day. Hannele burst into tears and wrapped her arms around me, blubbering that she was so happy for us before hugging Aydan as well and kissing his cheek. When Alastair hugged me, he lifted me off the floor, and I saw Gerridan over his shoulder handing Kenna a few coins.

I told Lyra later, by myself.

"Congratulations," she told me. "You know, witches who are with child are thought to be extremely powerful."

"Oh good, something else to learn how to manage," I said.

"It's just a bit of old folklore," she clarified with a chuckle. "Witches don't often have children of their own, so I think it's meant to be more of a commentary on the rarity of such a thing."

"Good," I joked. "I don't think I could add anything else to my schedule."

The morning we were due to set out for Nautia, we were up at dawn. Elise dressed us in black and gold. "For intimidation," she said.

When my hair was done, I strapped two daggers to each of my bare legs. Elise left the room to retrieve my dress, and Aydan made a point to double check my sheaths to make sure they were properly fastened. Once he confirmed they were functioning properly, he smacked my backside. I squealed and batted him away, making him laugh as he stepped out of reach. I didn't know if she heard or saw us, but Elise had an amused look on her face when she returned. She said nothing of it and helped me into my dress.

She chose some new armor-like pieces I'd recently commissioned to pair with it— a set of gold spaulders adorned with small lions' heads. A gold tiara, bejeweled with large chunks of black and white diamond—one of the more elaborate and expensive pieces we owned— was woven into my hair, and the dark makeup Isolde painted on me for the coronation feast had been duplicated.

Aydan wore a suit of black trimmed in gold thread and embroidered with his lion wreathed in roses on the breast. It was similar to ensembles he'd worn before, but this one had been specially made for today, with multiple daggers sewn into the lining at the insistence of the council. Each of us had enough weapons on us to take on a dozen mortals if need be, but the only visible weapon was a ceremonial saber on Aydan's hip.

"You know, I've always been fond of being prepared for anything," Alastair said from our bedroom doorway, watching me check Aydan's jacket to make sure all his weapons were hidden properly. "But this might be excessive. Even if they disarm you, you'll have your magic. They know that. They aren't going to pick a fight with you."

"King Mal used to brag in his addresses to the kingdom about his excessive stores of silver in case we were ever invaded by sorcerers," I said. "He was probably lying, but as my *sparring instructor* often says, it's best to have it and not need it—"

"Yes, yes, I get your point," Alastair said. "I just wanted to assure you that I don't get the sense of an impending ambush from the mortals. Prince Gram is eager for this meeting."

"Then hopefully today is a new start for both our kingdoms," Aydan said stiffly. "Let's get going."

We effuged first to Ayzelle, for a final send off from the council. Kenna stayed behind with Hannele, who had spent her morning running between her bathroom to vomit and the sitting room to argue with Gerridan that she was perfectly fine. Eventually she was convinced to stay, reducing our party to me, Aydan, Gerridan, and Alastair.

"The meeting with the Prince Regent is just that. A meeting," Declan reminded us as we all stood in the foyer of the King's Chambers. "Introductions only. As agreed upon by Your Majesties and the council, no negotiations will take place yet. Make no promises, accept no offers—"

"Thank you, my lord," I said with a dismissive tone. "We understand the objective."

"Forgive my caution, Your Majesty. This is entirely unprecedented. You *are* armed?"

"We are," I confirmed. "Careful Declan. That tone might have someone thinking you actually want us to return." Declan resisted smiling.

"Of course I want you and the King to return, ma'am. If you don't, I'll be out of a job."

I snickered. "If I didn't know better, Declan, I'd say you actually like me."

"Perhaps you've started to grow on me, ma'am."

When Alastair first started making his visits to Nautia, it had been agreed upon that the witches would raise their wards for exactly thirty seconds at the stroke of noon on the day he was to arrive, so that he could simply effuge to the palace rather than come on horseback. It was decided we would arrive in the same way, but that the wards would be altered so that we could leave at any time we saw fit.

We were instructed to arrive outside the southern gate to the Grand Palace. Barricades and guardsmen lined the area, keeping back what looked like hundreds of Nautians gathered to watch us. We were greeted by a collective gasp— their reaction to seeing us appear from nowhere. I made it a point to look at those who stood closest to me, giving them a tight-lipped smile. They just stared.

"Are you all right?" Aydan whispered, brushing my hand with his fingertips.

"I'm fine," I lied. "What about you?"

"The last time I walked through these gates, my mother was here to greet me." His voice was tight. "I worry about what the mortals may have done with her home. I never knew what they did with her body— if they gave her a pyre. My father was forced to flee without it." The gates opened, leaving me no time to reply. I squeezed his hand and hoped that said everything it needed to.

The four of us were now flanked by mortal guards as we walked forward onto the grounds. Standing at the palace steps was a slender man whose hair was a tawny color that reminded me briefly of Stefan. As we came closer, I recognized him to be Prince Gram.

I'd seen the prince only twice in my life: once, as a child, I accompanied Gideon to the capital square to run an errand and spotted a boy a few years older than me trying to outrun the guards.

"Seems the prince has grown bored again," was all Gideon had to say about it. Years later, Gideon and I were in the square again, this time to hear King Mal's Yule address. Beside him on the balcony stood Prince Gram, at full attention, apparently having outgrown his boyhood mischief.

Gram jaunted off the stairs, coming toward us with a bounce in his step.

"Greetings, Your Majesties," he said, extending his hand to shake Aydan's, then mine. "I am Prince Gram. Welcome to the Grand Palace of Nautia."

"Good day, Your Highness," Aydan replied first. "I am King Aydan of Medeisia, and this is Queen Shaye. You already know Lord General Alastair Greenwood—" Gram nodded in Alastair's direction with a smile— "and this is our Chief Advisor, Lord Gerridan Hollick."

"Welcome to all of you," the prince said earnestly. "As you can see word has spread that the King of Sorcerers would be arriving today." With his attention on me, he added, "And no one was truly sure until now, what the fate of Shaye Eastly was. It must have been quite the feat of magic that got you past our wards that night."

"Not so terrible a fate, I should say. Quite the rise in station, having been raised by your palace blacksmith."

"Yes," Gram said a bit grimly. "I assumed Mr. Gideon would come up. I am sorry for his fate. I was out voted by the council, and as I am not King— and my nephew is not of age— the majority could not be overruled. There was nothing I could do but accept the decision."

I stiffened. It was a topic I had been avoiding, even in my own head. Negotiations must take place; we must work toward a good relationship with Nautia— and so I must set aside the fact that my uncle had died a prisoner in this palace.

"Well," I said more darkly than I meant to. "As long as it was a fair vote." Aydan straightened beside me, and I heard Alastair inhale sharply.

"Your Majesty, I—"

"My apologies, Your Highness," I said quickly. "We are here not to dwell on the past but to look toward the future."

"Maybe so," Gram said kindly, "But looking to the past can help us understand what comes next. How can we know where we're going if we don't pay attention to where we started?" I nodded. "I am very sorry for your loss, Queen Shaye."

"Thank you, Prince Gram," I said. "Please, let's just continue." Gram turned and began leading us inside.

"Are you all right?" Aydan whispered again.

"Fine," I answered. "Let's go."

Prince Gram led us through the palace, showing us dining halls, an art gallery, and a vast library before we were brought to a council room of sorts. In the center of the space was an enormous mahogany table, long enough to seat fifteen people comfortably. The top had been polished so thoroughly I could see my reflection, while the edges and legs were carved with an intricate filigree not unlike Aydan's tattoos. Aydan ran his finger along the edge with a distant look on his face.

Before we could be seated, a servant boy holding a note appeared and gave it to Prince Gram with a bow. The Regent dismissed the boy and read the note quickly before saying to us, "I am dreadfully sorry, but I must attend to an important matter— please make yourselves comfortable. I'll only be gone a few minutes." He took off swiftly down a corridor, leaving us alone in the room with a pair of guards at the door.

"What are the odds this is a trap and that was staged?" Gerridan asked no one in particular.

"Zero," Alastair said. "That happens a lot. He's dealing with Callum."

"Is the boy so poorly behaved that he cannot be left alone?" Aydan inquired.

"Gram has ordered Gwendolyn—the witch that Callum is so fond of — to stay away from the young King. Callum waits until he thinks his uncle is too occupied to notice, and sneaks to her quarters to see her."

"The Prince Regent has let you in on his family troubles," Gerridan observed.

"We have an understanding."

"Mmm."

"Gerridan, this is not the time or place," I said.

"Speaking of time and place," my Chief Advisor hissed. "Perhaps next time we can make it *inside* the palace before you bring up your dead uncle."

"I wasn't exactly planning on that—" I snapped. But before we could continue our argument, Gram returned.

"Where were we?" he asked. "Ah— yes, please sit, all of you."

I had expected, with Gram bringing us to a council room, to be questioned directly about our demands and motives for meeting with Nautia. Instead, we spent the next hour having tea, and what felt like a friendly chat with the prince. He told us briefly about being raised by his brother after the death of their father. He asked me questions about life in Medeisia and how it compared to Nautia, and what I thought about Nautia's ability to form friendships with the Medeisian territories. I told him the truth— that while I felt that we as leaders of two very different nations could come to an understanding, it would take some time before the people of Nautia would come to terms with the changes.

"That's not to say they won't ever be receptive to change," I clarified. "But I grew up within walking distance from this palace, Your Highness. The people you rule over...they fear me. They fear my husband, and our people. To Nautians, sorcery is foreign and dangerous. Your family saw to it that we would always be viewed as a threat."

"I see," said Gram. "Perhaps we could show the people that you and King Aydan are not a threat to them?"

"How would you propose we do that?" Aydan asked.

"As Her Majesty has pointed out, her childhood home is just a short distance away. Let's take a walk. She can visit her old home, and her neighbors can see she is no threat to them."

"I— what, *now?*" Alastair's eyes went wide. "Your Highness, there is a crowd of hundreds standing outside the palace gates. I will not allow my King and Queen to be put in danger."

"We could effuge," Gerridan suggested. "If Their Majesties would like to make this excursion, that is."

"We would prefer no sorcery be used at this time," Gram said. "As Prince Regent, I could cause quite a panic if I suddenly disappeared with a group of sorcerers. But we could simply take one of the carriages."

"What do you think?" Gerridan asked Aydan.

"It's up to the Queen," Aydan replied. He then added in a low voice to me, "If it's too much, Shaye, we don't have to do this."

I considered it for a moment. It could be gut wrenching to see what remained, if anything, of my childhood home. But this might be my only chance to see it at all. And perhaps Gram was right. Maybe seeing me as my true self would help my old neighbors be the first to accept that Medeisia is not their enemy. I quietly loosed a breath.

"Will the carriage hold all five of us?"

It took half an hour to arrange the carriage and then only ten minutes to arrive at the edge of my old village. Children were playing in the road when we arrived, so we stopped with the intention of walking the rest of the way now that we were free of the crowds.

Gram exited first, and I heard a gasp from one of the children. "It's the prince!" Alastair left the carriage next, followed by Gerridan and Aydan, who then stood by to help me step down.

"Go tell mother!" The children broke out into a run upon seeing me exit. I didn't get a good enough look to know if I recognized them.

As we walked down the dirt path, my former neighbors came filing out of their houses while memories flooded my mind. The road was damp from the previous day's rain, leaving a familiar scent in my nostrils. As children we would dance and chase each other in the rain, letting mud splatter up to our knees and ruining our clothes. The village boys would form the mud into balls and launch them at the girls, sending us shrieking as we ran home to tell on them.

"You can do this," Aydan muttered. I realized that my nails were digging deeply into his arm. If he hadn't been wearing his jacket, I would have broken skin.

By the time we were approaching my house, every villager I'd ever known was standing outside of their home, watching. My breath hitched when I reached out to open the gate and found it squeaking like it had when Gideon came home that last day. I'd been turning the garden beds— which were now overgrown with weeds. The entire front garden was in disarray, unkempt and torn apart by the soldiers who had come raining down on us that night. The night I met Aydan, the night I learned that I was a sorceress. My eyes burned, and I walked to the front door, which was open. Or rather, I realized, it had never been fixed after being broken down. That final image of Gideon raising his sword to face what lay on the other side as the door blew off its hinges flashed in my mind.

As far as I could tell, nothing had been touched— by people, that is. By the look of it, some local wildlife might have taken shelter in the empty dwelling during the winter, but everything else remained intact. Aydan, Gerridan, Alastair, and Gram all stood back and watched as I wandered the front rooms of my old home. I stepped into the kitchen and saw that my skillets still hung on the wall. My apron remained on its hook. I took the fabric in my hand and felt the layer of dust and grime that had formed on it, ruining my careful stitching. The cupboards seemed to have been ransacked by whatever creatures found their shelter here, and so I turned the other way, starting toward the sitting room.

The fireplace, which I had almost always kept burning, sat empty, save for the cold pile of ashes at the bottom of it. Our chairs and the small tables beside them, like my apron, had succumbed to the dust, and I resisted running my hands along them. What I had been most concerned about was the books. Our precious books, lining the walls of the sitting room, remained undisturbed. I was certain the soldiers would have emptied out the shelves in search of contraband, but they hadn't even moved the books from our tables. The maps too, remained on the walls. Gerridan stared up at them.

"These are pre-Rebellion," he commented.

"Gideon always said not to mention them outside of the house," I told him. "It wasn't until I was older that he explained they could get him arrested." I noticed Gram seeming interested, squinting up at the frames. Before he could raise any sort of fuss about them, I waved my hand, and the maps were gone, sent back to one of the empty rooms in our chambers in Ayzelle. I didn't look to see his reaction to my magic before I waved once again, and every book in the sitting room was sent there as well. "My apologies for the sorcery," I said with a nod to the prince before walking past him down the hallway toward my bedroom. Aydan followed.

The bedroom was much the same as the rest of the house: covered in dirt. There was little to be seen here aside from the small bed and a wardrobe, as I spent most of my time in the kitchen or sitting room with Gideon, only coming in here to sleep. I opened the wardrobe and found dresses, blouses, and gardening trousers that all looked so familiar yet felt like they belonged to another person entirely. I supposed they did.

"You're very brave for coming here," Aydan said from behind me.

"Am I?" I said in a near whisper, looking around the room again and blinking back tears. "This house feels like a ghost." He put his hand on the small of my back. "I don't belong here anymore. Or maybe I never did to begin with. It's not home... I-I'd like to go home." My hands shook.

"We'll leave in five minutes," Aydan promised. "Let's leave on a good note with the prince and the villagers." I nodded, trying to pull myself together. "How can I help?"

"Just... give me a minute, please. Go talk to Prince Gram so he doesn't see me like this." Aydan wiped a tear from my cheek before kissing it and then left the room to do as I asked. I took a few breaths to gather myself then stepped back out into the hallway.

Directly across from my bedroom was Gideon's. The door was shut, as it always was. I could count on one hand the number of times I had even been inside his bedroom— most of them as a child, waking him to rescue me after a nightmare. Understanding this may be my only chance to see it, I pushed on the door and stepped inside.

The closed door had saved Gideon's bedroom from at least some of the dust, but there was still a thin layer of grime on everything. The room was simple, like mine—not much more than a bed and table on the far side, and a chest of drawers on the opposite wall. On top of the chest of drawers were a few items: a stationary box, a discarded pen, some loose copper pieces, and a sloppily folded handkerchief. Curious, I stepped forward and opened the stationary box, finding a single folded card. I opened it, and something fell to the ground. Before bending to pick it up, I read the uneven scrawl:

Gideon—

I'm writing to tell you that you have the happiest sister in the Known Nations. I've fallen in love with Lord Ronan Redfern, and we are wed. No one is more surprised than me.

Visit soon— I want to tell you everything.

Your sister always,

Lady Brina Redfern

"Alastair," I called out as I stooped to pick up the fallen item. He entered just as I had the chance to look at what it was: a miniature of Brina and Ronan's wedding portrait.

"What is it?" Alastair asked. I handed him the card.

"Wow," he breathed. "I haven't seen her handwriting in ages."

"Do you think there's more in here?" I asked, looking around the room for hiding spots. "If this was just sitting on the drawers, there might be more of her notes or something hidden somewhere."

I started opening drawers, only to be greeted with a few moths and dusty clothing while I searched. I found nothing among the few belongings, and moved on to the bedside table, opening the drawer there and finding a few spare candles. I moved to face Alastair again when my foot ran into something under the bed. He gave me a strange look as I bent down to reach for the item, which turned out to be a small wooden trunk. It was fairly heavy, but not so much that I couldn't lift it on my own and set it on the bed. I didn't pay much attention to the carved lid before opening it, hoping to find more letters from my mother, or other family keepsakes. Instead, it was a large drawstring bag made of black velvet. I opened that as well, revealing what must be thousands of gold pieces.

"What..." I whispered to myself while I reached into the bag and pulled out a handful. "...the fuck."

"Is that—?"

"It's gold," I confirmed. "Gideon didn't make much at the palace. We never had extra money— why does he have a trunk of gold?"

"Dunno— is there a label or something? Look under the bag." Alastair lifted the heavy bag while I peered beneath it, finding another folded card. I snatched it and flipped it open, revealing neater, sharper penmanship than my mother's:

For maintenance. —K.R.

Scowling, I pocketed the note and Alastair placed the bag back in the box. I let the lid of the trunk fall, then finally noticed the carvings. Forget-me-nots bordered the perimeter, and in the center, a red fox.

"What is all of this? What did the note say?"

I told him what it said, and that I didn't know what the purpose of it was. "But I'm not interested in this gold."

"We can't just leave it here."

"Fine," I said. "Just... carry the box." My general obliged.

We walked back down the hallway and straight through the front door without stopping to explain to our companions what I'd found. Instead, I walked through the garden, through the gate, and across the road with Alastair right behind me.

As I suspected, Cait's family was outside like the rest of the villagers. Her belly was swollen again, apparently expecting baby number six. Her husband the miller stood beside her— not the miller, I realized. Finn. Gods, he'd grown. He had to be fifteen by now, and just as he had the last time I saw him, appeared much older than his age. Finn's gangly limbs had filled out with muscle that indicated he must be working with his father in the mill by now, and his once generous smile was replaced with a scowl as he watched us.

Surprise— perhaps mixed with horror—washed over Finn and Cait's faces when I approached their gate and walked through it. Finn stepped in front of his mother, ready to take on Alastair and me if need be.

"I'd like to give you this, if I may," I said, gesturing to the box in Alastair's arms. Finn remained silent but took a step back and looked me up and down with a disgust that rattled me. His eyes flicked to the crown on my head. "Here— it's not a trick." I opened the box and hoisted the bag from it. I set it on the ground before them and, crouching down, opened it to reveal the contents without letting the other neighbors see. "Take it. Use what you need. Distribute the rest to the others if you want. Get ready for winter." I saw Cait's eyes widen over her son's shoulder.

"Why?" She nearly whispered.

"I don't need it." I shrugged. "I remember how hard the cold was here. Keep your babies warm and fed, Cait."

"No, but— why us?"

"You were my friend," I said. "Please take it and take care of yourselves." I returned the bag to its box. Alastair set it on the ground and we walked away without another word. We rejoined Aydan, Gerridan, and Gram, who had been standing in the road watching us. "Thank you for bringing me here, Your Highness, but I think I've had enough."

"May I bring you back to the palace for another cup of tea?" Gram asked.

"We'll wait for our next visit," Aydan promised, earning a strained smile from the mortal prince.

"Then I shall await a letter from Ala— General Greenwood to plan such a thing."

"It was a pleasure, Your Highness," I said. And before we could say anything else, Aydan took my hand and effuged us back to Ayzelle.

Declan and Dracus were the only council members remaining in the King's Chambers when we returned to Ayzelle. They had each taken up an armchair in the parlor but scrambled to their feet once we reappeared. The lords bowed to us briefly before Declan started in with his questioning. Gerridan did most of the talking, explaining our arrival, the movements of the Prince Regent, how many guards were present, and any other details the councilmen wanted to know. After a few minutes of listening, I stepped away, quietly excusing myself— though no one appeared to notice— and walked right out the front door of the chambers.

I moved swiftly down the corridor, nodding briefly at the guards who stood at the entrance to the north wing. I continued, passing courtiers who seemed startled to see me strolling through the castle without Aydan or a Cabinet member on my arm. I ignored their bows and curtsies, though I did make a point to nod politely to the servants who would stop and mumble, "Your Majesty," under their breath with their eyes positioned toward the floor. Finally, I arrived at the southern end of the castle, and turned down the corridor across from the Great Hall that I had not dared to enter since I was removed from it.

I stood before the beautifully carved, handle-less door to the Prince's Chambers. It had been repaired— or had repaired itself— after being blown apart by the King's Guard to capture me. It took me a moment of staring before I worked up the nerve to place my hand upon the wood and will it to let me inside. A brass knocker appeared, and without much further effort from me the door swung open. I sent in a few orbs of light, letting them float to the ceiling before I stepped inside, half expecting to see the dwelling ransacked, but just as the door had been repaired, so too had the beautiful rooms where I spent my first weeks in Ayzelle with Aydan, both of us prisoners of King Zathryan. The wine-red rugs in the foyer remained, as well as the sofas and armchairs in the parlor, the vases and knickknacks all in place. I stood in the center of the parlor for a few minutes, arms crossed over my chest while I stared at the space. A familiar wave of magic surged behind me and soon I felt Aydan's arms loop around my middle, pulling me back so I could lean fully against his chest. He kissed my cheek and let his chin rest on my head.

"I thought I might find you here," he said quietly.

"Sorry to disappear," I replied. "This just seemed like the next logical place to go."

"Oh?"

"I spent the last hour reliving my past. The next place I went was here, with you. Although I am cheating by skipping the week of walking and camping in the freezing cold." Aydan chuckled. I continued, "How badly did I mess all of that up?"

"What makes you think you messed it up?"

"Immediately jumping down Gram's throat about Gideon. Giving all that gold to Cait."

"I think we're in the clear," he said. "Things were bound to be tense at first. And that gold was in your house. Unless there's some Nautian rule I'm not aware of, you're allowed to give your money to whomever you'd like." I nodded.

"You're right," I sighed. "I suppose I underestimated how difficult this would be for me."

"All things considered I would say you're doing quite well."

"Thank you," I said. Wanting to change the subject before I could get misty-eyed, I gestured to the front door. "The wards are down on this place. I just willed the door open."

"They're not. I gave you access to the wards while we still lived here together, so you could come and go without me if you ever got brave enough."

"Sneaky prince," I quipped. Aydan nipped at my ear, making me laugh. "Even if I had been brave enough, I wouldn't have wanted to go anywhere without you. I was already in love with you while we were trapped here."

"I know." His arms tightened just slightly. "Me too." Sadness hung over me as I thought of all we missed, all the lost time between the two of us. In that moment I was truly grateful for the gods bringing us back to one another over and over again. His palms spread low on my belly, and I knew Aydan was grateful too.

Chapter Fifteen

"It just doesn't make *sense!*" Lyra slammed her book shut, startling Petyr, who had been coiled beside it on her desk while she read. The witch had assigned me the task of identifying the various dried flowers on a table in front of me, then labeling them with their name and uses in both healing and potions. It would have been an easy task, except that she had presented me with nothing but different types of blue flowers. "A challenge," she told me. "You're getting good at beginner work, let's see how you do with more difficulty." I'd grumbled to myself but managed to feel fairly confident that I was doing well. Catchfly wove herself around my legs while I worked, trying to get my attention after I scolded her for attempting to hunt Petyr.

I had officially been training as a witch for a little over a month now, since our return from Xarynn, and had not done much else besides memorizing herbs, continuing to try gaining control over the elements, and following Lyra's instruction that I keep my dream diary. Our lessons had stagnated as Lyra struggled to find answers about the dreams and I made no progress in elemental magic. So she had moved on to researching mindwalkers.

"What doesn't make sense?" I asked, looking up from my flower work.

"Mindwalking," she said. "Well— *your* mindwalking, I should say. But then again nothing about your magic makes any gods damned sense."

"My apologies," I said flatly.

"Sorry," she replied. "That was insensitive of me. It's not your fault."

"What's so different about my mindwalking?" I inquired. "Beyond being born with the ability, I mean."

"Well, that's just it." She flipped open the only book in all of Medeisia that contained any information on the topic. "It doesn't make sense that you were born with this ability. It's not like the elements. Once you have access to those and have trained yourself in their use, you can summon your chosen element at any time with the right spoken spell. Mindwalking requires ritual. Those who were very skilled in the art of mindwalking could eventually learn to maintain their hold over a person for longer periods of time, some even leaving their workspace and going about their lives while accessing someone else's mind. But for most who even attempted it, the spellwork was so complicated and dense that they never tried it again. Even if Lord Ronan had started learning to mindwalk a *decade* before his death, the idea that he might be skilled enough to maintain his hold on the power strongly enough to pass to you seems unlikely."

"That is strange," I replied. "But what does it mean for me?"

"It means that, even with the extreme limitations we already face regarding the study of mindwalking, I must once again find a way to understand how this skill has blended with your sorcery, and then teach it to you. The problem this time is that I've never mindwalked. No one I've ever met has, including the Mothers." I nearly shuddered at the mention of the three Queens of the Onyx Temple.

"Is it so important that I master mindwalking?" I asked, somewhat flippantly. "What does it matter if I slip into Alastair's head once in a while?"

"It *matters*," she said, standing and coming to examine my progress on the flowers, "Because the Lord General likely doesn't want you viewing his memories on a whim. It matters because the Children were not the only witches to use mindwalking, and one day you could come across someone with ill intent. You should know how to protect your mind from other mindwalkers as well as use the skill. And it matters, Your Majesty, because you brought me on to teach you about your powers, and this is one of them. These are not correct." She pointed her finger at my labels. "Start over." With a wave of her hand and a mumbling of a few words, my neat piles of flowers mixed themselves back up.

"This is ridiculous," I groaned. "I've been learning about these plants for a month. Can't we practice spells while we wait to figure out the mindwalking? Beyond the elements, I mean."

"No," she said. "Not until you master this."

"Why?"

"Because you've been learning about these plants for a month and you still apparently can't tell the difference between basketflower and blue thistle. Much of witchcraft requires more than saying words and pointing. Often we need physical items to complete our spells, and we need to be able to identify our needs without stopping to examine a text every step of the way." Her eyes drifted to my stomach, which was still flat but would likely start swelling any day now. "I understand that you have been distracted lately, but we have an objective here."

"Yes, 'don't die' and 'figure out my dreams'." Not sorting flowers.

Lyra stared at me for a moment before finally saying, "Why don't we take a break for a few days? I'll send you with some books to refamiliarize yourself with the herbs you need to know, and we can still consider them to be lessons." Her tone was curt enough that I knew I had angered her.

"Lyra—" I sighed.

"You can come find me when you're ready to take our work seriously."

I fell silent. She was scolding me. I had to admit, she had courage. Not many would be willing to be so harsh with a Queen, let alone the Queen of what was technically an enemy nation. She did not wait for me to speak again, and instead started making a stack of texts for me to take back to my room. She wrote a note with a few titles on it as well.

"The King tells me these titles can be found in the library at castle Ayzelle. If you would be so kind as to retrieve them when you attend your next council meeting, I would be grateful. I am told that only nobility can access the library." Dismissal. She was dismissing me.

I couldn't think of what else to do or say, so I simply said, "Fine. I'll see you later then." I gathered the books and the list of titles before storming out of the room with Catchfly on my heels.

"If it makes you feel better, I was dismissed from lessons constantly as a child," Gerridan said as we walked together around the merchant's square. I had left Lyra's room and stormed to my own, only to find myself pacing instead of studying. I went for a walk and ran into Gerridan, who was returning from dropping a few weapons with his preferred blacksmith for repair and had offered to accompany me to the bustling market on the outside of the Grand Palace gates.

"Exactly, you were a child— not the Queen. It's embarrassing. She threw me out and told me to find her when I was ready to *take things seriously*."

"Well, *were* you taking things seriously?" I glared at him but did not answer, and instead I turned my attention to a vendor who was selling honeycakes. I purchased two that were smeared with blueberry-and-basil jam and served wrapped in butcher paper by a young woman whose hands shook when I dropped the required copper pieces into them. I handed one to Gerridan before taking a large bite of my own, chewing angrily. "Look, you have a lot on your plate. It's easy to see where your lessons might not be getting the attention they deserve, but—" Gerridan dropped his voice as we continued our walk around the square. "—Lyra left her coven to help you."

"The Children—" I started to say around another bite, but Gerridan cut me off.

"The Children will kill her if they ever see her again. Hannele already told me of the horrors they put you through. What they put Lyra through when she was in their good graces. Can you imagine what would happen to her if they ever got their hands on her again?" I swallowed, guilt landing in my stomach along with the cake. "She made a deal with you at great personal risk to herself: a teacher in exchange for a better future between our peoples. If you aren't taking her teaching seriously, how can she expect that you will uphold your end of the bargain? I'm not saying it's been easy for me to accept a witch into the household, but Lyra has held up her end of the deal so far, and by the sound of it, you have not."

I finished the cake and banished the paper, chewing and swallowing before I answered. "If I admit you're right, will you stop making me feel so guilty?"

"I cannot make you feel any way you don't want to. But I'll stop talking if you buy me an ale."

"Deal."

Chapter Sixteen

I followed Lyra's instructions and continued with self-study, doing my best to memorize the herbs and flowers expected of me. Aydan had even provided me with some old books on healing he had stored away from his time in the army, which held great detail about the best ways to combine the plants for the maximum healing potential, as well as beautifully drawn illustrations of the mentioned ingredients. I became a nuisance to our friends as I asked them each to quiz me. Only Alastair and Kenna would oblige me, as Gerridan, Hannele, and Aydan often had to work away from the house. The six of us were hardly ever in the same room during the day unless it was time to head to Ayzelle to meet officially with the council each week.

This week, when it was time to go, I was sure to grab Lyra's list for the library. The meeting had come and gone quickly, with no news from Ayzelle, and nothing for us to report to them. The next visit to Nautia had not been planned yet, and until I was far enough along for Aydan and me to officially break the news about the baby, there was simply nothing beyond the day-to-day and weekly reports to discuss. Afterward, I informed Aydan and our friends that I needed to step into the library and told them I would be a few minutes behind them. Alastair offered to accompany me, and after a swift kiss from Aydan we went our separate ways.

The library was a vast room, nearly as large as the Great Hall, and filled to the brim with books. Floor to ceiling shelves lined the entirety of it, with several ladders on tracks throughout the space to allow one to find the titles stored up high. It all centered around an enormous white marble fireplace with armchairs and tables scattered around so people might use them for reading or study.

The only commoners allowed in here were the librarians—elderly mortals from the nearby villages who kept the library running smoothly. Aside from them, there were only a handful of visitors here today, all courtiers.

"Greetings, Your Majesty," a withered man said, bowing his head. "Is there something I might help you find?"

"Er." I shoved the list into the pocket of my dress. I did not know what the contents of these books were, but if the librarian knew them to be associated with witchcraft at all, it would not bode well for the head of House Redfern to be searching for them. "No, thank you. My general and I are just browsing."

"Should you require any assistance, you need only ask, madam," he said. He bowed his head again and walked away.

I pulled out the list. "We need to find these," I told Alastair before explaining why I didn't show the librarian. He agreed that it would not look good to be seen with the titles requested.

"This one," he said, pointing to the page, "I believe I've seen before. That would be over here—" We got to work searching for the titles, and despite the enormous space and vast number of books, they were quite easy to find. Soon we had Lyra's entire list. "Anything else?" Alastair asked before banishing the stack to my bedroom at home.

"No, I..." my eyes drifted toward the fireplace. Toward the brick wall behind it. I hadn't thought much of Lord Ronan since my last visit with him. Watching him speak to my mother, who was likely bewitched into thinking these things of her own accord, had been gut wrenching. Until now, his promise to prove how real he truly was had not crossed my mind. But standing in the same room as the fireplace, where he said his message would be waiting... "Hold on just a minute."

I walked to the fireplace and knelt beside it, counting four bricks to the left. It was firm, with no hints of cracking, but— there was something about it that piqued my interest.

"What are you doing on the ground?" Alastair asked, approaching from behind.

"I need... I need to do something, but I cannot tell you why and you can never tell anyone what I've done," I said. Alastair's eyes went wide.

"Shaye, are you—"

"Can I swear my best friend to secrecy, or must I invoke the Queen's Guard for that?"

"I—" he started, then sighed. "Fine, I won't say anything."

"Good," I replied. "Now watch my back." I turned to the bricks and placed my hand on the correct one. A humming erupted from under the bricks as something called for me to look further. Channeling my sorcery, a violet glow came off my hands, and in a blink the brick that had once been beneath my palm was gone. I reached my arm into the hole, all the way up to my shoulder.

"Shaye, what the *hell*—" Alastair hissed.

"Got it," I said, feeling a wooden box beneath my fingertips. I snatched it and brought it toward me. It was covered in an inch of dust, though I could feel there were once carvings in the lid. Power thrummed beneath my hands and the memory of another wooden box with a message from witches flashed behind my eyes. I couldn't open this here. Without much more thought I banished the box home, repaired the wall, and turned to leave. Alastair trailed behind me, gaping in confusion.

The next morning a bit of sunlight pouring through a gap in the curtains managed to find the perfect position to wake me.

The night before when we returned home to Sylvanna, I was suddenly overcome with a headache and a dull cramp in my stomach like I had eaten something rotten. Rather than join the others for drinks or reading, I elected to bid everyone else goodnight and go to bed early. Aydan had a cup of ginger tea sent to our room, which I sipped on while I changed. I woke briefly when he came to bed and said that he would be joining his grandparents for breakfast and did I want to come. The stomachache answered on my behalf, and I simply told him I'd rather sleep in.

Now, I covered my head with a pillow to block out the light. My headache had not subsided, and my stomachache appeared to be worse if that were possible. Catchfly was incessantly pawing at the floor beside my bed, trying to get my attention.

I groaned and sat up slowly. Aydan was already gone for the morning. I planned to send Catchfly from the room and then try to go back to sleep if these ailments would allow it. I pulled back the plush top blanket and nearly jolted out of my skin.

Red.

My normally white sheets were covered in huge red stains over the top of my lap. I tore the sheet from me and saw that my nightdress was much the same. Sweat beaded at my forehead, and I waited for my eyes to spring open and wake from another bad dream. I touched my lap— utterly soaked, staining my palms. Help— I needed help.

Shaking, I stood from the bed. Immediately, a rush of blood poured from me, trickling down my legs followed by an unpleasant sound that I realized was a blood clot hitting the floor. My stomach cramped again as if I were being stabbed.

I moved for the door, but with each step the edges of my vision blurred. When I finally reached the door, it took four tries to open it as the blood on my hands made the brass knob slip under my skin. Finally, I stepped into the hallway.

"Hello?" I rasped out as loudly as I could. "Is anyone home?" No one answered and I realized that I wasn't being loud enough. I had lost a lot of blood— who knew how long I had been bleeding before I woke? And now, as I stumbled shakily down the hallway, I could feel more slight gushes of blood leaving my body every few steps and I grew frightened.

It wasn't until I pushed my way into the sitting room that I found Alastair, standing with his back turned to me as he read from a stack of letters in his hands.

"Al—" my voice was nearly a whisper. He turned, a smile hiding on his mouth in response to whatever he'd been reading. That was immediately gone, and his papers fell to the floor when he saw me standing in my blood-soaked nightdress.

"Br—Shaye."

"The baby—" Tears spilled onto my cold cheeks. "Help. Please, help me—" I wobbled on my feet again and hit the ground before Alastair could catch me.

An hour later, Aydan came bursting into our bedroom, demanding to know what was happening.

It had only taken about a minute for the room to be filled with healers. Alastair had bellowed for the servants and sent them effuging for Jemma and her team. They'd flooded the room, immediately going to work examining and assessing me. Pain continued in my abdomen— contractions, Jemma corrected me when I told her. Then, she apologized and explained that she would have to examine me more closely. Alastair turned his back in an attempt to spare my privacy while staying close to my side as Jemma lifted my nightdress and felt around my abdomen to confirm whatever it was she needed to know. Her face was grim, but she did not show much emotion otherwise while she treated me. She gave me a cup filled with a sky-blue liquid and told me to drink it. "For the pain," she explained. I downed it all.

I felt no pain, but plenty of movement while Jemma delivered whatever was left of my baby. I felt my legs being moved to give her and her healing team more room, but I did not look to see what was happening beyond that. Alastair knelt beside the bed and stroked my face, bidding me to focus on him, his voice, rather than what the healers were doing to me. I couldn't even do that, and instead closed my eyes, letting tears spill out from beneath shut lids. By the time anyone had a moment to alert Aydan, Jemma was cleaning me up while the other healers murmured their sympathies and cleared the room of healing supplies. I caught sight of myself in our long mirror on the other end of the room when Aydan came flying through the door. I was white as snow. Gods, I had lost so much blood. My eyes were bloodshot, shining with tears, and the skin around them was red and blotchy.

"What's going on here?" Aydan asked, rushing to my side and reaching for my hand. I did not look at him as he held it. He stroked it with his thumb a few times before standing and looking between Jemma and Alastair, who were the last two remaining in the room with me. Alastair's shirt front was stained with my blood from scooping me off the floor and carrying me back here while yelling for the servants. "Al, what—"

"Your Majesty, I'm very sorry to have to tell you this..." Jemma began. She gave him nearly the same explanation that she gave me. I listened, staring directly ahead. "There was no indication that anything was wrong... based on the size of the remains I'd say it happened a week or so ago and we missed it—" At that, my eyes flicked to the white box that had been set on a table near the fireplace. Jemma had taken what was left of the remains and wrapped them in cloth, before offering to let me say a few words to them if I wanted. I could not— did not— bring myself to do anything else but squeeze my eyes shut and shake my head while Alastair continued stroking my hair. Instead, she had conjured the box and gently placed the poor thing in there before setting it aside. "—Very sorry. Her Majesty has lost a significant amount of blood and fluid. She'll need to remain on bedrest for the time being. I've prescribed a few herbs that I will leave with you." I saw her gesture to a variety of jars on my bedside table, though the only thing among them that my mind would recognize was the small bottle of lavender colored sleep tonic. I shut my eyes again, hoping to somehow tune out the sounds of Aydan and Jemma discussing my health. Alastair remained at my side, his hand now holding mine. He didn't say anything but stared ahead with a faraway look in his eyes.

Eventually, Jemma left. She offered to take the box with her. Aydan turned and lifted the box up, placing his hand gently on the top of it. For a second, I was terrified that he would open it to hold its contents, but instead he handed it to the healer, letting his fingertips linger as she took it from him. Jemma bowed deeply to each of us before shutting the door behind her.

"Thank you, Alastair," Aydan said tightly. "Could you give us a moment?" Alastair nodded. He kissed my head then squeezed my hand one more time before leaving without another word. I couldn't read Aydan's face from where I sat, but his eyes looked shiny. He sat beside me on the bed and I continued staring across the room. He leaned in and kissed my cheek.

"What will she do with them?" I asked quietly.

"There is a pyre near Ehnara's temple, for babies born sleeping. They'll be taken there and put to rest." I nodded, grateful that someone would think to put such a thing in sight of the mother goddess.

"I'm sorry," I choked out softly after a few quiet moments.

"You have nothing to be sorry for," he replied. "I'm just… I'm so thankful that you're all right." He ran his hand over my sweaty hair. "The most important thing for you to do now is rest. I'll take care of everything else."

"What do you mean?" I asked, finally turning to look at him. It wasn't grief or worry that etched his face. It was panic. Fear.

"I'm going to have Gerridan speak with Jemma's team and see what it will cost to keep all of this quiet," Aydan said. "No one needs to know." I blinked a few times. "I'd better go meet with him and get this done." He kissed my temple before standing. When he reached the door, he turned back. "I'll take care of this. It will be like it never happened," he promised, and then left me alone with a ball of anguish in my chest.

Over the next week, our friends each made a point to visit me during the day. Hannele and Gerridan were the first to do so, but upon seeing Hannele's swollen belly tears began to prick behind my eyes and I could no longer hold a conversation. They cut their visit short, and the next time Gerridan stopped by he came alone.

Kenna dropped off a stack of romance novels. "A distraction," she explained kindly. I was grateful, but they were of no use once Lyra came to visit. Since I was bed bound, the witch brought my lessons to me. She used the herbs prescribed to me as a learning opportunity and gave me assignments to research the magical correspondences of each one. She also delivered a book on dreams that she suggested I begin reading. I only had so much energy to sit up and read each day, so the lessons took precedent. When I could no longer focus, Alastair would sit beside me and read aloud from the texts.

Alastair canceled his next visit to Nautia in favor of spending his spare hours with me. He had lied and told Prince Gram he was ill, rather than expose my condition to the Nautians.

At night, Aydan would come home and join me in our bed. The first night, he assured me that Jemma and her team had been sworn to secrecy, and those who needed it properly paid off. "It will be like it never happened," he'd repeated. "No one outside of the Cabinet needs to know." The words cut through me just as much the second time I heard them. Aydan had also made it a point to assure me that we could try again as soon as I was healed. Heirs would come soon, and there was no reason to think that any of this meant there was a problem.

It was equal parts strange and heartbreaking when I realized that nearly everyone around me truly wanted to forget this ever happened. I did not see how I ever could. Even Jemma, when she would come to check on me, had stopped saying 'baby'. It was as if they were a disease I had been cured of rather than a searing, gut-wrenching loss of a potential future.

I was only required to stay in bed for a week, and I was soon out of the house returning to my normal duties while continuing Lyra's lessons on my own. The extended councils had all been told I was ill, even Solandis, to whom I assumed Aydan would tell the truth, sent flowers and a note wishing me a speedy recovery. The daytime distraction of our work was welcome, and slowly I began to fall into a new sense of normal.

My sorcery made quick work of my healing, and only four weeks after the miscarriage, Jemma declared me fully healed and told me and Aydan that we were free to try again if we wanted. I hid my hesitation behind a tight-lipped smile once I saw the eager look on Aydan's face.

That night he poured wine and lit candles and did all the things he used to do for me in an attempt to lead me back into intimacy. I tried to be present, but my mind wandered, wondering if I would fall pregnant again quickly. If the next time would be any different. Would there be a next time? Was that my only chance? I wanted so badly to want this as much as Aydan seemed to, so I made the same noises and faces I did before, which seemed to convince him enough to finish.

The nights that followed were less tender. When it was time for bed we would both go through the motions, pretending like we each didn't have other concerns on our mind: myself, still in mourning for what we had lost, while Aydan held nothing but determination in his stares, in the look on his face when he took me to bed. His only goal now, it seemed, was to produce an heir.

After a month of this, I could not bring myself to pretend any longer, and I denied Aydan for the first time. He did not push further, and simply kissed me goodnight before rolling over to fall asleep. I lay awake for hours before managing to do the same. I continued denying him. Despite his goal to impregnate me, Aydan did not push further for more, or even an explanation. Maybe he was as exhausted with this situation as I was.

After a week straight of denying Aydan's advances, I once again lay awake staring at the ceiling. An hour passed, and Aydan's breathing beside me turned steady and deep as he fell further into sleep. I got up from bed and tied a robe around my waist before summoning an orb of light to hover by my shoulder while I walked up the stairs. When I reached Lyra's door, I knocked softly, not wanting to wake her if she was already sleeping. She opened the door; Flames danced at her fingers to use as a light.

"Shaye," she said, looking me over. "To what do I owe the pleasure?"

"I'm ready," was all I said. She nodded and stepped aside to let me into her quarters."

"Then let us get to work."

Part Two

The Thread

Chapter
Seventeen

I tore through Aydan's wardrobe, digging around in the bottom compartments trying to find his Healer's case. In the weeks since I'd recommitted myself to my lessons with Lyra, I had withdrawn from my public duties as Queen. Aydan and Gerridan fed some lie or another to the council, and I managed to make do with attending every other official council meeting. Today, Lyra had been complaining that she was struggling to find valerian root and that there appeared to be a shortage among the herbalists when I remembered seeing some in Aydan's case. I left the lesson to come find it, thinking I would only be gone a minute or two, but now it had been twenty and I still had not found it but could not bring myself to cut my losses either.

"How many black jackets do you need?" I mumbled to myself as I tossed yet another one to the ground. With a frustrated sigh I waved my hand over the mess I made, and it all organized itself back into the wardrobe. The door snapped shut behind it. I glanced over at my own wardrobe and shrugged to myself. It was the only place I had not looked.

Minutes after I began my last-ditch effort to find the damned case, my fingers grazed something hard and for a split-second excitement filled me— until I pulled out a small, dust-caked wooden box. I recognized it immediately as the box I pulled out of the library wall. I'd nearly forgotten about it, with all that happened the following day. At first I wasn't sure I wanted to know what was inside, but then my fingers grazed the wood and I felt grooves in the lid as if something had been carved there under the filth. I blew at the dust but nothing happened, so I took it to the bathroom sink and dampened the lid just slightly before scrubbing at it with the hem of my dress. I didn't care much if the water ruined the box itself, I just wanted to see a glimpse of whatever message might be waiting for me. I scrubbed at the decades-old grime until I could make out an image that nearly caused me to drop the box on the floor: a fox, wreathed in forget-me-nots.

I rushed back to Lyra's quarters, slipping inside and shutting the door swiftly behind me. Lyra sat leaning in a chair with her boots up on the desk, allowing Petyr to climb up her arm while she spoke to him. "I understand that you're used to roaming to hunt darling but the gardeners fear you and I'll not have you hurt." She looked up upon hearing the door shut. "Ah, have you found the valerian root?"

"No. Can you keep a secret?"

"The Mothers didn't call me 'the keeper' for nothing," she replied with a hint of sarcasm. "Prisoners, secrets, ancient artifacts…"

"Fine, but will you keep *my* secrets?"

"Of course, Your Majesty." Her tone turned serious and she took her feet off the desk. "I'm here to help."

"Do you remember when you interrogated me back at the Onyx Temple?" I asked.

"Yes."

"Do you remember me telling you that I had dreamt of my father?" She nodded, and I proceeded to tell her about all the dreams I'd had of him since then, and what he said to me during each encounter. "He promised to prove to me that he was real by hiding this in the wall beside the fireplace at the library in Ayzelle. I found it the day before I—" I stopped myself from saying the painful words. "Before everything happened and I just sort of forgot about it. But it was *there* and it means he's… he's real, and I've been mindwalking in my sleep to see my father."

"This is mindwalking? You're sure?"

"What else could it be?" I said. "If I'm seeing his memories and I'm linked to his power somehow?" Lyra shrugged.

"When it comes to your abilities, I suppose anything is possible." Her attention turned back to the box in my hands. "So, what's inside?"

"I never opened it," I admitted. "The last time anyone in this house opened a box delivered by a witch it was full of fingers."

"Some of my finer work, if I do say so myself," Lyra chuckled.

"I'll pretend I didn't hear that," I said with a shudder. "I couldn't risk it being seen in the library, and then like I said I forgot about it, so I never looked inside."

"Well, let us find out then," she said, standing up and gesturing for me to set the box on her desk. Petyr remained wrapped around his witch's arm as she began muttering a spell to herself. White light engulfed her hands, ready to strike if whatever was inside could do us harm. She continued reciting her spell as I slowly, carefully pried the box open. Inside was nothing but a tattered, aged piece of folded paper. I snatched it from the box as Lyra stopped speaking and opened it so we both could see the single word written there:

Liar.

For the next two nights I pictured Ronan's face as I fell asleep, but it wasn't until the third that I found myself back in his study. More than half the tables were gone and those that remained were pushed up against the walls, creating a large empty space in the middle. Had Ronan not been standing there I would have thought the room was ransacked. He wore sparring clothes, and his auburn hair hung loose around his shoulders as he struck blows against an imaginary opponent, not unlike the punches and kicks I practiced in the ring with Gerridan. Suddenly, flames burst forward from his fist, but he smothered it in ice. He raised his hand upward and flowers sprung up from the stone floors before being choked with thorns that tore the petals from their stems. Another thrust of an open hand and every surface was covered in frost; what remained of the plants withered and froze, before he dusted his hands off on each other and the ice disappeared completely, leaving the room empty once again.

"How long has it been?" He asked without turning to face me. He conjured a towel from nowhere and wiped the sweat from his face.

"What the fuck is this?" I asked, pulling the note from my pocket. It was an experiment, keeping it there to see if it would arrive with me. I remembered my wedding ring was on my hand during my last visit and wondered what else might stay. I tossed the open note to his feet, with the word *Liar* facing up at him.

"An apt description," he replied. "You are no more a Vesper than I am. How long has it been?"

"A couple months."

"Hm. A bit over a week for me."

"Have you married m— Brina Eastly, yet?" I caught myself almost saying *my mother*.

"Ah, you saw that," he said. His face reddened slightly. "My apologies if you were present for anything er, particularly intimate."

"I was gone quickly after you accepted her...proposal." Ronan's head tilted at the way I said *proposal*, but he replied:

"Good... and no, we are not wed yet. We will have our ceremony at the temple next week."

"You will not even grant her a wedding?" I asked sharply. "Elopement is all you can manage in your plan?" Ronan looked confused.

"What plan?"

"Is it not your intention to enchant Commander Eastly into marriage?" I asked. Ronan looked aghast, and I immediately realized I had spoken too much.

"What the hell are you talking about, young lady? Is that— what is it you think I am?"

"My... friend told me once that he'd never heard of a witch with good intentions. You are a witch by choice sir, and in secret. It does not take much deduction to see that anyone you let in on your secret would be under your control."

"You are an admitted witch yourself, Lady Shaye," Ronan reminded me.

"I was born with these powers. I would not have chosen them of my own free will," I said.

"Yes, you did mention that." Ronan crossed his arms and leaned against one of the remaining tables. "I have not enchanted Brina Eastly into marriage. She is of her own mind, and I am lucky enough to be the man she desires, despite my choices."

"Then why rush the elopement?"

"There is some danger in her association with me. The faster Brina has the protection of my name and titles, the better. I offered to put a more traditional wedding together for her, but *she* insisted on the temple." I stared at the floor, mulling over his explanation, wondering why I felt such a strong urge to believe him.

"So, how did you know I wasn't a Vesper?" I asked finally.

"For one, the last living Lord of House Vesper claims he will never marry or produce children." How could that be? "But more than that, once you mentioned that you thought you might be mindwalking, I realized that you were using the Thread. You hail from House Redfern."

"The Thread?" I repeated.

"Many of the ancient Houses of Medeisia have... gifts, I suppose you could call them. Beyond the standard powers sorcerers are born with. Greenwood, Hazelwren, Redfern, Floinn... The royal House, Aevitarus, has access to raw magic— the pure essence of sorcery. It's why they've held the Crown for so long. That is what is at the core of the Eternity Throne." He paused to tie his hair back from his face. "If you're ever near that blue light, I suggest you steer clear." I fought to keep the corner of my mouth from tugging upward. "The Thread is what we call the power special to the Redferns. It allows us to call upon our ancestors in times of need. I haven't used it in centuries, and I've never been on the receiving end so it did not occur to me at first what you were doing."

"I didn't call upon you. I've been asleep each time we've spoken."

"But you were in need?" He asked. I thought back to my first couple of times meeting Ronan.

"I suppose I was in distress, yes."

"Well there you have it. The Thread found me, likely due to my being the first witch in the Redfern line— how does being a born witch work anyway? I suppose this means I will father children one day—" My heart leapt into my throat. He was about to put together who I was—"Have all my descendants been born with witchcraft in their veins? How many generations have held this secret?"

I nearly sighed in relief. "I don't know. I was never told about any of it. My parents are dead. I was raised by a mortal uncle who did not inform me of my heritage— I only learned of my sorcery after I reached adulthood."

Ronan threw me a strange look. "How? Your power did not appear to you earlier?" I shook my head. "Strange. I have not known a Redfern to make it to fifteen without their sorcery emerging." I shrugged.

"Perhaps the witchcraft slows down sorcery? I have no one I could ask. Redfern has... dwindled. We are no longer a great house of Medeisia." It was close enough to the truth that I wouldn't have to remember a complicated story if asked again later. I didn't actually know how many Redferns were left. I imagined most must have moved abroad to avoid Zathryan's wrath or changed their names to avoid the notoriety of their House. Ronan chuckled.

"There must be many generations between us then, Lady Shaye. I have enough cousins that the Redfern name will last well beyond me." I gave him a tight-lipped, humorless smile.

"So, no mindwalking then?" I asked.

"If you mean did you inherit mindwalking, then I don't see how you could have. I've never done it and do not intend to. Nasty, difficult spell work— there's a reason the Children don't do it anymore."

"The witch I met said that there had not been a witch worthy of the knowledge in quite some time. That their goddess Otana must approve of them."

"That witch is right," he said. "The Children I met believe they have fallen out of grace with their goddess, and they do not seem to mind. Their focus now is on Lord Thiirmot— I'm shocked you were able to find a witch in your time who even mentioned the goddess. The number of her worshippers now are dwindling." Curious.

"Is this the last time I'll see you?"

"That is entirely up to you," Ronan said. "The Thread is controlled by the descendant. If you find yourself in need, it seems your mind will seek me out."

"This was the first time I've ever done it on purpose. Could you tell me how I might do so again?" The words came out of my mouth before I fully realized what I was asking: To see Ronan again. On purpose. Guilt balled up in my gut.

"Drink a cup of cronewort tea before bed, and as you're falling asleep, picture who it is you're looking for and what you need from them." I nodded.

"Thank you, Lord Ronan. I'm sorry I lied to you."

"Do not worry yourself, young lady." Ronan waved me off. "Though if you're going to be hiding your craft as you are, I suggest you become better at it."

Eighteen

The next morning I stared at the ceiling while Aydan dressed. Most days I was still sleeping when he departed but after I left Ronan, I found myself mulling over everything that I'd learned. Most of it at least made sense. The Thread explained why Lyra couldn't understand my 'mindwalking' before— I wasn't doing it at all. Ronan's reaction to my accusation of bewitching my mother felt... genuine. Though, what did that say of Brina, if she could know what he was and still choose him? I doubted I would ever find out. Still, there was one bit of knowledge I'd gained from this most recent encounter with Ronan that puzzled me.

Aydan sat on the foot of the bed, lacing up his boots with his back to me. "Can I ask you a question?" I said suddenly. He startled. Silence had become part of our routine in the weeks since I recommitted myself to my lessons with Lyra, and I doubted he had even noticed I was awake.

"Of course."

"What happened to Kenna's father?" I asked. Aydan stopped what he was doing and sighed as he turned to look at me. "I know he was found dead in his home, and I know what was said about you afterward, despite there being no evidence—"

"It is not my story to tell, my love."

"That's what Gerridan said at your coronation."

"Good," said Aydan, returning to his laces. "It is not our story nor our place to speak about that man."

"But if there was some sort of accusation against you—"

"Shaye." Aydan's voice was firm. If he had it his way, this conversation would be over.

Carefully, I asked, "Kenna is older than you, isn't she?"

"... yes." His voice was tentative. Quickly, I scrambled for a lie that would explain my knowledge of her House.

"I was... reading. An edition of *Houses of Medeisia* that was published around when I was born. And it lists a Lord Vesper there as the last of his line. Why would it not list Kenna?"

Aydan sighed again. "I'm sorry. I cannot tell you those stories." Without another word he tied off his boots and walked out the bedroom door.

Later, I leaned against Lyra's desk and recounted my visit to Ronan. Her face remained quite neutral, considering what I said.

"I wonder," she said after I had finished telling her everything. "If this Thread is what is connecting you to Lord Ronan, and you have not inherited any form of mindwalking from him, what is it you were doing when you saw the general's memories?"

"Hell if I know," I said with a shrug.

"Could you ask Lord Ronan about it?"

I *had* asked for instruction on how to find him again if I needed to. "You're suggesting I seek him out on purpose to ask questions?"

"Was that not what you did last night?"

"It was, but—"

"But you were angry that he called you a liar after you had indeed lied to him, so that makes it okay." Lyra's fingers drummed on her desk. I chewed the inside of my cheek.

"You don't have to be right *all* the time, you know." Lyra smiled. "I don't know if it's a good idea to seek him out in my dreams— or, while I'm asleep. I suppose I'm not dreaming when I'm with him, am I?"

"How have your dreams been, by the way?" Lyra asked. "Have you been using your journal?"

I stared sheepishly at the floor. "I haven't stopped the new doses of the sleep tonic," I admitted. "I've tried, but the nights without it are... quite difficult." To my surprise, Lyra placed her hand on top of mine.

"I understand," she said. "Take the time you need. We have plenty else to worry about." I was about to thank her when a knock sounded on the door. Lyra and I looked at one another as if to ask if the other was expecting someone. I shrugged. She called out for the person on the other side to enter.

Kenna quickly slipped into the room and shut the door behind her. Her attention darted between Lyra and me, and she looked quite upset.

"Kenna?"

"I'm sorry to interrupt," she started, now staring at her feet. "But I needed to speak to you, Shaye. I suppose you might as well hear this too, Miss Lyra." That might have been the first time I heard Kenna say Lyra's name. "Aydan told me that you were asking questions about my father. About his death. Aydan and the others would never say anything without my permission, and I'm quite grateful for that, but I suppose it's time you knew. And it would be best if you heard it from me." She looked up at me. "I'm sorry I never told you this before, but if I'm being honest it was nice to have someone around who didn't know about my past."

"Kenna, you don't have to—"

"I know I don't. But you should still know. This is… difficult to speak of, so please just let me spit it out." She took a deep breath and crossed her arms over her chest. "I don't remember my childhood," she began. "That is to say, I don't remember specific details. I remember feeling scared sometimes. I remember feeling my mother's fear when she held me. I also remember feeling her love. I don't remember what she looked like, only that she was mortal. We never stayed in one place for too long— we were constantly moving around, constantly hiding. I never knew or understood why, until I was fourteen, and my father found us. She ran from him when she found out that she was pregnant with me and spent fourteen years in hiding. But once he found me there was no way to keep me from him. The day I met my father was the last day I ever saw my mother. I don't know what happened to her." My throat bobbed. "My father fed and clothed me well. He hired a private tutor to live with us and manage my studies. I became well versed in literature, mathematics, music, and languages. But I was never allowed to leave. I was never allowed to open the curtains. No one that he did not deem acceptable could know I was there. We had limited staff, and I certainly never saw any children my own age. I'd only been with him for two years when my powers emerged, and it became obvious quickly that I was a seer. My father was delighted. And that was when my real hell began."

Kenna paused and took a deep breath before explaining, "Seeing is more than getting snippets of future events or sensing certain types of magic. It also involves prophecy— specific predictions linked to a particular person or family. It's more accurate than the little cryptic messages I recite to people. Prophecy is something that comes naturally to seers, but it is still a skill that requires practice, and it is not an enjoyable thing. It can cause illness, weakness, paranoia… among other things. When I would grow too fatigued to continue practicing, my father would—" She cut herself off, wincing a bit. "He was not a gentle man. He did anything he could to motivate me. For a decade, I honed my skills, and learned to be a reliable seer and prophet. And it was then that my father could begin to make me earn my keep.

"He formed club of sorts. Of mortals from abroad who would pay my father for my services as a seer. I was highly sought after— prophecies are usually reserved for nobility. Most Medeisian Kings employ a seer on their council at some point or another.

"I didn't mind it much at first. It was exciting to see new people for the brief moments I was aware of them." Confusion painted my face. Kenna noticed, and explained, "Prophecy puts you into a sort of trance. I never remembered what I said when I told these men of their fates. We would meet and I would take their hands, and then I would wake up to them smiling and thanking me for their good news. Until the first time it went bad.

"A man came to see me for a prophecy, and when I woke he was seething. He struck me. I cried out for my father, and he simply looked at the man and said, 'This will cost you'." She took another deep breath. "I thought my father was threatening the man, but then he threw a coin purse at my father, and once my father counted its contents, he left the room and the man continued taking his rage out on me." Lyra shifted in her seat, and I felt anger rising from her. "I healed quickly, but after that, my father saw the value in allowing his customers to take their frustrations out on me, should they be unhappy with the message they received. After all, he saw no problem in beating me himself, so why should he mind if they did it too if it made him extra money? It went on for years. Maybe even decades, I'm not altogether sure. I had no concept of time, as I was kept hidden away. He never reported my birth, and so no one save for my mother and the people my father allowed into his estate knew that I existed. I don't even know if his friends knew that I was his daughter.

"I started to see a new customer. The son of a mortal man who had been visiting me from Sewyth for years. Kaid." A sad ghost of a smile danced on Kenna's face when she said his name. "He was handsome, and polite. Much younger than most of my customers. When he saw bruises on my wrists and neck, and my too-thin frame, he seemed horrified by my condition. He started traveling to see me sometimes twice per month, spending ridiculous amounts of gold just to be in the same room as me, probably to be sure I was still breathing. I was grateful for his company, and I became rather infatuated with him.

"One day Kaid came to see me, and when he arrived, he complimented my dress. My father was watching and saw when I blushed while greeting Kaid. He was livid." Kenna paused, running her hands up and down her arms, which were still crossed over her body, hugging herself while she stared at the floor. "He stormed right into the room where I was meant to be telling prophecy and screamed in my face that he was not running a brothel, and that I should not be behaving like a whore. Kaid tried to step between us and defend me, but he was knocked to the ground. My father asked if he thought he could pay for my body as well as my sight and Kaid told him 'Of course not', but my father called him a liar. I was made to strip naked before my father beat me senseless in front of the only… well, the closest thing to a friend that I'd ever had. Kaid was then beaten himself and informed that he and his father were banned from my services for the rest of time. I never saw him again."

Kenna's eyes shone and she continued. "I could barely stand after the punishment my father gave me that time. He would not allow the servants to bring me clothes. He came to check on my healing progress every other day or so, and made me stand naked, facing him in the center of the room with my hands at my sides. He would just…stare. Stand in the doorway and stare so hatefully at me, at my body, before he would turn an angry shade of red, slam the door, and retreat to his bedroom." My fingers were smoking. I was going to be sick. "Once I was well enough to walk around, I was allowed a nightdress to wear outside of my bedroom. I was not allowed to wear my real clothing until I was well enough to read prophecy again. One night, I was out of my room, taking a walk when I passed the library and saw a wide, open ground floor window.

"I didn't know where I was or how far I was from the next person and how many of those people would be willing to return me for a reward, but I ran for it. It was snowing, and I had no shoes with nothing but a nightdress on, but I ran anyway. I ran until I found myself on the grounds of the Grand Palace. I ran right up to the front doors and began pounding on them until the guards answered. I think I might have terrified them. I had no idea how badly I had been hurt, how awful I looked. Thinking back, I'm sure it appeared like I should be dead. Solandis and Priamos were in the Faelands, so the guards called for Aydan who came immediately." Kenna finally sat on one of the nearby cushioned chairs. "I didn't know who he was. I just thought he was a healer. When he tried to understand what had happened to me I became so hysterical that he called in Gerridan to help calm me down, and Hannele to sit with me while Aydan looked at my injuries. He thought I would feel safer with a woman present. I remember— I remember him saying quietly to Gerridan that he had not seen anything like my injuries since his time in the army. That first night they cleaned me up, got me some warm clothes, and brought me back to this house.

"It took days for me to come out of my room. He asked what had happened to me, but I couldn't tell him. And at that point I didn't even know if the things my father had done to me were wrong, I just knew I didn't want to go back to him. I had not told Aydan my father's name. He assured me that I was welcome in his home for as long as I wanted to stay, and that I would be safe from anyone who might come looking. He even went so far as to glamour me so that I could come and go as I pleased and not fear being seen while I was outside. Gods, to be allowed outside in the daylight was so strange," she added. "I was here for half a year, known only by my first name, and kept in glamours. In that time, Gerridan and Alastair taught me to fight. Aydan gave me books. Hannele showed me art and took me riding. My body got stronger and my mind became clear. I was given freedom, and friendship, and a life outside of my father's estate. But I knew he was close by, and as much as I wanted to disappear into my new face, my new life... knowing he was out there hung over me like a cloud.

"An eclipse festival was coming. The first in a while, and the first I would ever attend. My father had never spoken of such a thing,

143

so despite living in Sylvanna for close to two hundred years I had never heard of the eclipse festival. Aydan bought dresses for Hannele and me." The corner of Kenna's mouth ticked upward. "By then I knew he was a prince, of course, and I felt quite special to be part of his household— even glamoured, even hiding. They took me to the festival and for the first time I danced, and drank, and laughed not just with them, but total strangers— even flirted with a few of them. I met so many people and suddenly the world seemed so much bigger than I could have imagined, even having never left Sylvanna.

"A few weeks after the festival everyone came back to the house after a council meeting with Solandis and they were talking about a guest who had arrived unexpectedly to the council room, and how irritated they were by him. When I inquired who it was they were talking about, Hannele rolled her eyes and told me it was lesser lord who lived a few miles away. He only came around every few years and was awful the entire time. Lord Vesper." My hand rested at my throat and had covered itself in frost. I glanced at Lyra, who was ashen. Her full attention remained on Kenna. "I... I lost it. I completely lost my composure. I shook and sobbed uncontrollably until Gerridan could get ahold of me and calm me down. Once he did, we gathered around the dining table, and I told them everything I've told you today. When I finished my story, I broke down again, begging them not to turn me over to him. I offered myself as a servant, a slave, anything that would keep them from claiming whatever reward he would offer if they returned me to my father's estate.

"Of course they were all horrified, both from my story and that I thought they would even consider turning me over." She looked up at me. "Aydan was beside himself. He asked my permission to take this information to Solandis, but I was too scared that she would feel some obligation, or there would be some unknown law that would require her to return me to my father. I said no. I just wanted to stay glamoured and hide forever.

"A week or so passed and one evening I went to the sitting room to find Gerridan, Aydan, and Alastair all in sparring leather. Hannele was pacing around, looking nervous while they strapped weapons to themselves and checked each other's buckles. When I asked what was going on, none of them would say anything. Alastair tried to make up an excuse about sparring." Kenna scoffed a little. "Anyway, Aydan just told me not to worry, and that everything was going to be fine. Gerridan hugged me, and then they all effuged out of the house.

"Of course I immediately demanded that Hannele tell me what was going on. She tried to change the subject but she's about as good of a liar as Alastair. It took a bit of interrogating but eventually she told me that they were planning on intimidating my father into fleeing his estate— either through blackmail or physical threats. She said they had sworn to her that they would not truly hurt him unless they were in danger, but I knew right away that they would never convince my father to leave. I didn't care if they injured my father but I was terrified at the thought of one of my friends getting hurt because of me if it turned into a fight, and I knew that I had to go after them." The frost had crept upward, engulfing my arms completely, and the rest of my body shook. Lyra continued to look horrified. "Hannele got me to the front gate and then I made her leave.

"It took a while to get myself inside because I was so afraid of getting caught. I didn't know if he kept much of the staff without me there, but I had to be careful. I had no idea where the boys were but my best guess was that they would attempt to ambush my father in his bedroom. I started there but when I was nearly to the door, I heard a commotion coming from the other end of the house.

"I snuck into the parlor and found Gerridan pinning my father to the ground with his knee in his back." Kenna chewed on her lip. "I'll never forget the sight of it. Alastair and Gerridan got him up on his knees and stepped away so Aydan could start interrogating him. Asking questions about the seer he kept captive in his home. My father laughed and spat at Aydan." Kenna's arms uncrossed and she began fiddling with the fabric of her skirt. Her gaze dropped again. "Seeing that, seeing him laugh and spit at my friends— at these wonderful people who took me in and made me one of them... I stepped out from my hiding spot and my father glared at me, until I asked Aydan to remove my glamours." My heart pounded. "When he saw my face, my father's eyes went wide and then he started to laugh at me. He didn't waste any time calling me a whore. Asked if the boys took turns with me or if they shared me all at once." Kenna ran her tongue across her teeth. "I don't remember grabbing the dagger. But suddenly there was one in my hand and I was in front of my father. Before the boys could move my father lunged at me and I drove the blade into his chest." Lyra might have stopped breathing. "I took it out and I stabbed him again. He fell back and I tackled him, continuing to stab him over and *over*—" She stopped herself and ran a hand over her face. "The boys might have said my name a few times before I realized they were still right next to me. I raised the dagger again but Aydan caught my wrist and took it away. I froze, looking at my father's body as I sat on top of it, and I just— I burst into tears. Alastair picked me up and took me away from the body while Aydan checked for a heartbeat. I cried even harder when I heard him tell Gerridan that my father was in fact dead. Not from any feeling of loss— but it is a heavy thing to take a life.

"Gerridan held me for a long while as I sobbed. I soaked the front of him in blood and tears but he just let me keep going. I asked him later why he didn't use his power on me and he said that he could tell I needed to feel every bit of that night. Whatever that means.

"The boys got me home and had Hannele help me bathe and dress for bed. I was sure in the morning I would be arrested. But instead, I was brought before Solandis and Priamos to tell my story. Just the two of them, me, and Aydan. He bid me to tell them as much as I could handle. After I was finished Solandis charged me with manslaughter and then immediately pardoned me of the crime on the grounds of self-defense. It is recorded only in her personal diary, so that if an official complaint were ever made it could be proven to be a settled matter. She made me a Lady of Sylvanna and ordered the Vesper estate to be burned to the ground.

"I was introduced to the Sylvannian court as myself: Lady Kenna Vesper. Anyone who asked was told that I had been raised elsewhere and came to claim my inheritance following my father's death. There were a few who whispered about the strange circumstances, but other than a few rumors about Aydan getting back to Ayzelle, nothing ever came of it. The boys have promised to never say a word, and I prefer to forget that it ever happened."

There was a long silence as we all took in the story, and the change in the air after hearing it. "I'm sorry that happened to you, Ken," I said quietly. "And that I nosed my way into your business. But thank you for telling me."

"You needed to know," she said plainly. "That part of my life was fucked up. It's over and behind me, but it's still part of me. I control my life now. I own my body now. I decide what happens to me. Our family is the greatest gift I could ever hope for." She smoothed out her skirts and stood up. "I've taken up enough of your time. I'm going to let you get back to your lesson." She turned to leave, but Lyra stood and crossed the room to close the space between them. She took Kenna's hand.

"Lady Kenna," she choked out. "I am so sorry. For the way I spoke to you the night before the wedding. I teased you for having a charmed life, but I didn't—"

"There's no way you could have known," Kenna said softly. She glanced down at her hand being held by Lyra. "It's all right."

"It's not."

"I haven't exactly been forthcoming," Kenna replied.

"If I could have gotten away with it, I would have done the same to Deimos," Lyra admitted.

"Sounds like your husband and my father were cut from the same cloth." Kenna looked up at Lyra's face. "I should really be going now." Lyra let go.

"Of course. We should get back to it."

"I'll talk to you later, Shaye." Kenna nodded at my teacher. "Miss Lyra."

"Goodbye, Lady Kenna." The seer shut the door behind her, and Lyra stared blankly at the wood for a moment before turning back to me. "Cronewort tea, was it?"

It took a day to get ahold of cronewort, but the next afternoon I was drinking a cup and then lying down on the floor in Lyra's quarters. She made a nest out of several pillows and blankets, trying to promote a relaxing environment.

"I can't sleep if you're staring at me," I told her, keeping my eyes closed.

"You also won't be able to sleep if you keep talking."

"Maybe it has to be nighttime."

"Maybe you have to be *quiet*—"

I pushed up onto my elbows and glared at her. "You know, there are some who would call the way you're speaking to me treasonous."

"Lucky for my pretty neck you don't agree with them, Your Majesty," Lyra replied. "Now lie down, picture your father's face, and *hush*." I did as I was told, grumbling a few choice words a moment before falling silent and focusing on my breath:

In, two, three, *out,* two, three, four... *In,* two, three, *out,* two, three, four... *In,* two, three, *out,* two, three, four—

I stood in the darkness outside of Ronan's study. Gods, it had worked.

I stepped into the room and realized after a second that Ronan was not there. Strange, to think of him anywhere else but here. I glanced around the room, walking the perimeter slowly and examining the shelves of books, herbs, trinkets, and candles. With all the talk of Ronan's dark purpose I would have expected there to be more sinister items placed around the room. Instead, I almost felt the need to double check I wasn't in an elderly mortal healer's cottage. The only things making it clear to whom this room belonged, were the sword hanging above the door, and a peculiar jar. It was filled with what looked like... clouds. Looked like them because they *were* clouds. This was the storm I had watched him conjure in my very first visit, before I even realized who I was seeing.

"That's a fun little trinket," Ronan said from behind me. I jumped, then turned to face him. His face had more color to it than I was used to seeing. He looked well rested. "I trapped the weather in the jar, and now the clouds tell me if trouble is near." The clouds in the jar were bright white and puffy, like the spun sugar treats I often saw children buying in the merchant square.

"And is there trouble now?" I asked, turning to face him.

"No." He grinned. "No trouble today, Lady Shaye."

"You... you look well," I commented.

"I— thank you. We've just returned from one of my country estates."

"We?"

"My wife and I." Another smile. It was so genuine, so... Gods, he cared for her. Something in his face— it wasn't an act. There would be no purpose in lying to me about it.

"Congratulations," I said. "So it has been a week or more since you've seen me, correct?"

"More." He nodded. "Almost two. And you?"

"I was here the day before yesterday."

"Interesting— and you have need of me so quickly?" His tone was nearly teasing.

"I— well, my teacher. The witch I met when visiting the Children. She had a question for you, regarding the Thread."

"Oh?"

"Yes." I cleared my throat. "We wondered if there were other ways to make connections with the Thread that you did not explain before. You see, we first thought that I had mindwalked when I accidentally saw a memory in my friend's own mind."

"What exactly do you mean, you 'saw a memory'?" Ronan crossed his arms and leaned back against one of his tables. Pure curiosity danced in his eyes.

"Well, my friend has the ability to share images in their mind with others—"

"Ah, you know a Greenwood then," he interjected. "If it's Vera, well, bless your patience." He laughed and gestured for me to continue.

"But when they tried to show me the image, I experienced the entire event from their eyes. Like *I* was my friend."

"Did you have control over what they did?"

"No," I said. "I had no control over what they did or said, I only experienced the event as they did."

"Then you were not mindwalking," Ronan said plainly. "Mindwalking entails having control over the person you're walking with. What was it your friend was showing you that first time?"

"Family. Someone I lost." Not a lie, technically. I wasn't sure why I cared whether I was lying to him, but I hoped he couldn't tell.

"I hope it was a good memory to experience, then." There was an awkward pause and then he said, "To answer your question, that is not something I have ever heard of happening with the Thread. However, it could simply be the convergence of the two gifts."

"What do you mean?"

"I mean your Greenwood friend can push forward an image from their mind as they saw it, and the Thread allows you to contact your ancestors. Perhaps it is some melding of the two that you experienced. It certainly sounds unique— I doubt you would be able to do such a thing with anyone but a Greenwood." The corner of my mouth quirked upward at that. I liked the idea of something special for just me and Alastair. Not that I could ever tell him how I'd learned such a thing... Oh. Oh gods. How was I going to explain this? How was I going to explain to Alastair and Aydan, and the rest of my family that I had not been mindwalking, but using plain sorcery all this time? And how would I explain how I even *know* this? "Lady Shaye?" My breath became ragged. My vision blurred, and I half expected to reappear in Lyra's quarters but instead I heard Ronan snap, "Lady Shaye, get ahold of yourself!"

I blinked and looked up at him. Then I realized why he had spoken so harshly. My arms had encased themselves completely in ice, all the way up to my shoulders and threatened to climb up my neck. Once I became aware of it, the ice immediately felt heavy enough to topple me over, which it nearly did, before Ronan murmured something, made a pushing motion with both of his hands and the ice turned to water, freeing my arms but leaving the sleeves of my dress soaked. I shook the excess water off my arms and let it drip into the puddle I now stood in. Before Ronan spoke again he pointed his finger, and a blast of warm air dried me. "Are you all right?" He asked.

"I'm fine— just a bit panicked, is all." He looked at me expectantly, so I explained, "It was concerning when I first learned of mindwalking, and now it does not appear to be much of an issue for me. But my friends— they were so sure that I am a mindwalker. They think my teacher can help me learn to use it—"

"Your friends know of your powers…I suppose they'll be disappointed they can't use it to their advantage?" Ronan asked darkly.

"No— gods, no." I shook my head. "They're terrified for me. If they had it their way, I wouldn't have access to witchcraft at all." Ronan made a face like he might not believe me, but I ignored it. Instead I changed the subject, plucking at my sleeve. "How did you do this?"

"You'll have to be more specific. Clearly you have access to elemental magic, so you should know what I did."

"I do. But I'm afraid it's proving difficult to control. As I've told you before, there is no other sorcerer I know who has these powers, and much of what my teacher tries to show me is unsuccessful. I speak the words and nothing happens."

"Interesting," he said.

"You say that a lot," I commented.

"I find you quite interesting, Lady Shaye." He pondered a minute. "What has your teacher shown you?"

"She's attempted to address the elements a few times, to no avail. That is the most urgent matter. Mindwalking has gone nowhere— now we know why. Mostly she has me keep track of my dreams, and I've learned much about the ties between the craft and healing," I told him.

"Why are the elements so urgent? And why dream tracking?"

"The elements are what sent me on my search for a teacher to begin with," I explained. "They tend to burst out uncontrollably, and when they do it's a heavy drain on me. I've wound up unconscious for days at a time." He looked alarmed at that. I didn't bother telling him that the first time I saw him was during such an event. "And I am plagued by nightmares. I have been since I first came to Medeisia. I took a tonic for a while, but my teacher thinks they're worth examining. I've been on it again for the time being, but when I'm ready I'll start tracking my dreams again."

"Again— interesting." Ronan smirked once more. "It does seem rather dire for you to learn then. I suggest you tell your teacher that the answer may not lie solely within whatever books she's likely tearing through. It will likely require an open mind and a strong imagination."

Then, before I could stop myself—before I even realized what exactly I was saying— I blurted, "Could you teach me?"

He stared at me for a moment. "You have a teacher."

"I know," I said. "But she does not know what it is to blend sorcery and witchcraft." What was I doing?

"I do not know how the magic of a born witch functions."

"Perhaps not, but you're the first sorcerer to use and master the craft." He clenched his jaw at that. "You would have a better chance than anyone of helping me figure out how to tame this."

"Is that all that you want— to tame it? Keep it under lock and key and never let it out?" He asked, taking a step forward. "Or do you want to control your power? Wield it, and give it a purpose?"

"I want—" I took a deep breath, and let my eyes shut for just a moment. What was I *saying*? "—I want it to have a purpose. If it's here, and I must have it either way… I suppose giving it that would be a worthwhile task." Ronan rubbed at his face. He looked like he was regretting ever speaking to me in the first place. A long silence followed while he stared at me.

"Fine." Anxiety filled my chest. "I will do what I can to help you, Lady Shaye."

"It is… kind of you, Lord Ronan, to take on such a task."

He waved me off. "I've taught before. Admittedly, not this subject matter. But once we find a way for you to do spell work it should not be an all too difficult thing to accomplish." I remembered then that it was Ronan who oversaw Aydan's training as a child. "Return home, and tomorrow use the Thread to come back. Hopefully it will only be a day or two difference here. Tell your witch I will require her help in supplementing your lessons."

"I will," I said. "Thank you again. I will see you soon."

"Goodbye, Lady Shaye."

"Just so we're clear," Lyra said, pinching the bridge of her nose. "I sent you to ask a question of Lord Ronan, and now you've recruited him as an additional teacher?"

"That sums it up fairly well, yes," I said as I methodically peeled the skin off a fat green grape.

"Well isn't that simply fantastic." Lyra sighed. "You're going to get me killed."

"No one is going to kill you." I rolled my eyes.

"The King would have me executed on the spot if he knew I was overseeing these visits with your father."

"He would not," I said. I threw a grape at her. "Aydan likes you well enough."

"There is not a single member of your Cabinet, Your Majesty, who would give a fraction of thought to dumping me back at the Five Peak Summit the second you gave word to do so."

"That's not true," I argued. "Kenna would give at least a *fraction* of a thought." Lyra smirked, and I could have sworn a rosy hue stained her brown cheeks.

"Perhaps a fraction," Lyra agreed. Then, remembering herself, she cleared her throat and said, "Now, we need to come up with a plan for you to transfer information between Ronan and I…"

I listened while she plotted and planned. And although guilt still swam in my belly, for some reason I could not explain, excitement grew there too.

Chapter Twenty

The next day, I woke just before sunrise. The spot next to me was empty and cold. Aydan must have left a while ago. Rather than try to go back to sleep, I stood from the bed and found a dress in my wardrobe. I threw it on and ran a brush through my hair before leaving the house and taking off into the crisp morning air.

I wasn't sure why I was so intent on seeking Aydan out. I had been fine with our recent silence in the mornings and evenings, and during the day we both had so much on our plates that we would not have had time to spend together even if we wanted it. I never would have thought that I would be grateful, or in any way fine with having so much distance from my husband. But then again, I never thought I would grieve so deeply for something I never even saw or held. And I never thought that he would not seem to grieve at all.

The clanging sound of metal-on-metal rang in my ears well before I reached the sparring ring. I continued my approach, and soon saw that Gerridan was in there with him. Both men had removed their shirts and sweat glistened on their skin in the gray-pink glow of the morning light, despite the cool temperature. Gerridan swung, but Aydan blocked the blow. He swung his own blade in a circle, forcing Gerridan's to make the same motion before the blade flew from his hands. Aydan yelled as his foot rose and he kicked Gerridan square in the chest, knocking him off his feet— and certainly, I thought, knocking the breath from his lungs.

Before Gerridan could collect himself, Aydan tossed the sword aside and tackled his friend, pinning him completely to the ground before punching him in the jaw. He got in a few more blows before Gerridan wrapped his legs around Aydan's waist and twisted the both of them around, flipping so Gerridan was now pinning Aydan down. Gerridan only got in two strikes before Aydan snatched his wrist, stopping the third blow. He'd bested him again, but instead of taking over and continuing their fight, Gerridan rolled off and they both collapsed on the floor of the sparring ring almost as soon as I arrived at the gate.

I stood there timidly, not sure if I should enter. They appeared to be finished with their fight but Gerridan and Aydan had been known to keep going until forced to stop by Alastair, who did not appreciate their competitive nature.

Aydan stood up a few seconds later, then turned to offer Gerridan his hand. He took it and allowed Aydan to pull him up. They each clapped the other on their shoulder and grinned stupidly at each other as if they were teenage boys who'd just been boxing rather than the two most powerful men in Medeisia. The sun was rising higher now and Aydan's brown skin shone in the golden morning light, accenting his tattoos and his muscled body, which had grown more defined since I last paid it any attention. Clearly he'd been sparring more often than usual. Gods, he was beautiful. Gods, I missed him.

At the other end of the ring, Gerridan took a drink of water then handed the canteen to Aydan, who swigged as well. As Aydan drank, Gerridan spotted me. I watched as he said something to Aydan and then jerked his chin in my direction. Aydan turned and saw me as well. He knit his brow and wiped his mouth with his bare arm as he started toward me. I opened the gate and entered the ring.

"Shaye," he said when he was close enough for me to hear. "Is everything all right?"

"I— yes, everything's fine. Just wanted to see you."

"Oh?"

"Yes. I don't want to interrupt though. I can head home—"

"You're not interrupting," he blurted. "We've finished for the day. Even if we hadn't, you're always welcome. To watch, to join us."

"Thank you," I said shyly. His arm in the sunlight caught my eye. "Did you get a new tattoo?"

"Oh— sort of," he brought his arm forward so that I could see. "I was with Priamos last week and some of the Sylvannian commanders were getting theirs updated to match their rank. I was offered some updates now that I am King. I didn't see the harm."

The formerly black filigree was now accented in gold ink, creating depths and dimensions that had not existed previously.

"It's beautiful," I said. "I— I'm sorry I didn't notice."

"It's okay," Aydan replied. He reached forward carefully. A single curl had been sitting in front of my shoulder, and he lifted it with a knuckle, letting it loop around his finger. "We've been busy. Too busy." Guilt pooled in my gut. If he knew what I was doing with my days— what I would be doing again as soon as I returned to Lyra's quarters today, he would be equally livid and devastated.

"We have," I nearly whispered. I felt tears pricking behind my eyes. "I miss you." His hand moved from the curl to cup my cheek.

"I miss you too, my love." He pressed a kiss to my forehead and I let my arms loop around him. He wrapped me in his own arms and held me against his chest. He asked, "Do you want to go home? We have time before we need to get ready. We could spend some of it alone without Gerridan pretending like he's not watching us." I huffed a laugh.

"That sounds nice," I said. "I'm ready for the day but I can help you prepare for whatever meetings you have today." Aydan pulled back a little to look down at me.

"You're joking, right?" He asked. I just stared at him. "Shaye— we're due to meet with Prince Gram by noon."

"What? No— no, we're not supposed to meet again until..." I wracked my brain, trying to remember a date. Alastair had told us, at one of the handful of Cabinet meetings I'd attended since starting in on my lessons, that he and the Prince Regent figured out a date. It was— oh. "Oh my gods, that is today, isn't it?"

"How could you have forgotten?" Aydan asked. "Shaye, have you even read through the notes Alastair has been keeping for you? This is all we've discussed with the Cabinet for weeks now."

"I know," I groaned, feeling like an idiot. "Aydan, I'm so sorry— I'll stay behind. I'm clearly unprepared."

"No, it would look worse if you didn't show up. Alastair already canceled one of his visits. If you don't show up this time it will look like something's wrong." He took a deep breath. "Let's just... let's just go home. We'll relax a bit before it's time to leave— I'm sure everything will be fine. Gerridan will be handling most of the negotiation anyway."

"If I have the time, I should go over at least some of the notes. Besides, I need to let Lyra know I'll be gone so we can rework my lessons. I'll have to meet with her when we return." He looked like he was going to object to my plan but instead Aydan nodded.

"I'll meet you there in a bit," he said. "I might go one more round with Gerridan."

"I'll see you in a little while then." Aydan kissed my forehead once more, and I effuged back to the house.

We arrived outside the gates of the Grand Palace of Nautia as we had done before. Elise dressed us all in black again, and just like last time, Kenna remained behind with Hannele. The only difference in our current visit, it seemed, was tone. According to Alastair's notes, we were going into this meeting prepared to start some real negotiations. Today we would be flat-out requesting the return of the Eternity Throne.

Gram, pleasant as ever, greeted us once we were inside the gates.

"Your Majesties, my lords," he said with a dip of his head— as much reverence as he was willing to show monarchs of another nation. "I am glad to see you're all well."

"Thank you, Your Highness," Aydan replied. "We're all thrilled to be here."

Gram led us to the same room we were in last time. Today Aydan did not pause at the sight of the table, nor did he seem to give much attention to anything we saw in the palace. He was good at this part, I realized. He and Gerridan enjoyed negotiation like this nearly as much as they enjoyed a physical fight. I felt my palms frost over. "May I offer you all any refreshment?" Gram asked.

"No need, Your Highness," Gerridan said, "We are quite eager to begin."

"By all means." Gram bid us to sit. He did the same, leaning back in a chair on the opposite end of the table. I noticed no one joined the Prince Regent.

"Will your council be coming?" I asked.

"It's just me today," he answered with a warm smile. He gestured for Gerridan to begin.

"Thank you." My Chief Advisor cleared his throat. "Our initial requests today are threefold. Firstly, we request the immediate return of the Eternity Throne to the Crown of Medeisia. Secondly—"

"Your Highness?" A servant stood in the doorway. Her hands were clasped in front of her, though even from where I sat, I could see they were shaking. "I am so terribly sorry for the interruption, but the King is on his way."

"The King is here," a deep voice corrected from behind the girl. The voice did not match the gangly body and boyish, acne-stricken face it belonged to. As King Callum stepped into the room, Gerridan, Alastair, and Prince Gram all stood, while Aydan and I remained in our seats.

"Your Majesty, we did not expect you," Gram said in a tone that seemed to indicate that he may have ordered his nephew to stay away entirely.

"Well, since you've placed guards around Gwen at all times, my only choices for something to do today were to sit in my chambers alone or see what's happening with the so-called Old Ones." Callum nodded toward Aydan and me, the most he had acknowledged any of us since entering.

"Callum, this is not the time or place to discuss it," Gram said softly as he turned himself and his nephew away from us. "There is much at stake here."

"Yes, much at stake with *my* kingdom," he replied, not bothering to lower his voice. "I ought to be allowed to weigh in. In a few months you won't be regent any longer anyway."

Gram hissed, "Fine. But sit and keep your mouth shut. I will not be embarrassed in front of our guests." The boy-king sat, looking smug, while Gram had gone a bit pale. He took his seat beside his nephew and said, "Please continue, Lord Hollick. My apologies."

"Not at all." Gerridan folded his hands on the table. I glanced at Alastair— his eyes darted between Gram and Callum, as if anticipating a larger fight to come. "Our second request is for Nautia and Medeisia to draw up plans for mortal family reunification." Confusion painted the Nautians' faces. Gerridan explained further, "Much of our mortal population was separated from friends and relatives during your rebellion. Leaders among Medeisian mortals have told us that they would like the opportunity to explore family ties that may still be present here in Nautia."

"That separation was due to their disloyalty to their own kind," Callum chimed in. Gram glanced at his nephew. My face went hot. The Eastly family had been among those who left the former capital. "Perhaps they should have thought of that before following your King like dogs."

"The separation was due to an act of treason from your ancestor, King Callum," I cut in. "The mortals that followed King Zathryan to Ayzelle displayed tremendous loyalty and bravery."

"If that's what you want to call it."

I opened my mouth to respond, but Aydan's hand squeezed my knee. I slid my gaze to him and I saw his head shake slightly, just once, while he kept his eyes forward. A warning to remain calm.

"Third," Gerridan continued smoothly, "The Crown requests the immediate de-warding of the border between Medeisia and Nautia." It felt like the air had been sucked from my lungs. I had missed that request in Alastair's notes.

"What purpose would that serve?" Gram asked. He sounded genuinely curious. Meanwhile, Callum had a bemused smile on his face and dramatically planted his elbow on the table, resting his head on his fist.

"Our nations share a cultural history," Gerridan replied. "Medeisians and Nautians were not always enemies, but fellow countrymen, and we believe it would be a step in the right direction to allow for the crossing of borders for mortals and sorcerers alike."

"You see, uncle?" Callum said to Gram. "Open borders, sorcerers pouring in and out, doing as they please to our people, on our land…"

"Your Majesty, reintegrating our peoples would dispel much of the fear of sorcery your people hold," Gerridan responded calmly. "My King and Queen bear no ill will toward you or the people of Nautia."

"I understand that," Gram said tentatively. "And I believe that *you* bear no ill will toward us, Your Majesties. However, the immediate opening of the borders is not something that I or my nephew will agree to today."

"May I ask why?" Aydan asked. It was the first he had spoken since the discussion started.

"Frankly, without any form of trade agreement or tangible reason for the border opening, such an act would most likely cause unrest here," Gram explained. "Regardless of the cause of such feelings, the people of Nautia are fearful of Medeisia, of sorcerers and sorcery in any capacity. Even our meetings and the planning that has taken place between Alast— the general and I have been met with great suspicion. Without some form of gain on our end, it would appear that my mind is being controlled by the Crown of Medeisia."

"Careful uncle, you'll give them ideas," Callum said.

"You'll be happy to know, Your Majesty, that such a thing would be impossible," I said coldly, locking eyes with Callum. Aydan gave another warning squeeze, which I ignored, batting his hand away from my lap. Amusement danced in the Mortal King's eyes.

"Oh?"

"Mind control is not among the capabilities of sorcerers. Your witches, however, are more than capable of such things."

"What are you implying?"

"I'm not implying anything," I said. "Only suggesting you check your prejudices before you accuse my court and my husband of approaching these meetings with anything but good faith."

"Your husband's father was a tyrant to the mortals he ruled over," Callum countered. "Your court speaks of my family's rebellion without stopping to remember that it was not without cause. Your husband's name is all over Calvin Thandreil's journals— his pitiful attempts to *negotiate* with us while offering nothing of benefit. Looks like some things never change when you're immortal."

"Calvin Thandreil slaughtered my husband's mother, Queen Astra." I felt sparks fly from my fingertips and I buried my hands deeper into my lap. Aydan stiffened beside me. "His men pulled her from her bed as she slept and dragged her and her ladies to the Great Hall before he slit their throats. Tell me, little boy, does her blood still stain the floors?" Gram's face drained of any remaining color. I felt the tension building in the room, and a nearly unnoticeable flicker of movement from Alastair told me he had unsheathed his dagger and was now hiding it in his sleeve. Callum had the same stupid taunting look on his face.

"A necessary move," he said. "No matter how unpleasant."

"*Callum!*" Gram looked mortified.

"Yet you call *us* violent, call *us* unpredictable," I snapped. "When all we have asked for is the opportunity for a better future between our people. You've been allowed to remain a sovereign nation since your rebellion—"

"*Allowed?*" Callum barked a laugh. "We've had to remain warded, isolated from the rest of the world—"

"Your wards are not as strong as you think they are," I countered. I felt Aydan's eyes bearing into me as if he could will me to stop speaking. "Your witches are fooling either you or themselves when they tell you you're safe here." Callum and Gram both paused at that.

"What are you talking about?" Gram asked softly. His eyes moved between Alastair and me. Alastair shifted uncomfortably in his seat.

"All those wards do is prevent us from effuging over the border. There was no incredible feat of magic the night I escaped from your soldiers. I walked into Medeisia on foot," I told them, my voice falling low. "Do you think that we could not march an army here if we so desired? Do you think that a nation of millions of sorcerers— that my husband, our family—could not shatter those wards in minutes if we decided we wanted to? You are here, you rule yourselves, because we have allowed you to do so. Because we want peace."

"Peace?" Callum scoffed. "Claim what you want, but those who want peace do not generally threaten to raise armies against people they want as allies."

"Medeisia has never attempted to retake Nautia with violence," I reminded them. "Yet your forces have crossed our borders in attempts to expand your territory."

"We've done no such thing," Gram countered sharply. He looked uncomfortable, but until now he had not worn such a look of outrage. "The wards have always been intended to keep us in as much as they have been to keep you out. They've only ever been lifted to allow these meetings and for your general's diplomatic visits."

"Thirty-three years ago, Nautian mortal forces attacked Ayzelle," Alastair said calmly.

"My mother was a commander for the Ayzellen army," I added. "She defended her capital, and her King, with honor. She helped defeat your forces and drove them out of Medeisia."

"I do not doubt that your mother was an honorable woman, Your Majesty, but Nautia has never attacked Ayzelle, or any other

161

part of Medeisia." Gram's careful tone was infuriating. I slammed my hands on the table and rose to my feet.

"*You lie*," I snarled. "For what purpose?"

"We could ask you the same question," Callum said. He stood. "We're done here."

"Agreed," Gerridan said. Aydan stood beside me now. He placed his hand on my shoulder, pulling me back gently. I straightened, taking my palms away from the table. My handprints had burned themselves into the surface. I saw Gram's eyes widen when he noticed the marks. "Your Highness, we thank you for your consideration of our requests, and hope that you will also consider continuing our discussions in the future." Gram dipped his head, and before it rose back up, we were gone.

We landed in the sitting room, and I was still fuming. I brushed my hands over my skirts, attempting to get them to stop smoking. Aydan whipped around to face me.

"What the hell was that?"

"I don't know," I said. "But they were fucking infuriating—"

"*You* were fucking infuriating, Shaye," he snapped. "You absolutely botched that discussion."

"Excuse me?" I asked, taken aback. "I defended your plans and your intentions from that—that—"

"That *child* who was looking to get a rise out of you?"

"That child is a cold, cruel little fucker who needs to be put in his place by someone who can do so." I balled my hands into fists at my sides while Alastair and Gerridan stood watching, looking mortified as Aydan and I argued.

"You implied that if they do not fulfill our requests that we would take action against them. You turned a negotiation into a list of demands, you turned it into blackmail."

"Look, I'll admit I got emotional. It's certainly a setback but—"

"Shaye, it's not a fucking setback, you may have ruined this entire mission!" Aydan threw his hands up. "Unless we craft a perfect apology, unless we yield most of our requests, I doubt they'll ever speak to us again."

"If my calling out that little prick and reminding him what we're capable of is enough to ruin this mission then perhaps it's not worth pursuing," I snapped back. Aydan clenched his jaw, and I regretted my words almost immediately.

"How dare you?" He was nearly whispering. "You know what this means to me."

"I do," I said. "I'm sorry. But in the worst-case scenario, we wait a few decades and try again with the next generation of Thandreils."

"No, the *worst-case scenario* would be the Nautian witches bettering their wards and sealing us out completely. The Thandreils would then warn their children and children's children of us, of our tricks and threats, and we never get another opportunity to make things right with the mortals."

"Look, I can't change what I've done. Let me try to make it right. I'll draft the letter—"

"No." Aydan cut me off angrily. "You'll stay out of it."

"Don't talk to me like—"

"Alastair will draft a letter to Gram. He has a good relationship with the prince, and with any luck he can smooth this over. If they ever deign to meet with us again, you'll show up and stay quiet so Gerridan can negotiate on our behalf."

"What was the point in having me anointed if you were still planning on ordering me around?" I spat. "If you want me at *any* meeting, with anyone, I will speak when I please, whether you like it or not."

"Then perhaps next time you won't be invited." Flames engulfed my hands. "Put that out. Your witch needs to get ahold of your tantrums—"

"My *what*—"

"Aydan darling, time to take a walk," Gerridan suggested as the flames crept further up my arms.

"Fine." Aydan stormed out of the front door. I stared after him for a moment before turning back to Gerridan and Alastair.

"I'm sorry," I said. The flames quieted and turned to smoke. "He's right, I let my emotions get the better of me."

"I'm sure we can fix it," Alastair said despite the unsure look on his face.

"And I'm sorry you had to see... well, *that*." I gestured toward the door where Aydan left. Gerridan grimaced. "I've never seen him that angry."

"Being in the Grand Palace has been a lot for him," Gerridan said. "And well, hearing you recount the details of Astra's murder to make a point may have set him off. Doesn't excuse the way he spoke to you now, but..."

Shit. "I'll talk to him when he gets home," I sighed, noticing the time as the clock chimed. "I still need to have my lesson with Lyra. I'll see you all for dinner." Alastair waved and I started toward the stairs. Gerridan followed.

"I'm just going to check on Hannele. Though at this time of day she's probably napping."

I reached the hallway first and rapped my knuckles on Lyra's door. No answer. I frowned, and Gerridan paused beside me.

"Strange," I said. "She's always in her room."

"Maybe she's having a nap too," Gerridan suggested. "Try again." I knocked loudly once again and called the witch's name. I tried to turn the handle but it was locked.

"Lyra, are you all right?" I called through the door. Just as I was about to knock once again, the door flew open. Lyra appeared to be out of breath and her hair was messy.

"Hello," she breathed. "Everything's fine. Just need a minute to, erm, prepare. I'll be ready for you in a few—" She tried to shut the door again before I could respond but I grabbed it to keep her from closing it completely.

"Lyra, what's going on?" I felt Gerridan shift defensively beside me. Whether he thought Lyra was a threat or suspected something else, I didn't know.

"Nothing, Your Majesty. Just, erm, organizing my supplies. I'll be ready for you shortly—"

"There's someone else in there," Gerridan said.

"There's not—"

"I can see movement."

"Step aside, Lyra," I said.

"There is nothing to be concerned about—"

"We need to see inside your room," I insisted, pushing the door all the way open.

Gerridan was right. Lyra was not alone. My breath hitched, and my eyes widened at the sight: the bed in disarray, clothes and jewels strewn about. A chair lay on its side on the other end of the room. And sat on the foot of Lyra's bed in the center of it all was Kenna, completely naked except for a white sheet she had wrapped around her body. "Oh. Gods, I'm so sorry. I thought—" I stepped back out of the room and shut the door behind me. Realization seemed to wash over Gerridan and me at the same time, and when I turned my eyes toward him, he was shaking in silent laughter.

When he finally regained control of himself, a stupid grin remained plastered on his face as he said, "Let's take a look at those deeds."

Chapter
Twenty-One

Dinner was tense that night.

Aydan and I could barely look at one another. I was surprised to even see him at the table. Alastair had not joined us, instead opting to get started on his apology letter to Gram. Gerridan grinned to himself periodically, thinking of his winnings. I had asked him to keep things quiet until the following day so I could talk to Aydan first. The news about Lyra and Kenna might have stayed quiet had the pair not arrived at the table together. It was the first time Lyra had joined the rest of us for a meal since arriving in Sylvanna. Aydan had taken one look at them before glancing at me for confirmation. I nodded once and returned my attention to my plate of roast venison. I heard Aydan sigh, but he did not otherwise comment. No one did. Hannele looked confused as she tried to make pleasant small talk with Lyra and Kenna. Gerridan seemed as though he might explode if someone didn't mention the obvious, but they never did, and he would not break his promise to me.

Later that night, Aydan and I prepared for bed in silence. I never did get my lesson from Lyra, so to make up for it I read from one of her books while sitting by the fireplace. Catchfly took a rare break from sleeping directly in front of it and hopped into my lap. After a few minutes of listening to him rustle around the bathroom, I heard Aydan make his way to the bed. I set my book down and turned to speak to him, but he had already banished the orbs on our ceiling and left me in the dark with nothing but the glow of the fireplace.

Aydan was already gone when I woke the next morning. I dragged myself into the bathtub and washed quickly, wanting to get my breakfast with Gerridan over with as soon as possible so he could pick a property and be done with it.

I didn't bother calling for Elise or Isolde, and when I finished with my bath I dressed in a pair of sparring pants and one of Aydan's shirts. I sat at my vanity to braid my hair, and noticed a folded sheet of thick, cream-colored paper and a white flower. The page read:

> *I'm sorry for the way I spoke to you yesterday. Let's talk*
> *tonight.*
> > *All my love,*
> > *-A*

I sighed, relief washing over me. We'd both been so wound up after Nautia. I didn't blame him for being so angry; I probably would have said something similar. Now I was anxious for him to come home so we could talk. Maybe we could fill some of this space between us.

"That's the one." Gerridan's eyes twinkled as he pointed to the deed of a riverside manor owned by House Redfern. By me.

"You're absolutely positive?" I asked, holding up my pen. "I've never even seen this place, I have no idea what sort of condition it's in."

Gerridan considered. "Would you have time tomorrow to allow me to view it?"

"I have time right now," I said, glancing up at the clock. "Lyra and I aren't meeting for a couple of hours. We could effuge there and view the property before I sign it over."

"Hannele has an appointment with Jemma in a few minutes," he explained.

"I'll go," Alastair said, rounding the corner into the dining room. "I can escort Shaye and we can assess how much it would take to make it livable."

"Would you really?" Gerridan said. "That would be very helpful, Al, thank you."

"I *could* go alone, you know," I said, looking between them. "I don't need an escort everywhere I go."

"It gives us something to do." Gerridan winked.

"And it keeps you out of trouble," Alastair said more seriously.

"I don't need to be kept out of trouble," I countered. Alastair snorted but didn't say anything else. I wasn't sure if I should be offended or not.

Alastair and I effuged directly outside the gates of the manor. As we walked up the stone path toward the dwelling I took in my surroundings. Strange. Everything from the grass to the path we walked on appeared to be in good condition. I'd expected broken, misplaced stones, overgrown greenery, and vines covering windows. Instead, everything appeared to be as I would have expected it to look when Redferns still dwelled here.

Alastair moved to open the door for me, but it would not budge. Thinking it might be jammed, he thrust his shoulder into it, but nothing gave.

"Wait," I said as he was gearing up to hit it once again. "Let me try something—" I placed my palm on the door, and sure enough, it unlatched and opened for us immediately. Alastair gave me a look. "Aydan had a similar ward on his old chambers in Ayzelle," I explained.

"You've never been here."

"It's probably some ridiculous Head of House thing." We walked into the foyer, and I was surprised, once again by the good condition of the space. The floors were covered in pale blue rugs, and fine paintings decorated the walls. Straight ahead was a large staircase that appeared to mark the center of the house, splitting off at the top to lead to opposing wings. Orbs of light hung in chandeliers, and from where we stood I could hear a fire crackling in the next room.

"Shaye, we need to get out of here," Alastair hissed at me.

"Why? It's mine." I gestured to the preserved decor. "Clearly whatever sorcery was used to keep this place running worked— quite good luck for Gerridan, don't you think?"

"It's not sorcery keeping this place running. Someone lives here. They must."

"Don't be so paranoid—" Footsteps came bounding down the hallway toward the top of the stairs. Alastair's arm shot out and quickly pinned me against the wall, where he stepped in front of me. I only had a small dagger strapped to my leg but I unsheathed it anyway and gripped it tightly in my sweaty palm.

"I don't see how anyone could have gotten in," said a vaguely familiar voice.

"Sir, I heard banging on the door and then *voices*—"

"I'll certainly take a look but I'd be shocked if it was anything other than a— what in Ehnara's name are you doing here?" The voice was only feet away from us, clearly only spotting Alastair. I squeezed my way out from behind him, sheathing my dagger and showing my empty hands as I dipped my head in embarrassment.

"We are incredibly sorry, we did not realize this place would have anyone living in it—"

"My gods— Your Majesty, what are you..." I looked up and saw an incredibly pale, uneasy-looking Knox Redfern. Beside him stood an elf woman who appeared to be a servant. Knox turned his head to her and said, "Camilla, a pot of tea if you please. The Queen is here."

Chapter
Twenty-Two

Minutes later Alastair and I sat on one side of a small table in the parlor, while Knox Redfern took up the other side. Camilla delivered tea service with shaky hands and looked like she might crumble when I offered her my thanks.

"Excuse my frankness, Your Majesty," Knox said once Camilla had left the room. "But I can only assume you have come to take the manor as your inheritance and remove us from the dwelling. We will vacate at your command, but I do wonder if you will grant us a few weeks to make other arrangements."

"I have not come to force anyone to vacate," I said. "I did not know anyone lived here. I was simply coming to take a look at the property, and if it was rather run down, assess what it would take to restore it."

"I see," he said. "Do you plan on doing the same with your other properties?"

"Are there people living in those as well?" I asked. He nodded.

"All but Woodrest—the forest house," he said. "It is a beautiful place, but most of us would prefer not to be so far away from the others."

"Others?" I repeated. "How many Redferns remain in Sylvanna?"

"Oh, er, none but myself, Your Majesty. It is just a few members of staff at each property. The rest of the members of House Redfern have relocated to the Elf Kingdoms, though many of us stay in touch." Knox poured a cup of tea and passed it to me.

"I see." I paused to mix milk and honey in. "And are the other properties well-maintained by the staff?"

"As much as they can be, Your Majesty. Markets are reluctant to allow Redfern goods to be sold in their stalls, so we tend to simply trade amongst ourselves and keep up the properties as best we can."

"Yet you have enough income to keep staff employed?"

"We have downsized quite a bit. The remaining housekeepers earn just a modest wage but are also given a place to live and all their other needs are accounted for," said Knox. Noting the skeptical look on my face he added, "House Redfern has plenty, Your Majesty. The ledgers show that we have enough gold to continue like this for another century, if need be."

"I certainly hope it doesn't come to that," I said. Knox raised an eyebrow. "You have committed no crime other than sharing a name with Lord Ronan. It is unfair that you have been so shunned. I do know a bit about what that is like." Knox grew solemn.

"Yes, I heard of your struggles when you first arrived back in Medeisia. After the fact, of course," he added quickly. "It was only confirmed to us that you were back in the country after the members of King Aydan's Cabinet were announced. Had we known that you were being held by Zathryan, House Redfern would have intervened."

"And done what, exactly?" Alastair chimed in. "You have no standing militia, none of the commoners yield to you, and you have no political sway. All that would have done was prove to Zathryan that House Redfern was rising up against him once again—"

"We never rose against the King to begin with. Ronan loved him, and thus we all loved him." Knox's teacup rattled against the saucer.

"Ronan was charged with treason. He was plotting a coup—"

"Enough," I said. "We all know the charges brought against Ronan. There is no reason to bring them up now." To Knox, I added, "I appreciate that you would have wanted to help me. It is clear that Lord Ronan was dear to you."

"We were like brothers," Knox confirmed. The three of us sat in uncomfortable silence for another moment before he added, "Your Majesty, I do want to apologize to you for my behavior the first time we met. I am prone to episodes of...recklessness. Sometimes once an idea gets into my head I cannot shake it, no matter how poor of a decision it might be— though, I hardly ever think in the moment that it is a poor decision. I normally take a tonic for it, but I ran out and it would be several days before I could get more. It is no excuse. I had no business being in Ayzelle, and I certainly would never intend to frighten you the way I did. I only wanted to show you a bit of your family history, but that was obviously a terrible idea. I am incredibly embarrassed and sorry."

"It's nothing," I said earnestly. "No harm done. Though I hope you have found more reliable access to your tonic?"

"I have, Your Majesty, thank you."

Another silent moment passed, and I said, "I thank you for your hospitality my lord, but we had better be going." Knox rose to his feet.

"If I might bid you to stay a moment longer, there is something I would like to give you." I looked to Alastair, who did not appear pleased.

Still, I replied: "By all means." Knox strode quickly to another room. He was gone for several minutes and we heard quite a bit of rustling around. Alastair's dagger found its way into his hand once again. "Do you really think that's necessary?"

"I don't really care, I'm not risking it," he said. "We should have taken off the second we heard him coming."

"I think he's probably harmless."

"Probably," Alastair scoffed as Knox returned to the room. A large wooden trunk floated in behind him and set itself down before me.

"Here we are," Knox said. "The rest of your inheritance."

"I don't need to take anything else from House Redfern," I said. "I have plenty of money."

"This is not money," Knox said. "These are heirlooms from the Eastly family. Your mother left them in my possession a few months before she died."

"Why would Brina have left anything with you?" Alastair snapped before I could speak.

"We were fairly close." Knox shrugged. "As close as we could have been in the short time I knew her. I visited my cousin Ronan often and was present at his wedding. They were doing renovations on their home and Brina asked me to store these items here until she had enough space for them. She said she planned on saving all of this while she and Ronan grew their family, and then dividing the items between her children when they came of age." To me, he said, "Of course that time has come and gone, Your Majesty, but these remain yours all the same." I dragged my fingers along the lid of the trunk.

"Did she want a large family?" I asked.

"She said she did," Knox replied. "She told me that she adored her brother, but since he was so much older, wished she'd had many siblings to grow up with herself." My heart ached for the dreams Brina did not get the chance to fulfill. All because her husband wanted more power. Guilt wrapped around the heartache as I thought of the Thread, and the request I had made of Ronan.

I lifted the lid, revealing many packages wrapped in cloth to protect the items inside. I unwrapped a few, finding modest jewelry, a hand mirror, and a set of combs that must have belonged to some Eastly woman from a generation or two before. I pulled out a ring box, expecting to find some other simple piece inside, but when I opened it, I found a gold ring topped with a light pink pearl, surrounded by a dozen or so tiny white diamonds. It was familiar, and I wracked my brain trying to remember where I might have seen it before.

"That's her wedding ring," Alastair blurted, and I was taken back to the memory he showed me, of seeing Brina for the last time. The ring that had caught his eye when she admitted she'd married Ronan months before and did not tell him. "Why is that in there?"

"Not sure," Knox said. "I remember her telling me her fingers were swollen and her rings would not fit anymore. Perhaps she put it in the trunk so it wouldn't get lost during renovations." I placed it back where I found it.

"We really should be going—" I shut the lid of the trunk. As I raised my hand to send it back home, I noticed a carving on the top corner of the lid, almost like a stamp. It was the fox wreathed in forget-me-nots again. "What is that symbol? I've seen it a few times now." Knox peered over and looked where I was pointing.

"Oh, that is the sigil of House Redfern. The red fox is the representative of our house. The forget-me-nots were added by Ronan's mother."

"Why was the Redfern sigil carved in the top of a box owned by my uncle? A box filled to the brim with gold? He never knew any of you." Knox lowered his gaze and did not speak. "*Knox.*" He nearly flinched at my stern tone. Alastair's normally tan face had lost most of its color.

"When your parents... died," he hesitated on the last word, like it was still painful for him to speak about. "You were taken. No one knew who took you from castle Ayzelle. Our House was in disarray as our family in Ayzelle and Xarynn were forced to flee the country and those of us who remained here worked to find you without running into the King's men who were looking to do the same thing. We felt it would be our duty to take you in and care for you. After a few months I thought the worst must have happened, and Ronan's line was wiped out completely." Knox took a deep, shaky breath as if trying not to cry. "And then, when the rest of the Sylvannian Redferns had gone and I was alone, I received word from someone— I still do not know who they were— that you were safe in Nautia."

"You *knew*—"

"You must understand, Your Majesty, that there would have been no way for me to retrieve you without King Zathryan taking notice, and I knew that his attention would not result in anything good. It was clear, once I knew where you were, that remaining among mortals would be the safest thing for you, until your sorcery emerged. The person who alerted me to your location told me where we could send information, and promised that it would be given to the correct person. I made a gamble and sent a sum of money to be used for your maintenance as you grew up. It was my honor, and my obligation, as your father's kin, to ensure that you were well cared for."

For maintenance, that note had read.

Signed K.R...Knox Redfern.

"When I did not hear from you or your uncle, I assumed that you found a way to subdue your powers enough to remain where you were, or that you had fled to the Faelands to remain in hiding." Knox looked devastated.

"How would my powers have been subdued?"

"I have no idea, Your Majesty, I simply had no other explanation for why you were able to remain hidden for so long. In our family, our powers tend to emerge well before one comes of age—not that it is a bad thing that they did not in your case, Your Majesty," he added, seeming worried that I would be offended.

"We really must be going now," Alastair announced. He stood and offered me his hand. I took it, mulling over everything Knox had just said.

"It was an honor to speak with you, Your Majesty," Knox said as he bowed low. When he rose, he added, "Should you ever find yourself in need of me, I am at your service."

"Thank you, Lord Knox." I waved my hand over the trunk, sending it to one of the spare rooms in our chambers at castle Ayzelle rather than the house. "I will send for you should the need ever arise." Knox dipped his head again, and we were gone.

Alastair and I arrived outside the front door of our home. I turned to him immediately and said, "You will not speak of that."

Alastair sighed. "Shaye, Aydan really should know that there are people still dwelling in your estates."

"I don't use them. Who cares? They've done nothing wrong."

"Squatting on the Queen's property feels rather wrong to me. And then to trouble you with those stories—"

"Alastair, once again I am asking you as your friend to just keep this between us. I do not want to ask as your Queen."

"Fine," he said. "But I don't like it."

"Me either," I replied. I opened the door and stepped inside to find Zale and Isolde darting around the foyer and the sitting room. Isolde seemed to be gathering blankets while Zale made his way to the staircase holding a tray that held an empty bowl, a steaming kettle, and what appeared to be folded hand towels. "What's going on?" I asked when Isolde looked up and saw us.

"Oh, Your Majesty," she said breathlessly, "Princess Hannele is in labor."

"Isn't it a bit early for that?"

"Two weeks or so, yes. But the healers do not seem to be concerned by the timing. Jemma is upstairs with her. Lord Gerridan and Lady Kenna are there as well."

"Where is Aydan?" I asked. Certainly he would want to be here for this. Alastair stepped around me and made his way up the stairs.

"The King is in Ayzelle. A message has been sent but he has not yet returned. I expect he'll be here shortly one way or another." I nodded.

"Do you need any help?"

"No, Your Majesty, I am almost finished here and then I will take these to Elise to be cleaned and warmed for the babe. Seems we may still have a few hours to go, but it's best to be prepared."

"Good," I said, taking a deep breath. "Just... just do whatever needs to be done, I suppose. You know more than I do." Isolde dipped into a curtsy before returning to her work. I made my way upstairs as well, but rather than follow the others into Hannele and Gerridan's bedroom I knocked on Lyra's door. She cracked it open and peered out, opening wider when she saw it was me.

"Are you avoiding all of that too?" she asked, motioning with her head to the other end of the hallway. "Kenna said I should join everyone but it's not really my place."

"I don't know that I'm ready to be around that," I admitted, wrapping my arms around myself. "I know she's one of my ladies, and it's probably a huge insult for me to miss the birth but I just..."

"I'm sure the princess will understand." Lyra stepped aside to let me in. "Should we pass the time with some cronewort?" It was probably not a good idea, but I nodded and stepped inside anyway.

When I arrived in Ronan's study he was already there, pouring over his books as he often did.

"It's been three days," he said without looking up. "Has it only been the one for you?"

"Two," I corrected. "I could not make it yesterday. An emergency with my work."

"Still, we're getting closer. I think if we set our meetings for regular intervals, we might be able to straighten out the time difference." He closed his book and looked to me. "Are you ready?"

"I suppose I'd better be," I replied. Ronan smirked.

"I'll go easy on you, Lady Shaye."

For the next hour, Ronan coaxed my elemental magic out of me with various techniques that I recognized from my first lessons with Lyra. Like Lyra, Ronan wanted to see what I could control of each element. Though I had a bit more control than I once did over *when* my witchcraft made its appearance, I still had little say in what my powers did when they were present, and the strength behind them.

Ronan gave me words to say to attempt to summon fire, and as I expected, nothing happened. However, when he formed a storm cloud behind my head without me noticing and thunder sounded suddenly in my ears, ice formed on my hands and shot up my arms in surprise.

"Interesting." Was all he had to say most of the time. He took notes in a journal as he observed my abilities. I was panting by the time we were done, desperate for water, though I could not seem to drink anything while using the Thread. "That may change as you use it more," Ronan informed me. "The family histories claim that one's presence can grow stronger the more they use the Thread. Right now, if you touch me, I cannot feel you. But as time goes on we may be able to shake hands as teacher and pupil."

"Who did you visit with the Thread?" I asked. "You told me that you had never been on the receiving end before I arrived, so I assume you've been the visitor?"

"I have," he confirmed. He crossed his arms and sat back against a table. "Just once. My mother, Aoife... I had not seen her in a long time before she died. She was very sick, very old, and chose to not let the healers cure her. By the time I made it to her deathbed she was hardly conscious with all the medicines she'd been given to take away her pain, and I did not get to say my true goodbyes. So I went to see her on what she'd always told me was the happiest day of her life: the day she married my father. I didn't speak to her. I just watched. She was so young— only twenty when she married him. But they had centuries together after that, and they were happy for most of them."

"I'm sorry you lost her," I said. He waved me off.

"It's been three hundred years, Lady Shaye. I've learned to cope." He sighed and straightened. "I think that's all I need for today. I'm going to take my notes here and compare them to some of my texts and see what I can come up with. Come back tomorrow— well, *your* tomorrow. We'll see what happens here—"

"Darling, are you talking to someone?" I jumped. Brina had entered the room so quietly that neither of us heard her. Ronan glanced sidelong at me, clearly trying to decide what he should tell his wife, if anything, about the Thread.

"Only myself." He grinned at her. "Helps me think."

"You're a strange man, Ronan Redfern," Brina teased. I tried willing myself back to Lyra's bedroom as my mother kissed her husband. When that didn't work I stepped to the back of the room, pressing myself against the wall to give them as much privacy as I was able. She pulled away and asked, "Have you made any progress?"

"Yes and no," he said. "I can tell when he's not himself. But I still cannot prove it, and that's the key. He won't believe anything is wrong, and I must be able to show the other lords and ladies that the King is not in his right mind." Was that his plan then? To try and convince the nobility that Zathryan was mad, and could not be trusted to rule? I had to admit it was a smart plan— as long as Ronan could convince the lords and ladies of the court that Zathryan was unfit, it wasn't as if Zathryan could do much to deny it. A madman would certainly not admit to his own madness. But why bother with witchcraft, if that were the case? One could frame a King for madness without forbidden magic, couldn't they?

"What would they need to see in order to believe you?" Brina asked. "How do you prove something like that?"

"I think…" Ronan sighed and leaned against the table again. "I think I may have to appeal to Prince Aydan after all. I've written a letter. I was going to have you check it over before I send it to Sylvanna tomorrow." Brina blanched.

"Do you think he'll meet with you? It's been so long."

"I know. I can only hope he will see that I did not advocate for his banishment." Ronan gazed at the floor.

"I'm sure he knows that. You were close once."

"I can only hope," Ronan repeated. Brina stepped closer to him and wrapped her arms around his middle, pressing her face into his chest. He kissed her hair. "What time is it? Have you eaten?"

"No, that was why I came to find you," she said, pulling away so she could look up at him. "I've had the cooks prepare your favorite tonight."

"Oh? What's the occasion?"

"You'll have to wash up and join me to find out," Brina answered, waggling her brows.

"Lady Redfern, you torture me with your surprises," Ronan chuckled. "But as always, I am intrigued." He followed her to the door, and right when he opened it I found myself lying in the center of Lyra's bedroom once again. She was crouched beside me, shaking my arm.

"What?" I mumbled groggily, sitting up and rubbing my eyes. Someone was knocking on the door.

"That," Lyra said, pointing to it. "I didn't think you wanted your Cabinet to see this just yet."

"No, I don't. Thank you." I stood as the knock persisted. I motioned for Lyra to open the door, and when she did, Kenna rushed inside.

"What took you two so long?" She asked. "The baby is going to be here any second."

"Sorry, we couldn't break concentration," I explained vaguely. Reality washed over me and I remembered what was happening before I drank the cronewort. "How's Hannele?"

"She's doing wonderfully. Started pushing a few minutes ago. We're all in the sitting room, waiting. I thought you'd want to be there."

"Yes, yes of course." The three of us left Lyra's bedroom and joined the others downstairs. Alastair and Aydan both had drinks in their hands. Alastair poured one for Kenna and for Lyra, but I turned him down when it was offered to me. I didn't see Gerridan, and almost asked where he was before realizing he must be in the room with Hannele. In Nautia, men did not watch their wives give birth, but in Medeisia many chose to be right there at her side. I sat beside Aydan, though we did not look at one another. I wondered if he was as nervous as I was. I felt him put his hand on my knee, stopping my leg from bouncing— I had not noticed that it was doing so.

Only five minutes or so passed before we heard Gerridan's bedroom door open, and a small cry echoed down the stairs. All of our heads turned toward the sound and we watched in silence as Gerridan bounded down the stairs with an enormous grin plastered on his face, which was blotchy and tear stained. He stopped when he reached the center of the sitting room.

"A boy," he breathed. Alastair all but leapt from his seat and hugged Gerridan, nearly lifting him off the floor. Kenna stood waiting for them to finish before kissing his cheek, then made a show of handing Alastair a coin purse. Lyra just stood back with her hands clasped at her chin.

Aydan hugged his friend. "No son could ask for a better father," he said. Tears spilled onto Gerridan's cheeks once again.

"His name is Drystan," he choked. "He's small, but so strong. Hannele is doing great— gods, she was amazing. She's asking for you all to come up and meet him."

We all filed up the stairs, following Gerridan to the bedroom. I remained in the back while the others stepped inside. Jemma passed us as she left to give everyone privacy for a few minutes.

Hannele was beaming as she held her son. Her hair was mussed with dried sweat and while she looked like she had been awake for days, she looked more beautiful and in love than I had ever seen her. Gerridan went quickly to Hannele's side and kissed her cheek before she handed the babe off to him. His attention darted between the two of them as if he could not tell who he was more in awe of.

Alastair and Kenna stepped forward to take a look at Drystan. Kenna stifled an excited gasp as she looked down at him with shining eyes.

"Gods, Hannele, he's beautiful," she said, looking back to our friend.

"Thankfully he takes after his mother," Gerridan joked. Alastair rested his hand on Gerridan's back before taking his turn to admire the baby. He reached his hand forward and touched the boy's tiny foot with what now seemed like enormous fingers.

"Aydan, Shaye, come take a look," Alastair said without taking his eyes off Drystan. I had not realized that Aydan stood beside me. He seemed apprehensive but stepped forward with his hands clasped behind his back. I took a deep breath and crossed the room as well.

Drystan Hollick was one of the prettiest babies I'd ever seen. My only comparison being the village babies in Nautia whose births I was present for prior to ruining my reputation. He was tiny, with balled up fists held by his chin, heart-shaped lips and a tuft of curly black hair atop his head. He slept in his father's arms as if that were the safest place in the world— and I knew that for Drystan, it always would be.

"Do you want to hold him, Shaye?" Hannele asked quietly from the bed.

I didn't. The thought terrified me if I were honest. But I didn't know how to deny such an offer from a new mother. "Oh, I- erm," I fumbled, and before I could form any sort of useful answer, Gerridan placed the baby in my arms.

He seemed smaller in my arms than he had just by looking at him. My eyes welled up immediately, but I did not dare let

Gerridan or Hannele see. I locked eyes with Aydan for a few seconds. He appeared ashen, and we both quickly looked away.

"My turn!" Kenna announced while reaching for Drystan. I gladly handed him over before offering my congratulations to Hannele and Gerridan once again. I kissed them both before excusing myself and leaving the room.

The door shut behind me and I let a choked sob escape my throat. The door opened again and I hurried to gather myself before anyone could see me ruining my friends' happy moment.

"Are you all right, my love?" Aydan placed his hand on my back, but I stepped out of the touch.

"Of course. Just a little emotional. It caught me off guard."

"I thought perhaps being around the baby had upset you."

"Why should it?" I said more sharply than I'd meant to. Though, by the look on my husband's face I could see that my true message had been heard loud and clear: please change the subject.

We stood in awkward silence for a moment before Aydan said, "Listen, about yesterday. Like I said in my note, I'm sorry for the way I spoke to you. There are better ways to express anger, and you deserve more respect than I showed you."

"It's all right," I said.

"I'm sure everything with Nautia will work out one way or another," he said.

"I hope so." I cleared my throat. "I'm feeling rather tired. I think I'll go lie down."

"Of course," Aydan said stiffly. "I'll see you in a few minutes. I'm going to say goodnight to everyone."

"I'll see you then," I told him. He moved like he might lean in to kiss me, but I had already turned to walk away. I made my way to our bedroom, and once I'd changed into a nightdress, I spent the rest of the night pretending to be asleep.

Chapter
Twenty-Three

I was in Lyra's quarters before the sun rose, steeping the cronewort myself while I waited for her to arrive. She did not answer when I knocked, but I could not bring myself to return downstairs. When I found her bedroom to be empty, I realized she must be next door in Kenna's, and helped myself to the kettle she had enchanted to always stay warm. I sipped the bitter tea and stopped to stroke a finger down the length of Petyr's body while he soaked up the winter sun in the windowsill.

Had I not known the snake was a familiar, I would have found him quite unnerving. The change in temperature did not seem to affect him, and his stare hinted that he might comprehend what humans said to him— a perfect spy for his mistress, should she ever need one. Perhaps one day he would teach Catchfly a thing or two. The fat gray cat hardly left the hearth in my bedroom these days.

I drained the last of the tea. Lyra still had not returned, so I lay down on the floor and focused my mind toward Ronan.

I found him sitting on the floor in his study with his back to the wall, a book open in his lap.

"I saw you the day before yesterday," Ronan said before snapping the book shut. I spotted the title: *Heart of Thirst.*

"I saw you yesterday afternoon," I replied. "Is that... a romance novel?" He chuckled.

"I needed a break from the spell books and histories," he said, holding up the volume. "I found this one in the bottom of my wife's wardrobe. She claims to have no idea how it came to be there, and I would never call Brina a liar, but I must admit I recognize some of the heroine's techniques." He laughed again, and I couldn't help but stare. A fearsome traitor, one of the most powerful sorcerers to ever live, the disgraced Head of House Redfern—reading romance novels. Making teasing jokes about his wife, whom he seemed to adore. Behind his laugh I spotted some restlessness in his eyes.

"Something's wrong," I said. "Why are you acting strangely?"

"Ah," said Ronan, halting his laughter, "You've caught me— my mind is elsewhere, young lady. My apologies."

"I'm sorry to have interrupted your day then," I replied. "I'll leave you to your book—"

"No, no," he said as he stood up and set the book aside. "You've made the effort to come here. Let's see if we can make any progress."

The next hour held many of the same tests and experiments we did the day before. This time, Ronan gave me words for summoning each of the elements, not just fire. None of them worked. Next, he asked me to show him what it looked like when I attempted to simply will each one into being. Each element made a sort of appearance eventually, but none were in my control. Ronan had to step in each time to tame my power into submission.

"I'm sorry," I panted after he had subdued my windstorm down into a tiny breeze that eventually subsided.

"Why should you be?"

"I'm making a mess of your study, for one," I said, noting the scattered supplies on the floor. "And I'm not making any progress here."

"It's your second lesson," he said. "I can't expect you to master your abilities, which we know very little about, in a matter of a few hours. You should not expect it either."

"I know I shouldn't." I dragged a hand down my face. "I'm just tired. I'm so tired of not knowing how this all works. It seems to be only a matter of time before something slips in front of the wrong person, or I lose control and really hurt someone."

"I can imagine that would be quite exhausting," he said kindly.

"I thought going to the Children and finding a teacher would fix everything, but it's been months and I've made no progress. Don't get me wrong, Lyra is wonderful, but she has not been able to help me tame the elements, and I am growing fearful that I may never do so." I fiddled with my braid. "I've studied, I've practiced— I've done everything but go to the temple and appeal to the gods themselves."

"Lyra— the keeper is your teacher?"

"She is. You know her?"

"Of her," he corrected. "I've only seen her twice, in my visits to the Children. I'm just surprised that she was allowed to help you. The Mothers and her husband appear rather possessive of her."

"They are," I said. "She wasn't allowed. She helped me escape their captivity." Ronan's eyes widened in surprise. "If you ever see them again, stay clear of Deimos. He's a bad man."

"Noted. Though I doubt I'll be traveling for a while. I was given some rather important news and must stay near home for the time being."

"Oh?" I asked. "Is everything all right?"

"Yes, everything's fine," he said with a smile. "I was just—"

But before he could finish his answer I was torn from Ronan's study and back into Lyra's room.

I was soaked, freezing, and completely confused. "What the fuck—"

"Shaye, thank the gods." Kenna stood over me with an empty bucket, which by the feel of my sopping clothes, had just recently contained ice water.

"Pigeon, you don't understand—" Lyra swept into the room but stopped upon seeing me awake and dripping. "Shit."

"Does someone want to tell me what's going on? Why were you passed out on the ground? You looked *dead* and you had an empty cup in your hand. I thought you'd been fucking *poisoned*, Shaye, you scared the shit out of me." Lyra and I locked eyes. She shrugged in a way that seemed to say, *Your call.* I sighed.

"Sit down," I said. "There's something I need to tell you."

It only took half an hour or so to tell Kenna about the Thread, and how she had been wrong about my abilities. She only interrupted me once, when I finally explained that I was not a mindwalker after all, to say, "Everything you and Alastair told me matched what I was taught about mindwalking—"

"I know," I said. "We all thought the same thing, but we were wrong. Mindwalking is something else altogether." I continued explaining my deal with Ronan and Kenna's eyes went wide. When I finished, she let out a low whistle, looking between Lyra and me. She stopped on her lover.

"You should have told me," Kenna said. "But I understand why you did not."

"You don't think I'm crazy?" I asked.

"Of course I think you're crazy," she replied. "But you're in a shit spot with an opportunity to achieve what you've been hoping for all this time... I do think you should tell Aydan at some point though."

"I know," I said. "I will. Things have been strange between us—"

"Obviously." I shot her a dirty look. "I have eyes, Shaye."

"I do not want to add this to the list of difficult topics we need to work through just yet," I continued. "I need to give this a chance to work before I let him try to talk me out of it." Kenna nodded.

"I don't like the idea of keeping things from him, but I can see why you feel you need to. I won't say anything unless ordered to reveal what I know." A fair enough promise.

"Thank you, Ken."

"Just be safe and tell the truth as much as you can. All these lies run the risk of taking you over." She hugged me before leaving, and I couldn't help but notice she did not do the same with Lyra. On her way out the door Kenna called over her shoulder that we should eat, and that she would have breakfast brought up to us while I mulled over what she'd just said.

"So," Lyra said once we were alone. "Did you learn anything in your lesson today?"

"What happened to you?" The first words out of Ronan's mouth the next time I arrived in his study were sharp.

"No calendar tally today?" I joked. His eyes bore into me. "What's wrong? Has it been a long time?"

"It's only been one day," he admitted. "But you were mid conversation when you *screamed* and disappeared. You shouldn't be able to be pulled from the Thread very easily, so something must have happened— what was it? Were you hurt? Did someone— how long has it been?"

"It's only been a day for me too," I said. "My friend found me passed out with an empty cup in my hand, and apparently thought I had been poisoned. She dumped ice water on me."

"I see," said Ronan. "And you are such an important woman that poisoning was the first thought a friend would have upon finding you in such a state?"

"I suppose," I replied. Ronan looked at me expectantly. "I'm... in government."

"Ah, well then, your friend may have been right to suspect poison. All the council members in my time are asking for it." I snorted.

"Were you... concerned? About me?"

"Would that be so surprising? I've taken you on as my pupil, and you are my descendant, no matter how distant. I'm sure you can understand why I would want to ensure your wellbeing." I nearly blushed.

"Thank you, I suppose." We paused for a moment before I broke the silence by asking, "What was it you were going to tell me before I left?"

Ronan's mouth twitched. "Tell you what: if my idea for today's lesson works, I'll tell you."

"You were going to just tell me yesterday."

"Perhaps I was," he teased. "But today is a new day and you are nosy enough—"

"—Excuse—"

"—that I know this will be excellent motivation for you." I narrowed my eyes at Ronan, and he grinned.

"What is it you want me to do?"

"I believe the solution to controlling your elemental magic may lie in how your powers have presented themselves in you to begin with." I stared at him, waiting to understand. "Your sorcery is blended with witchcraft. Of course your additional powers cannot be controlled by spoken spells, or by the willing of sorcery— we must blend the two techniques."

"...How?"

"Witches believe that their spells are spoken in the language of the gods, and to speak these words is to make a direct request to the highest authority to grant them use of it. What if, instead of speaking the words aloud, you silently requested that the goddess of witches allow you to bend the elements to your will?"

"What, just say the spell in my head?"

"No, make the request in the common tongue, in your head. Like a prayer."

"You think I should pray to Otana for control of the elements?" I didn't even pray to my own gods.

"More or less."

"Where should I start?"

"Fire seems to come to you with the most ease," Ronan offered. "Ask for that." I nodded, steadying myself where I stood. He stepped back a few feet, giving me plenty of space should flames appear *too* easily.

Otana, I thought, mimicking the priests' and priestesses' prayers that I had heard before. *Hear me. Grant my prayer. Bring fire to me.* Nothing. *Otana, allow me to command flame.* My palms heated, but still no spark. Frustrated, I looked to Ronan, who gestured for me to continue. I took a deep breath, closed my eyes, and gave something else a try: *Mother Ehnara and Father Lehrun. Goddess Otana. All the divine, all who granted me power, please: allow me to wield what you have gifted me. Make me a vessel for spark and flame.*

"Lady Shaye, look." I opened my eyes and dancing in my outstretched palm was a gentle flame. Not sparks or wild blazes, but something safe and warm. A symbol of life. "My gods, it worked," Ronan said. I thanked the gods in my mind and the flame extinguished itself.

"I had to ask them all," I explained. "Lehrun, Ehnara, and Otana. I asked all of them, and that's when it worked." Ronan nodded.

"Makes sense, I suppose."

"*Now* will you tell me?" I asked. Ronan's eyes sparkled.

"I suppose you've earned it." A smile crept onto his face. "In six months' time, I am to be a father." Dread filled my stomach. In six months' time I would be born.

And Lord Ronan would already be dead.

As it turned out, I was a quick learner.

In the months that followed, I truly mastered control of all four of the elements at my disposal, and once I had done that, Ronan could finally show me how to *do* something with them.

Fire, of course, came easiest to me. I had already managed to light fireplaces and lanterns before learning to make a request, so now I was just learning to guide it with more precision. Ronan initiated my lessons while I used the Thread, then when I was back in Lyra's quarters, she continued by showing me practical tasks to apply the skills to.

Earth came easily as well. Plants grew from seed before my eyes, at my command. It was also the only element that I could not produce from nothing— plants, soil, or rocks had to be present in order for me to command them, but I soon found that my power could just as easily command the stone of castle floors and walls as it could a boulder from the garden.

Wind and water both eluded me for weeks. I had produced each only with extreme emotions like sadness or fear, and so to try and produce them from nothing, with a purpose, proved to be a challenge. They each came to me eventually, water arriving first and pouring from my palm like a faucet, then allowing me to weave the stream around my arm like a liquid snake.

Wind was much more modest in its arrival, simply fluttering around me, lifting the petals of flowers I had just grown off the table and spiraling them around Ronan and me where we stood.

Ronan taught me to blend the elements— like using wind and water to create the storm cloud I watched him make the first time I ever used the Thread or allowing the wind to feed a flame and make it grow larger. He showed me what he had learned of potion making and healing, collaborating with Lyra using me as a conduit between my teachers to deliver messages. My now extensive knowledge of herbs and other plants impressed Ronan, and he showed me how to use potions to enhance the effects of other spells, giving me recipes to make with Lyra and practice at home. The more time I spent with Ronan, the stronger my grasp on the Thread became. I was learning so much, so quickly, as if everything I'd ever learned about magic had prepared me for this.

One day, I stood in the center of Ronan's study wearing sparring clothes, panting as I made what felt like my millionth attempt at fighting a dummy he'd brought from the sparring ring. All the tables had been banished to wherever he sent such things, and it was just me, facing the dummy as Ronan spoke the instructions in my ear once again:

"Grow the vines and choke him with them, turn water into ice to cut them away. Then set him alight and blow out the flames."

"Got it," I said with some irritation.

"You can do this, Shaye." He'd stopped calling me 'Lady' weeks ago. "Just make your requests, and then let the power flow from you."

"Hush, you're distracting me," I snapped. I could almost sense the half-smile I was sure would be painted on his face as he stood behind me with his arms crossed.

I took a deep breath and said my prayer to the gods. From what had seconds ago seemed to be empty pots of dirt, thick, thorned vines burst forth and wrapped themselves around the straw-filled dummy, constricting it until the seams pulled. In a slicing motion Ronan taught me the week prior, I threw blades made of solid ice to cut the vines, letting them drop to the ground, motionless. Then, with an underhand thrust of my fist, the dummy burst into flame. Ronan straightened as he put himself on standby in case the blaze got out of control. Then, with a sidelong wave of my arm, a powerful gust of air moved through the room and the fire went out like someone blowing a candle. Surprised laughter erupted from my throat as I whipped around and faced Ronan.

"You did it," he grinned.

"I did it!" I nearly squealed, and without thinking, I jumped forward and threw my arms around Ronan. He squeezed back for just half a second before pushing me away.

"I can feel you," he said, wide-eyed.

"I can feel you too," I said, stepping back and staring where I had just had my arms looped around him.

"You've gained a lot of strength here," he said, seeming to consider each word carefully. "How is it back home?"

"My powers have never been stronger," I said. "My craft and sorcery alike are potent and well within my control."

"And what of your physical strength?"

I hesitated a second too long. "What of it?"

"Shaye." I met Ronan's scolding with forced aloofness.

"I'm *fine*."

We weren't actually sure if I was fine. I was eating, drinking, and sleeping— I finally told Lyra to drop it and that I would not be giving up my tonic any time soon— but regardless I was deteriorating. I stopped training with Gerridan and Alastair ages ago, and thank the gods I had, because I doubted I would be able to hold up a waster these days, let alone an actual sword.

Hannele had taken Gerridan and Drystan to her family's home to visit and give the rest of us a break from Drystan's incessant, colicky cries. This left Kenna, Lyra, Alastair, and Aydan to watch me steadily losing weight and gaining large circles under my eyes. Kenna of course knew everything, but the men were in the dark. I caught Aydan watching to make sure I swallowed my food on more than one occasion, and once I overheard Alastair privately scolding Aydan for allowing things to get this bad. I wasn't able to hear much of his reply, but Aydan seemed to indicate that my anointed status meant his hands were tied.

Ronan raised his eyebrows. "I've looked better," I admitted. "But as I said, my power has never been stronger. I finally have a grip on it. I'm not being drained every time the elements appear, *and* I control when they do so."

"Perhaps we should take a break for a few days," Ronan suggested.

"Please, Ronan, I swear I'm fine," I pleaded. "I'm finally getting this. Don't take it away."

He sighed deeply. "Do me a favor and take one day off. Just one," he added when I started to protest. "Do something that doesn't involve the Thread. Read up on your dream issue— hell, I'd prefer you skip lessons altogether and read that trashy book you like so much." I scowled at his mocking of *Enchanted, Enchanting.* "Just take a break. You've earned it. And I will still be here for you when you come back."

"Fine," I said with a sigh. "I'll see you after tomorrow then." Ronan put a hand on my shoulder and squeezed.

"It'll be good for you." He paused to chuckle at himself. "Sorry," he said. "I don't mean to sound like your father." I blanched when he said that but forced myself to smile anyway.

Chapter
Twenty-Four

The next day, upon hearing that Lyra had been given the day off, Kenna whisked her away to Xarynn for a day on the water. Lyra looked concerned when I jokingly told them to not let the Duke see the two of them together but shook off the worry quickly before vaguely mentioning some berries and herbs that needed replenishing in my potion making case. I promised her I would refill them before Kenna glamoured her and effuged them both to Xarynn.

I smiled a little to myself. It was nice to see the two of them together, even if it meant I had lost my bet with Gerridan.

When I finally got around to talking with him after Drystan's birth, I explained that the only Redfern estate I could give him with a clear conscience was the forest house, Woodrest. Gerridan had just laughed, still euphoric over the birth of his son. He told me to forget the house, and that it didn't really matter to him. That night, I signed the deed over to him anyway and had it delivered to him with my seal and a note that said, *A gift then.* When the Hollicks finished their visit with Hannele's family, they went to their new estate instead of returning to our home. I made sure to send Knox Redfern a note letting him know that Woodrest was no longer the property of House Redfern, and to let the rest of my remaining relatives know to steer clear, should they decide to return to Sylvanna someday. Knox replied quickly, letting me know that the information had been passed along, and reminding me that he was at my service should the need ever arise.

Now, I walked along a dirt path alone, carrying a basket and a pair of gardening shears. I did not know if I would find enough of Lyra's requests to require the basket, but I thought it would do well to be prepared. After only a couple minutes of walking I found myself a bit winded and cursed the effects of the Thread on my body. My now too-thin frame struggled to carry me for any sort of distance, and I had to stop a few times to take a break before I reached the berry patch I was searching for. I clipped a few stems that held fat clusters of strange orange berries that would be mashed into a paste and put into jars for later.

I only managed to find one of the herbs, but happily discovered a patch of wild spotted mushrooms that Lyra constantly complained were too hard to find. I gathered as much as would fit in the basket and I started on my walk back home. The basket, though it and its contents totaled only a few pounds, felt like it was filled with bricks as my frail arm struggled to carry it. I tried rearranging it several times before finally giving up, panting with my hands on my knees. I sighed to myself.

"Alastair?" I called out. In an instant, my general was beside me with his hand at his hip.

"What's the matter?" he asked, looking around for some danger or another, but only finding me struggling to catch my breath.

"I don't want to hear your scolding," I said through sharp breaths. I pointed to the basket that lay discarded on the ground. "Will you please help me carry that home?"

Alastair scowled, confused. "This?" he asked, bending down to grab it. He lifted the basket with ease. "Shaye, you're kidding, right?"

"No, I'm not." I took a seat on a large boulder. "I'll be behind you in a moment—" Alastair scooped me into his arms and began walking home. "Alastair put me down."

"No, Shaye, I'm done." He glared straight ahead, not looking at me as he fumed. "Whatever the hell you're doing to yourself stops now. I'm taking you to Aydan, and we are getting you to a healer right this second—"

"I wish to invoke—"

"No."

"Alastair Greenwood, you swore an oath to me," I said. "Now honor it and put me the fuck down."

"You are so frail you cannot carry a basket of herbs without becoming winded," he said, stopping in his tracks but not putting me down just yet. "We've all been watching you waste away for months, and Aydan says his hands are tied, but I don't particularly care. You're right, I swore an oath— and right now protecting you means protecting you from yourself. So we will go to Aydan, and—"

"No, Al, please. Don't take me to Aydan."

"What else am I supposed to do, Shaye? You won't talk to me. You won't talk to anyone but Lyra and Kenna, it seems. You spend your days shut up in that room with the witch, and you come back to us looking the way you do. What are we to think?" The worry in his voice was clear.

"If I—" I paused, trying to find the words. "If I tell you what I've been doing, will you put me down and stop all this talk about taking me to Aydan?"

"Put you down, yes," Alastair said, and he did so. "But I will wait until I hear what you have to say before I agree to keep Aydan out of this."

"I suppose that's fair." I held out my hand. "Let me effuge us back to the house and we'll talk in Lyra's room, where we won't be disturbed." Tentatively, Alastair took my hand and we arrived in Lyra's study. His nose instantly crinkled.

"It smells like an apothecary in here," he complained. I took the basket from his hands and placed it on the desk. I sat down in Lyra's normal seat and indicated that Alastair should sit in the one opposite from me. Petyr snoozed in the windowsill. I began to pick the berries from their stems and set them in a bowl. "So?" Alastair said expectantly.

I sighed while I continued working. "When Stefan Whittaker and I had our final argument, I was unconscious for a few days, do you remember?"

"I will never forget it, Shaye. You know that."

"Well, while I was asleep, I found myself in the dark…" I proceeded to recount the story as I told it to Kenna a few months prior. Every encounter with Ronan, all I had learned of the Thread, and mindwalking, and my connection to Alastair's powers as well. I told him of my additional training with Ronan, and how I had mastered all the elements while learning from my father. I did not tell him how I reluctantly, against my better judgment, had grown to enjoy Ronan's company, and look forward to our meetings. I did not tell him how disappointed I had been when Ronan told me to take a break today, and that I found myself missing him, even now.

When Alastair seemed skeptical, I gave him a demonstration of the request, showing him my control of each element. He just sort of blinked at me, realizing what I was saying.

"You are not a mindwalker," he said.

"That's correct. We were confused by rumor and our own lack of understanding of the craft."

"You've mastered the elements," Alastair added.

"More or less," I said.

"And you've done all of this under the instruction of your dead father."

"Yes," I breathed. "Alastair, you have to believe me."

"Oh, I believe you," he said, leaning back fully in his chair. "You have control, which you didn't before. And it explains your physical state. I just... I hate this so much, Shaye. I cannot even put it into words."

"I know you do," I said. "I know everyone will. That's why I've kept it to myself."

"He's a traitor, Shaye."

"It's... all very complicated."

"He consulted witches—"

"And so have I," I replied.

"Not to usurp the throne. Not to gain power. Only to control what he has plagued you with." Alastair leaned forward in his seat. "If he loved your mother as you claim he did, he would not have put her in the position he did. She is dead because—"

"Because she refused healers. Because she was stubborn."

"Because she would rather be dead than live without him," Alastair corrected.

"Yes, and she did not think of her daughter. She could have lived for her one connection to him and she did not. Don't sit here and paint him to be the ultimate villain and her his victim. She was no such thing— she knew exactly who and what he was before she married him, and she did it anyway." I clenched my jaw, and I thought I saw him do the same. "If you're going to run and tell Aydan, I suggest you get on with it."

"I'm not going to tell Aydan," Alastair said. He saw my confusion and explained further, "I was only going to do it if I found you were endangering yourself. I'm not a fan of your appearance right now, and I will be keeping an eye on you. But you do not seem to be in any immediate danger." Relief washed over me.

"Thank you, Alastair."

"You should tell him, though."

"I know— everyone keeps saying that. And I will, at some point." I fiddled with my wedding ring which had grown loose in the past months. "I don't know that he'll believe me."

"I'm sure if you just spoke with him, he would listen."

"Maybe," I said. I ran a hand over my face. "Look, I'm going to go ahead and make a visit right now anyway. You can stay if you want, but I'll essentially be sleeping so there won't be much to do."

"I'll give you privacy," Alastair offered. "Maybe I'll join Aydan and Gerridan."

"What are they up to today?"

"They're at the Grand Palace. Lady Hazelwren is there to discuss taxes on her village's wheat production with them and Solandis. It should take most of the afternoon."

"Right," I nodded. "Well, let me know if there's anything I can do. And tell Lady Reyna I said hello."

"I will. Be safe, Shaye."

"Always," I told him before finding a teacup. "I'll see you in a bit."

I was alone in the study. Of course. Ronan thought we weren't meeting today. He was likely taking some time with Brina or catching up on other things. He had hinted that some of his other work had been lacking. I toyed with his trinkets and ran my fingers along spines of books for a minute, waiting to see if he would walk in. Just when I was getting ready to return home, the door opened.

It wasn't Ronan, but Brina who stepped inside and slammed the door behind her. A thick, choking sob ripped from her and she had to steady herself on a table to avoid hitting her knees. I watched, fascinated and horrified as my mother cried thick, fat tears. I didn't know how to help her. As I stared, I realized I recognized her dress, of all things. It was flowy and purple, with glittering purple combs holding her hair back—

Ronan came flying through the door. Once it was locked behind him, he approached his wife and tentatively placed his hand on her back. She turned and pressed her face into his chest.

"I'm sorry," he murmured. "Brina, I'm so sorry." He kissed her hair and that was when he noticed I was in the room. His eyes widened and I mouthed *I'm sorry* to him. When I moved to leave I suddenly could not. The Thread would not release me.

"It's Alastair, Ronan. I can't even tell *Alastair* the truth. Though it's not as if there's much to tell— he seemed to already know your secrets—"

"Brina, I promise when this is over we will find a way—"

"Is it ever going to be over Ronan? You refuse to make a move. You've been planning and preparing for years and now you've come to a halt."

"This is delicate, darling, I cannot just walk in and—"

"Then drop it. Resign tomorrow and make good on your promise to take us away from court." Brina gripped the front of Ronan's shirt. He placed his hands around her own.

"I wish I could. But I must finish what's been started." His eyes were shiny and his face was etched with grief.

"Then finish it. Please, before it gets worse. Meet with the prince as soon as you can and get his help." Ronan nodded.

"Before the month is out. I promise."

"Thank you." Brina took a deep, shuddering breath. "I think I will go home and lie down." Ronan traced a knuckle along her cheek.

"That's a good idea. We'll have a quiet night... I'll be home shortly, I just need to finish up a couple of things here. And I'll make sure the stables know to give Alastair and his companions anything they might need," Ronan said. He let his other hand rest on Brina's belly. "I love you."

"Me too," she said. He bent down and brushed a kiss against his wife's lips before bidding her farewell. As soon as the door was shut, he turned on me.

"I told you to stay home today."

"I know, I'm sorry. I didn't mean to intrude. I've just..." I took a deep breath. "I've had a strange afternoon."

"You and me both," he said. He pulled out a chair from one of the tables and gestured for me to sit. I did, and he took the chair on the opposite side. A kettle, cups, saucers, and small pitchers appeared on the table. "I don't feel like teaching today."

"I don't much feel like learning." I reached for a cup and found that I could grasp it. "Things are not very pleasant at home, and I found myself wanting to be here instead. I'm sorry to have interrupted your day." Ronan poured dark tea into my cup.

"Don't worry yourself over it." He poured his own. "Is there anything I can do to help? You aren't being hurt, are you?"

"No, nothing like that." I watched as Ronan stirred milk and honey into his tea before passing the dishes to me. He looked at me politely, waiting to see if I would continue. I focused my attention on my teacup, stirring in my own milk and honey as I said, "My husband and I... We've grown distant. I— we— lost a pregnancy earlier this year. I'm afraid I've let it affect me for quite some time now." Ronan's face softened.

"I'm very sorry to hear that, Shaye."

"Thank you," I said. We each sipped our tea in silence for a few seconds before I sat my cup down on my saucer and looked at Ronan. My father. My teacher. This man who had no reason to give me the time of day and yet he took the time to teach me what he knows of his power, to help me master myself. This was not an evil man. So why, *why*, is he betraying his friend? What could the throne bring him that he did not already have? "Ronan—" I started, then paused. I had been so careful these months, to not hint what I knew of Ronan's plans for Zathryan. But maybe... could I change things? Could I change my parents' fate?

"What is it?" He asked, noticing the worry on my face.

"I know what you're planning, and I am begging you not to go through with it."

Confusion painted over his features. "I'm sorry?"

"I— I know that you intend to remove Zathryan from the throne and take his place. You must stop whatever plans you've already put in motion. This will not end well."

"Shaye, what in Ehnara's name are you talking about? I'm not— I would *never*—" He took a deep breath. "I am *not* trying to take the throne from Zathryan. He is the rightful King, and the best friend I have ever had— practically my brother. I pledged myself to the Crown's service at his coronation and stood witness at his wedding. I was the first to hold his children after he and his wife— I held him when his wife was killed. How could you think—" Realization washed over him, halting his rambling. "This is the reason House Redfern is no longer one of the great houses, isn't it? I am to be accused of treason?" I nodded.

"All I have ever been told of you is that you are a traitor." Ronan put his head in his hands.

"I must move quickly then and be more careful. No one else knows anything besides Brina and me. If I move her to one of my estates— maybe I can convince Knox to take her to Sylvanna—"

"What are you saying?" I asked. "If your plan is not to take Zathryan's throne then what is it?"

"I am trying to save his throne," Ronan said. "There are already plots in place against him— someone in his own court—" He let his hands ball into fists on the table. "I am not the first sorcerer to learn witchcraft." My eyes widened, and my hands gripped my teacup almost tight enough to shatter. "I grew suspicious of... someone. And when I confirmed their plans to myself I knew that I could not stand against them on my own, not without more power at my disposal. Not if I could not at least match them in a fight. I used to think there must be many of them, to be so organized, to have so much control— but in recent months, I have become convinced that it is just one who has taken up the craft." As he spoke, I remembered what he said to Brina, the first time I saw them together, back when I still thought I was mindwalking: *There are people. Here. With plots against Zathryan. They've utilized this knowledge already, in secret.* I thought at the time he had been lying to Brina, and I did not truly register what he said. But now— "If I attempted to uncover what I knew and could not defeat them, Medeisia would be left with no protection. I sought out the Children because their access to elemental magic seemed to be the best defense I could think of against the power I believe this person has obtained."

"...You don't want the throne for yourself?"

"No, Shaye, I never have. I have only wanted to save my friend."

"Why not tell the Cabinet? You are the Chief Advisor, you are not without your influences," I said.

"The Cabinet has been reduced to only myself and the Crown Princess. The extended council is of no use. I have contacted Zathryan's son, Prince Aydan. He is the only person who might be able to help me rally forces to take on this traitor. But I cannot ask in a letter, we have to meet in person—" Oh gods. Oh *gods*—

"That is why you've requested all these meetings with him?"

"Yes," he breathed. "Shaye, you must believe me."

"I do," I said. "I promise I do. But if you are to change things, you must be careful. Ronan, please, you must make sure you're not caught."

"I will. I should receive a response from the prince within the next day or two, and I will make quick work of what must happen next." Tears pricked behind my eyes, and I hoped that this wasn't a mistake.

"You're a good man, Ronan," I said. He reached out and squeezed my hand.

"That's all I've ever tried to be," he said. "Go home and rest awhile, Shaye. I'll see you tomorrow."

When I woke back in Lyra's quarters, Catchfly was curled into my side. I let my hand run over her smooth fur a few times before I sat up, realizing what I had done. Had anything changed? Would I even know if it had? I still only remembered a childhood with Gideon, being rescued by Aydan... Aydan. I needed to tell him about this. Distance between us be damned, he needed to know the reason behind those meetings. He needed to know about everything.

I did not think I had the strength to effuge to the Grand Palace, but luckily when I emerged from Lyra's room I could see from the light pouring through the windows that sunset was approaching. Aydan would be home by now, likely in his study organizing whatever notes he might have taken during his meetings today. I could hear pots and pans being stirred in the kitchen and knew that dinner approached. It had been so long since I'd seen Zale and Tory, I realized. I made a note to stop in the kitchen when I was through talking to Aydan and say hello to them. Isolde was setting plates on the table while Elise followed her with the silver. Both stopped briefly to curtsy as I passed, heading down the hallway toward Aydan's study.

I paused outside the door, standing there with my palm on the handle, and took a deep breath. It was time to tell the truth. I was ready to tell the truth. I was ready to have my husband back. I knocked and opened the door at the same time, saying as I stepped into the room, "My love, can I speak with you—" I stopped short.

All the air seemed to be sucked from my lungs as I beheld the scene in front of me:

Aydan, standing in his study, with Lady Reyna wrapped in his arms.

The King of Nautia

Part Three

I sat cross-legged on my bed with stacks of papers spread out around me. Most of the documents were Alastair's reports on his trips to Nautia, while others were reports from the treasury, correspondences from courts abroad, and anything else I might need to know for the council meeting tonight. Catchfly padded around the bed, occasionally stepping on my piles. I would shoo her, swatting gently at her feet so she would move, but then she'd be back again minutes later on another stack. Eventually I stopped paying her any attention and she sniffed at me before leaving the bed altogether to find a spot of sunshine to lie in.

I looked at the clock and saw that I only had another thirty minutes or so before I needed to get ready. Absorbing this information all at once was proving next to impossible. I had spent so much time focusing on my studies with Lyra that Cabinet documents had fallen to the wayside, and now I risked looking like an idiot in front of Declan and the council.

There was a knock at the door. Probably Alastair, coming to alert me of the time.

"Come in," I called as I shuffled through the treasury reports. When I didn't hear Al's heavy footfall enter the room, I looked up. Gerridan was standing in the doorway.

"Hello Shaye," he said. His voice was somber.

"Gerridan." I set the papers down. "What are you doing here?"

"I thought I'd check in on you before we meet with the council. We just arrived a few minutes ago."

"We?" I repeated, peering over Gerridan's shoulder and into the hallway.

"Me and Kenna," he clarified. "She's talking to Alastair. Hannele is home with Drystan. Ay—the King will arrive in a little while."

"You can say his name," I sighed. I made a show of picking up my paperwork and continuing to shuffle through it, in hopes that Gerridan would take that to mean I am busy and should not be disturbed. Instead, he continued to stand in the doorway, not saying anything.

"You've checked in on me," I said. "If there's nothing else you need to tell me then I'll see you—"

"When are you coming home? It's been over a month."

"I am home."

"Ayzelle is your capital, it is not your home," he insisted. He was right, but I certainly wouldn't be telling him that. Sleeping alone in Zathryan's former chambers these past weeks had been unsettling and lonely. "Shaye, Aydan's a wreck—"

"And how do you think I feel?" I snapped.

"If you would just talk to him..."

"I said everything I needed to say." A knot formed in my gut as the images flashed in my head. It had been weeks, but each night the scene played over and over in my head as I tried to fall asleep:

Aydan and Reyna both looked up and met my eyes as I gaped at them. Quickly, I shut the door and turned on my heel, rushing toward the sitting room, toward the front door. I needed to get outside—

"Shaye!" Aydan's voice called out from behind me. "Shaye, don't go—" Tears blurred my vision as I continued. I kept blinking, waiting to wake up gasping in bed, hoping that this was a dream. I walked right into an end table and stumbled forward, barely keeping myself upright before Aydan caught my hand. "Shaye, please—"

"No," I choked out, trying to pull my hand from his grip. He held on. "Let go."

"Just let me explain—"

"No. Let me go."

"I know that looked bad. I know you're angry—"

"Fuck you, Aydan," I spat through tears, trying once again to pull my hand out of his. He still did not let go, and continued pleading for me to stay, so

I began shoving his arm as hard as I could. My weakened physical state barely got a reaction out of him, but the panicked look in his eyes grew more desperate. "LET GO OF ME!"

Faster than I could blink, Alastair and Gerridan effuged into the room, each with a dagger drawn. Both had appeared, scanning the room for danger, for some intruder attacking their Queen, and instead found me sobbing, with Aydan still holding on to me and pleading for me to stay.

"If you'll just listen—"

Gerridan sheathed his dagger and approached us, placing his hand on Aydan's arm. "Aydan darling, you need to let go of her." As if woken from a trance, Aydan dropped his grip immediately and looked down at his hand.

"I'm sorry," he sputtered. "I didn't— I don't know—"

Alastair approached me, stepping between Aydan and I, keeping his back turned to his King. "What do you need?"

"I need to get out of here. I can't... I can't stay here." Aydan tried to move around Alastair, but Alastair simply stepped in front of him, keeping him blocked from my view.

"Then we're going," Alastair said. "Do you want to gather your things?"

"Shaye, it wasn't what it looked like," Aydan said from behind Alastair. Rage ran through my core upon hearing those words.

"Oh? And what did it look like, Aydan?" I snapped. White-hot anger boiled in my chest. "Because I know what it looked like to me." For the first time in months, fire roared uncontrolled out of my palms.

"What have you done?" Gerridan asked sharply.

"He was in there with Reyna," I said through tears and gritted teeth.

"It wasn't... my love you have to believe me, there was nothing happening—"

"Because I walked in."

"No, no that's not—"

"Do not try to convince me that I didn't see what was right in front of me—"

"We're going," Alastair said. He still stood between us, but it did little to calm our fight. "I'll come back for your things, Shaye." I nodded, still crying as he gripped my shoulder and effuged us to the King's Chambers in Ayzelle.

We landed in the parlor, and an inhuman sob tore from my throat. I buried my face in Alastair's chest and he patted my back, letting me cry until I was spent. He offered to help me to the bedroom but the thought of sleeping in the bed alone had been too much. Instead, I lay on the sofa and told Alastair what I had seen while he sat on the floor beside me. I cried again as I described seeing *the pair of them with so much emotion etched on their faces while they held each other, Aydan's arms wrapped tightly around Reyna's waist while hers looped around his neck. Alastair did not speak. He just listened and offered his hand for me to hold while I told the story.*

Eventually I fell asleep. I woke in the morning covered with a quilt from one of the bedrooms and Catchfly curled between my feet, apparently having arrived in the night.

Alastair had gone back for the rest of my belongings, as well as a sealed letter from Aydan. "I told him I would bring it. You don't have to read it," he said. I picked it up and tossed it in the fireplace, unopened.

"You'll have to speak to him eventually," Gerridan said. My mind returned to the present and I pursed my lips.

"I'm aware. I wasn't intending on giving him the silent treatment during a council meeting." The council had not been made aware of our living situation. Strife between anointed monarchs would not be well received.

"I meant beyond the council."

"There's a visit to Nautia coming up too." Alastair's apology had been accepted the week before, and he was now planning a good time to hold our third meeting with Gram.

"Stop with the sarcasm, Shaye," Gerridan snapped. "He never meant to hurt you."

"I know." I stood up from the bed, noticing the time once again. "I have to start getting ready."

"Will you please just hear him out?"

"I'll think about it," I said. Gerridan nodded, realizing that was the best answer he was going to get from me.

"I'll leave you to dress then," he said. Before walking out the door he added, "I miss you too, Shaye. We all do." Gerridan shut the door behind him, and I stood alone, blinking away new tears.

With minutes to spare, I arrived in the foyer of the King's Chambers wearing a deep red gown that fell off my shoulders, exposing much of my scarred back. My hair was held away from my face by pins adorned with black pearls in lieu of a tiara, but I didn't bother with any other jewelry, save for my wedding ring, which I had not been able to bring myself to remove.

I met Alastair in the foyer. He wore what he typically did for these meetings, a more formal version of the leather training clothes we normally donned in the ring. They were lighter and more comfortable than wearing armor, but still showed off his rank as Lord General. "You look nice," he said when I entered.

"Is *nice* really all you can muster?" Kenna said from where she stood. Alastair shrugged. "You look incredible," the seer told me.

"Well, thank you both, but I think I've made us run late so we should get going." Kenna had been here this morning, when she effuged Lyra into the King's Chambers to conduct my lessons. Alastair offered to move Lyra into the Chambers with us after we first arrived, but she had elected to stay close to Kenna rather than try to move her entire study across the country. So each morning the witch effuged to me and we continued expanding on what she and Ronan had taught me in the past months.

I had not used the Thread since the day I left Sylvanna. I was afraid of what I might find if I went back to Ronan's study. In the month since I had last seen him, I waited for something to change, and it did not. Everything I knew of Ronan's fate remained the same. His plans did not work.

"They'll be in the corridor outside the council chamber," Kenna informed me.

"That's fine."

"If you're uncomfortable we can do it without you," Alastair offered once more.

"I'm fine," I assured them. "We can get through one meeting. Let's go." I headed out the door and the pair of them followed quickly behind.

When we arrived at the council chamber, Aydan and Gerridan stood in the corridor, talking in low voices. They looked up upon hearing our footsteps, and I saw Aydan swallow as his breath hitched. He looked me up and down before swallowing again.

"Sorry we're late," I said, looking mostly to Gerridan. "I struggled with the pins," I added, gesturing to my hair.

"You look beautiful," Aydan blurted. I met his eyes, and my face grew hot.

"Thank you," I said quietly. Silence hung over us for a moment before Gerridan cleared his throat.

"Well," he said. "We should probably go in." I nodded and we all fell into rank.

Standing beside Aydan, I couldn't look over to him as I lifted my arm and placed it on top of his. As we walked inside, I hoped he couldn't feel my hand shaking.

The meeting was a disaster.

None of my studying had prepared me for what Lord Aren, the master of our treasury, brought to the table: ending discussions with Nautia altogether. Alastair had been the first to object, but we allowed the lord to speak before arguing too strongly. It seemed that the treasury was apprehensive of our negotiations and thought that Aydan's attachment to the Eternity Throne would cause him to offer up too many of our resources in exchange for an heirloom.

"You forget, Lord Aren, that the throne is not just some trinket from my childhood home," Aydan said. "And it is not all that we seek in our discussions with the mortal kingdom. We have explained many times that peace is our goal with the Nautians."

I remained quiet while various council members voiced their concerns, and Aydan or Gerridan responded with reasoning for why we should continue. Eventually Aren yielded and it was agreed upon that we would carry on, but it was clear that we had very little support from the council, and therefore the nobility in general. We left the council chambers with little hope that we would continue to have any support at all if the next visit to the Grand Palace went poorly.

We did not linger in the corridor. Alastair escorted me back to the King's Chambers while Kenna stayed with Gerridan and Aydan. I retreated straight to the bedroom and sat down in front of the vanity to start plucking the pins from my hair. When I'd nearly finished, there was a knock at the door.

"I'm fine, Alastair," I called out.

"It's me." Aydan's voice was muffled through the door. "Can I come in?"

I stood and took a few deep breaths before replying. "Yes."

He entered looking like he had not expected to get that far. Aydan shut the door behind him slowly, staring at me. After a moment of silence, he finally said, "Shaye, I can't tell you how sorry I am." When I didn't reply, he added, "I know it sounds ridiculous, but... nothing happened. Nothing was going to happen."

I nodded, keeping my eyes fixed on a spot on the floor, my arms crossed over my chest. "Is that all?"

"I'd like you to come home."

"I can't do that," I said.

"We can't fix this if we're living across the country from one another. Come home. Please."

"No." Anguish threatened to crumple Aydan's face. Silence hung in the air again, and then I added, "*We* don't need to fix this, Aydan. You do."

"And how do you expect me to do that if you won't be in the same room as me?"

"I don't know."

"What is it you want then? This— separation? Forever? There are no avenues for monarchs to divorce. Our oaths bound us magically, it's not just some frivolous thing we can walk back on—"

"I don't want a divorce Aydan, and don't start accusing me of not taking our oaths seriously. I didn't get us into this mess."

"I sought comfort from a friend because my wife was nowhere to be found," Aydan said.

"Oh, fuck off," I snapped. "If you're here to make this my fault then you can just go back to Sylvanna—"

"You've barely looked at me in months, Shaye," he continued. "You've been so wrapped up in whatever it is you do with Lyra that I can count on one hand how many times you've touched me in half a year."

"You're standing here telling me that I didn't walk in on anything more than a friendly hug, and yet you're also telling me it's all my fault because we haven't had sex as often as you want?"

"I'm not talking about— Shaye, you used to touch my hand when you walked past me in a room. Kiss me when you came home for the day. Let me hold you at night while we slept. But it's like you've built up this wall around yourself and no one is allowed inside. We promised to be partners in everything, but you haven't let me."

"You can sit there and list off all the ways I've broken our promises, and maybe you're right, but I wasn't the first one to do it," I said, staring at the ground again.

"What are you talking about?"

"When I lost…" The words stuck in my throat. "When I lost the baby, your first concern was making sure no one knew what a disappointment I was." He blinked at me. "You saw that I wasn't dying and then you hurried off with Gerridan to pay off the healers and keep our dirty little secret from getting out. You kept saying you'd take care of it. That it would be like it never happened."

"Shaye, I never thought you were a disappointment," Aydan said quietly. "I thought that keeping things quiet would make it easier for you. Court has already given you enough grief for being a Redfern, I didn't want rumors flying about your ability to produce heirs—"

"*My* ability to produce heirs? Or yours?" He stared at me. "Your parents struggled for nearly a century before conceiving you and Irsa… how would that make House Aevitarus look to the court, to find that a second generation is struggling to produce heirs?"

Aydan was quiet again. He bit the inside of his cheek. "I'm sorry that I made such an awful moment worse for you. I thought I was doing what was best, but it's clear that I was wrong." More silence. I didn't know what to say anymore. Our conversation wasn't going anywhere. I started to open my mouth to say just that when Aydan said, "Just know Shaye, that no matter how you feel about me now, I love you. I always will."

"Gods, Aydan." I shook my head. "I didn't leave because I stopped loving you." I stepped forward, and before I realized I was doing it, I kissed him.

When I pulled away, surprise was written on Aydan's face. He swallowed, and then took my face in his hands and kissed me back. I let him, deepening the kiss until my hands began searching for the hem of his shirt. I found it and pulled it over his head, revealing his bare chest. Aydan turned me around. He began loosening the laces on the back of my dress, pressing kisses to my neck as he did so.

When the mass of red fell off my body, Aydan scooped me up and carried me to the bed. He lay me down on top of the blankets and wasted no time in going to work between my legs. I gripped my hands in his hair and cried out as he brought me just to the edge before rising and slamming into me, sending me over completely. He kept going, gripping my leg, kneading into my backside as he thrusted, sending me over again before he finished too, spilling into me while he buried his face into my neck.

He rolled off of me and we lay there, chests heaving, with nothing but the sound of our breath surrounding us.

"That was nice," I said, breaking the silence. Aydan took the hint.

"I suppose I should be going now," he said with his eyes still closed.

"That's probably a good idea."

"Of course." He clenched his jaw and stood up from the bed before reaching for his discarded clothes.

"I'm just not ready," I said. "I need more time."

"Take all the time you need," he said stiffly as he pulled his shirt back over his head. "I'll be waiting when you're ready." He fastened his pants and laced up his boots in silence. When he finished, he approached me and kissed my hand. "Goodbye Shaye."

"I do love you, Aydan," I told him.

"I love you too." And then he was gone. I sunk down into the sheets and waited for sleep to take me. It never did.

Chapter
Twenty-Six

Aydan and I tried to speak twice more in person over the next few weeks. Each time we devolved into an argument and left feeling more frustrated than ever. He held firm to his story that he was discussing personal matters with Lady Reyna, and that upon seeing him so distraught she hugged him, right when I walked into the room. The emotion on their faces, according to him, was from their discussion about me, and not anything to do with each other. She was just a friend, offering her comfort to someone she cared for.

The thing was, now that the shock had worn off, I believed him. I believed every word of it, but it did not shake the sense of betrayal that filled my chest every time I saw him. Not because I truly thought Aydan was being unfaithful to me, but because he had sought comfort and advice from the one person who he knew could make me doubt him. I wanted to overcome my jealousy of Lady Reyna, but the thing inside of me that still told me I was not fit to be Aydan's wife, not fit to be a Queen, anointed or otherwise— it was all rooted in her. He knew what seeing them together like that would make me think and feel if I saw it, and he did it anyway.

The day after our second conversation, which led to me screaming at Aydan to get the hell out of the King's Chambers, I sat at lunch with Kenna, Lyra, and Alastair. Alice and Amelia, two of the Ayzellen servants that I liked, had been tending to us while we stayed in the chambers. They'd dropped off lunch and quickly left to finish cleaning another part of the dwelling and try not to appear as if they were eavesdropping, which they most certainly were. With a wave of my hand, I shut the dining room doors behind them from where I sat.

"I'm going to use the Thread today," I announced. Kenna nearly choked on the bite of bread she had just taken.

"Are you sure that's a good idea?" Alastair asked. I nodded.

"I know I'm still a bit frail, but I need to check in on him. I need to make sure he's still... there. And if he is, maybe get some more answers about who exactly he's fighting." I had told them all what Ronan and I discussed, what I had learned of his true plans. Alastair was reluctant to believe me, but trusted me enough to accept what I said.

"I have to return to Sylvanna after we're finished," Kenna said. "We have preparations to make for the Nautia visit."

"I have to prepare as well," Alastair added. "The council wants an updated explanation of the safety measures we'll be taking."

"I'll stay with her," Lyra said to them both.

"I don't need a nanny," I said.

"Well, I need something to do so I'll be nannying for as long as you're with Ronan today." I rolled my eyes.

"Fine, do what you want. We'll set up after lunch."

Ronan looked terrible when I arrived in his study. He was pale, with dark circles around his eyes and looked as if he had not slept in days. He startled when he saw me.

"Shaye," he breathed. "It's been nearly two months. I thought..."

"It's been almost the same for me. More trouble at home. I needed time, and I thought you'd be away meeting with the prince anyway." He nodded.

"I see. That did not go as planned," he said. "The prince has been unable to meet with me, despite my urging at its importance."

"Then you need to come up with something else," I said sharply. "Find another way, find someone else to tell."

"There is no one else."

"Appeal directly to Solandis," I said.

"She will not receive my letters. I've tried—"

"Then tell the fucking King himself," I snapped. "At least *try*—"

"Do you think I am not trying?" He threw his arms out, exasperation painting his face. "Shaye, I sought out a coven and

215

learned forbidden magic so that I could *try* to have a fighting chance against this threat. I am doing my best—"

"Do better. Your family deserves more than this outcome." Ronan scoffed.

"I am sorry that you do not get the privilege and money that once came with the Redfern name, but—"

"I am not talking about our House, I am talking about your wife and your child, Ronan! They deserve more than this."

"Do you think I don't know that? My child will arrive in a matter of weeks, and I am here, studying, practicing, trying to give myself any edge I can. But I don't think I can do it alone, Shaye." Ronan's voice cracked.

"Ronan," I said, my own voice breaking. "Take Brina and leave Ayzelle. Tonight. Go to Sylvanna, go to the Grand Palace and tell them yourself what is happening. I'm begging you." He just stared at me, defeated. "Ronan, I— I lied to you. Or, you believed things about me and I let you make assumptions, because I thought it would be better that way."

"What are you—"

"I'm not some distant descendant of yours. You assumed it, and I never corrected you. I'm sorry." Tears welled in my eyes and before I could stop myself, I blurted, "Ronan, I'm your daughter."

Any remaining color left Ronan's face. "How…"

"That's why no one knew how to manage my powers. I am the first born witch. I inherited everything you learned from the Children as I did your sorcery. That's why the Thread brought me to you so easily. I am yours and Brina's daughter."

Ronan's breathing was ragged. "You said your parents were dead. That you were raised in the mortal kingdom and kept from your heritage."

"I was." The tears spilled over. "If you continue on your path the way you have, you will never fight your enemy. You will not defeat them. You are going to be caught practicing witchcraft, and you will be tried for treason."

Ronan's eyes were shining now. "What happened to Brina?"

"It doesn't matter. You still have time to change it. Please, just change it, Ronan. I want to know you. I want to have been raised by my parents. Just— just change it, please," I begged, fully crying now. "Take a chance and tell Zathryan, or Irsa about this threat. Tell Declan or Dracus. Make an announcement in the Great Hall for all

I care, just stop letting it be a secret. Whoever it is, whatever you know, will remain in the dark. The knowledge will be lost with you."

A loud knock sounded on the door, and both our heads snapped toward it. Ronan wiped at his face, trying to collect himself. "That'll be Brina," he murmured. I stood against the back wall as I usually did when she arrived. As Ronan reached for the handle, I spotted his jarred storm on the bookshelf turning black as lightning crackled within it. He opened the door, then immediately attempted to slam it shut again. I watched as a slender brown hand curled its fingers around the edge of the door and pushed back against him.

Princess Irsa managed to shove Ronan aside and step into his study, looking around at the shelves, her face smug. "Well, well," she said sarcastically, "This is quite the cozy setup."

"Your Highness, I must ask you to leave."

"Oh, no, I won't be doing that," she smiled sweetly. "Not until I get what I'm looking for."

"And what might that be?"

"I think you know," she said, dragging her fingers along the spines of the books. "Then again, you know so many things, Lord Ronan, that I wonder how you can keep it all straight."

"I don't know what you mean," my father said. "But this is my private study—"

"On my father's property. Which means it's *my* property if I wait long enough." She chuckled. "And I have all the time in the world." Irsa moved to stand in front of Ronan, and she placed her hand on his chest, dragging her fingers upward until she traced up his neck and brushed them along his hair. "I know you know my secrets, Lord Ronan," she whispered. "I know what you've been up to in here."

"I don't—"

"You think I am so *wrong* and so *bad* for working to remove my father from his throne," she said, keeping her hand in his hair. "But you don't even know the half of it."

"Why don't you tell me?" Ronan let a fake smirk form on his face.

"Where's the fun in that?"

"Princess, please—"

"Oh I *love* when you call me Princess—"

"Stop." He stepped out of Irsa's touch. "Why are you doing all of this? You're next in line to the throne. All you have to do is wait long enough and it's yours. Why go through all the trouble of getting covens involved? Why hurt your father this way?"

"Because I can," she grinned. "Oh, my lord, I have so much to tell you." She placed both her palms on my father's chest this time and I felt my own hands grow hot. "We could be unstoppable, if you joined me." One of her hands traveled downward, toward the waist of his pants. He caught her wrist.

"I am not interested in your plans, or your advances," Ronan said firmly, dropping her hand and stepping back. "I am loyal to your father, and to my wife."

"Noble Ronan Redfern, blindly faithful to an old man and a *mortal*," Irsa mocked. She reached again for his face, and yet again he caught her wrist.

"Yes, I am. And if you think for one second I will let you get away with these plots against your father—"

"I already have."

"*Irsa*—"

"I thought I'd stop in and give you a chance to put your hard work to good use, and if I was lucky, you might fulfill a fantasy or two for me." She winked, and Ronan looked like he might be sick. Irsa sighed dramatically. "But alas, you've disappointed me yet again. I suppose I'll have to meet with my father and the King's Guard and tell them—" she forced herself to take a few ragged, gulping breaths, and suddenly tears welled in her eyes. Her voice shook as she brought her hand to her mouth and whispered, "—and then I found him in his study... practicing *witchcraft*. I am so sorry to be so emotional, I don't— it was just so *awful*—" She stopped and straightened herself. "Oh, wait, of course." She laughed. "I've already done that." She snapped her fingers.

The door burst from its hinges, and before Ronan could react, he'd been tackled to the ground. The guards slapped silver cuffs on his wrists before dragging him back up to his feet. My father's eyes were wild, glaring at Irsa as she sobbed quietly into a handkerchief. "It didn't have to be this way, my lord," she choked.

"Come along, Lord Redfern," the guard holding him grunted. "Don't make it harder than it has to be."

"My wife— where is my wife?" Ronan asked. When no one answered, he barked, "*Where is Lady Redfern?*"

"She will not be harmed, Lord Ronan," another guard said. "Let's get moving."

Ronan shot one last look in my direction. We locked eyes for just a few seconds, and then I was gone.

Chapter
Twenty-Seven

I gasped as I sat up straight, ripped from my visit to Ronan's study.

"Hey," Lyra said, coming to my side immediately and placing her hand on my back as I began to cry. "Hey, it's alright. You're safe. You're at home—"

"It was Irsa," I choked out between the tears. "Irsa was the one plotting against Zathryan. She intended to stage a coup and remove him from the throne."

"The Crown Princess?" I nodded. Lyra's eyes widened. "Then that means…"

"We need to speak to Aydan."

An hour later, Lyra and I sat across from Aydan in front of our bedroom fireplace in Sylvanna. His hands were clasped together with his chin resting upon them, listening quietly as I told him everything about my lessons with Lyra, then with Ronan, and what I had learned about his family.

"…you see, the only reason Ronan sought out the Children to begin with, was in an attempt to gain enough power to match Irsa. He couldn't expose her and risk a fight that she would win, and succeed in her coup against your father, without first being able to ensure your father's protection. She found out and exposed his connection to the Children and framed him for conspiracy against the Crown."

Aydan was silent for a long moment, and then said quietly, "So you're telling me that the Crown Princess of Medeisia was plotting to overthrow the King, before framing the Chief Advisor and having him executed. And that you saw all this while in a... *trance* under Lyra's supervision?"

"I... yes, I suppose that's what I'm saying. Yes."

"I see." Another long pause, and then, "Gerridan."

In an instant our friend was walking through the bedroom door, a quizzical look on his face when he saw the three of us together. "You called?"

Aydan looked me in the eyes, while a deep sadness swam in his own, before answering with lethal calm, "Take Lyra into the Crown's custody. She is under arrest."

Dread took root in my chest. Ice formed around my hands, and I leapt to my feet. "No. You will do no such thing Gerridan—"

"Gerridan," Aydan said firmly, now standing as well. "The witch has corrupted your Queen. Take her into custody—"

"She has done *nothing*—"

"—where she will await trial for crimes against the Crown."

Gerridan looked back and forth between us. Bound by oath to follow both of our orders, my dear friend surely never anticipated such division between us. I met his gaze and pleaded with my eyes. He looked apologetic as he moved toward us anyway. "Gerridan, please."

"Lyra, come with me."

Lyra, though ashen, did not plead, or cry, or even tremble. I threw my arm out in front of her as she moved to step forward.

"*No,*" I said again. Aydan took a step toward me.

"My love, if you don't stand aside, I will have to move you myself."

"Aydan," I choked. "I know— I *know* it seems impossible; I know things have been difficult between us the past few months—"

"Because we've given a witch, who was once in charge of your imprisonment, free access to your mind every day for months. Who knows what else she has planted, what memories she has created and erased within you—"

"That is not what happened—it's— oh if you would just *listen*—"

"I spent the last hour listening to your tale, which I will remind you involved the defense of a known traitor and the slander of my dead sister, without interruption. Irsa and I had our problems but to accuse her of treason is outrageous." My husband turned his attention back to Gerridan. "Go ahead."

I stepped between Lyra and Gerridan, giving the advisor and Aydan one last pleading look. "Don't make me do this."

"Place the witch under arrest—" Gerridan stepped forward while Aydan reached to take me by the arm.

"*Alastair!*" I called out.

In no more than a few seconds, Alastair was storming into the bedroom, sword already half drawn, eyes darting around at the scene before him. "What is this?"

"Al, I—" I met Aydan's gaze once again. One last hope that it hadn't really come to this. "I wish to invoke the Queen's Guard," I said. "Protect Lyra at all costs."

Alastair blinked slowly, just once, before turning to face Gerridan. The men reluctantly, horribly, both drew their swords completely.

"Is she worth this?" Aydan snapped at me. "The Crown pitted against itself, our Cabinet at each other's throats?"

"The truth is." I swallowed. "Alastair, I ask that you use violence only as an absolute last resort, to defend yourself or Lyra from harm." The general nodded, taking a step between me and his friends. "Please remove Lyra from the house and take her somewhere safe." Aydan clenched his jaw but did not order Gerridan forward as Alastair reached his hand back. Still silent, Lyra grasped it and the pair disappeared, effuging to anywhere but here.

Now it was just me facing Gerridan and Aydan in my bedroom, while my mind raced through the options of what might be next. I prepared myself to hear Aydan give the order for my arrest, for Gerridan to step forward and lock me in a room for my own protection.

"Leave us, Gerridan," Aydan said instead.

"Aydan, I—"

"I'd like a word with my wife," he said calmly. "Go home to your family. We'll see you in the morning." Gerridan hesitated but bowed to each of us anyway before effuging from the room as Alastair had done. Aydan stared at the spot where he had been standing for a moment before turning his attention to me. "You lifted my wards."

"Just enough to effuge," I said before snapping them shut again. "I didn't think you'd let Alastair and Lyra walk out of here without a fight, and that's the last thing I wanted."

"Clever." Aydan sat back down in his armchair and reached for a bottle of liquor that sat on the table between us. I returned to my chair as well, watching while he poured two glasses and floated one of them into my hand before draining his own and refilling it. I knocked back the contents of my glass as well, attempting to shake my nerves. I watched while Aydan poured and drained two more servings of the alcohol before he simply held the glass in one hand and traced the rim with the other. "How did we get here, Shaye?"

"I don't know anymore," I admitted. "But I know that everything I've told you tonight is the truth. I'm begging you to believe me."

"I believe… I believe that you believe what you've been told. I believe you've been fed a very convincing story. Your whole life here has had the shadow of your father's crimes lingering over you and I can imagine wanting to believe that he was not a villain after all."

"Nothing I say will convince you, will it?"

"There is nothing to be convinced of. The truth is what it is," he said flatly. "You've admitted to letting the witch have free reign of you in an unconscious state for months now. I mean, just *look* at yourself Shaye. You're not well."

"And you're looking for anyone to blame for it," I replied.

"Who else is there to blame, besides the two of you?" Aydan said. "Do you know what these months have done to me? Watching you waste away before my eyes? After… after the baby, I expected it would take some time… before you were back to your normal self. But this—Why do you think Reyna was in my study that day? I've been preparing to wake up one morning and find you dead beside me, and she's the only friend I have with experience losing the only person they've ever loved."

"You don't get to spin this as me stepping out of our marriage in favor of the craft— there is one way to master these powers, and one way only. You agreed to me learning from the beginning—"

"*It was supposed to make you better!*" He shouted, slamming his glass down on the table so hard it nearly cracked. "Before the witch came along, it seemed every other week you were collapsing due to an outburst of magic. I finally agreed to you learning because I thought it was the only way to ensure that your powers didn't kill you. Yet here we are, worse off than before. You *did* set our marriage aside in favor of the craft, you've set *everything* aside. You haven't been to a council meeting in weeks. Are you even aware that we return to Nautia tomorrow?" He rubbed a hand over his face, and his voice grew softer. "I can't stand to see you this way. It feels like living with a ghost. You haunt me, Shaye, with the memory of a wife I barely had."

I stared at my too-thin hands, clasped together in my lap. "I don't plan on dying any time soon."

"No one ever does, my love."

I stood and crossed the space between us while he moved to grab his drink. Before he could take a sip, I took the glass from him and set it down on the table. I took his hand in my own, and he did not pull away. Instead, Aydan's other hand gripped itself into my skirts and he pulled me into his lap, where I wrapped my arms around him and buried my face into the crook of his neck. His arms held me tightly at the waist. It didn't take long to feel teardrops falling on the top of my head and rolling down the back of my neck, while my own tears dampened his shirt.

We remained like that for hours, holding one another, afraid of what we may have to face if we let go too soon. I didn't know if either of us ever fell asleep, but before long, the gray glow of morning came peeking through the curtains and it was time to set out for Nautia.

Chapter

Twenty-Eight

We had already parted and begun our preparations by the time Elise's tentative knock sounded. Aydan was bathing, so I bid her to enter.

"Your Majesty, is everything alright?" she asked, poking her head through the bedroom door. She looked surprised to see me there.

"I... Yes, everything is fine Elise, thank you. I'm happy to dress myself this morning, but the King and I could both use a strong cup of tea if you wouldn't mind bringing a tray."

"Well— of course I will, Your Majesty, but— did you know the Chief Advisor and Lord General are both asleep in the hallway?"

"What?" I stepped out of the bedroom to see Gerridan and Alastair sat against the wall, the former sleeping with his head on the latter's shoulder. Alastair began to stir. I sighed. "Go ahead and have tea delivered to their rooms as well. Thank you, Elise."

"Your Majesty." Elise curtsied and disappeared.

Alastair's eyes opened fully, and upon seeing me stand before him he shot to his feet, nudging Gerridan awake as he did so. Gerridan shook off sleep as he stood as well, both men looking at me expectantly. Finally, Alastair said, "Are you going to explain what the hell happened last night? Are you all right?"

"I'm fine. Aydan's fine." I looked to Gerridan apologetically. "I'm sorry to put you in the middle of us like that. Aydan's in the bathtub if you want to speak with him."

Gerridan sighed. "I'm sorry it came to that— whatever happened." I just nodded, knowing my voice would break if I spoke.

Gerridan squeezed my arm before walking past me into my bedroom, shutting the door behind him.

"Well?" Alastair asked once we were alone.

"Where is Lyra?"

"In the care of Knox Redfern."

"Good." I nodded. Alastair continued to stare at me until I began to tell him all I had learned the night before. "... Aydan now believes that Lyra has corrupted my mind through our lessons— He believes Lyra to be responsible for my physical condition. He thinks I'm dying, wasting away in front of him."

"Your looks certainly aren't doing you any favors," Alastair replied, looking me up and down. I hit his arm. "But— you're sure? It was truly Irsa?"

"Yes. I watched her taunt him. She was trying to seduce him into silence and bring him to her side, but..." I paused, unsure how insane this would make me sound. "He loves my mother. He loves Zathryan. He'd never betray either of them."

"But... what is there to be done, Shaye? They're already gone. All of them. What good does it do to drag this out and pit the Crown against itself?"

"My father gave his life trying to protect the Crown, and the people of this kingdom. My mother gave her life trying to protect me. It would be an insult to their legacy to allow this lie to continue. The truth still matters, Alastair. People deserve to know it, and my family deserves to have its good name back." He nodded somewhat reluctantly before loosing a breath.

"So what next?"

"Go get yourself ready for the Nautia visit. I'll effuge with Aydan and the others, you stop at Knox's to fetch Lyra. I would prefer to have her at my side while I'm outside of Medeisia just in case the King's Guard is looking for her. I will still require her protection via the Queen's Guard," I told him. "You'd better fill Kenna in on everything as well. I'm sure she's upset that Lyra didn't come to bed last night."

Alastair pulled his watch from his pocket and glanced at the time. "We'd better get moving if we don't want to be late. I need to freshen up."

Elise returned to the hallway carrying the tea service tray and passed by me and Alastair, stopping briefly to curtsy. I bid Alastair farewell and thanked him before following Elise inside.

Chapter
Twenty-Nine

A couple of hours later I was nearly dressed.

I'd returned to my bedroom and dismissed Elise, pouring tea for Aydan myself and setting it on the table by the fireplace. He and Gerridan were speaking in hushed tones when I entered, and the Chief Advisor was quickly dismissed. His eyes swam with pity as he bowed his head in my direction before leaving the room. Aydan's tale of events must have made me out to be quite the victim. My husband briefly met my gaze. He didn't say anything as he crossed the room to drink his tea while I made my way to the bathroom.

After a bath and cleaning my teeth, I selected a gown. As I had done for all the other visits to the mortal kingdom, I wore black. This one had a bodice made of feathers and a skirt that glittered at every catch of light. The material hissed when it dragged across the stone floors of our bedroom. I pinned my hair up on top of my head in a style simple enough to manage on my own before placing the black and white diamond tiara in front of it.

It was when I stood to finish lacing the back of my dress that Aydan finally came to my vanity. I struggled to reach behind my back and fumbled with the ribbon, trying to pull it tight enough to stay on my body but not so tight that the ribbon tore. Though my body had begun to fill out again when I stopped using the Thread so often, I was still so much thinner than I used to be that I knew I would soon need to request alterations on all my clothing.

"May I help?" Aydan approached me and gestured like he wanted to apply a glamour.

"I don't see why not," I replied. He waved the hand he gestured with and immediately I felt the effects of a glamour fall over me. I looked in the mirror and saw that my face and chest had filled back out. Muscles appeared where they once were along my shoulders and arms. My bones were no longer the center of attention. Once the glamour was complete, Aydan began to untie, then re-lace the back of the dress. When he finished, I thanked him.

"Happy to help," he said, then bent down and pressed a swift kiss to the top of my head before returning to silence.

We arrived at the open gates to the Grand Palace that afternoon as we had with every previous visit to the former capital. Aydan and I stood side by side, and my hand rested formally atop his. Gerridan accompanied us, while Alastair went to fetch Lyra. They arrived in Nautia seconds after we did, to my surprise, with Kenna in tow. Both Gerridan and Aydan's faces hardened, but the pair did not look at or otherwise acknowledge the new arrivals as they fell into rank behind us.

"What is this," I said flatly under my breath as Alastair approached my side.

"New recruit. I told Kenna what happened, and she has demanded I let her join the Queen's Guard."

"Thanks for filling me in, by the way," Kenna hissed from behind me.

"There wasn't exactly time to announce the issue to the household," I replied. "Everyone is safe— and there's no need for you to join my guard. Let's just get through this meeting." I didn't look at her, or at Lyra, who remained silent at the rear of our party. Before Kenna could respond, we were bid to enter the grounds of the Grand Palace by the mortal guards.

The guards led us through the doors, but rather than take us to the council room we had always met the Prince Regent in, they led us past the corridor and toward a large, ornately carved door that, in Sylvanna, led to the Great Hall. I slid my gaze to Aydan, who seemed to be confused, then to Alastair, whose hand now rested at his hip, fingers grazing the hilt of his shortsword. It seemed my Cabinet was stuck in a place between confusion and vigilance as we continued stepping forward toward the door and silently prepared for what we might face when we entered the room before us, while doing our best not to tip off the guards.

However, when we stepped through the door, we were not met with anything but what appeared to be an empty throne room. Aydan's breath hitched, and we stopped a few paces in while the door shut firmly behind us. His eyes were glued to what sat upon the dais on the other end of the room.

"Is that…" I started. Aydan nodded.

The Eternity Throne hummed with power. Having gained access to the powers of House Aevitarus at my coronation, I felt what Aydan no doubt was feeling as well: an ancient pull, a vibrating in my blood that bid me forward to claim the inheritance that so rightfully belonged to our House. The King's seat of power was not particularly ornate, despite being made of solid gold. The true power of the Eternity Throne lay in the magic that lived within it, and all it represented to sorcerers the world over.

It had not been more than a couple of minutes when a door beside the dais opened, and in strode Prince Gram, looking flustered and glistening with sweat.

"I cannot begin to apologize enough, Your Majesties. It was not my intention for you to be blindsided like this, but His Majesty King Callum elected to hold today's meeting in the throne room, and my objections were unfortunately not taken into account."

"They weren't?" Alastair blurted with a familiarity he hadn't used with Gram in front of the rest of us before.

"No. They weren't." Gram sighed. "The King's eighteenth birthday was three days ago. I am no longer Regent of Nautia, and it seems I am to be pushed out of the council altogether."

"Your Highness, should I be concerned about the safety of my Cabinet today?" Aydan asked plainly. "It does not bring me any comfort that we weren't informed of your removal, or the change of location—"

"I have no reason to believe that there is anything to worry about," Gram assured him. "My nephew is simply throwing his weight around with me. He's angry that I held what he deems to have been too much power over the past few years, and now he wants to show me who is in charge. He understands the historic nature of this exchange, and he is just as eager as me to move forward with an alliance. As far as a lack of communication, I'm afraid there has been so much happening that needed my attention that it simply slipped my mind."

I looked around to my friends and I could feel them preparing their defenses for what may come next but kept their composure in front of the prince.

"Should we expect King Callum soon?" I asked after a moment of silence.

"He should be here any moment," Gram said, looking around the room before pulling a watch from his pocket and glancing at the time. "He had a council meeting to complete before joining us here."

"And he has allowed you to remain for these discussions?"

"Yes, given my history of correspondence with your Lord General, and what has been a good working relationship between myself and Your Majesties so far, His Majesty thought it would be beneficial for me to attend today—" Gram replied.

"My apologies, Majesties, for my tardiness," Callum's voice boomed from the door behind us. He entered with no guard, only flanked by a pair of witches who walked several paces behind him. "I'm afraid my previous engagement could not be put off any longer. I *do* hope we haven't offended you with lateness or locale." He smirked at the last word, as if knowing the call that the throne was sending out to Aydan and me.

"No offense at all," Aydan replied with a charming, diplomatic warmth, "Only embarrassment that we were not made aware of your birthday, so the Crown could have presented you with a gift."

Callum waved my husband off. "No need. I've been gifted with all I require." I thought he might be making a dig about the Nautian Crown, or the Eternity Throne, but I glanced at Gram, whose face was painted with confusion, and I knew that couldn't be what he was saying. The boy-king gestured to his witches, who began to mutter quietly, and soon enough a long table and enough chairs for all present appeared. "Shall we begin?"

Chapter Thirty

The meeting dragged.

Callum allowed Gram to remain present for the discussion but was clearly only doing so to placate us. Gram's input was brushed aside or ignored at every opportunity— the young King was indeed attempting to reclaim his power. His witches, who joined us at the table, contributed nothing to the conversation, but stared at my Cabinet from the moment we all sat down, giving us all a sense of unease.

Callum and Gram both shot down the idea of fully reintegrating Medeisian and Nautian cultures at our previous meeting, so Gerridan started with the return of artifacts belonging to House Aevitarus. The Eternity Throne was of course at the top of the list, followed by heirlooms belonging to Queen Euna and a cache of weapons that had belonged to Medeisian royalty long before House Aevitarus had even taken the throne.

"So you'd like me to give up a fortune of gold and weapons? Not likely." Callum smirked.

"Your Majesty, the return of these artifacts— which I will remind you have no use to mortals outside of monetary value— would be compensated with an economic boost that your kingdom has not seen since its formation," Gerridan insisted. Gram slid his gaze to his nephew and saw what I did: an aloof, lazy grin plastered on his face.

"Your Majesty, it would not hurt to hear what they have to offer in exchange for these trinkets." Callum rolled his eyes and gestured for Gerridan to continue. I wanted to slap him.

Gerridan cleared his throat. "In exchange for the return of the Eternity Throne and other Medeisian artifacts, the Crown would be willing to allow Nautia to trade within our borders. You would be allowed to establish trade in all of our territories including Xarynn, which would of course open the possibility for imports from Auperene, Keotis, and Sewyth if you so desired." Gram's eyes widened and he bent his head low in Callum's direction.

"Nephew," I heard him murmur, "This is a very generous offer. The potential revenue would more than make up for the loss of gold from returning—"

"Quiet, uncle." King Callum fixed his attention on us. "It *is*, as my uncle says, quite a generous offer. However, due to our need for protection since the revolution, we have had wards at all of our borders— which you well know. Our former routes to your territories haven't been touched since the wards went up. They are grown over, eroded, or have been flat out destroyed in the last century. So, you may allow us to trade all we want but it will take decades to reestablish those routes—"

"If I may," Aydan cut in, "That problem was considered as well. The Crown would be willing to offer Nautia a grant of up to half a million in gold for the purpose of updating or rebuilding former routes. We can also offer the assistance of our builders' magic, if you think Nautian workers would be willing to work alongside sorcerers." I nearly gaped at him. Had this number been discussed, and I'd missed it? Callum seemed to be mulling the information over when a guard entered the throne room.

We watched as the guard approached his King, leaned down and whispered something in his ear.

"Good, send her in," Callum nodded. He glanced toward us while his guard turned to follow orders. "We'll have to table this discussion for now. The reason for my tardiness has arrived."

Gram looked panicked. "Callum, what are you talking about? This is the best offer you will ever receive in hopes for an economic future for this kingdom, in exchange for a chair that means nothing to us. Sit down and—"

"Uncle, I will remind you again that you are no longer my Regent. You remain my only heir for the time being, so I won't have you hanged for your insolence yet but give me an order one more time and you'll spend the next year shivering in the dungeons." Gram blanched at Callum's words. "Now, if you'll excuse me, I will return momentarily with a surprise. Perhaps she can give some insight to these offers from Medeisia." Callum left the table, following his guard with a smooth stride toward a door on the other end of the room.

"I cannot begin to apologize enough—" Gram started, but the door opened, and our attention turned to the person who entered.

We all fell silent. The only sound to be heard was the clicking of heeled shoes on the shining stone floors, followed by the light swishing noise of skirts brushing along behind. As the woman who now approached, clinging to Callum's arm, came into clearer view, Aydan leapt to his feet, nearly knocking his chair over and looking as though he might be sick.

"Uncle, ladies," Callum started, nodding in the direction of the witches who sat at the table beside him, then looked to us, "And of course our honored guests from abroad, the secret is out. I'd like to present my wife, fresh from her coronation: Gwendolyn, the first anointed Queen of Nautia."

Loose sparks shot off from my fingertips as I stood to join Aydan, staring in disbelief at the sickly-sweet smile of Irsa Aevitarus.

"Callum, you can*not* be serious," Gram started in frustration, turning his attention to the pair of them. "To allow Lady Gwendolyn to be a distraction to you is one thing but to *marry her*?"

"Her Majesty, Queen Gwendolyn— as you will refer to her henceforth, uncle— has been approved by my council, over which you no longer preside." Gram gaped at him.

"The people will not allow themselves to be ruled by a witch, Callum. We are *mortals*. Their magic stops them from aging— you *know* this. If you have had her anointed as you say... she will outlive you, and rule alone. Nautia will not stand for this," the prince said.

"It sounds," Callum drawled, "Like you are saying that *you* will not stand for it, uncle. I'm sure you don't need to be reminded that to openly defy the anointed monarchs is an act of treason." Gram did not reply, and instead averted his eyes to the floor, fuming.

Every member of my Cabinet was now on their feet. The words exchanged between Callum and Gram had reached my ears, but I did not linger on them. None of us took our eyes off Irsa, who continued smiling at us— a taunting grin, waiting to see what we would do. Aydan just kept blinking, sweat now covering his brow. Gerridan, Alastair, and Kenna all had their hands hovering at their hips, ready to draw blades if necessary. Lyra seemed to understand that something was very wrong and had begun muttering spells under her breath. I felt layers of protection beginning to coat all of us and prayed it would be enough to get my family out of here safely.

"Irsa..." Aydan breathed after moments of staring. "Irsa, I don't... I don't understand..."

"It was truly agony to have to wait so long," Callum spoke over the top of us as if he hadn't heard Aydan. "As Regent, my uncle would not allow me to marry. He claimed it would be inappropriate, as I was not of age. He also believed that a witch as powerful as my Gwendolyn couldn't possibly return my affections—"

"Stop talking," Irsa said sweetly. Callum's mouth immediately snapped shut, and he stared ahead with a glazed over, contented look, as if he had not just been mid-sentence.

"What is happening here?" Gram looked frantically between his nephew and my family.

"It seems the cat's out of the bag," Irsa replied, not taking her eyes off us. She stared icily at Aydan. The other witches were on their feet, looking to Irsa as if waiting for instruction. "Doors," she said, and her companions each waved a hand. One by one, the doors sealed themselves with a *thud*. Irsa waved her own hand and the chairs and table vanished, leaving us all standing with nothing between us.

"Lady Gwe—Your Majesty," Gram corrected himself, "The Medeisians came here as honored guests, you cannot show them this level of hostility—"

Without a word, Irsa flicked her wrist and knocked Gram off his feet. His head hit the floor with an unsettling crack. Alastair took an impulsive half step forward but did not leave my side. Bewildered, Gram looked up at Irsa from the floor, and blood trickled down his forehead. Callum did not react to anything that was happening in front of him. He simply stared at Irsa with that same dazed look of adoration.

"Irsa," Aydan managed to choke out again, this time taking a step toward his twin. I put my hand on his arm to stop him.

"Surprise, brother," she grinned horribly at him. Then, looking at me, she added, "And you've brought my new sister along, how thoughtful."

"What is this?" Aydan asked. "Why are you here? You— the attack—"

"Oh, that?" Her girlish laugh was unsettling. "Yes, my distraction was effective, wasn't it? A perfect escape while you and father were busy with your little castle."

"You were *dead*, Irsa. There was a funeral."

"Glamours work on corpses." Irsa shrugged. "Not for long, of course, but long enough to have witnesses see their poor Crown

Princess broken and mangled by those nasty, nasty mortals before tossing her on a pyre."

"Why." I gritted out, the image of her hands running along my father's chest flashing in my mind along with that awful smile that was plastered on her face in front of me.

"Miss Redfern," Irsa crooned. "Or are you still pretending to simply be an Eastly?"

"Queen of Medeisia," I replied. Her eyes sparkled.

"For now, sister." Irsa's gaze landed on Alastair, whose sword was fully drawn now, his attention locked on the two witches flanking her. "No need to worry about them, general," she said, and with a wave of her hand the pair were gone. Not effuged, not killed, just simply removed, as if they had never been there. "See? Now it's just us, cozy as can be—"

"Why are you doing this, Irsa?" I asked again.

"Don't you see?" The grin was back, this time laced in rage. She glared at me, then her brother. "*He* was given everything that belonged to me from the minute we were *born*. Our father made him the priority, preparing him for the Heirs' Duel the second we showed a speck of power— and for what? Because he was male. That's all my father needed to know to decide that my brother was *special*. And he ate it up— the praise, the attention, the tutors, the gifts from our father. Arrogant prick didn't even have the decency to die when we finally did duel." I could feel Aydan shaking beside me. The hatred in Irsa's eyes did not give me confidence that we'd walk out of here in one piece if she had her way.

"How did you learn witchcraft?" I asked, hoping to distract her. "I know that you tried to usurp your father and got mine out of the way in the meantime. I know that you found a teacher somewhere. Was it a coven?"

Irsa smirked. "Smart girl. I thought you might have figured that out. It was the Wives of the Unseen Moon," she said flatly. Behind me, Lyra inhaled sharply. "Shortly after our thirteenth birthday, my father brought me and Aydan along on a visit to Xarynn. We were sent to the shore to *have fun*, as if either of us were capable of playing like normal children. We fought, and I ran off, only intending to hide in the caves for an hour or so— long enough to scare my brother. Soon enough I'd gotten myself turned around, scraped up and shivering until, from the darkness, emerged my future.

"I ran nearly headlong into Eda. I thought she was a ghost or a monster at first, I was so scared. But she took one look at me and guided me back to her home. For the first couple of days, I was terrified. But soon they showed me their ways— the old ways— the divine right to learn and wield their craft. I committed myself to their cause and soon returned to my father. When I was deemed well enough to return to my usual lessons, Eda was conveniently hired as my tutor, and my training began.

"I remained naïve I will admit. I never wanted to believe that Aydan would actually go through with the duel, despite Eda's warnings. But then, on our eighteenth birthday, the night that father was to announce me as his heir and officially title me Crown Princess, he strolls in like it's nothing, and challenges me for my place in the succession. He *graciously* allowed me to strike first and strike I did. He was knocked out, twitching on the floor when I moved to make my final blow— but Lord Ronan stopped me, nearly tackling me to the ground before I could. I wouldn't have been shocked if that was the moment that Ronan decided not to trust me," Irsa mused. "But it was decades before he suspected any of my plans for father were serious enough that he should take action."

The doors opened and guards flooded in, taking position around the perimeter of the room. Prince Gram was back on his feet and had slowly made his way to our side of the room while Irsa had been talking, following Alastair's silent instruction to get behind Kenna. King Callum remained beside his wife, his face vacant and bemused.

"I suppose your marriage is a trick as well?" I continued, motioning to the young King. "Do these guards know that you aren't their true Queen?"

"Oh, but I am," Irsa laughed. "That's the fun of it. The Prince Regent did half the work for me in his attempts to keep the King and I apart. The boy has a rebellious spirit. He was bound to go against whatever rules the prince put in place. All I had to do was flirt with an adolescent and promise him my heart— isn't that right sweet thing?" She looked to Callum, who smiled back at her.

"Yes darling."

"Well, my heart wasn't the only thing I promised," Irsa chuckled cruelly while her husband returned to staring. "Pussy is an excellent motivation for young men—"

"That's enough," Gram snapped as he stepped out from behind Kenna, who gripped his sleeve to stop him going too far. "You're disgusting. You— you're—" Irsa threw her head back and laughed as Gram stammered at her. "This marriage will be annulled. You will *never* rule over Nautia."

"Can't be annulled," Irsa sighed. "It's already been consummated— that's what led to Callum's tardiness. Don't you know your own laws?"

"You're lying," Gram replied.

"Get him out of here," I murmured to Alastair. "He's going to get himself killed."

"I'm trying," Alastair replied shakily, "There's too many guards now to make a move."

"As you well know, Your Highness, I must now be treated as if I'm carrying a prince until proven otherwise." Irsa rested her hand low on her belly, mocking Gram's outrage.

"Irsa, your quarrel is with Aydan and me," I interrupted, stepping forward. "Let my Cabinet escort Prince Gram—"

"No, sister, I don't think I will. The prince is much too fun to toy with. And I'd like your Cabinet to stick around as well. I think they'll be interested to know how much they've failed in protecting their precious monarchs." I felt new wards snap down around us, and immediately Lyra began casting under her breath, attempting to reverse them.

"My Cabinet has never failed me," I told her. Irsa cocked an eyebrow, but before she could reply, a roar erupted from beside me as Aydan's power engulfed him in blue light, which he shot toward his sister. She blocked the blow lazily, muttering spells I'd never heard before as she reversed Aydan's attack back toward him. He stormed forward and I rushed to follow, despite Gerridan's attempt to stop me. Flames surrounded my hands, and I turned the floors beneath us to ice. Irsa's guards did not move, and neither did our Cabinet. Callum was unfazed by the magic being cast in his direction while his bride did not deem it necessary to move from beside him to prevent an accidental strike. Aydan wasn't noticing any of this, I realized. His shock and despair had turned to fury in the face of his twin's deception, and he was out for blood.

Whether seconds or minutes had passed in our fight, I did not know, but soon Irsa, despite the slight sheen on her forehead, appeared too bored to put up much further effort. A red light erupted from her palm and into Aydan's chest, sending him toppling to the floor.

I screamed Aydan's name and halted my attack on Irsa. I fell to my knees beside him, gripping at his jacket collar, moving to feel for a pulse.

"He's breathing," I heard Lyra say from the other side of Aydan. I didn't see her move toward us. I didn't look to see if her face was painted with concern. I just watched as she tore his shirt open, and saw a raw, blistering wound over his heart that seemed to be smoking. Lyra's hands immediately became encased in white light that she placed over it. "I've got him," she promised.

"We need to get him out of here. You all need to get out of here."

"If one of us can crack the wards we can all get out. Distract the bitch and we'll work on the rest." I nodded, rising slowly, and turning to face her.

Irsa feigned a pout, making a show out of peering over my shoulder to check on her brother's condition.

"Lucky you, to have found one of the Children," she commented. I requested flames to engulf my hands once again.

"I required a teacher, so I found one."

"I did wonder how you would gain control," Irsa said. "I didn't expect that you'd be so stupid as to go directly to the source, but recklessness is certainly an Eastly trait. As much as being a born witch is now a Redfern trait."

"What do you mean, you wondered how I would gain control? There's no way you could have known— I didn't start displaying power until—" Gears turned in my head, trying to understand. Irsa watched, waiting for realization to spark, once again feigning disappointment when it didn't.

"Nothing? Oh, sister, you're going to have to catch up to speed." She called out over her shoulder, "Bring it in." A guard opened the door and I felt my Cabinet shift behind me, as we all awaited whatever it was that was coming toward us. The dragging sound of heavy metal on stone floors indicated that it was perhaps a weapon of some kind. Something of use to her brand of witchcraft. When the guards parted, I stumbled backward, nearly falling over my skirts to land beside Aydan on the floor. Led into the throne room, locked in heavy shackles at the wrists and ankles was a bruised and bewildered looking Stefan Whittaker.

"Stefan?" I nearly whispered.

"Oh good, you can recognize him. I asked the guards to keep the face pretty, but you know how those things go."

"What have you—"

"My influence over my father kept my eyes on most of the goings-on in Ayzelle, though when needed I could transfer some of that influence where it was necessary," Irsa explained. "The Prince's Chambers were nearly impenetrable. My little brother is quite the master at wards, I'll give him that. Breaking those wards would have been too suspicious, but it was expected that father would place a guard— his most trusted guard— in charge of such a person of interest. I had father place the captain in the chambers, then watched from his mind as he watched you reading your little books, lounging like a queen even back then." Influence over her father… watching from Stefan's mind… Irsa watched with a gleeful look on her face as what she was saying sank in. "Mindwalking is such a useful tool, I must say," she said with a grin. It was all I could do to not let my mouth fall open in shock. "After I staged the mortal attacks and set my plan in motion here, I kept my hold on Captain Whittaker to keep my eye on you."

Bile rose in my throat. Stefan had never been my friend, my confidant. It had been Irsa. Irsa was a mindwalker. Stefan's last words to me rang out in my mind: *She's right there and I can't see her…* Gods, she'd had a hold on his mind until—

"And then when you confronted the poor captain about father's orders— or what father thought were his orders, anyway— and had your little outburst, you managed to rip me out of his feeble little mind. Snatched him up when your Cabinet shipped him off to

Xarynn. Luckily the drearies are such faithful allies. I certainly couldn't risk the healers at Ironridge getting to the bottom of his madness."

"Your father's journal…" I tried to understand what she was saying. I felt the wards begin to flicker and hoped she didn't notice. "When you say you were influencing your father…How long were you controlling his mind? When was the last time Zathryan made a decision for himself?"

Irsa smirked. "On and off following the Heirs' Duel. I took full control around the time of Ronan's first trial. Couldn't have Papa getting a soft spot for an old friend—"

"How many?" I spat. "How many innocent people's minds have you warped into doing your bidding?"

"Oh, ten, twenty or so, over the years. Once I figured out how to do it, I must say it was a useful tool to have on hand. The first time I took full control was a bit of a mess— Calvin Thandreil was difficult to keep a hold of."

"You… You're lying."

"Why would I? I've told you everything else willingly."

"I have no reason to believe anything else you've said today either. You wouldn't have driven your family from their home. You wouldn't have killed your own mother—"

"My mother's death was not part of the plan," Irsa snapped. Had I struck a nerve? "Thandreil got loose from my grasp and took matters into his own hands." The sounds of metal-on-metal began to ring out behind me, and I knew my Cabinet was finally taking on the mortal guards. The wards flickered again. I didn't dare look and risk breaking Irsa's concentration on me. "In the end, I'll get what I wanted the whole time. If not through Calvin, then through a different Thandreil." She stroked Callum's arm and he looked down at her adoringly. Stefan remained behind them, shaking and looking around the room. Irsa continued taunting me. "I learned my lesson after your bitch mother ruined my last attempt at blaming my death on mortals." I knew she was trying to get a rise out of me, trying to make me lose control and attack her. She was trying to make me careless. I had to keep her talking. The second she turned her attention on the fight, or on Lyra still trying to help Aydan, we would be done for. "I thought dying in battle would be the easiest way to do it— but then my father forbade me from the battlefield and my hands were tied. So, I tried giving Commander Eastly orders that would lead to an attack on the castle. She was young and inexperienced. It should have been an easy task. But somehow, she managed to defeat my soldiers and make herself a *hero*, despite her insubordination."

"What do you mean *your* soldiers?" I snapped.

"It takes a lot of effort to control that many minds at once— I couldn't use Nautians and risk someone slipping away from me. It turns out mimicking the Nautian uniform is quite easy— I was able to disguise all my friends from the Unknown Territories."

"The night you faked your death, were those mortals your friends too?"

"Oh, I didn't need them that night," she laughed. "The same methods I used to convince sweet Calvin Thandreil to attack the capital worked all over again. I suppose when the Crown treats an entire population like shit it's easy to direct your anger where you want it."

"And you were controlling your father, ensuring his treatment of the mortals so that when the time was right, you could sic them on castle Ayzelle," I said.

"Clever, sister. No wonder my brother jumped on the chance to marry you— smart as a whip, and so pretty. For now, anyway."

"Why?" I asked, ignoring her threats. "You could have waited for Zathryan to die—"

"Because I *wanted* to," she snapped. "Because I wanted my brother to get a taste of all he coveted, and then rip it out from under him like he deserves."

"Aydan did nothing but listen to your father."

"He was old enough to know better," she spat. "He was father's pawn and mother's favorite. All I *had* was my birthright, and he tried to take that too."

"So now you settle for being the anointed Queen in a foreign land?" I asked. "Prince Gram was right— Nautia is no longer home to sorcerers. They will not take kindly to being ruled by an immortal."

"They won't have a choice," Irsa said.

"I wouldn't have pegged you as being satisfied with gaining power through marriage," I continued as the fight behind us got louder.

"My power is my own. The Wives of the Unseen Moon assisted me by aiding the mortals in their rebellion, and then by keeping tabs on the royal mortals until the time was right for me to make my appearance in court. The Thandreils only ruled Nautia because I allowed them to, and now they've served their purpose." She turned her attention back on Callum. "Haven't you, sweet thing?"

Callum blinked a few times, shaking his head slightly as Irsa released her hold on him and clarity replaced the clouds in his eyes.

"Gwendolyn, what's happened?" He asked, taking in the room. Aydan was beginning to stir, and I sent up a small prayer of thanks to whoever might be listening. I finally gained enough courage to glance behind me and saw that several Nautian guards lay on the floor while my friends continued to fight. Though Kenna's side was darkened and wet with blood, she did not waver in her defense of Gram, who was frantically trying to stop the guards from pursuing us while he sought a weapon of his own. Blood trickled down Gerridan's forehead as he fought back-to-back with Alastair.

A loud cracking sound, like thunder, paired with an ominous red glow, sent everyone— even the guards—turning toward Irsa and Callum.

The room, and everyone in it, was painted in the red light. Callum, now of his own mind, was tearful as his eyes darted around the room and found Gram.

"Uncle?" He called out. "Uncle, I don't understand—"

"Let the boy go, Irsa," I yelled. "Your fight is with us. He has done nothing to you."

"Oh, but it's just so fun to watch them beg, don't you think?" She stroked Callum's face and his lip quivered.

"Gwendolyn, I thought— you said…"

"Oh, sweet baby, I say a lot of things," she replied dismissively. "Flowery promises of love and forever made in dark corridors should never be taken too seriously. You've served your purpose now my dear, and truly, I thank you."

Tears spilled over on Callum's cheeks as Irsa's hold on him forced him to his knees. The boy-king sobbed, begging through gritted teeth as his eyes met mine, *"Please—"*

Time halted, and the air seemed to be sucked from the room. My ears could not make out any sounds— just a ringing, followed by Kenna's voice making a long-ago premonition:

Kings will fall to their knees before you.

Irsa flicked her wrist, and Callum's head twisted, snapping his neck before he fell motionless to the floor.

Chapter
Thirty-Three

The ringing in my ears continued. A wild grin spread on Irsa's face while she watched me stare at the limp body of Callum Thandreil ten feet in front of me. The ringing faded and was soon replaced by the anguished screams of Gram from behind me. I looked back, only to see the mortal prince clawing at Alastair's arms as my general held him around the waist, keeping him in place. I paused to lock eyes with Gerridan, then Kenna, and hoped that my stare conveyed my plans well enough. I glanced at Lyra, who had managed to wake Aydan fully and was helping him to stand now. Despite his ragged breathing, his blue light engulfed his hands, while the pool of white Lyra had placed on his chest remained floating there like a bandage. His eyes searched around the room before landing on me, and a sigh of relief escaped him. A second later, I felt the wards lift completely, and all hell broke loose.

The guards turned again on Gerridan and Kenna, while Alastair effuged away, dragging a still screaming Gram with him. Lyra formed another white light, this time encasing Aydan in a dome of it, while she began to defend its perimeter. He was keeping the wards open, I realized. He'd lifted all the wards and was using the last bit of his strength to give us time to escape. Even depleted, Aydan's anointed power was incredible.

Which meant mine was too.

I turned on my heel only to find that Irsa was standing only about a foot away from me. I engulfed one hand in flames and the other in blue light that quickly became crackling lightning— only to have her hit me with a ball of red light that knocked me off my feet. My body crashed into the floor, and I rushed to get back on my feet before launching a wall of flame at her, which she blocked. I sent another at her, and another. Another. She blocked each one, laughing as she did so. The fight behind me seemed to be getting louder, closer, but I didn't dare to look back. It wasn't until I saw Alastair appear behind Irsa and grab Stefan before disappearing again that I realized my friends would get out of here, and that was all I needed. I knew Lyra would take Aydan, and I would take Irsa down on my own.

Suddenly, my eyes were wrapped in darkness. I heard nothing, saw nothing, but felt a breath on the back of my neck, as if someone was standing an inch behind me.

"Sister," Irsa's voice whispered in my mind. "We shouldn't be fighting."

"You shouldn't have tried to harm the people I love," I breathed back. "You shouldn't have killed a child right in front of me."

"My true quarrel is with my brother," she continued. "And if I'm to understand it, he has not exactly lived up to your expectations. Join me. You liked me when I wore the captain's face, and I think you'll find that I'm quite interesting company to keep—"

"Go fuck yourself."

"Such *language,* Your Majesty," she chuckled. "I can respect your position, but I hope you can understand mine: if you are not by my side, you must be out of my way. I tried, before things ever got this far, to chase you out of my hair— such dreadful dreams I've sent you over the years, and they've never managed to scare you off. I cannot make you leave, brave girl, and so I must destroy you."

My vision returned, and chaos continued to reign around us. Lyra lost hold of the perimeter around Aydan, and they were both fighting the guards now. Alastair had returned to the fight to help now that Gram and Stefan had been taken to safety. "Dearest sister," Irsa crooned. Her voice wrapped itself around my senses again, echoing through the madness. "By the end, you'll be begging me to take you." In lieu of a reply, I let blue light surround my body before sending a beam of it at her, finally striking her in the chest. She fell backward, and I felt the wards flicker back into place for just a second before lifting again. Aydan's hold was faltering.

"*Get out of here!*" I roared to my friends as I conjured the blue light again. Irsa was scrambling to her feet. Flame encased my right hand while ice encased the left. I sent a wall of each in her direction, trying to keep her from standing, though she blocked both easily. I geared up for another shot, and she blocked it as well. Finally, she sent a blast of red light toward me and it was my turn to block with the blue Aevitarus light once again.

My power surged, and then wavered before I found my strength again. I geared up to put more effort behind the blast when I felt her doing the same. Everything, I would give everything to see Irsa defeated here and now. I filled my lungs with one last deep breath, channeling every ounce of the power at my control toward my hands—

Like a ton of bricks, something crashed into my side, bringing me down to the floor, knocking the wind from me as my stomach dropped. When I landed, my back crashing into the ground, I looked around wildly and realized I was no longer in the Grand Palace of Nautia, but the parlor room of the King's Chambers in Ayzelle.

"*NO!*" I roared. Flames and lightning burst from my palms as I moved to stand. Strong arms pinned me to the floor. Alastair, I realized, was straddling me, his grip tight on my arms as I thrashed and struggled beneath him. "Get off of me," I snarled. "Take me back— I almost had her—"

"No, you didn't," Alastair said through gritted teeth as I continued fighting him, "You were losing. We lost— we all lost—"

"*Take me back!*"

"No." He gripped me harder as I tried to fight him off again. "Stop it Shaye— it's over—*IT'S OVER.*"

I felt my nostrils flare and the sound of my shallow, gulping breaths became the only thing I could hear. The flames in my fingertips subsided and were replaced by ice creeping up over my palms as dread, rather than anger, filled me.

"I had her," I whispered to myself, "I could have—"

"You were killing yourself," Alastair replied. "She was letting you wear yourself out. The fight was over before it started." We sat in silence for a minute before Alastair was satisfied that I had settled, and he released his grip on my arms. He stood and held out a hand to help me to my feet as well.

I looked around the room and saw my friends, sitting in ripped, dirty clothing, shaken by what had just occurred. I glanced at the clock. Two hours. We left for Nautia only two hours ago.

"Shaye," said a hoarse voice. I turned and found a somber looking Gerridan, his hair caked in blood. "I need to go to Hannele. Tell her what's happened."

"Go ahead," I said softly. "I'll need you again tonight, if she can spare you."

"I'll be back as soon as I can." I scanned the room while Gerridan effuged away.

"Where's Aydan?" I asked no one in particular. Alastair, who still stood beside me, pointed in reply. I followed where he indicated, to see Aydan sitting against a far wall with his head in his hands.

I approached and knelt before him, placing a hand on his head. He looked up at me, his dirty, bloody face stricken. "Shaye," he croaked. "I-I don't—"

"I know."

"Irsa, she—it was her. My mother. Nautia. The whole time—"

"I know."

"Your father," he murmured. "Gods. The Crown murdered him." I brushed my fingers through Aydan's hair.

"No," I said. "Just Irsa." We were silent again, and Aydan clutched at my dress like he'd done the night before, as if he were afraid I would disappear if he let go.

"Shaye," he murmured after a minute. "Shaye, if Irsa is alive, then— then I am no King." I tilted his chin to face me.

"You are," I told him firmly. "You are Aydan Aevitarus, anointed King of Medeisia. You were chosen by the gods—" He brushed my hand away and moved to stand. "Aydan—"

"I need a minute," he choked, moving to walk toward our bedroom. I placed my hand on his arm.

"Aydan, I believe in you," I whispered. "And I'm going to try to believe in myself, too. I am this nation's Queen, and I intend to keep leading, even if you cannot." Aydan didn't reply. Instead, he moved my hand, pressing a kiss to the top of it before walking away. I watched after him until I heard a door shut, then turned back to the room.

Kenna lay on a sofa, her shirt discarded while Lyra muttered spells and white light poured from her palms, healing the seer's wounds. Lyra glanced up at me, holding my gaze for just a second before bowing her head. Alastair joined Gram on the opposite sofa, his arm wrapped around the prince's shoulders as he sobbed softly into his hands.

Stefan stood alone, looking shaken as he took in his surroundings. I approached and touched his arm. He flinched. "Do you know who I am?" I asked when he turned his attention to me.

"Miss Eastly?" He blinked. I sighed.

"She's done a number on you, hasn't she?" I said mostly to myself. My friend— or at least, the face of my friend. It was clear that my friendship with Stefan had been entirely fabricated by Irsa. *She* cleaned my wounds and brought me extra food. *She* led me through the gardens, kissed me, and bid me to abandon my position as Chief Advisor. I did not allow myself to dwell on what she may have done with me once we were alone and away from Ayzelle had I fallen for her trap. "I was Miss Eastly when we met, yes," I told Stefan. "You've been held against your will by the former Princess Irsa. We thought her dead, but she was away, plotting and taking control of your mind to get to me. I am now the anointed Queen of Medeisia, upon my marriage to King Aydan."

He blinked. "Zathryan..."

"Dead," I told him, more bluntly than I'd meant to. "For almost two years now. Also orchestrated by Irsa." Stefan was quiet. "You're safe now, here with us," I assured him. I snapped my fingers once.

"Your Majesty?" Elise appeared beside me. She looked around the room, at the Cabinet in disarray. "What on earth—"

"Elise, please find a room where Lord Stefan can bathe and get some rest," I told her. "He's had quite the ordeal." Despite the shock painted on her face, Elise didn't question any further, instead simply bidding Stefan to follow her down the hallway. Stefan, to his credit, did not hesitate for more than a second before following, seeming to deem us safe enough to trust for now.

I approached Kenna, whose wound seemed to have closed well enough with Lyra's help. "How bad is it?"

"Not very," she replied. "It wasn't deep, he just grazed me with his blade while I was distracted with someone else. It didn't feel right to use magic on mortals at first but after a cheap shot like that I suddenly had a clear conscience—"

"She'll need to stay off her feet as much as possible for a few days," Lyra clarified before adding. "Shaye, you need to know... the Wives are the worst of us."

"I guessed as much," I said. "Do you have any idea what their numbers are? Where in Xarynn are they located?"

Lyra shook her head. "That's the problem— they're not a coven like the Children are, it's more of an ideology. A system of thought. The clan that Deimos hailed from followed the philosophy of the Wives. There's no knowing how many there are out there."

"The witches employed at the Grand Palace have always claimed to be of the Wives," Gram croaked from behind me. Alastair's arm was still around him; his face was blotchy and red. "My ancestors had an understanding with them. They were the ones to assist in the revolution from the beginning."

"So, it seems, was Irsa," I finished, running a hand along my face. The chamber door opened.

"Oh my gods—" Hannele swept into the room, looking around at the damage to the Cabinet. Gerridan followed, shutting the door behind him. I felt him strengthen the wards.

"She insisted," Gerridan explained.

"It's fine, I need you both," I said. "How quickly can you gather the councils?"

"Which one?"

"All of them. The extended councils of all territories. As well as the Duke of Xarynn, Lord Priamos, and Lady Solandis. I need them here in the Great Hall, tonight."

"What will you tell them?" Hannele breathed.

"I'm going to tell them everything."

Gerridan worked his magic and in no time, it seemed that I was being informed of the first arrivals in the Great Hall. I sat with Gram while he did his best to recall Irsa's roles in the Grand Palace throughout his life. She'd always gone by Gwendolyn, he explained, and until Mal's death had remained particularly demure. Unlike the other witches, she seemed to travel often, but it was always with the permission of the King.

"We were told not to concern ourselves with what the witches did," Gram explained. "They were there to serve the King and the King alone— not the rest of the royal family. Prior to becoming Regent, I can only think of a few times in my life that I even interacted with any of them."

"Would you be willing to repeat this information to my councils?" I asked. He nodded solemnly.

"However I can be of use."

"We will win back your crown," I promised. He blinked at me, puzzled. "You are the rightful King of Nautia, Gram. Medeisia will fight for you as we fight for ourselves. That is my promise to you." Realization washed over his face, and he sat back in his seat with a hand over his mouth. I waited for a moment, trying to string together something kind to say, but before I could, Gerridan was there, placing his hand on my shoulder to get my attention.

"It's time," he said. "Solandis just arrived with the Sylvannian council."

"Oh," I said, looking down at the gown I still wore, tattered and ruined from fighting with Irsa and being tackled by Alastair. My arms and forehead were scraped, and I could feel dried blood flaking above my eye. "I don't suppose any of us have time to change."

"They're all very anxious," Gerridan replied. "Hannele is waiting with them, but they're all demanding to know what's happened."

"Of course," I said, standing up and smoothing out my skirts to the best of my ability. "How do I look?"

"Like we all do— like we just got our asses handed to us."

"Fair enough." I made my way to the door and my Cabinet followed, bruised and battered as they were. I threw one last glance toward the hallway leading to the bedroom, but Aydan had not stirred since retreating there. Reluctantly, I squared my shoulders and led the Cabinet forward.

When we arrived, the Great Hall was buzzing with dozens of voices speaking over each other. Hannele was doing her best to keep everyone calm, but the knowledge that something so severe had occurred to warrant my summons of all the councils had created somewhat of a panic. I hesitated at the door and forced myself to take a few deep, shaky breaths. My legs would not move.

"I don't know if I can do this," I whispered, regretting my decision now that I was faced with carrying it out.

"You can." Gerridan placed his hand on my back and I turned to meet his eyes. "We'll be with you the whole time."

"They're not going to take this well," I told him. "This could go very badly for me."

"We'll get you out of there at the first sign of trouble," Gerridan said. I nodded, still feeling a bit shaky. "I won't let anything happen to you, Shaye."

"I know you won't," I said. He moved his hand from my back and held out his arm for me to take. "I know."

We entered, and the room fell silent at the sight of a bloodied, disheveled Cabinet— and no Aydan to be seen. Solandis met my eyes, a question painted on her face. I responded with a nod, hoping I conveyed the right message: *He's okay.*

"Your Majesty," the Duke of Xarynn spoke, cutting the silence, "What on earth has happened here? We've received no information other than a demand that we come immediately. Where is the King?"

"Your King is indisposed," I replied as I sat on my throne. The rest of my Cabinet, joined by Gram, fell in place around the dais. "There is no need to be alarmed by his absence. He is simply resting after our ordeal tonight."

"And what ordeal would that be?"

"I will tell you, if you stop interrogating your Queen long enough to let me speak, Edwin." The Duke looked as sheepish as I imagined he was capable and stepped back. "Now," I said, taking a deep breath and looking out at them all hanging on my every word—

Footsteps sounded from outside the door, and to my surprise, Aydan swiftly entered the Great Hall. He remained as bloodied as the rest of us but held his head high as he entered and approached me.

"My apologies," he called out, loud enough for the hall to hear while keeping his eyes on me. "I needed a moment to gather myself, but I am here now. With you." I replied with a slow nod, and Aydan sat down beside me.

"Thank you, my lords and ladies, for your patience with us. I have a story to tell you," I started. "And like all stories, the best place to start is the beginning. Or as close to it as I can come." I took a deep breath. "When I first came to Medeisia, I was plagued with nightmares…"

It took over an hour to tell them everything: from my nightmares involving Aydan, to my visions of my father, the search for the Children and bringing Lyra home with us— to the revelations made today in Nautia. When necessary, Gram spoke and confirmed the pieces of Irsa's story that we were not present for.

The lords and ladies of the councils, to their credit, did not interrupt or cry out their disbelief. As I finished my story, the room remained silent.

"Princess Irsa is alive?" One of the Sylvannian ladies finally called out.

"She is," I confirmed.

"I don't suppose there's any way to prove this?"

"Without inviting her here to kill us all, no, my lady, I don't believe there is," Gerridan replied on my behalf.

"There is one thing that may sway you," Aydan said. "He's been kind enough to wait outside while we spoke. Lord Stefan, if you please."

Despite his clear hesitation, Stefan stepped into the hall, greeted by alarmed murmurs.

"As you can see, Stefan Whittaker is alive, having been held captive by Irsa—"

"You expect us to believe in the innocence of Lord Ronan?" Lord Aren called out. "For thirty years, his treason has been known, and now his daughter admits to the same crime, *admits* to bringing a witch into our midst, and we are supposed to believe the Crown Princess is the aggressor?" The lord sputtered, addressing the room. "I'm more inclined to believe that this witch has enchanted the current Cabinet and usurped our rightful Queen!" Aydan opened his mouth to argue, but I placed my hand on top of his to stop him. Arguing would make me look more guilty than I already did. "And what's more— the Wayward Prince sits beside her! He tried to take the throne from the Crown Princess once— we were all there. Aydan Aevitarus has had his sights set on the throne since he was a child. Of course he would ally himself with the Redfern heiress, an admitted witch, to take it. If Princess Irsa is indeed alive and well, then these two belong in the dungeons—"

"That's enough, Lord Aren." Lord Declan stepped forward, hand raised to stop Aren from speaking further. Declan looked at me briefly before turning to the crowd of gathered nobles. "As you all know, I served King Zathryan faithfully from his marriage to Queen Astra until his death. I led his council in Nautia, I helped form the new capital here in Ayzelle. I voted to ban then-Prince Aydan from Ayzelle following the Rebellion, and I voted in favor of Lord Ronan Redfern's execution—"

"Your voting record is not the topic at hand, Declan," Aren grumbled.

"It isn't, but I thought those too young to remember or who were not present during those votes ought to know where I stand in terms of loyalty and the law." He cleared his throat before continuing. "The King and Queen have brought us all together to hear an unbelievable story— truly unbelievable— knowing that many, if not all of us might react as Lord Aren has. Queen Shaye knows the opinion this court has of her father and of her House, and yet she sits before us advocating for truth—"

"An. Admitted. *Witch.*" Aren cut in again.

"Yes, an admitted witch. Accompanied by one of the Children. And yet the Cabinet stands before these gathered councils begging for us to believe them, rather than simply enchanting us to do so. There would be no purpose in her admission if the Queen had ill intent. You may believe her story or not, but I will stand before this hall and declare with certainty that I believe Queen Shaye." Declan glanced at me again and bowed his head slightly while the crowd began to whisper amongst themselves.

"As for the legality of their position," he continued, "You will find that the Old Laws are very clear: the one who is anointed before the gods shall rightfully rule the kingdoms of sorcery for all of their days. The Crown Princess abandoned her birthright, and King Aydan was anointed in her place. The gods did not reject his anointing, nor Queen Shaye's after him. Therefore, it is they who must hold the Eternity Throne. I pledge now, as I always have, my loyalty and my life to the Crown of Medeisia." Declan dropped down to one knee, his head bowed, and his fist over his heart. My breath slowed as one by one, the gathered councils fell to their knees, pledging themselves anew to me and Aydan, until finally Aren was the last lord standing. Fuming, he turned on his heel before effuging out of the hall altogether.

The Guard and a few scattered lords moved as if to follow him but I said, "Let him go. I will not force anyone's loyalty. Those of you who declare it tonight, I thank you, and expect that you'll uphold your oaths. But those who do not wish to make them in the first place will not be forced." The rest of the hall now stood, looking at me and Aydan expectantly. "Now, I ask the lords and ladies of each territorial council: return to your borders and strengthen your wards. A new checkpoint protocol will be delivered to the captain of each guard by morning. Lord Declan will outline and deliver this by first light." I made eye contact with my head of council, and he responded with a nod. "I ask that all patrons remain in the capital for the next few hours. We will continue our discussion in the council room. It is time to prepare for war."

It was nearly dawn by the time we all made it back to our rooms.

Aydan and I both elected to remain in Ayzelle for the time being. It didn't feel right to leave the capital tonight. Solandis and Priamos had returned to Sylvanna but I knew they would not be returning to the Grand Palace for quite some time. If I knew anything about Solandis, she would be meticulously inspecting the wards at all her borders before she would allow herself to rest.

It was decided that before we raised our armies over the next weeks that our focus, first and foremost, must be defense. Gram had informed us that the standing armies in Nautia were far more vast than they allowed anyone to realize. That alone under Irsa's command would be enough to cause alarm, but her influence over any witch or coven adhering to the philosophies of the Wives would be enough to destroy us all if defenses were not taken seriously. In the morning, Gerridan would be sending out alerts to Auperene, Keotis, and Sewyth, allowing them to prepare their defenses as well. Knowing Irsa, her sights would not end on Medeisia, and notice from us now might just be enough to gain assistance from our allies should we need it in the future.

Now, we returned to the King's Chambers. Gram and Stefan were both given rooms here with us while the rest of the family returned home, save for Alastair, who remained in the sitting room. When I told him to try and rest, he just nodded and continued staring down the hallway toward Gram's room.

I didn't bother calling for Elise. The gown I still wore was practically falling off my body now, and it was simpler to peel what was left of it off me than to call her in to help. Catchfly meowed and wove herself through my legs while I wrapped a robe around my body. Concern radiated from her, and she seemed to be asking what happened. "I'll tell you in the morning," I mumbled. Grouchily, and with a bit of a huff, she walked away to find a better sleeping spot.

I bathed, cleaned my teeth, and brushed my hair, trying to keep the past few hours from taking over my thoughts while I completed my mindless grooming tasks. When I emerged from the bathroom, I found Aydan sitting on the foot of the bed, still in his tattered, bloody clothes. He stared at the floor.

"You should take a bath," I said as I sat down beside him. "You'll feel better once you're clean." Aydan nodded, but continued staring, not moving. He blinked, holding his eyes shut for just a bit too long to be normal. "Aydan?"

"I'm fine," he breathed. "I'm just… very tired."

"Here." I flicked the covers back on the bed. "You should lie down then."

"I don't— I should go out to the sitting room with Alastair."

"You should sleep in a bed," I said. With a wave of my hand, I was able to remove most of the grime from his skin and clothes, though they remained torn. "You need to get some real rest, Aydan. You nearly drained yourself today." Without further protest, he let me take his arm and help him to lie down beneath the blanket. I pulled it back up over him, and by the time I banished the lights and made it to my side of the bed, his breathing turned deep and steady.

I woke early the next morning. It took me a moment to realize that everything I remembered from the previous day had in fact occurred. Irsa was alive. Stefan was alive. We were on the brink of war. Aydan—

I turned over to find that Aydan was awake as well, staring up at the ceiling.

"I've been laying here for about half an hour, trying to come up with an apology that could possibly be enough," he said without turning to face me. "You told me what Irsa was, and I didn't listen."

"I didn't know she was alive," I said. "You believing me wouldn't have helped anything."

"Maybe." He turned on his side to face me. "I have been a terrible husband."

"I haven't exactly been the best wife."

"You were trying to uncover the truth. You were doing what you needed to control your power. When you were up against Irsa... gods, Shaye. Lyra has taught you well."

"In the spirit of honesty, I suppose I should tell you that Lyra was not my primary teacher," I said. "Ronan taught me to wield my magic properly." He nodded, remembering what I told him of the Thread.

"I'm sorry for his fate. I'm sorry that I believed the lies about him."

"You had no reason to think Irsa was lying. She was the Crown Princess— of course you thought she was telling the truth. You had no way of knowing how much control she had over your father."

"I know I didn't. But I should have." Aydan fell silent, and I did not try to argue with him. Everything was still too fresh. He would need time.

After a moment I said, "What now?"

"Now, we do our best to defend our people. Gerridan will alert the other Known Nations today. We will do whatever it takes to defeat Irsa and get Gram home to Nautia to take his place as King."

"And what about us?"

"I'm afraid I have no idea where to start with us," he said. "What were you thinking?"

"If you'll have me, I would like to come home." Aydan brought my hand to his mouth and brushed his lips on my knuckles.

"Of course. Of course you can come home."

"I'm sorry I shut you out." I gulped. "I blamed you for my pain—"

"The blame was deserved," he interjected.

"Not all of it," I said. "You were scared. You were trying. And yes, you should have done things differently... But I was keeping secrets long before that. And if I'm being truthful with myself, maybe somewhere deep down I knew it would be easier to keep secrets, to learn about my family, learn from Ronan— if I kept you at a distance." Shame washed over me. "I hated it. I hated myself for doing it. But as long as I was able to blame *you*, I felt like I could justify my actions." I fell quiet again. Aydan chewed the inside of his cheek.

"Nothing more than that hug happened between me and Reyna," he said.

"I know," I replied.

"But I knew it would hurt you if you learned I was confiding in her," he admitted. "I wasn't *trying* to hurt you, but... it did cross my mind that at least if you found out and were angry, it would mean that I had your attention. I'm not particularly proud of that thought process, but here we are." He swallowed. "I never imagined that you would think I was being unfaithful to you." Aydan let go of my hand and rubbed my bare arm. "You're all I've ever wanted, Shaye."

"Me too," I said. He tucked a curl behind my ear.

"It seems neither of us has quite lived up to our public vows nor our private ones," Aydan said. "We should just start over, and let things go back to how they were."

"I don't think we can do that," I said. Aydan faltered. "We've learned too much from our mistakes," I explained. "We are not the same people we were when we made those vows. We cannot be what we once were, but I think we can become something better than that." My husband nodded.

"'Better' sounds perfect to me," he said. Then, tentatively, Aydan leaned forward and pressed a chaste kiss to my mouth. I kissed back, for just a second before pulling away. I curled myself into Aydan's side, laying my head on his chest while he wrapped his arm around my shoulders. We lay there together in silence for a long while, savoring what could be our last moments of peace.

A few hours later Aydan and I stood hand in hand outside of Knox Redfern's home. I knocked on the door, and Camilla answered it. Her eyes widened at the sight of us, and she dipped into a curtsey.

"Hello Camilla," I greeted her warmly, "Is Lord Knox at home?"

"He is, Your Majesties." She stepped aside. "Please, come in. He will be thrilled to see you."

When Knox arrived, he was startled to see me, and even more so to see Aydan. I thanked him for housing Lyra, and he denied requiring any thanks, insisting that it was his pleasure to do my bidding. Then I told him about my use of the Thread, to which he blanched, and when I told him everything else I had learned about my father, he nearly fainted. "So we were correct? Ronan was innocent?"

"Yes," Aydan said. "The Crown executed Lord Ronan based on a lie told by my sister. Ronan was working tirelessly to protect my father's throne, and Irsa won out. I am sorry. I wish I had known sooner."

Knox sank slowly onto one of his sofas and ran his hands over his face. "I cannot believe it," he whispered. "I-I *knew* that he was not capable of such things, that there had to be a misunderstanding, but— Princess Irsa? I would have never guessed."

"Neither did we," I said. "She is a clever woman. She will put up a difficult fight."

"So we are at war then?" Knox asked. I nodded. "House Redfern remains at your service, Your Majesties. Whatever we can provide, it is yours." Knox bowed his head to us both.

"Good," I said. "Because I have a request to make of you, cousin."

"Anything, Your Majesty," he said.

"We require a new master of the treasury on our council and wondered if you might take the position." He blinked several times.

"I'm afraid I don't understand."

"Lord Aren has fled Medeisia, I assume to Nautia to join Irsa's ranks. We require a new master of the treasury. We are at war, as we said, and war is expensive," Aydan explained.

"But— my apologies, Majesties, but I still do not understand why you would ask me," Ronan said.

"House Redfern has not generated significant income in over thirty years," I said. "And yet you have managed our funds so well that not only have the vaults not been emptied, but you keep a staff and maintained thirteen different properties on my behalf." Knox straightened. "Now, I know that it is a lot to ask, as taking this position will require you to take up residence at castle Ayzelle, but—"

"I accept your offer, Majesties," Knox interrupted. "No further explanation needed. I thank you for your trust in me, and the opportunity to return our good name to our House."

"Good," I said. "Thank you. I also thought you should know that effective tomorrow morning, no marketplace in Medeisia will be permitted to deny a vendor's goods based solely on their name." Knox looked like he might cry. "Redfern goods must be allowed to be displayed within any marketplace that your goods could reasonably be sold in. I cannot take away the customers' personal biases but getting your products in the stall is a start."

"It is, Your Majesty. I cannot begin to thank you—"

"There is no need," I said. "Though I do wish you would call me Shaye in private."

Knox chuckled. "I will do what I can," he said. I glanced at his clock.

"We must get going," I said, pointing out the time to Aydan. "Cousin, thank you again for meeting with us, and accepting our offer. We ask that you—and Camilla, if you wish for her to accompany you— arrive at castle Ayzelle in one week. You'll join us for council meetings the day after you arrive."

"I look forward to it, Your— Shaye."

"Goodbye Knox," I said.

Aydan and I returned home, while Alastair remained in Ayzelle to keep an eye on Gram and Stefan. I knew I would need to speak to them both soon and include Gram in our plans moving forward.

The rest of the afternoon was spent approving Gerridan's letters to the Elf Kingdoms and the Faelands, ensuring that we stressed the urgency of the situation as well as clarifying it. A vengeful princess back from the dead was a difficult thing to explain in a single letter.

We also met briefly with Solandis, who displayed to us the capabilities of the new wards she had put in place herself. Only Aydan or I could effuge freely over the borders of each territory, as we would need to meet with their patrons frequently as we moved forward.

Our last task of the day was to meet back in Ayzelle with Alastair and Captain Adler to discuss a potential site for Irsa's first strike. It was decided that the eastern villages would be given extra protection from the King's Guard, just in case. Anyone who wanted assistance moving westward toward Xarynn and away from the Nautian border would be given help doing so.

By the time we made it home once again that evening, I had to stop myself from plopping down on one of the sofas in our sitting room. There was one more thing I should do on my own. Aydan told me he had a few things to attend to but would be done shortly. I bid him farewell as Elise rounded the corner. "Would you like something to eat, Your Majesty?"

I rubbed a hand over my face and said, "Not right this second, Elise. I'll get it myself when I'm hungry."

"If you have no further use of me then, I will retire to my room for the night."

"Of course. Thank you, Elise." She left and, realizing I had no more excuses, I effuged to the meeting I could not put off any longer.

The last time I was here, I was nearly delirious from exhaustion and pain, and so I did not notice the well-kept grounds, the carved gates, and endless bushes of Sylvannian roses. I walked a stone path straight to the front door and knocked three times. The same servant who answered last time opened the door and I realized I didn't know her name. She looked just as shocked to see me now as she had that day.

"Your Majesty," she said, dipping into a low curtsey, "To what do we owe the pleasure?"

"I've come to speak with Lady Hazelwren, if she would be so kind."

"I—Yes, of course, Your Majesty. Please, come in and I will fetch my lady." The servant led me to a parlor and curtsied again before leaving.

While I waited, I observed the room's thoughtful décor, and tried to shake my nerves.

"Your Majesty?" Reyna said from the doorway. I faced her and clasped my hands in front of me.

"Hello, Lady Reyna," I said in what I hoped was a warm tone. "My apologies for the intrusion, but I did not feel that this could wait—"

Reyna took a knee. "My Queen, I must extend to you my deepest apologies and renew my House's oath of loyalty to you. My friendship with the King has never extended beyond that, and I am deeply ashamed that I allowed myself to exhibit behavior that could call that fact into question."

"I believe you, my lady, and accept your apology," I said. "But that is not why I'm here."

"Then why..."

"May we sit?" I asked. Reyna rose to her feet.

"I— yes, of course." She gestured to a pair of cushioned chairs and we each took a seat.

"Lady Reyna, I've come here today to ask your forgiveness."

"I don't understand," she said. "What for?"

"Whether you knew it or not, I have placed undue blame on you for my own... insecurities," I began. Reyna looked puzzled. "The knowledge of yours and Aydan's previous betrothal was difficult for me to bear. But that was my fault, not yours. I knew— I *know* that the two of you are friends. But, seeing you together that day—"

"Your Majesty, you must know, I did not mean anything by it—"

"I know—"

"The King was just so upset, and I embraced him without thinking of what it would look like," she said thickly. "I am... I am so ashamed of myself for putting us in that position. For causing you to have any doubt in the king. We were speaking of his fear for you—"

"Reyna. It's all right."

"It's not," she choked. "I want to be a friend and servant to the Crown, and yet *this* is how I allowed myself to behave. I hope to one day earn your trust again, Your Majesty, and perhaps be welcome in your court."

"Reyna, you are already welcome in my court. The Crown needs you. War is coming. We will need your council, and your assistance in defending our home," I told her. "I hope to one day earn *your* trust and friendship. I have yet to deserve it."

"Your Majesty..." Reyna looked uncomfortable. "I'm afraid I don't know what to say."

"I don't either," I admitted. "I simply wanted to get that all off my chest. I appreciate you letting me do so. I will leave you to your evening now." I stood, and Reyna followed suit. When we reached the door, I told her, "I hope to hear from you soon. We would love to have you and Calliope for dinner."

"You honor us, Your Majesty." She curtsied.

"Just Shaye," I said for the second time that day. "In private, my friends call me Shaye."

Reyna loosed a shaky breath and dipped her chin down. "Thank you, Shaye." I squeezed her hand.

"Goodnight, Reyna."

When I returned home, the house was dark, except for a faint glow coming from our bedroom. I followed it and found our armchairs and side tables in front of the fireplace were gone, having been replaced with a table set for two, with covered dishes, white linens, and lit candles atop it. Catchfly greeted me, weaving around my legs before I crouched to scratch her head. Aydan came striding from the bathroom, looking like he just finished changing.

"Ah, you've caught me," he said. "I thought I might have more time when I realized you'd left. Where did you go?"

"I went to speak to Reyna," I said. Aydan's brows rose. "I felt that a conversation between us was overdue."

"And how did that go?"

"Well, I think." I looked around the room. "What is all of this?"

"It's not quite as elaborate as my set up the night before our wedding, but I thought perhaps this time we could actually spend it alone. Together." He went to the table and pulled out a chair for me. I sat, and he took the other. Suddenly ravenous, I uncovered the dish and found a bowl of a simple rabbit stew, not unlike the first meal Aydan and I shared together in Ayzelle.

We ate in near silence, only occasionally speaking to make small talk, as if we were mere acquaintances, and not husband and wife. It felt strange to be near Aydan after all this time apart. I struggled to find words to say and felt myself going red with embarrassment as I wracked my brain for something to talk with my husband about.

He noticed my agitation and placed his hand over mine. "It's all right," he said. "We will get there. Better than before, remember? We have to start somewhere."

"Better than before," I agreed, and warmth filled my chest.

This was what we were fighting for. Not just our kingdom. Not just the Crown, or even the Eternity Throne. Irsa would be fighting for retribution. She sought a day of reckoning that would never come. But us? We would fight for truth. We would fight for our family. We'd fight for the future— and we would do it together.

Thank you for reading!

This book fought tooth and nail to exist. I am so incredibly lucky to have dedicated readers and friends who have helped me make this one happen— you all know who you are.

As always, reviews on Amazon and Goodreads are appreciated! To find out about current projects, follow me on Twitter @NCHayesAuthor. To see book photos, cool fanart, and awkward selfies, follow me on Instagram @nc.hayes.

Shaye and Aydan will return in book three of The Redfern Legacy: *The Eternity Throne*.

Cheers,

N.C. Hayes

N.C. Hayes lives in Arizona with her husband, children, and the things that go bump in the night. *The Queen of Reckoning* is her second novel.

www.ingramcontent.com/pod-product-compliance
Lightning Source LLC
Chambersburg PA
CBHW031025260626
47153CB00017B/2121